The
Dogs
of
War

The Dogs of War
Copyright 2016 by Matthew McCain

Published by Piscataqua Press
an imprint on RiverRun Bookstore, Inc
142 Fleet St. | Portsmouth, NH 03801
www.ppressbooks.com

ISBN: 978-1-944393-03-8

Cover photo: Shutterstock/Dmitrijs Bindemanis
Editing assistance: Tom Holbrook

Printed in the United States of America

THE DOGS OF WAR

a novel by

MATTHEW McCAIN

piscataqua press

To my grandfather:
The real Ray and my real hero. Thank you for watching over me like a
father…and maybe now you'll get your damn knee fixed.

&

For Chris:
Who gave me something when it felt like I had nothing

Chapter 1: Just Another Friday

The phone rang to 'Ray's Auto/Body' shop twice. Ray was just about to pick it up on the third ring, but enough time had passed for Ray to realize that next ring wasn't going to come. But if it suddenly rang again then Ray would know it would become another busy day...just not at the body shop.

In a way, Ray really didn't want it to ring. He was still pretty tired after finishing up the job that Joey gave to him last week. It was times like this when Ray started to think about just giving it up and retiring. It was easy back in the day but now (especially after reaching fifty) it was just taking a toll on him every time he suited up...not to mention it was getting hard to hide the grays that were beginning to appear on the top of his head.

Ray took a quick glance out of the window in his office and saw his team working on a few cars inside the shop. He smiled because for a brief second it almost felt like that was his normal life. But that train of thought quickly derailed when the phone rang again.

Ray quickly lost the smile on his face when the loud phone rang from his desk. Even though Ray didn't really want to pick up the damn thing he knew that if he didn't pick it up, Joey would call Paul Roader (a bitter rival of Ray and his team and the last thing he wanted was to bang into Roader at some bar in the middle of the city and pretend to be happy while Roader when on and on about how good the job went) so in the end Ray swallowed his doubt and quickly picked up the phone.

"Yeah?" Ray asked in his deep serious voice.

"I need you guys down here at the Mall of America ASAP," Joey said in his professional voice.

"Equipment?" Ray asked.

"Bring the kids and bring the toys. The party requires them," Joey said.

"Alright, you got it."

"Meet me at the far entrance of the place. Gray undercover cruiser."

"Give us fifteen."

"Make it ten," Joey said right before he hung up.

Despite the arthritis slowly creeping up into Ray's knee he quickly got up and walked out to the guys in the shop. He walked over to a bell that was hanging right by his office and rang it twice. The guys in the shop quickly stopped what they were doing and looked up.

"We're moving out!" Ray yelled.

The men (who looked like your average Joes) kicked it into high gear and ran into the break room. On the far end of the room was a large cabinet. The newest to the group, Kevin Bear, quickly opened it and started throwing the bulletproof vests at each of the guys behind him. The wild child known as Tommy got his first.

"Alright! Time to blow some shit up!" he screamed.

"What do we need?" Kevin Bear shouted to Ray.

Ray quickly turned his head before entering his office. "Get the big stuff! Sounds like we'll need it!" He shouted back.

Kevin smiled. "God I love Fridays."

Kevin threw another vest over to Bob Tiggs (another guy thinking about change before he hits Ray's age, which he was approaching quickly). Bob quickly put it on and lit up a cigarette.

"You do know that's bad for you right?" Kevin asked.

"You do know your hair makes you look bad, right?" Bob asked.

"Fuck you, Bob," Kevin said as he smiled.

Kevin had some type of genetic problem on the top of his head that caused parts of his hair to turn white. That wouldn't be a problem for him if he was Ray's age but, since he was only twenty-six, every time someone said something he couldn't help but get a little pissed. But since he's been working with Bob for close to ten years he's just gotten use to it.

Kevin threw the last vest to Jasmin, or as Bob calls him 'the foreigner'. Jasmin quickly caught the vest and put it on.

"We always get a call when I'm in the middle of lunch. It's like Ray knows when I'm on break," Jasmin said in his Bosnian voice.

Bob chuckled as he loaded his assault rifle.

"Just look on the bright side Jas..." Bob said.

"What's that?" Jasmin asked.

"At least that vest still covers your gut," Bob said.

"Wow Bob," Jasmin said.

Bob laughed as Jasmin looked down at his stomach. He couldn't deny that Bob was right. Jasmin had kinda let himself go, but Jasmin told himself that he could still get the job done...course he was still kinda hungry.

While the guys got ready in the break room, Ray was getting his gear on in his office. He was in the middle of loading his pistol when his long time friend (and right hand man) Steve Bright came walking in.

"What's the job this time? Another wild ride in Bosnia?" Steve asked as he took off his shirt and changed into his uniform.

"All Joe said was Mall of America," Ray said as he holstered his pistol.

"Always nice to get a close to home job for a change."

Ray smiled as he looked up at Steve. "You know I use to look like that," Ray said.

"Look like what?" Steve asked.

"Like you. Use to have the six-pack and everything. Course I didn't take my shirt off every three seconds," Ray said.

Steve chuckled. "Please, the only six pack you've ever had was the ones you bought when you were a teenager," Steve said.

"What makes you think I don't have a six pack now?" Ray said.

"I'm sure you probably do...in the little refrigerator you keep behind your desk," Steve said as he smiled.

"Remind me to fire you when we get back."

"Will do...you know you say that every time we suit up for one of these little adventures," Steve added.

"Don't worry...one day I'll actually remember," Ray said.

The two of them finished suiting up and walked out to the body shop floor and walked over to an all black van. The guys in the break room came out around the same time.

"Kevin, get on the internet and find out what's going on at the Mall of America. Maybe we can get an idea of what's going on before we get there," Ray said.

"You got it," Kevin said as he took out his cell phone.

"Why would Joey be at the Mall of America?" Bob asked.

"No idea. You know how Joey works. He pops up everywhere. Look what happened in Syria," Ray said.

"Guy must have a good travel agent," Steve said as he got into the passenger seat of the van.

"Everyone ready?" Ray asked as he got into the van.

"Ready when you are chief," Tommy quickly said in excitement.

"Tommy, make sure you try not to get us killed like last time okay?" Ray asked.

"I'll do my best," Tommy said with a smile as he loaded his pride and joy of a shotgun.

Ray started the van and drove out of the shop. The metallic black van sparkled as the sunshine beat down on it. Clearly anyone could tell that the van had been babied it's whole life. And the large painting of a vicious bull dog with saliva drooling from its angry teeth made it stand out like no tomorrow.

"Kevo, find anything?" Ray asked as he looked in the rear view mirror.

"...Um...ah..." Kevin said out loud as he read.

"Um...ah...ooh..." Bob said making fun of Kevin.

"Yeah, found it...oh shit!" Kevin said.

"I know what that means," Tommy said.

"What's it say?" Ray asked.

"Armed gunmen enter Mall of America. News is reporting that the local and state police are already on the scene along with hostage negotiation and S.W.A.T.," Kevin read on his phone.

"So why would they need us? Sounds like they have plenty of people there," Jasmin asked as he put a piece of gum in his mouth.

"The Russians got a point there. Why would Joey need us?" Steve asked.

"Well, after working with him all these years I figured it's either one of two things. Either A: not much is going on in the world..." Ray began to say.

"Or B?" Steve asked.

"Someone important is in there," Ray finished as he looked at Steve.

Steve sighed (knowing that Ray was right) and then looked out the window.

"Oh it's gonna be a long day..." Steve said.

II

Even though Kevin had given them a list of people who were already there, nothing could prepare them for when they drove up to the top of the street that looked down on the mall.

"Holy shit," Steve said in amazement.

Police cars, ambulances and undercover cars surrounded the place. There must have been a good one hundred cruisers surrounding the large building. And with four helicopters flying around it looked like a war zone was underway. Even the guys in the back took a second to look.

It wasn't anything Ray hadn't already seen before but most of the time Joey was giving him jobs outside the country, so seeing all that in the States definitely took him by surprise for a moment.

"Alright guys...this is it," Ray said as he started driving down the hill.

"Guess you can believe some of the things you read on the Internet," Steve said.

"I wouldn't know. I don't have internet," Bob said in the back just before taking another puff from his cigarette.

"Knowing you, you probably don't even have cable," Kevin added as a joke that got a few laughs.

"Nope. Waste of time," Bob quickly said.

"You're something else Bob," Steve said.

"But that's why we love ya," Ray said.

Bob shrugged his shoulders. "Wish I could say the same."

As the van finally made it down to the end of the hill both Ray and Steve started looking around.

"Where'd he say he be?" Steve asked.

"The far entrance," Ray said as he turned the wheel to the left. "Gotta be down here."

"Hope you're right. Looks like it'd be pretty easy to get lost."

"No I know where I'm going...I think," Ray said.

As Ray accelerated on the gas a sharp pain came from his knee. Normally, the pain started off slow (giving Ray a chance to prepare for it) but this time it came sharp and fast. Once he felt it, he quickly grabbed his knee and attempted to caress it while letting out a fairly quiet groan of pain. The guys in the back didn't hear it, but the same couldn't be said for Steve. Ray slowly looked at Steve and saw that Steve was looking at his knee.

"Still haven't fixed that yet huh?" Steve asked as he looked back out the window.

"When would I've had time to do that?" Ray asked in pain.

"Maybe you should consider taking a vacation," Steve suggested.

"Yeah...maybe one day." Ray said to shut Steve up.

The van pulled into a rather empty parking lot on the far edge of the mall. Five police cruisers covered the entrance but the rest of the parking lot didn't have many cars and that made finding Joey's car easy for Ray.

"There he is. Guys get ready," Ray said to the guys in back.

Bob, Jasmin, Kevin and Tommy quickly put on goggles to cover their faces and each picked up their guns as Ray pulled up to the undercover police car. Leaning up against the hood of the car was a man dressed in a suit with gel all in his hair. Steve got a good look at Joey before putting the goggles on. Once Ray stopped the van and put it in park they all got out.

Ray opened his door and looked around as the police sirens echoed all around him. He suddenly looked up when a helicopter flew past him. Then he focused his attention to Joey (and the pain in his leg) as he walked over to him.

"What's going on here Joey?" Ray asked.

Joey looked at Ray and then looked at the entrance of the mall.

"You said fifteen minuets...it took you seventeen," Joey said in a serious voice.

Ray shrugged his shoulders. "Traffic was bad." Ray said.

Joey looked at Ray and then looked at the guys standing next to him in their all black uniforms (the goggles made it damn near impossible to see who they were).

"I see you're boys are ready to invade Chernobyl," Joey said.

"They always are. So how about we cut the small chat and you just tell us what we're doing here. This doesn't seem like a regular job you'd give us," Ray confessed.

Joey took out his cell phone. "Around two hours ago sixteen men armed with AKA-47's ran in there screaming and lighting up the place. According to some of the people that came out all the security officers are dead and so are a few civilians."

"How many civilians inside?" Ray asked.

"In the middle of the summer and on a Friday? I'm sure you can figure that out for yourself...now since you guys are going in...like that... make sure you watch your fire for civilians. They're already shaken up and between you guys and the actual bad guys in there they probably aren't going to know the difference. Best intel is that many of the shooters will probably be in the security office..." Joey said as he began tapping the screen of his phone.

Ray looked at Steve in confusion and then looked back at Joey.

"...That's it? That's all we're here for?" Ray asked.

Joey lifted is eyes off his phone and looked at Ray for a second.

"You really think I'd call you here just for that? The local P.D. could handle that..." Joey said as he handed his cell phone to Ray.

Ray grabbed the phone and blocked the glare of the sun from the screen. The screen showed a picture of a beautiful young teenage girl. She had a pink sweatshirt on and long black hair running down to her shoulders.

"That's Cassidy Roux...also better known as..." Joey began to say.

"The Secretary of State's niece," Steve finished for Joey.

Joey looked up at Steve.

"Yeah..."

Bob sighed.

"Well now we know why we're here," Bob said.

"This just got a little more complicated," Kevin said.

"Tell me about it," Steve added.

Ray looked back at Joey as Joey took the phone from him and started texting.

"Let me guess: she's inside, isn't she?" Ray asked.

"You know teenagers nowadays. They don't listen for shit. So the job is simple: find her...and kill everyone who gets in your way. I'll send this picture to your phones."

"Alright...how we getting in?" Ray asked.

Joey pointed to the entrance right in front of them. Ray turned and looked (along with the rest of the guys).

"Joe, you know that's not how we do things. Nobody knows about us in case you forgot," Ray said.

"The local P.D. has already been notified that someone from...'higher up' was coming down to take care of the situation. Right now their orders are to simply make sure no one goes in or out," Joey quickly said.

"Just like that?" Ray asked.

"Just like that. I recommend you use silencers until you get close enough to the head honcho calling the shots in there."

"You have a name on him?" Kevin asked.

"At the moment...no. You're just gonna have to wing it this trip," Joey said.

Bob sighed loudly enough to make sure Joey could hear it and walked away. Kevin followed. Joey watched them walk away and then looked back at Ray.

"Look Ray, you know I don't like telling you how to do your job but my orders come from someone a lot higher up than me. It's simple: find the girl and...keep one alive. That way we can just make sure this isn't something bigger," Joey said.

"You know you're being very cryptic with me right now," Ray said.

"Well...for now you just have to go with it. Just do what you do and you'll be fine...I gotta head back to Washington." Joey started walking over to his car.

"Hey Joe!" Ray said to him.

Joey looked up.

"When this is done...you and I...we gotta talk," Ray said.

Joey shook his head. "We'll be in contact." Joey got into his car, started it and drove away. Ray made sure he watched Joey as he drove away. Even though Ray didn't want to admit it to himself, deep down he knew this whole secret thing was starting to become too much to handle. Ray was so busy in thought, he didn't even see Steve stand next to him.

"You know I don't trust that kid," Steve said.

"I trust him...I just don't trust his resources."

"You still wanna do this?" Steve asked.

Ray turned and looked at Steve. "You ask me that like we actually have a choice. Let's just do this and I'll deal with Joey later."

"Fair enough. You should know though...the guys are getting tired of these wild goose chases with this guy," Steve said.

Ray didn't say anything as he walked over to Bob and Kevin (because honestly he already knew. Hell even he was getting tired of doing jobs and being kept in the dark about all of it). But Ray knew that this wasn't the time to worry about that. It was time to save Cassidy first. Ray walked over to the guys as he put his goggles on.

"Okay here's the plan. All of us are gonna go through this entrance like Joey said but were gonna split up. Bob, you and Kevin are gonna head left when we get in, me and Steve will head right. If you run into anyone, hit them with a silencer; Joey was right about that part."

"What about me and Tommy?" Jasmin asked.

"I want you two to guard the entrance when we go in. The clowns in there know they can't leave through any other exit so there gonna try and come through this one when the time comes," Ray said.

"That's all I get to do?" Tommy asked.

"You have problems, don't you?' Jasmin asked Tommy.

"No! I just want to be a bigger help."

Ray looked at Tommy. "Tommy you'll be keeping our exit intact. Trust me that's a huge part of this."

Tommy shook his head.

"Everybody ready?" Ray asked.

They all nodded their heads and Jasmin threw up a thumbs up sign.

"Alright...let's do what we do," Ray said as he cocked his gun.

Ray turned to the entrance and began to walk toward it with the rest of the guys.

"You think the food court is still open?" Jasmin asked Tommy.

"Do you ever stop thinking about food?" Tommy asked.

III

When the team walked inside the mall looked like a ghost town. Bags and purses were scattered everywhere along with a few dead bodies. They all quickly noticed how quiet it was. Ray didn't show it but he was nervous. He knew that at any moment someone could pop out of one of the stores and open fire at them. But he tried to forget about that as he turned to Jasmin and Tommy.

"Okay you guys make a stand here. Bob and Kevin take that way. With any luck this should be able to go nice and smooth," he said.

Jasmin and Tommy stood over by the doors as Bob and Kevin walked down the long hall. Once Bob and Kevin made it down halfway Ray and Steve started to head down the opposite hall.

"You really think this will go over smooth?" Steve asked.

"Course not, but I can't tell them that. They'd freak out," Ray confessed.

"Your knee feeling any better?" Steve asked.

"Not really."

"So where would a teenage girl hang out?" Steve asked.

"Victoria Secrets?" Ray asked.

Steve looked at him.

"You really don't know much about teenagers nowadays do you?"

"Well where do you think they would be?" Ray asked

"I read that the youth of America like to drink tea nowadays so she probably would've been at a store that sells tea," Steve said very professionally.

"Bullshit. Even I don't drink tea."

As Ray turned away from Steve he quickly noticed a man holding a machine gun walk out of a store. Ray quickly grabbed Steve and both dropped down to their knees. The man didn't see them, that was for sure, but he was starting to make his way over to them.

Both Ray and Steve quickly ran over to a wall for cover. Once they were behind it, Ray very carefully stuck his nose out to see if the guy was still walking towards them; he was.

"How you wanna do this?" Ray asked.

"I'll handle it." Steve whispered as he took out a knife.

Ray rolled his eyes. "You and knives."

Steve moved over to Ray's spot and got ready to take action the moment the poor bastard walked over. As the footsteps got closer and closer Steve's heart began to pound heavily. Ray stepped back to give Steve some space. Ray knew that this was gonna be messy.

And sure enough it was. The moment the man walked past the wall Steve suddenly jumped out of cover and put his hand over the man's mouth. The man quickly resisted but Steve immediately shoved the knife into the man's throat. Blood poured out and slowly the man stopped moving. Once Steve felt like there was no more life in the man he dropped him, and the lifeless body fell onto the floor. Then Steve looked at Ray.

"See? Nice and easy," Steve said.

Then suddenly a man cocked a machine gun and aimed it at Steve.

"Do not move," the man said in a foreign accent.

Steve slowly put his hand up in the air.

"Drop the knife," the man ordered.

Steve looked down and dropped the knife. Steve looked at the man and into his eyes and realized he had just sealed his own fate. The man cocked his gun and was just about to shoot when suddenly a bullet blew out of the side of his head. Instantly, the man dropped dead on the ground. Steve wiped the blood off his face and looked at where the shot came from.

Ray was still aiming his silenced pistol at the dead man. Once he made sure the guy was dead he slowly lowered it and then looked at Steve. Steve bent down and picked up his knife as Ray walked over to him.

"Nice and easy huh?" Ray asked.

"Oh shut up," Steve said.

Ray smiled as Steve patted him on the back and then the both of them started to walk down the hall again as blood poured out of the two men they had just killed.

Meanwhile Kevin and Bob were talking, but it was about something entirely different.

"I banged the shit out of her, you wouldn't believe it, Bob," Kevin said to Bob as they looked around.

"Bullshit," Bob quickly said.

"And why don't you believe me?" Kevin asked.

Bob stopped in his tracks and turned to Kevin.

"Because a guy with a face like yours doesn't have a chance with a piece of ass like hers," Bob said.

The brutal honesty made Kevin's mouth drop.

"Nice Bob. And after everything we've been through." Kevin started walking again. "I mean you can't deny that we've been through a lot."

"Yeah well that's coming to an end pretty soon," Bob stated.

That actually surprised. There was no doubt that Bob was pretty miserable in life, but it always seemed like he enjoyed being with the guys, so hearing that really took Kevin off guard.

"What are you talking about?" Kevin asked.

"I'm thinking about leaving," Bob said.

"Why? I thought you liked...doing this. You thinking about working for another group? Please don't tell me you're leaving us for that Roader guy," Kevin said.

"You kidding? Ray would cut my head off if I left him for Roader. I'm thinking about leaving all this for good...I'm getting to old to keep doing this."

"Oh come on, Bob. You know you're only as old as the woman you feel," Kevin said as he patted Bob's arm.

Bob chuckled.

"You're disgusting you know that?"

"Oh that's nice, first you call me ugly and then you call me disgusting. I see how it is," Kevin said.

Back at the entrance, Tommy was playing on his cell phone while Jasmin was putting money into the vending machine. As the change went into the machine it was so loud it almost echoed throughout the hall. It even got Tommy's attention.

"Could you be any louder?" Tommy asked.

"Dude I'm hungry. I didn't get to finish my lunch today," Jasmin admitted.

"Well didn't you have a big breakfast? You Russians are suppose to eat good in the morning right? You probably what...sacrificed a chicken, took off all the feathers and then ate the whole thing right?"

Jasmin let out a big sigh.

"How many times do I have to tell you guys I'm not Russian? I'm Bosnian!" Jasmin pretty much yelled.

"Same thing," Tommy said.

Jasmin shook his head in annoyance and then pressed a few buttons on the vending machine for a candy bar. The candy bar fell and made a louder noise then when the change went in. Once he grabbed the candy bar he walked back over to his post. Tommy looked up at him when Jasmin got back to his spot.

"What'd you get?" Tommy asked.

"Just a candy bar," Jasmin said.

"Nice, you couldn't even get a bag of chips so we could share?" Tommy asked.

"Dude I didn't know you were hungry," Jasmin said as he bit into the candy bar.

"And now you can't even split the candy bar. Thanks friend." Tommy said. Tommy shook his head in disgust and then looked up. His eyes grew big with fear. "Jas!"

Jasmin looked up from taking another bite of his candy bar. That's when he noticed a man with a machine gun patrolling the area. Quickly both of them ducked down for cover.

"You wanna shoot him or let him pass?" Jasmin asked.

"Shoot the fucker!"

Tommy put his shotgun to the side and then took out his handgun.

"Shit!" Tommy said loud enough for the man patrolling to hear.

"What?"

"I didn't bring my silencer. You're gonna have to shoot him," Tommy said in disappointment.

"Don't worry, I'll take care of it," Jasmin said.

Jasmin took out his handgun.

"Oh shit," Jasmin said when he looked at the tip and realized he didn't have his silencer either.

Tommy rolled his eyes.

"Oh this is not good," Tommy said.

While Tommy and Jasmin were discovering they were heading up shit creek and were about to get stuck, Ray and Steve entered a store that was clearly a teenager store. Ray covered the right hand side while Steve covered the left.

"Clear on this side!" Steve said.

"Same here, check the back," Ray ordered.

Steve headed for the counter. As he approached he heard a noise come from behind the counter. He quickly aimed up his gun and slowly proceeded behind the counter and found a young blonde hiding behind it. When she saw Steve in his goggles she quickly gasped in fear. Steve rushed over to her.

"Please don't hurt me. My name is Katie. I'm sixteen years old. I have two dogs, three cats, no boyfriend and I still live with my parents," She quickly said.

Steve was confused.

"Huh? What? No I'm not gonna hurt you," Steve began to say. He looked up to see where Ray was. "Ray!" Steve yelled.

Despite his knee killing him Ray quickly ran over.

"What's up?"

As soon as Katie saw Ray she screamed again.

"Please don't hurt me. My name is Katie. I'm sixteen years old. I have two dogs, three cats, no boyfriend and I still live with my parents," She quickly said again.

Suddenly Steve put his hand over Katie's mouth and looked up at Ray.

"You have a picture of that girl?"

"Yeah," Ray said.

He took out his cell phone and brought up the picture. Then he handed the phone to Steve. Steve quickly grabbed it and showed the picture to Katie.

"Have you seen this girl at all today?" Steve asked Katie.

Ray thought it would be a long shot that Katie would remember. There's so many people in the mall everyday it's hard to remember every face, so Ray thought it was just a waste of time as he watched Katie look at the picture.

"Um...actually yeah. She was in here when the shooting started," Katie said.

Ray looked right at her. "Do you remember where she went?"

"She ran out of the store...but she probably didn't go to far," Katie said.

Ray sighed in disappointment as he looked up. But once he looked up he quickly pushed Steve and Katie behind the counter when he saw two armed men walk into the store. Ray got down on his stomach as Steve put his hand over Katie's mouth. Katie began to cry.

"Shh," Steve whispered into Katie's ear.

It was clear that the two men were walking toward them and it was clear the men weren't very happy about the job as they argued to one another in a different language. Ray aimed his gun for when the two men approached the counter. Suddenly the whole situation changed when Ray heard one of them say a familiar name.

"...Cassidy." One of the men said.

Steve slowly looked at Ray. Ray looked at him.

"Shit," Steve whispered.

Katie started crying harder as Steve pressed his hand down on her face. Then suddenly Steve started to feel something warm going onto his pants. He quickly looked down to see that Katie had wet herself...and all the urine was being picked up by his pants. Steve looked at Katie.

"Really?" Steve asked Katie as she cried harder.

Then suddenly one of the men stepped behind the counter and Ray fired two shots with his silenced pistol. Both bullets hit the man in the chest. As soon as he fell the other man quickly raised his gun but Steve jumped up (while still holding Katie) and fired three times into the man's stomach and chest. The man groaned and quickly fell to the ground. When Steve let go of Katie she dropped back down and started to cry. Ray slowly stood up and looked at the dead men and then looked at Steve as Steve reloaded his gun.

"They know Cassidey's here," Ray said. He bent back down and grabbed Katie by the arms.

"Okay...Katie...here's what I want you to do: I want you to stay right here. Do not move, do not make noise. Just stay here until the police come in alright?" Ray asked.

Katie wiped her eyes and shook her head up and down.

"Okay. Thank you," Ray said as he quickly got up and left.

Steve bent back down and looked at Katie.

"Thanks for the memories sweetheart." Steve said. Then he stood back up and ran over to Ray.

"Which way, right or left?" Steve asked.

"The closest exit is down to the right. She must've gone right," Ray said.

"You sure?"

"Nope. But that's all we've got," Ray said.

"Alright. Hope you're right."

"So did she really..." Ray started to ask.

"Yep, all over me. And we're not talking about it," Steve said.

"Oh, we gonna talk about it alright," Ray said as he chuckled.

"You really are an asshole, aren't you?" Steve asked.

As Steve and Ray headed closer to where they thought Cassidy would be, Tommy and Jasmin were still trying to decide on what they should do about the man walking over to them.

"What do you wanna do?" Jasmin asked.

"We can't shoot him. It'll be to loud," Tommy said.

"So...what do you wanna do?" Jasmin asked again.

"We'll just have to do it the old fashioned way," Tommy said as he grabbed his shotgun from his side.

Jasmin shook his head as he waited for the man to walk over and right when he did Tommy suddenly stood up and hit the man in the face with the butt of the shotgun. The man groaned in pain and dropped his machine gun. Blood started to trickle out of the man's noise. Then Tommy jumped onto the man's back and started punching him. Jasmin watched in almost amazement. Tommy then quickly looked at Jasmin as he started to loose his grip on the man's back.

"Little help would be nice, Jas!" Tommy shouted.

The man elbowed Tommy in the stomach and Tommy fell onto the floor. As Tommy held his stomach in pain the man quickly went to grab his gun but Jasmin suddenly got up and body slammed the man into a wall. The man was clearly in pain, but since he was a good six foot five and was built like a tank he easily grabbed Jasmin's hand, bent it so he could turn around and punched Jasmin in the face twice. After the second punch Jasmin fell to the floor. Tommy knew it would be the only time the man would be venerable so Tommy lunged back up and jumped on the man again and started punching his head.

Jasmin slowly got up and once he did he returned to the man and started punching him as hard as he could. The man groaned in pain after each hit but just as Jasmin went to punch again, the man ducked and Jasmin ended up punching Tommy in the face. Tommy fell off the man and back onto the floor.

"Oh shit," Jasmin said.

The man laughed and then Jasmin went to punch him again but the man blocked it and started punching Jas in the face.

"Stupid American!" The man said with an evil chuckle as he punched Jasmin.

IV

As Ray and Steve came to the end of the hall they realized there were only a few stores left to look before they had to enter another corridor. Ray stopped. It took Steve a few seconds to realize Ray had stopped but once he did, he stopped too.

"What?" Steve asked.

"She wouldn't have made it this far. She's gotta be somewhere around here," Ray said.

"Where then?" Steve asked.

Ray started to look around. There was a very small frozen yogurt shop to his right and then a kitchen store to his left. Ray could clearly see no one was in the yogurt shop so he looked in the windows of the kitchen shop. He almost decided to go back to a few other stores that he passed but suddenly he saw someone move in the window.

"Steve! In here," Ray said as he ran into the place.

Steve quickly followed Ray into the store. They looked around. It seemed empty but Ray was sure that he had seen someone move. He then walked over to the counter and saw movement again. He aimed his gun up and slowly walked to the other side of the counter. When he got to the back he couldn't believe what he saw. There must've been a good thirty people hiding behind it. Ray quickly lowered his gun and then took off his mask when he realized people were frightened by it.

"It's okay I'm not gonna hurt you," Ray said, as he looked at all the people.

"Please don't hurt us," one customer said.

"I won't. I'm looking for a Cassidy. Is anyone named Cassidy here?" Ray asked.

Nobody said anything at first but then suddenly a hand slowly went up. Ray focused his eyes on her, then sighed with relief. It was Cassidy, the girl he was looking for. He quickly ran over to her.

"Cass! Come on I'm here to help you. I work for your father," Ray said.

"You know my Dad?" She asked.

"Well...just trust me, come on! Everyone else stay here and don't move. You'll be safe here!" Ray ordered.

He grabbed Cassidy's hand and took her out of the store. Steve looked at Cass and then looked at Ray.

"Now where?" Steve asked.

"We get the hell outta here! Let the police deal with the rest," Ray said as he ran down the hall with Cassidy.

After five punches in a row, Jasmin fell to the floor with a headache. The man quickly walked away from him and then picked up his machine gun.

"Like I said...stupid American," the man said as he cocked his gun.

He then aimed the assault rifle at Jasmin. Jasmin braced for impact as his stomach grumbled from hunger. He closed his eyes and waited to hear the sound of gunshots...and they came. But it wasn't from a machine gun. It was a handgun. Jasmin quickly opened his eyes to see the man get shot seven times in the chest and face by Tommy. Tommy kept firing until the clip in his gun was empty.

The sound of the gunshots echoed in the mall. Ray and Steve heard it and so did Bob and Kevin. Once he was out of bullets Tommy lowered the gun and went back to holding his stomach on the floor.

"Oh shit," Ray whispered.

"That can't be good," Kevin said as he and Bob stopped dead in their tracks.

Suddenly out of nowhere a good ten men entered the hallway and started shooting at Bob and Kevin. The same thing happened to Steve and Ray. Kevin and Bob ducked and started to run back down the hall.

Ray kept running with Cassidy by his side. He fired a few shots, but the person doing the most shooting was Steve. Steve was walking backwards as he fired at the men with his machine gun. He killed two of them and the rest all ducked for cover. Steve quickly reloaded his gun and spun around to catch up with Ray and Cassidy.

Tommy slowly got back on his feet and walked over to where he dropped his shotgun while Jasmin crawled to his spot and picked up his machine gun. He wiped the blood off his lip and looked at Tommy.

"Thanks."

"Don't thank me yet," Tommy said as he looked up and saw both Bob and Kevin running towards them.

"What happened?" Bob shouted.

"Just fucked ourselves is what happened," Tommy said.

"Where's Ray and Steve?" Kevin asked.

"Right here!" Ray sshouted as he entered the hall at the same time.

Bob noticed Cassidy was with her. "Now what boss?" he asked.

"Cover us!" Ray yelled as he ran to the exit of the mall.

Kevin quickly stopped running, turned around, got down on one knee and aimed his gun down the hall.

"You got it," Kevin said as he closed one eye and looked into his sight.

Bob stopped and aimed his gun down the hall. Tommy stood up and did the same thing. Then Jasmin slowly stood up and cocked his machine gun. Steve took a deep breath and followed. It was clear that a lot of people were coming down the hall by all the footsteps and shouts.

"Cover your ears!" Ray said to Cassidy as they were running.

"Why?" She asked.

Suddenly all the men chasing Kevin, Bob, Steve and Ray entered the hall and were met with incredibly loud gunfire. When the firing began Cassidy quickly covered her ears as she screamed.

"It's gonna be loud!" Ray shouted.

Kevin sprayed bullets all over the place, hitting four people in the chest, neck, leg and stomach as Bob fired and killed two people with headshots. Having just got his ass kicked, Jasmin was having a hard time steadying his gun due to the adrenaline running through him, but was able to shoot one guy in the eye. And Tommy finally got to get his fix. He fired his loud shotgun into the people and blew everything—from chests and fingers to legs and heads—away.

While everyone else just shot at random, it was Steve that made sure every shot he took was lethal. Steve got mostly headshots (a couple chests but mostly heads). And once the last man went down, after having a chunk of his head blew off by the power of Tommy's shotgun, they all stopped firing and took a moment to enjoy the peace and quite. In the distance one man who was injured was slowly moving and Steve aimed in his scope and gave a gentle exhaled before firing one shot into the man's back.

"...Hey weren't we suppose to save one?' Kevin asked after a long pause.

"Whoops," Steve said as he turned and started to walk toward the exit. Kevin chuckled.

"Yeah...that's what I thought," Kevin said as he and Bob followed Steve toward the exit.

Tommy cocked his gun and wiped the sweat off his face and watched Jasmin as he walked over to the man that had beaten the crap out of him. Jasmin aimed his machine gun and fired multiple times into the dead corpse. Tommy jumped from the loudness of the gunshots. Jasmin lowered his gun and then started to walk over to the exit.

"How yeah feeling?" Tommy asked.

"I got my ass kicked...how do you think I'm feeling?" Jasmin asked.

Tommy chuckled as he patted Jasmin on the back.

"Don't worry about it, bud. You'll be able to kick someone's ass one day. And by the way...thanks for punching me in the face! It was a nice wake up call you jerk!" Tommy said.

"...Yeah sorry about that." Jasmin said.

"Really? That's all you're gonna say is sorry? I don't know how you do things in Russia but we treat others with respect in America."

"I'm not Russian!"

"Close enough!"

Chapter 2: Thoughts Of Retirement

After Ray and the guys handed Cassidy over to the authorities, they decided to stop for a bite to eat (Jasmin's idea). First they all decided to go for a sit down meal but in the end Bob convinced everyone that a bar would be the best place to go and relax. While Kevin was buying a round for the gang Ray's cell phone began to ring. At first he couldn't hear it, due to all the noise coming from the bar, but once he reached down to his pocket and realized his phone was vibrating he picked it up.

"Yeah?" Ray asked.

"It's me," Joey said.

"Hey. We took care of it. The girl is all set," Ray said.

"I know. I just got off the phone with my boss. You busy?"

"Not really...why?"

"Come outside..."

Ray started to look around.

"How do you know..."

"Because I know everything. Meet me outside. We can have that chat you wanted," Joey said.

"...Yeah okay. I'll be right out."

Ray took a sip of his piss-warm beer and then headed outside without anyone noticing him leave (with the exception of Steve). As Ray walked outside he looked up into the night sky; blues and pinks filled the sky from the sunset. When he finally looked down he saw Joey standing next to his car which was parked next to the van. Ray walked over to Joey but almost had to limp because of his knee.

"I thought you were heading back to D.C." Ray said.

"What can I say, this city has grown on me. Lord knows I come here enough."

"Yeah...I know," Ray said.

"Secretary of State is glad to have his niece back. Said if you need anything to just let him know," Joey said.

"Any idea who the hell those guys were?" Ray asked even though he really didn't want to know.

"There's a couple thoughts floating around. We probably won't have anything concrete until the morning."

"They were looking for her," Ray added.

"...What?" Joey asked.

"Overheard some of the guys talking and they mentioned her name. There's no doubt they went looking for her."

"...Okay, I'll pass that information along. You know it would've been nice to be able to talk with one of them but according to sources at the mall...there's not very many people able to talk."

"You'd have to talk to the guys. They did the shooting," Ray explained.

Joey shook his head.

"Make sure you keep an eye on them, especially that Tommy character. I can't keep letting him slide like I have," Joey said.

Ray shook his head as he kicked a rock around at his feet.

"I'll keep an eye on him."

Joey cleared his throat and fixed his tie and then looked back up at Ray.

"So what did you wanna talk about?" Joey asked even though he had an idea of what it was going to be about.

"I uh...don't think I can keep doing this," Ray confessed with shame.

Joey didn't say anything at first. He let it sink in. Then he shrugged his shoulders.

"You'll have to be more specific, Ray."

"You know what I'm talking about Joe."

Joey shook his head.

"...Okay. Why now?"

Ray put his hands up in the air.

"Look at me. There's nothing left. Everyone thinks I run a body shop. My own family doesn't even know about what I really do. I know you're still new to this but I've been doing this with the guy before you and the guy before him. I've pushed my family so far away that it feels like I may never be able to reconnect with them. I know it may be too little now but if I keep this up I'll be too late. You can't beat the clock, kid. You'll understand that, as you get older. It's not like I'm some spring chicken."

Joey didn't say anything. Honestly what could he say? He knew exactly where Ray was coming from. But in the back of his mind he also knew what Ray and the guys were doing every time they went out.

"I'm sorry but I can't do this anymore. I've lost enough as it is," Ray said as he started to walk away.

"Let me ask you something," Joey said.

Ray stopped and turned around.

"Why'd you decide to do this for all these years?" Joey asked. "I know we've only been working together for a few years, and when I took this job I was told not to ask any questions, but just tell me that."

Ray sighed.

"Because I saw what the world was turning into. I saw the cruelness that mankind can do...and I also knew back then that I had a baby girl at home. And to just walk away from it and hand her a world that was bound for disaster, when I could've made a difference, wouldn't have been right. If something happened to her...it...it would've been my fault because I would've known that I could've changed the world but I choose not to." Ray was trying to hold back tears.

Joey sighed and looked down. Ray continued.

"But now? She's grown up. I don't see her, I don't talk with her but every time I go out there...all I do is think of her. Sometimes it feels like I go one step forward and an asshole with a gun pushes me two steps back. I know that's not the answer you wanna hear but sometimes the truth hurts a lot more then any lie you could come up with."   Joey took his hands out of his pockets and walked over to Ray.

"You save the world every time you go out there. I know you don't get credit for it. I know you'll never be remembered for it, but there's a side of history that isn't written down...but if it was...your name would be all over it. You know man, I've talked to my boss about telling people about you guys, but...he just wants you guys to be safe. I know that isn't right but every time I have the conversation with him...I do agree with him at the end."

"...Yeah. So would I," Ray said.

"But listen, if you want to leave, I can't stop you and even if I could I wouldn't. You've done a lot for your country. And it's because of you that your daughter doesn't have to worry about some terrorist evening up a score every time she goes out. You may not see it but you've been a big part of her life. After all these years...how many times have you stopped a possible terrorist attack? How many lives have you saved?"

"I don't keep count of the lives I've saved...I keep count of the ones I've lost," Ray said.

"Nobody said this would be easy...so if you decide this is what you really want then by all means go for it. I won't stop you," Joey said.

Ray shook his head.

"Thanks."

"But I will need a favor from you if you decide to go."

"What?"

"You're gonna need a replacement," Joey began to say.

"...Well I love all the guys, but if I had to choose..."

"You wouldn't be able to choose," Joey interrupted.

Ray gave Joey a funny look.

"What? I built this team to what it is today and I can't decide who takes over?" Ray asked out of frustration.

"If it was up to me..." Joey began to say before he got interrupted.

"Yeah, yeah. If it was up to you the whole world would be sunglasses and limos. Just cut the shit and tell me what I need to hear."

"I had a feeling you would come to me and tell me this, so I mentioned it to my boss and he's already found a replacement for you. But we'd like you to train him before you decide to go," Joey said.

Ray put his hands in the air.

"So what am I suppose to do, just shit on the rest of the guys while some guy fresh out of the academy takes my place?" Ray yelled.

"I'm sorry Ray. I didn't want it to be this way. I tried to change it but it's out of my hands," Joey confessed.

Ray started to walk around as he tried thinking about the whole situation.

"Then I don't want any part of it. I'm not doing that to the guys," Ray said as he started to walk away again.

"This is happening with or without you. Now wouldn't you want the guy in charge of the team to be taught by someone as good as you? Because if you leave right now and walk away...I guarantee you you'll be questioning it for the rest of your life. Think about your daughter..." Joey said.

Ray quickly walked over to Joey and grabbed him by the collar of his shirt. Joey could see the anger in his eyes.

"Don't ever talk about my daughter. You haven't earned the right! You came to me! Not the other way around," Ray shouted.

Joey swallowed hard but kept his cool. He knew this wouldn't be easy to begin with anyway.

"You know you're just like the rest of the assholes in Washington. You fuck up the world and then put people like me in harm's way to try and fix it. You're no better then the rest of them. And I was a fool to think you'd be any different," Ray said.

Joey inhaled deeply.

"I need an answer Ray," Joey said as he looked into Ray's eyes.

Ray suddenly let go of his shirt.

"I'll do it, but on one condition."

"Name it."

"I don't ever want to see you again. This is over," Ray said with anger.

Joey looked at him.

"Fine...you train this guy...you make him the best and you won't see me ever again."

"Have him come to my shop in the morning," Ray said as he turned his back to Joey.

"He's there now."

Ray turned back to Joey.

"Like I said I had a feeling you'd be saying this to me," Joey said.

Ray shook his head and walked away. Joey exhaled as he thought about trying to say something to change the situation but he knew it would be better to just let it go, so Joey got into his car and drove off and accepted the fact that the only man in the world he thought was a hero never wanted to see him again.

When Ray got back into the bar pretty much everyone was cocked. While Kevin and Bob joked to each other, Tommy was trying to hit on some chick who was clearly twenty years younger then him while Jasmin was passed out at the bar. As soon as Ray walked in he picked up his beer and drank it. Steve instantly knew something was wrong.

"Hey. Everything alright?' Steve asked.

Ray sighed and he reached down and rubbed his leg.

"I gotta head to the shop," Ray said.

Steve looked surprised.

"Why? It's almost nine o clock at night."

"Something came up," Ray said as he finished his beer.

"By something you mean Joey? That kid is going to run you into the ground," Steve said as he chuckled.

"It's not Joey. It's something I did," Ray said.

"Oh...you wanna go at it alone?"

"No not really," Ray said.

Steve patted him on the back.

"I'll meet you in the van."

Ray smiled as he watched Steve head for the door. But he quickly lost the smile when he thought about some new guy taking over the team when it should've been Steve that was chosen. But Ray had been working with these guys long enough to realize that once a decision was made, that was it. Ray put down his beer and walked over to Bob.

"Make sure everyone gets home safely alright?"

"Yes sir!" Bob said half in the bag.

Ray patted his shoulder.

"Good job today," Ray said right before he walked out of the bar.

When Ray walked outside and over to the van he saw Steve standing outside holding something in his hand. Ray had to take a few steps before he realized that he was holding a file.

"What's that?" Ray asked.

Steve looked up.

"Dunno. Found it on the windshield," Steve said just before handing it to Ray.

Ray took the file and opened it. Inside was a picture of a very young man in a military uniform. After the picture was a bunch of papers and copies of college degrees and life history.

"Who's...Johnny Torque?" Steve asked as he read the name on the top of the picture.

"We're about to find out," Ray said.

"What?"

"I'll explain on the way," Ray said as he got into the van.

II

While Ray tried to explain the situation about him leaving to Steve, across the ocean, in a different time zone, in the deserted city of Chernobyl, in a rundown apartment complex overlooking the nuclear reactor that wiped out the city, a dark and very dangerous man known by his friends and victims as Dutra sat at his desk and looked across the lost city.

Many throughout the world consider what happened in Chernobyl as a horrific accident, but Dutra looked at it with admiration. He was fascinated by the fact that a manmade chemical could betray its own creator and prove it was stronger then the mind of scientists (and not to mention that Dutra was a firm believer that there are simply too many people in the world).

But a knock on his door quickly brought him out of that rather disturbing train of thought. Even though he heard the door open he didn't bother to greet Vincent, his longtime associate and muscle that went with him everywhere. Vincent walked up the desk and stood in a military type posture (from the posture, to the bald head and massive muscles, Vincent was clearly an AWOL marine).

"Good news or bad?" Dutra asked.

"We lost her," Vincent said.

Dutra didn't say anything for a moment; he was too occupied with looking at the view. But once he did Vincent could clearly hear the anger in his voice.

"How?"

"Still trying to figure that out. But whoever it was were able to kill all of our men and rescue the girl."

Dutra started biting his fingernail.

"Local cops wouldn't be able to take down twenty of my guys...no," Dutra slowly said.

"You think it's them?" Vincent asked.

Dutra slowly swiveled his chair around so he could look at Vincent.

"...Yeah."

"You want us to put things on hold?"

"No. We proceed as planned. The girl was just going to be used as a diversion anyway. Give the orders to stand down until I get there." Dutra stood up.

"Not sure I know what you mean by that, sir."

"...I'm going back home. Tell Street to meet me in New York," Dutra ordered. "You want me to come with you?" Vincent asked.

Dutra smiled. It was the type of smile that provided compassion but also a dark shade of mystery.

"Of course. Gonna need all hands on deck for this next job."

"You think they'll suspect anything?" Vincent asked knowing that Dutra reassuring him would keep Dutra in a positive state (because nothing was worse then when Dutra was angry).

"The beauty of the American dream is that Americans firmly believe no superpower could ever match them and over time...if people think like that long enough...their guard slowly goes down. This is the perfect opportunity to prove them wrong. And trust me Vincent...once this is over...a new dawn will rise," Dutra said as he patted Vincent on the arm.

Dutra walked over to the door to the office and shut the lights off.

"Tell the boys downstairs to get my helicopter ready," Dutra instructed as he walked out of the office.

"Yes sir."

Even though deep down Vincent actually thought his soul wasn't as tainted as Dutra's...it honestly was just as dark. Vincent hadn't killed nearly as many people as Dutra had but he never tried to stop Dutra...and had no intentions of ever trying to. In the end, no matter what Vincent tried to tell himself when he couldn't sleep, he was still just as hell bound as Dutra was.

III

While Dutra and his men headed to the nearest airport, back at home Ray and Steve were just getting back to the shop where they were about to meet the 'new guy' Joey had sent over. Ray knew that Steve wouldn't be happy about the decision and sure enough Steve wasn't.

"I'm not mad at you; please don't think I am...it's just that I was suppose to take over when the time came," Steve said in a pissed off voice as they walked Into the dark shop.

"I know Steve. I tried telling Joey that but...you know how kids are today. They couldn't give two shits on our advice. Let's just get this over with, meet this new guy and next time I talk to Joey I'll tell him he isn't gonna cut it," Ray said to try and calm down Steve, even though he knew it wouldn't work.

Steve shook his head in anger.

"I told you not to trust that kid," Steve said.

"...Yeah I know." Ray said as they walked over to his office.

"So you really gonna do it this time?" Steve asked Ray.

"Do what?"

"Retire? I know you've been thinking about it for a while now."

"Why does everyone keep saying that?" Ray asked.

"I don't know why everyone else thinks that but I'm sure you know why I think that," Steve said.

"My knee is fine. It just gets stiff once and a while!" Ray shouted.

"That's what she said," Steve said right before he laughed.

Ray couldn't help but laugh too.

"You're a piece of work," Ray said.

"Well I was taught by the best," Steve said.

"I taught you how to shoot. I never taught you how to be disgusting. You learned that all on your own."

"No, believe it or not I use to be a very polite guy," Steve said.

"What happened?"

"I met Bob," Steve said as he smiled.

Ray shook his head.

"Yeah I can understand that." Ray opened the door and turned the light on into his office.

When the light kicked on it lit up the room to reveal a very muscular man sitting in a chair across from Ray's desk. Both Ray and Steve instantly knew it was that Torque kid from the file. Obviously that picture was taken rather recently. Torque quickly looked up when the two walked in. Ray met his eye contact.

"You know the polite thing to do is to wait outside until someone let's you in," Ray said in a rough voice.

Torque shook his head.

"Yes sir, but my orders were to wait in your office sir," Torque said.

Ray waved his hand in the air as he sat down.

"First things first: stop calling me sir. It's degrading and makes me feel old," Ray quickly said.

Torque was just about to reply 'yes sir' but was able to bite his lip before his mouth opened, so he just shook his head and looked down. Ray let out a deep breath and grabbed the file from Steve. As soon as Steve handed the file to Ray he started to stare at Torque. Clearly it made Torque uncomfortable, and he wore a nervous look on his face. Ray opened the file and placed it down on his desk.

"Quite impressive I'll give you that. Three Purple Hearts, two Bronze Stars and one Silver Star. Clearly you know how to handle yourself with a gun."

"That or you know how to give one hell of a blowjob," Steve added.

Torque looked up at Steve. Steve had a small trace of a smile on his face. Torque clearly knew that Steve was only there to give him shit. But Torque tried to stay focused on Ray.

"Let me ask you something Torque: when they sent you down here what did they tell you about what this was?" Ray asked.

Torque cleared his throat and made eye contact with Ray.

"They...uh said I was about to move all the way up and yet still feel like I was at the bottom," He confessed.

Ray shook his head.

"Well, whoever told you that wasn't bullshitting you that's for damn sure. In fact that pretty much hits the nail right on the head." Ray looked down at the file and began to read some of it.

Torque swallowed again and looked down.

"...You don't have much family," Ray softly said to himself.

"No sir. I mean no." Torque quickly corrected himself.

"Says here you were a sergeant when you were over in Iraq...three tours of duty...even talks about giving you the Medal of Honor for saving four of your own guys..." Ray said as he looked up at Torque.

"Hope you didn't come here to try a get more awards because if you did...you might as well leave now," Steve said.

"With all due respect friend I came to talk with Ray. Nobody asked you to be a part of this," Torque shot back.

Filled with rage Steve suddenly grabbed the chair next to him and gave it a toss across the room. It made a loud bang as it hit the wall.

"I don't know who you think you are boy but you're fucking around with someone who you shouldn't be fucking with!" Steve said as he walked over to Torque.

Torque quickly stood up and got into Steve's face.

"I could say the same," Torque said.

Ray slowly stood up.

"Guys..." Ray started to say.

Steve rolled his eyes.

"All you young guys are the same. You think just because you joined the army, fucked a couple nurses and played ball together makes you a real veteran. You probably didn't even pick up a weapon. Did yeah sport?" Steve asked.

Torque kept his eye contact with Steve.

"And don't even try to stare me down with the thousand yard stare. I see more wiping my ass in the morning then you have any day of the week."

"Surprised you can still wipe your own ass, Gramps," Torque said.

And just like that whatever was holding Steve back disappeared into rage. Suddenly Steve threw a punch and hit Torque right in the face. The force form Steve's right hand knocked Torque to the wall as his lip began to bleed. Ray quickly stepped in.

"Hey!" Ray yelled.

Torque bolted for Steve, but before he could get close to him Ray grabbed him and threw him back down into the chair. The moment Ray saw Torque land in the chair he turned and pointed to Steve.

"Get out," Ray said.

"Oh come on, you really think I'm gonna let this pussy talk to me like that?" Steve yelled.

"Steve! Out!!!" Ray ordered.

Torque looked up at Ray as he wiped the blood from his lip. Steve put his hands in the air and went for the door. Ray kept his eyes on Steve as he swung open the door and slammed it shut. Then Ray looked back down at Torque, then walked back over to his desk and sat down as the pain from his knee began to take over his anger. Underneath the desk he began rubbing his knee.

"I don't know where you were taught but that's not how we do things around here! Around here you're no better than any other guy! Look at me Torque!" Ray shouted to get his attention.

Torque looked at Ray.

"What we do together is the same thing you did overseas only a hell of a lot more is at stake! If we fuck up the world ends and none of us will be around to see another tomorrow! And I am NOT gonna let some young punk ruin what's taken me years to build up! Do you understand me?" Ray shouted.

Torque didn't say anything.

"Do you understand me?!" Ray shouted as loud as he could.

"Yes!!!" Torque shouted back.

Ray exhaled and tried to cool off before he said anything else. Torque did the same. A good five minuets must've gone by before Torque spoke.

"You know my generation may act cocky but I'd like you to look me in the eye and tell me you didn't act the same way when you were our age. And if you can tell me you didn't then I'll walk out of here right now." Torque said.

Ray was going to say that he never was but quickly decided not to when he realized that would be a lie. Ray never bragged about what he did in the war but even he couldn't deny that when he came home he thought everyone else who stayed behind were beneath him.

"You know you guys say that all we did over in Iraq is walk down streets and fuck nurses and horny villagers. Did some of the guys do that? You're damn right they did! Some guys didn't give a shit. All they wanted was the pension that came with signing your life over for two years. Did some of us see action? No! And I wish to God I could say I was one of those guys that hadn't but I can't. I saw everything. From the massacres to four-year-old kids firing guns at us. I've done things that will never come off my soul. Who do you think had to kill those kids who were firing at us? Who do you think had to hold his best friend in his arms and lie to him saying that he would be alright when I knew deep down he was a goner? In any war it's kill or be killed. Weather it was Vietnam or Iraq; war is war..." Torque said.

Ray slowly lowered his head and looked down at the file as his Torque's words sunk it.

"And you don't have to respect me or any of the guys that came back. That's fine by me. Hell I don't even respect half of them, but by God at least respect the fact that some of us did what we had to do." Torque wiped the sweat off his face.

Ray didn't want to admit it but the kid was right. War is war no matter where you go. The mission is the same no matter where they send you; kill the guy in front of you before he gets the chance to kill you first.

After waiting long enough Torque shook his head and started to get up. At first Ray didn't even see him. Ray was too busy thinking about what his soul had gone through. And a lot that Torque said he went through was the same that Ray went through. But when he finally noticed that Torque was walking to the door Ray knew he had to say something before Torque left.

"I got drafted for Nam back in sixty-eight..." Ray began to say.

Torque stopped in the doorway. He didn't turn around but he did stop. He would've turned around but he didn't want Ray to see that just bringing up those memories in a couple sentences started to bring tears to his eyes.

"...I had just married my wife at the time. We were gonna wait but after I found out...we thought it would be best to do it while I was still around...and so we did. We got married, went on our honeymoon and eleven days later it was time to say goodbye," Ray said before he paused.

Torque lowered his head into the darkness of the shop. Ray looked at Torque and then looked down at his desk.

"When I said goodbye to her...just before I got onto the plane...I balled my eyes out. I was positive that I would never see her again. I couldn't tell her that but deep down I didn't have to, But the last thing she said to me was 'I'll see you soon'. And then I left for two years," Ray said.

Torque wiped his eyes and slowly turned to Ray. When Ray saw him turn he looked up at him.

"I saw a lot of shit in those two years...I did a lot of shit in those two years. I saw people slaughtered, too. I didn't have kids shooting guns at me but I had them dropping grenades in our boots. But somehow I got promoted to sergeant too which is a slick way of them saying 'congratulations now you get to go to the front lines and be the first the set of boots on the field'..."

Torque swallowed as Ray's eyes began to slowly gloss over.

"The last place I went was in this shit storm called the A Shau Valley. Our boys had been getting shot up pretty good around there...so when we landed, we got orders to take a hill numbered '937'. At first it wasn't too bad but as we slowly made our way up the hill we found out those gooks were tucked in there good. Two moments stand out where I thought I was gonna die. The first was when we radioed for air support. Seemed like a good idea at the time but when the choppers came down they couldn't tell who was who and ending up killing more of us then they did of the enemy..."

As Torque imagined it he began to close his eyes. Ray's eyes started to get glossier.

"...The second is when I lost my main gunner...Private Praft...good kid and a solid head on his shoulders. He was the only person I can say was a friend there. Some nights I would stay up talking with him about what we had back home and it would always make everything seem okay...almost like the light at the end of the tunnel was close enough to see. When I got promoted I made sure he stayed with me. He was a good friend but man was he a better gunner. That kid was like a tank. He just kept going and going. I always knew I would be okay as long as I heard him shooting. But on either the fifth or sixth day of fighting I suddenly stopped hearing his gun...so I slowly turned around. For a brief second I thought maybe he was just reloading but my gut told me something else. You know your heart may lie but your gut never does...and sure enough when I turned...I saw that he had taken a bullet to the chest. I'm not gonna lie I panicked. I quickly grabbed him and took him over to this small blown up tree that was just outside the shooting zone. I looked into his eyes and I promised him...I gave him my word that I would be back for him...so I left him, walked up that hill and killed every fucker that caught my eye. It didn't seem like that long of a fight maybe a couple minuets or so and once I realized no one was moving I told the guys to get up there and get to the top of the hill. And I kept my word...I went back to him...but it was too late...Praft was gone..."

Torque wiped his eyes and quietly sniffled.

"...I've always kept my promises but I wish to this day I would've promised to get back to him while he was alive. Maybe that would've put me in high gear to finish the fight faster so I could tend to him...but war has a funny way or creating more questions than answers," Ray said as a tear rolled down his face.

Once Ray felt tears in his eyes, he knew he wasn't going to be able to get to sleep that night on his own, so he opened his desk and took out a bottle of whiskey. He quickly opened the cap and took a mouthful and swallowed hard.

"I had seen death before. Hell it was everywhere I looked, but when I looked into his eyes...it was something else. A part of my soul died in his eyes when I saw how lifeless they had become. That's something you don't forget. Not even time can take away that. It may blur the edges but you can still make out the picture. When we got to the top of the hill I looked around at what was left. I did a head count and made a ballpark guess as to how many we lost...I wasn't off by much. 600 of us went up...less then a third came back down."

Torque wanted to say something but he just didn't know what. What could he say? But how could he not say anything?

"While we waited for the choppers to pick us up I thought about what we wanted to call the hill. We threw a few ideas around but once someone threw the name up...it instantly clicked; course I never liked the name but hey all the other guys didn't seem to mind it. And once I left there and got home to see my wife and baby girl, I went back to dealing with normal problems like bills and money. I was hell bent to leave the war life behind me but then I got a knock on my door one afternoon and was told about the money I could make if I stayed longer...so I decided to keep doing it...and it's a decision I regret every day of my life. It started off small and before I knew it, it became what it is today... I didn't choose this because I enjoyed it, I did it because I wanted my family to be supported and most of all protected...and they are...I just lost them along the way...I guess even if you survive Hell...it still takes a piece of you." Ray took another sip of whiskey

"...I'm sorry, Ray." Torque said.

Ray shook his head.

"A lot of people have said that to me...you might be the only person I actually believe." Ray said.

Torque shook his head.

"Listen tell that guy...Steve, I said sorry for me, will yeah?" Torque asked.

Ray finished taking another sip.

"Tell him yourself tomorrow. 6am." Ray said.

It took Torque a moment to realize what Ray was saying then it finally hit him.

"You got it." Torque said just before he started to walk into the darkness of the shop.

But Torque didn't get to far. He had one last question for Ray.

"Hey Ray?" Torque asked.

Ray swallowed another mouthful of booze.

"Yeah?"

"Just out of curiosity: what did you guys end up naming the hill?" Torque asked.

Ray sighed.

"...Hamburger Hill...see you tomorrow kid."

Torque smiled in the darkness.

"Thanks Ray," Torque said softly.

"Oh you won't be thanking me tomorrow," Ray added.

And with a smile on his face Torque walked out of the shop while Ray spent a large part of the night drinking his whiskey and looking back at all the decisions he's made in his life; proving that no one ever really leaves Vietnam.

Chapter 3: Code Five

Torque kept his promise. He was at the shop exactly at 6am. And Ray kept his promise too. The training course that he set up in the back was good enough for even the army to train in. Most of the obstacles were made from old piece of shit cars but Ray knew it would work (after all he still had the scar on his arm from when he had to do it).

The course started off rather normal: run around the entire center three times, then head down to the pit where Torque had to climb up four cars that were stacked on top of each other. Then he had to jump down, pick up the silenced machine gun (because God only knows what would happen if they decided to fire a machine gun without a silencer in the middle of the city) and take down the targets while not hitting any civilian targets that popped up out of nowhere.

As Torque made his way further into the obstacle, the guys stood near the top and watched. None said anything but all were impressed by just how well Torque was doing. Even Bob was (and that's saying something because not too much impresses Bob).

"Five bucks says he shoots the civilian behind the car," Kevin said.

"You're on," Tommy said.

"Make it twenty," Jasmin said as he took a sip of his soda.

"Jas! As much as we love ya, you can't bet on it," Tommy said.

"Why the hell not?" He asked.

"Because you shot the target too on your first try!" Bob said.

"Oh you guys suck. You really expect me to believe that none of you shot the target when you were down there your first time?" Jasmin asked.

"Oh course we did! But we only wounded the target. You blew its goddamn head off!" Tommy said.

"Screw you guys." Jasmin took another sip of soda.

"Don't feel bad Jas..." Ray said as he put his sunglasses on.

"Yeah coming from the guy who built the damn thing. That's not saying much," Jasmin said as he looked back down at Torque who had just shot a target with a double tap.

Steve turned away from Torque and looked at Ray.

"Putting a target there was a real shitty move, Ray. Even I shot the damn thing," Steve admitted.

Ray looked at Steve and leaned closer to him.

"Yeah I know, I shot the bastard too," Ray said.

Steve suddenly got confused.

"How the hell did you manage that? You put it there!" Steve said.

"What can I say Steve, it pops up quick," Ray admitted.

Steve chuckled as he turned and looked back at Torque.

"Alright here we go," Steve said.

Down in the pit Torque walked over to an old Ford car that had last seen the road sometime in the mid 80s. Suddenly, a bang from behind Torque grabbed his attention and he quickly turned and aimed the gun where the sound had come from. The moment he turned around the target of a black civilian popped up. Out of the corner of his eye Torque saw the target come up and suddenly dropped to the ground and fired one shot at the target.

"Ooohhhh!" Everyone yelled from the hill.

When Torque heard it he looked up at them for a moment and then looked back at the target.

"You had to make it a black man, didn't you?" Steve asked Ray.

Ray sighed.

"Oh come on don't start this conversation again. I told you it was the last target in the package!" Ray confessed.

"Sure it was you racist bastard," Steve said.

"Shut up Steve," Ray said as he chuckled.

Torque quickly stood up and walked over to the target.

"Oh shit," he said when he realized it was a civilian.

"Come on Torque, sprint to the finish!" Ray yelled from the hill.

Torque quickly put it into high gear and started running to the finish. And when he started running all the jokes quickly went aside...and everyone dropped their jaw.

"Holy shit," Kevin said as he watched Torque run to the end.

When he ran past the red line that was spray-painted on the ground he put his gun in the air.

"Time!" Ray yelled as he looked at Bob. "Bob what was the time?"

Bob stopped the timer in his hand and looked at it.

"One minute and two seconds."

"Christ what was the old record?" Tommy asked.

"...One minuet and six seconds," Ray confessed.

Steve sighed.

"Big deal, I could do it that fast if I wanted to," Steve said in a cocky voice.

"Wasn't your time one minute and fifteen seconds though?" Ray asked Steve as Steve started to walk over to the body shop.

"Yeah it was, but remember my leg hurt that day? I bet you I could do it just as fast now or if not faster," Steve said.

"Liar," Ray said as he smiled.

"Alright I want my five bucks!" Tommy said.

"Bullshit I want my twenty!" Jasmin said.

"Jas no way man! I made the bet first," Tommy shouted.

"I thought Kevin made it first," Bob said.

"Hold on guys," Kevin said as he looked through binoculars.

"What?' Ray asked.

"Look for yourself," Kevin said right before throwing the binoculars to Ray.

Once Ray caught them he put them to his eyes and looked at the target. He slowly exhaled when he realized the target didn't have a bullet hole in it.

"How the fuck did he do that?" Kevin asked.

"How'd he do what?" Jasmin asked as he took a bit of a candy bar.

"He didn't hit the target," Kevin said as he walked away.

"I thought he fired a shot, no?" Bob asked Ray.

"Must've missed," Ray said as he lowered the binoculars.

Tommy shook his head before looking at Jasmin getting ready to bite into the candy bar.

"Jasmin do you ever stop eating...like ever?" Tommy asked.

"I have a high metabolism," Jasmin said.

Bob chuckled under his breath.

"Jas...I hate to break this to you but if you had a high metabolism you wouldn't be approaching three hundred pounds," Tommy said.

Jasmin was going to reply but decided he'd rather finish the mouthful of candy bar he had instead of engage with Tommy, so instead he just flipped up his middle finger. Ray couldn't help but laugh. And that's when he started to really think about leaving these guys. At home sitting in the dark it seemed like a great idea, but when he was actually with them he couldn't imagine it. Deep down he didn't want too either.

Inside the shop Steve had just walked in to take a leak. He almost made it to the door when the phone rang. He suddenly stopped dead in his tracks. The phone rang again and Steve counted down the seconds to see if it was gonna ring again...and it didn't. Suddenly Steve ran over to the phone and waited for it to ring again...and sure enough it did. He quickly picked up before the ring had the chance to finish.

"Yeah?" He asked.

"Steve it's Joe, where's Ray?" Joey asked

"He's outside watching that GI Joe that you sent over," Steve said in a pissed off voice.

"Well go get him. I need to speak with him." Joey said.

Steve sighed.

"You know Joe after what happened between you and him last night, I think you better just give the man some space," Steve said.

"...Listen Steve..." Joey began to say before he got interrupted.

"No you listen Joe! Ray's out there doing what you asked...again. So if you have an issue you bring it up to me."

Joey sighed. He knew he wasn't gonna get anywhere with Steve. It was clear that Ray had told him about everything that was going on.

"My boss wants a meeting with Ray over in D.C." Joey began.

"For what?" Steve asked.

"That's all I know. But we need him here today..."

"...What about the rest of us?"

"We need you too. We need all hands on deck for this...Steve...it's a code five."

Even though Steve was pissed at Joey for forcing Ray to train the very same man that was gonna be replacing him he quickly pushed those feelings off to the side.

"We'll be there in an hour," Steve said right before hanging up.

Steve had been in the business long enough to know what Joey meant by a code five. Steve had only worked on a code five once damn near twenty years ago when he just started out with Ray. It was serious then and judging by the tone of Joey's voice it was serious now. While Steve took a moment to process everything, Kevin walked into the office.

"Dude you wouldn't believe the shit I just took. I swear it looked like a babies arm...what's wrong?" Kevin suddenly asked.

"Get your shit ready. We're moving out," Steve said.

"What?"

"Get your gear and round up everyone else's. We got a code five." Steve said as he quickly walked out of the office.

"What's a code five?" Kevin yelled to Steve as Steve ran outside.

Because he was so use to Steve never explaining himself, Kevin shrugged his shoulders and began to round up the gear for the guys as he tried to think about what a code five was.

Back outside the guys were trying to make it seem like Torque could've done better (despite the fact that none of them ever came anywhere close to finishing the obstacle course as fast as he did).

"Sloppy," Bob said.

"Not to mention you shot a hostage," Tommy added.

Out of breath and covered in sweat, Torque exhaled deeply and tried to not let the negativity get him down because despite what they said in his gut he knew he did pretty good. He picked up a bottle of water and took a large mouthful as Steve came running over.

"Bob, Tommy, Jas, new boy! We got a job! Get suited up and be ready to go in five!" Steve ordered.

The guys quickly took off but just as Torque was walking away Ray quickly grabbed his arm.

"I'll tell you right now: if that's all you can offer me...then I'm not impressed. Get your head in the game kid or you'll be left out on the sideline," Ray said with a serious look on his face.

Torque shook his head and ran to the shop to get ready. But as soon as Steve came over, Ray quickly told him what he really thought.

"Kid is amazing. Even I couldn't do that when I was his age," Ray said as he lit up a cigar.

"You probably don't even remember how you were at that age."

Ray rolled his eyes. If any of the other guys said that to him, he probably would've sucker punched them, but since Steve was a close friend (and only a couple years younger then Ray) he let it slide.

"So what's up?" Ray asked.

"Just got off the phone with Joe..." Steve began.

"I don't even want to hear that kid's name. I told him I was done," Ray said.

"Ray..." Steve softly said.

Ray looked into Steve's eyes. Steve was known for a lot of things and the honesty of the eyes was one of them.

"...Ray it's serious. Joey just said a code five."

When the words clicked in Ray's head, he quickly filled with fear.

"Where we going?" Ray asked as he exhaled.

"D.C. Guess we're meeting with Joe's boss."

"Sullivan? Oh shit," Ray softly said.

"What?" Steve asked.

Ray took another inhale of his cigar.

"I haven't had a face to face with Sullivan in years...might actually be serious this time around," Ray admitted.

"When was the last time you had a meeting with him?" Steve asked.

"...Gotta be close to three years now," Ray confessed.

And suddenly Steve saw the other side. He clearly remembered what the last code five brought.

"Come on let's go!" Ray said as he began to run to the shop. "When does he want us there?"

"ASAP." Steve said as he followed Ray.

"Alright let's get moving then."

II

While the guys grabbed the gear and headed to D.C. (and while Kevin and Tommy tried to figure out what code five meant), Dutra had finally made it back to the states. When he stepped off the plane at LaGuardia he was met with not only twenty of his finest men but also his second right hand man and muscle: Street. As soon as Dutra saw Street (mostly because of the shine his bald head gave off) he quickly walked over to him and they shook hands.

"Welcome back, sir," Street said firmly.

"Everything ready?" Dutra asked.

"Ready to roll, just waiting for the order," Street admitted.

Dutra took a second to watch all the people moving all about the airport. Street (much like Vincent) knew that when Dutra was in deep thought it was best to wait for him to say the next word. The last time someone tried to interrupt Dutra while he was thinking, it ended with a bullet in the head for that poor bastard (Dutra took it as a sign of disrespect).

"Take a look around Street," Dutra ordered.

Street slowly turned to the crowd and started to watch the people moving all about the busy airport.

"Mexican's, sand niggers, black niggers, fish heads, cunts and towel heads... living together like one big happy fuckin family...makes me sick. But you know what bothers me the most?" Dutra asked as he watched a young black girl texting on her phone.

"What's that boss?" Street asked.

"It's that they choose to come here...to the land I grew up in. They get tired of tainting their own country so they decide to come here and taint this one. Motherfuckers." Dutra put on his sunglasses.

"That's a strong way to look at it. Couldn't agree with it more."

Dutra slowly took his eyes off of the black girl and focused on a Jewish family.

"The sign on the Statue of Liberty might as well say 'Give me all your low lives, your careless and retards'. They all think the American dream is alive and well...but little do they know they're the reason it died in the first place. America needs to be looked at in a different light and when we finish this job, as God as my witness it will be. The light will be so blinding, those who survive the blast will be left with dead families and broken dreams. Then maybe they'll realize it was best to stay in there own fucking country. You know the old saying, though, Street: sometimes you have to start over to make everything right..." Dutra said as he looked around in disgust.

"I understand boss," Street said.

"Vincent call yet?" Dutra quickly asked.

"Yes sir, about five minuets before you landed."

Dutra grew a smile on his face.

"Right on time...did you know that if the man who had shot Regan aimed just a little more to the left, Regan would've been killed instantly?" Dutra asked.

"No. No I did not, sir," Street said.

"It's amazing to think how close some people get to changing the course of history and just as they get within reaching distance they fuck it all up...least that won't happen to us. Not this time," Dutra said as he started to walk away.

Street ordered the men with him to follow as he caught back up to Dutra.

"What do you want us to do?" Street asked.

"We go on with the plan, so get me to the office. A lot to do so we'll need to start moving the guys and set everything else up. Any calls for me?" Dutra asked Street.

Street quickly dug into his jacket pocket to take out the piece of paper that he had written down everything to tell Dutra.

"...Uh yeah, you had three. One was Zachary Noel; he said Boston P.D. was closing in on his merchandise..." Street began to say.

"Let them. Zac's no longer a resource to us anyway. In fact have one of the guys make an anonymous call to the Boston P.D. and have them check out 457 Front Street; apartment 16. If the dispatcher asks, have the guy simply say Zac's most valuable resources are there...who else?"

"Next was Jessica Dean. She wanted to let you know that the check we handed her for the weapons had bounced..."

"Shit, write her a new one...can't burn that bridge yet. You said three, that was only two."

Street looked down at the paper (even though he already knew the last name on the paper), but he didn't want to say the name out loud so he didn't. Dutra noticed that Street hadn't said anything, so he stopped walking and looked at Street and got ready to ask him again when he saw the paper in Street's hand. Once Street noticed Dutra saw it, he handed the paper over to him. Dutra grabbed the paper and took a look at it.

When he read the name in his head, he did his best to play it smooth and hide any type of nervousness, but it didn't work. Street clearly saw some trickle of fear in Dutra. Once Dutra took a hard enough look at the paper, he slid it into his pocket as he made eye contact again with Street.

"When did he call?" Dutra asked.

"This guy Stone? Uh...late last night. Wanted me to tell you that when you land to give him a call...after he called, Vincent ran a check on him..." Street confessed.

Dutra shook his head in anger.

"Yeah...heard a few of the things he's been associated with, but you know, Street, they say blood makes you related...loyalty makes you family. I'll take care of this."

"You're still planning on dealing with him after all the stories about him?" Street asked.

"The man is a sick bastard...you wouldn't believe half the shit he's done...but we'll cross that bridge when we get to it. Come on, take me to the office," Dutra said.

The two walked out of the airport with their army of hired guns like they owned the place. Even though you could never tell it, Dutra was happy to be back in the States. He was tired of taking jobs overseas. The money was a lot better, but Dutra was no longer in this for the money because if there's one thing that Dutra loved more than money it's power. And once this job was done, it would be clear that a new superpower had arrived in the United States. One that could get things done, one that could get through barriers and most of all, one that was about to take the top spot on the F.B.I. most wanted list. And in the deepest part of Dutra's twisted mind that's exactly where he wanted to be all along.

III

While Dutra headed to his office building in New York with Street so they could go over the plan one last time, Ray and the rest of the guys made it to Washington. By the time Ray parked the van, he had a major headache (due to the fact that he couldn't stand listening to Jasmin going on and on about his early life back in Bosnia. It wasn't that Ray didn't care it was that Jasmin had a very special way of making any story drier then a week old piece of dog shit).

"Thank Christ! If I had to stay in that van one more second I probably would've shot him," Steve confessed as he slammed the van door shut.

"You're telling me. I would've had you shoot me too while you were at it," Ray confessed.

"You should've said something. I would've been glad to."

Ray turned around to see the guys were following him, all except for Torque who was standing at the back on the van looking around. Ray turned back to Steve.

"Steve, take the guys in. I'll catch up with you in a minute," Ray said.

"Alright. Let's go old timers!" Steve yelled to the guys.

"Hey fuck you Steve, you're thirty years older then me!" Kevin said.

"And yet you have more white hair then I do."

Bob, Tommy and Jasmin suddenly lost it, instantly laughing. And once again Kevin rolled his eyes.

"You know what Steve, when you have a kid—if you can still get it up to have a kid that is—I hope the fucker is uglier then the hair growing in your mom's ass crack," Kevin said as he walked in.

Steve chuckled and patted him on the shoulder. Steve took one last look at Ray before he went inside. Ray was about half way there when his knee suddenly filled up with pain. He instantly stopped and put pressure on it with his hand.

"Son of a bitch!" Ray said in pain.

For a moment he thought the pain wasn't going to go away, but once it finally did he took a deep breath of relief and then walked over to Torque who was busy looking around at all the tourists, traffic and men in suits.

"You coming or what?" Ray asked.

Torque looked at Ray for a moment and then looked back to the street.

"Yeah...was just thinking," Torque said.

"Thinking about what?" Ray asked.

"Nothing. Just a personal thing..." Torque said to keep his privacy.

Ray was gonna order Torque to tell him but decided not to. If anyone knew that some things are best left inside it was Ray.

"Listen...I wanted to say thanks for not telling the guys about a code five...because I know that you know what a code five is...am I right?" Ray asked.

"Yeah. Never been on one but I know what it is. You think it's serious?" Torque asked.

"They usually are...I just don't know how serious though. Hoping it's just a wild goose chase," Ray confessed.

Torque shook his head.

"Is it ever?" Torque asked.

"Nope. And since Sullivan is conducting this, that means we're all screwed. You may not have to take my place kid. We all may be dead come tomorrow," Ray said as he slowly walked away.

Torque was good at keeping calm during a crises but his mind wasn't. It roamed like a bipolar patient off there meds. All Torque could do was prepare himself and hope that the situation wasn't as bad as his mind thought it would be. And after he took one last look around he went inside and caught up to Ray. The place was crawling with people running around.

"Where we heading?" Torque asked.

"My guess would be the situation room. That's where I went last time during a code five," Ray said.

"How long ago was that?" Torque asked out of curiosity.

"How many fingers you have?" Ray asked.

"Ten..." Torque slowly said.

"Add in a few toes too. It's been a while, let's say that."

Even though Ray still was pretty bitter about getting to know the kid, he actually kinda liked talking to him. Course he just wouldn't confess that to himself (and he really couldn't either. He still had major doubts about the whole situation. Not to mention he was trying to avoid telling the guys about it). The conversation quickly ended when Ray and Torque started to hear yelling and shouting down the next hall. Ray was going to try and avoid it (most likely two senators trying to show who has the bigger dick) but once he heard Kevin's voice he knew that wasn't the case.

He ran into the next hall and saw Steve, Bob, Jasmin, Kevin and Tommy arguing with some very familiar people. Even though the five of them were out numbered none of them—particularly Kevin—seemed to care. And when the guy Kevin was talking to made a sexual gesture to him, Kevin suddenly punched the man in the face.

Ray and Torque quickly ran down to them. As they were running they saw the guys that were with the poor bastard Kevin had just hit start grabbing Kevin, but Bob stepped in and punched one in the face while one punched Steve in the face. Steve fell back to the wall and then leaped onto the man.

"Hey!" Ray yelled at them.

Even though Ray yelled at the top of his lungs, that didn't stop Kevin from getting down on the floor and starting to punch the guy in the face as hard and as fast as he could. But that all ended when Ray finally reached him. Ray grabbed Kevin by the shirt, quickly stood him up and pushed him onto the wall.

While Ray was dealing with that, the guy Bob had punched walked over to Ray and started to make a fist. He quickly relaxed his wrist and fell to the floor when Torque punched him in the jaw. Ray let go of Kevin and looked at the huge fight in the hall. Ray then tried to grab Bob after he punched a guy in the stomach. He lost his grip for a moment, but was then able to get his hands around Bob's chest. He was so busy that he didn't even see a rather tall and older man (Ray's age) enter the hallway.

"My guys stand down! That's an order!" The man yelled.

As soon as Ray heard the man's voice he realized it was Roader. The men obeyed Roader's order right away. Ray kept his eyes fixed on Roader.

"Pull your heads out of your asses and remember where you are!" Roader shouted as Joey and another man, clearly his boss Sullivan, walked into the hallway.

"Well glad all of you have finally met," Sullivan said as he walked past Ray, opened the door to the situation room and went in.

As Joey walked by he looked at Ray but Ray made sure he didn't make eye contact. Joey really wanted to say something to Ray, but he knew it wasn't the right time or place, so in the end he remained silent as he walked past. Ray looked at the guys.

"My team head in and cut the bullshit," Ray said.

The guys headed in and remained silent. All except for Kevin. As he walked in he looked at the guy he had punched. Even though the man had a bloody lip he gave Kevin a sarcastic smile.

"Fuck you, Jimmy!" Kevin said.

"Kevin! Cut the shit!" Ray ordered.

Kevin shook his head and went in.

"My team: follow." Roader said.

Roader's team nodded their heads and went in. Roader walked over to Ray.

"Well, well Ray. Long time no see," Roader said.

"Yeah you too. What are you doing here?" Ray asked.

"Something about a code five. Sullivan personally called me in this morning," Roader explained. "Any idea why?"

Ray wasn't positive but he had a gut feeling it had something to do with the men in the mall who wanted the Secretary of State's niece. But Ray wasn't going to tell Roader that.

"No idea. When did you get back? Last I heard you were somewhere in London..." Ray said to be polite.

"Got back a week ago," Roader said.

"Fun trip?"

"Guess you could say that..."

"Glad to hear," Ray said as he walked into the situation room.

Roader shook his head with a smile as he followed Ray in, and closed the door behind him. Even though Ray always did his best to be hospitable, Roader always had the sense that Ray wasn't his biggest fan. Years ago he told himself that one day he would question Ray about it, but since then the timing for each of them was never right. He hoped the day was coming for that conversation to take place.

The men from each team sat around the large circular table inside the badly lit situation room while Ray and Roader remained standing. Sullivan waited for everyone to sit down before he began. While everyone was getting situated Ray couldn't help but keep looking at Joey, almost in anger. In a way he did feel betrayed, but past all that he knew that it wasn't Joey's fault. He just couldn't think about that. Once everyone sat down, Sullivan turned on the projector that was on the middle of the table.

"Paul...Ray..." Sullivan said.

Ray nodded his head at Sullivan while Roader gave a light wave. Sullivan then turned to the men at the table.

"Gentlemen, you're probably wondering why you've been brought here...and the answer is simple..." Sullivan said as he picked up the clicker for the projector and pressed a button on it.

The first slide was a satellite picture of Iraq.

"You're here so I can personally show you that the world is in a fine state. First the good news: we've got terrorists running around and blowing shit up in Iraq, only a matter of time before we send troops in."

Sullivan began before he changed the picture to a shot of Egypt. "We have a civil war happening in Egypt..."

While Sullivan was talking Ray stayed focused on the slide show while Roader was looking at each of Ray's guys. Sullivan then switched the picture to a shot of Korea.

"And we have tensions mounting in Korea, but that's not why I brought you here..."

Sullivan then switched the picture on the projector to a picture inside the Mall of America. The picture was of all the dead men inside of it that Ray and his team had killed.

"Early yesterday morning a team of highly trained individuals entered the Mall of America and started opening fire. While many of us here in Washington were hoping it was simply nothing more then a horrific one-time thing...that's not the case. Inside the mall was Cassidy Roux...the Sectary of State's niece. In a happy world that just would've been a coincidence, but based on Intel provided by Ray and his team it's clear that the men were after her," Sullivan said.

Steve slowly turned and looked at Ray as Steve finally started to put the pieces together before Sullivan said it. The look on Ray's face made Steve realize Ray had already had an idea of what this was all about.

"Now the question is why they were after her. While myself and the F.B.I. try and figure that out, I've brought you here because, as some of you know, the President will be having a press conference later today at the Lincoln Memorial. Our concern is that if these people went after Miss Roux, then they might try to go after the President during his speech," Sullivan explained.

"Have you brought this up to the president?" Roader asked.

"Several times, but he insists he wants to carry on with the press conference. The man is a stubborn son of a bitch. So I've called you guys in as extra security for today. All of you will be blending in with the crowd. Let me say this right now...we do not have any indication that something will happen. We just want to make sure everything goes smoothly."

"Any ideas about who was behind the attack at the mall?" Ray asked.

Sullivan changed the projector picture again to a list of names.

"Several. And as you can see it's going to take time to check all of them out, so a rather large piece of the F.B.I. will we working on this during the conference. So we'll be short handed. That's where you all come in. Many of you will be in the crowd, but I'm assigning some of you to roof tops to overlook...so Ray, Paul I'm gonna need names of your best snipers when the time comes."

Joey had a feeling that someone was watching him and sure enough when he turned and looked at Ray they made eye contact. With the look in

Ray's eyes Joey knew exactly what Ray was feeling. But he knew that he couldn't let that cloud his judgment on a situation like this.

"But you must have an idea of who was behind this," Roader said.

Sullivan sighed and then turned the picture on the projector to a security picture of a man in a ski mask.

"This man is based out of Russia. Info is very slim on him but from what we've gathered he goes by the name 'Vacca'."

"Never heard of him," Steve said.

"Not surprised...aside from selling guns in Russia we know he also did some work near Bosnia," Sullivan said.

Sullivan bringing up Bosnia brought a lot of memories back for Ray; hell that's how they ended up with Jasmin (during the seizing of a warhead, Ray and the guys ran into heavy resistance. It was so intense they almost left when a sniper from out of nowhere began taking each of the targets that were shooting at them out. That sniper turned out to be Jasmin. Originally Ray just said thank you but Jasmin was persistent about leaving the war riddled country and asked if he could go with them).

"So he's an arms dealer?" Roader asked.

"To a certain extent yes. But recently close sources have said that he's stopped all that and is currently working on something on a much larger scale that involves recruiting people to join him. That's all we know as of now."

"Any idea on where he is?" Jimmy asked.

"All intel says he's gone underground," Sullivan confessed.

"Is there a chance he's in the U.S.?" Ray asked.

"It's possible but slim. I don't think he'd risk coming into the country for any reason. But like I said we just don't know yet," Sullivan said.

"What time is the conference?" Ray asked.

"It's set for five this evening." Sullivan said.

"All right, my guys will be here." Ray said.

"So will mine." Roader said.

Sullivan nodded.

"All right then. We've got less then two hours to set it up. Ray, who on your team do you want on sniper patrol?" Sullivan asked.

"Jasmin and Bob," Ray said without hesitation.

Both Jasmin and Bob nodded an agreement.

"Alright and who on your team Paul?"

"Jimmy and myself will take that. Use the rest for whatever you need them for."

"Alright guys, thank you for doing this. Let's get moving then," Sullivan said.

Once the meeting finished up everyone headed for the door. As soon as everyone got into the hall Ray and Roader began making orders.

"Bob and Jas, go with Sullivan. The rest of you follow me," Ray said.

"While Jimmy and myself are gone I want you guys to head up to the Secret Service office," commanded Roader. "Anything they want you to do, do it. No questions asked, understand?"

As Ray started to walk away he looked at Roader as he was giving out the orders. When Roader made eye contact with Ray he nodded at him. Ray returned the gesture.

"Alright guys, let's move! Not a lot of time," Ray said.

Once Ray and everyone got back out side and over to the van the questions began for Ray.

"You want us in our uniforms?" Kevin asked.

"No. We don't want to attract any attention. We wanna blend in with the crowd," Ray quickly said.

"Take it that means no toys?" Tommy asked.

"No toys! Side arms only," Ray said as he opened the passenger door to the van and started to dig into the glove box.

"Well this day isn't turning out like I thought it was going to be," Kevin confessed.

"When do they ever?" Steve asked.

Ray walked back over to the guys with radio sets in his hands and then started to give them out.

"So what's the plan?" Torque asked.

"Steve and Tommy will be walking around in the crowd. If you see anything don't hesitate to make a move, just try not to make it obvious," Ray said.

"You sure you want Tommy to be doing that?" Kevin asked.

The guys chuckled.

"Hey! That hurts my feelings, Kevo," Tommy said.

"You don't have any feelings," Steve quickly reminded Tommy as he whacked Tommy on top of the head.

Ray handed the last radio set to Torque.

"Kevin I want you near the side by the president at all time. Your job is to watch him at all times," Ray said.

"Sounds easy enough," Kevin said as he put the radio into his ear.

Ray then turned to Torque.

"Torque and I will be covering the front. Now remember like Sullivan said, there's no immediate danger that we know of, but better safe than sorry. I want everyone on the top of their game. Understood?" Ray asked.

"Yes sir," The guys said.

"Hopefully with any luck we'll all be back home tonight. Everyone ready?" Ray asked.

They all shook their heads.

"Alright then. Let's do this."

IV

As Ray, Roader and the rest of the people in charge of the president's safety quickly started to set up for the press conference, Dutra had made it to his office in the skyscraper Street owned and ran a 'coffee importing' business out of. Normally when Dutra came back to the States after being away for as long as he had, he took the time to relax and rest, but this time was different as he stormed into his office and went over to his desk with Street trailing right behind him.

"How was business overseas?" Street asked.

"Good. Should have the shipment later on in the week. I want double the amount of people there this time. I'm not letting whoever jacked my shipment last time do it again. Speaking of which, any leads on who the hell that was exactly?" Dutra asked.

Street sighed because he knew the shit storm that Dutra was about to say when he heard the answer but Street had to tell him.

"We're still working on it. What we've gathered so far is that mostly likely it was some type of government agency...right now..." Street said before Dutra interrupted him.

"So in other words, you still have no fucking idea."

"Yes sir." Street said.

Dutra was furious but knew now wasn't the time to get into the discussion. Other bigger and more important things were already underway.

"We'll deal with that later, right now let's focus on today. How many men do we have in Washington with Vince?" Dutra asked.

"Twenty on the ground ready to go."

Dutra thought about the number. At first it seemed like a good solid number he could live with but Dutra's paranoia slowly started to creep up into his twisted mind and once it did nothing on the face of the earth could stop it.

"Get the helicopter ready. And tell some of the guys downstairs we're moving out," Dutra demanded.

"Where should I tell the pilot we're heading?" Street asked.

Dutra slowly prised his eyes off his desk and looked at the rather gorgeous view of the city beneath him. The sun reflecting off the large skyscraper windows made most of the top half of the city look like a mirror.

"Well since it's such a nice day out, what better way to spend it then taking a trip to the nation's capital?" Dutra asked.

Street got confused for a second.

"Sir, wouldn't the airspace be closed?"

"It would but if you decide to fly low enough under the radar, then nothing is closed," Dutra said with reassurance.

"I'll let him know," Street said just before walking out of the office.

Once Dutra was alone in the office he walked over to a large cabinet and opened it. Inside was damn near every weapon Dutra had used in all the years of being in the 'coffee business'. He then very carefully picked out which one he wanted to take with him. In the end he decided to go with his pride and joy, an F-2000 assault rifle with a state of the art tactile scope mounted on the top (the very same one he used in Burma only a few months ago that ended with the deaths of twenty-two people).

Once he picked out his main weapon he then decided on a side arm, a Walther P99 AS. He had only gotten it a few weeks prior so he hadn't had the chance to test it out, but figured this would be the perfect opportunity to do so.

And once he was done, he put on the top-of-the-line bullet proof vest, loaded his weapons, grabbed as many clips for each gun that he could fit into his case and then headed for the roof where the chopper and his men were waiting to get on with what would become the most devasting day in Washington D.C. history...and Dutra couldn't have been any more excited.

Chapter 4: Space In The History Books

Back in D.C. a large crowd was already beginning to form in front of the Lincoln Memorial as newscasters began to announce the president's conference. The conference was still about an hour away at this point but there were well over a thousand people anxiously waiting and the crowd was only expected to grow (the American people seemed to really approve of the job President Harris had done in the past three years).

"Look at all the people already," Kevin said as he, Ray and Torque walked up to the Lincoln Memorial.

"Yeah. Don't think this will be a walk in the park. If someone is out there with a gun it's gonna be damn near impossible to find them," Torque added.

"See that's the problem with you guys. You always look at the glass half empty," Ray said.

"What, you don't agree?" Kevin asked.

"I didn't say that but I didn't say it out loud. You gotta be optimistic in a line of work such as ours," Ray said.

"Well there's being optimistic and then there's being realistic," Kevin said.

Ray shook his head. Even he couldn't come up with wise advice for that one.

"Ah true. We're pretty much screwed," Ray said as he put his hand to the radio in his ear. "Steve how you guys doing?"

"Approaching the Lincoln Memorial now. A lot of people here already. It's gonna be tricky," Steve said over the radio.

"10-4 just keep your eyes out," Ray said.

"You too, old man."

Ray then pointed to the right hand side of the Lincoln Memorial.

"Kevin take the far right hand side. Torque and I will head up front where the President will be," Ray said.

"You got it," Kevin said before running off in that direction.

Torque then looked at Ray.

"So Ray, let me ask you something since we got time to kill."

"What's up kid?"

"I know you don't approve of me taking over. You know I get that but I'm hoping you'll give me the chance to prove myself," Torque said.

Ray looked around for a moment before he responded.

"You know Torque you seem like a solid guy. I mean that. You got skill for sure from what I've seen and read on your file, but a file doesn't mean shit to me. Call me old school, but I believe you have to see it to believe it and right now I haven't seen it. But I'm fair. I give everyone a shot, but if you fuck it up, that's on you. One shot and that's it just like in combat; if you miss the target you might as well kiss your ass goodbye."

"I understand...I won't let you down," Torque promised.

"And as far as taking over my place...I'm not gonna lie, kid, I don't approve of it now and I can't see me approving of it in the future. I built up what we are today and I'm proud of that. I've worked with these guys for years. Steve was the first to join and him and I have a bond like no other...truth is... I wanted him to take over. You know he's been with me since the beginning and to see him getting sidelined isn't right. Steve will never say it because that's the kind of man he is but I will: he deserves it."

Even though most people in Torque's generation wouldn't approve, he honestly did. He knew Steve was getting the shaft but he also knew there was nothing he could do. The choice was made. All he could tell himself was that he would show not just Ray but all the guys that he could live up to the expectations that Ray had given.

"And I gotta tell yeah man; and you're probably not gonna like the answer. If something changes and I'm given the choice to decide on who gets my spot...I'm going with Steve. Hope you can understand that because if you can't, you might as well leave us now," Ray confessed.

"I do Ray...but if it turns out that you can't, I just want you to know that I'll spend however much time we have together to prove to you I can handle whatever the world throws at us," Torque firmly said.

"Alright kid. I actually believe you." Ray looked back at the crowd that was still growing in size.

"You don't trust a lot of people do you Ray?" Torque asked, even though he knew that he might be crossing the line.

"After being in this business for all these years if there's one thing I've learned it's you can never trust anyone...learned that the hard way in Berlin," Ray confessed.

"Well shit happens right?' Torque asked.

"Yeah, still have the scar to prove it," Ray said.

Torque started to look at the crowd. It took a second for his eyes to adjust to the sunlight bearing down on his face.

"So what's your deal with Roader? Got the feeling like you two don't seem to get along very well," Torque asked.

"It's not that we don't get along; it's just that I like to handle things differently then he does. Not to mention he brags about everything he and his team does. 'Oh I saved the president, oh I saved a village in Germany'."

"Well not gonna lie if I saved the president I would want to brag about it too," Torque mused.

"Yeah, guess I would too. Lucky bastard that he is. But even I can't deny that the guy is good. Maybe even better then me. I can't take that away from him," Ray added.

"Takes a strong man to say that Ray."

"No it takes strong alcohol to say that."

Both of them laughed as they started to head down to the crowd.

"Alright kid let's just get this over with," Ray said.

II

As Ray and Torque made their way to the front of the crowd, across the street on the top floor of a four story building Jasmin and Bob got their sniper rifles into position...as they bitched about the heat of the sunshine.

"Jesus Christ, I'm sweating my fucking balls off," Jasmin said.

"Oh grow a pair, Jas. Try been stationed in fucking Egypt for six months," Bob replied.

"Man screw that," Jasmin said as he put a bullet into the rifle.

"That's what I said everyday," Bob said as he lit a cigarette.

Jasmin looked up at him when he heard the flick of Bob's lighter.

"You know that's really bad for you."

"Keep it up and I'll give you something that's bad for you," Bob shot back.

"You don't really like me do you?" Jasmin boldly asked, even though he kinda already knew the answer.

"Let's put it this way, Jas: I wouldn't take a bullet for you but I'd shoot the guy that shot yeah, if that makes you feel better." Bob said.

"Well that makes me feel a little better," Jasmin said.

"Well good, that's why I'm here."

Suddenly Jasmin's cell phone rang to the ringtone of classical music.

"Really? You save the world for a living and your ringtone is elevator music?" Bob asked.

"It relaxes me," Jasmin said while he took the phone out of his pocket.

Bob rolled his eyes as Jasmin answered his phone.

"Hello?"

"Jas it's Ray. You guys in position?" Ray asked.

"Yeah Bob and I are on the roof of the building just across the street," Jasmin explained.

"Alright. Torque, myself and Kevin are up at the front of the crowd. Steve and Tommy will be walking around just to keep an eye out. Can you see Roader from your position?" Ray asked.

Jasmin quickly stood up and started to look around at other rooftops.

"Uh...I can't see them but there's other buildings taller than the one we're on, so maybe they're on one of those," Jasmin said.

"Okay you see anything keep me posted," Ray said.

"Roger that."

Jasmin hung up and put his right eye into the scope.

"That Ray?" Bob asked.

"Yeah, just checking in."

Bob shook his head.

"Guy does nothing but worry. Some days I feel bad for him."

Meanwhile down on the street the place was filling up like lifeboats on a sinking ship. Steve almost lost Tommy a couple of times in the crowd.

"Holy shit!" Tommy yelled to Steve as they walked through the crowd.

"This is nothing, Tommy! It'll get worse trust me!" Steve yelled back.

Tommy was going to reply but he got distracted by a woman with incredibly large breast.

"Oh, wow, I want those," Tommy said.

Steve was looking all around but honestly couldn't see much due to the fact that nobody was standing still (not to mention the noise was really starting to pick up).

"Can't see a damn thing, can you Tommy...Tommy?"

Steve turned around when Tommy didn't respond and had to really look for a second before he spotted Tommy. But once his eyes locked onto him they quickly rolled. There was Tommy standing dumbstruck just looking at the large set of tits. Tommy must've been only seconds away from drooling.

"Tommy!" Steve yelled as loud as he could.

Tommy suddenly stopped looking and ran back to Steve.

"Steve did you see the pair of tits on that chick?" Tommy asked with excitement.

"Not now Tommy...but yes, I did."

"I would get into politics for her," Tommy said.

"There really is something wrong with you, you know that right?" Steve asked.

"What can I say? Boobies make me smile."

"Isn't that the fucking truth," Steve said under his breath before reaching to the radio in his ear. "Ray you copy?"

"Yeah go ahead, Steve," Ray said.

"Not gonna lie it's been tough to see more then two feet in front of me," Steve said, almost with worry in his voice.

"Just keep your eyes out, Steve. If anyone can do this, it's you," Ray said.

"You make it up front yet?"

"Yeah, just got here."

"Anything?"

"Yeah, a shitload of people!"

"I know huh? Since when did America start giving a shit about politics?" Steve asked.

"Must've been recently. Sure as hell wasn't ten years ago."

"Alright we'll keep looking. Hope you got a plan B up your sleeve because if we miss something you're gonna need one."

"Don't I always?" Ray asked.

"Roger that."

"Stay sharp."

Ray lowered his hand off the radio in his ear.

"Who was that?" Torque asked.

"That was Steve," Ray said.

"Where is he?"

"Somewhere behind us," Ray said before putting his hand back to his radio. "Kevin, come in."

"Yeah what's up Ray?"

"You make it to the spot?"

"Roger that. Nothing on my end."

"Okay hopefully it stays that way."

"10-4." Kevin said.

The guys kept their post for about a half hour looking around trying to find some type of danger but no luck. Their attention was quickly taken off the job when the president's limo pulled up to the large crowd. Suddenly the crowd went crazy and sirens from the police escort echoed throughout the street. Ray quickly looked over and reached up to his radio.

"Sullivan, the president just arrived," Ray said into his microphone.

"Alright, this is where I need your eyes Ray. Protect the president at all cost," Sullivan said to increase the drama of the situation.

"You got it. Jas? You see the president yet?" Ray asked.

"Roger that. He just stepped out of the limo. He's headed your way now," Jasmin said.

Ray quickly turned to Torque.

"Alright kid this is it," Ray said.

The president made his way through the crowd as he shook the hands of the people he walked by. The crowd was excited but it was nothing compared to when he walked up to the stage. The whole placed rocked with cheers.

Ray focused on the president and was impressed by the suit he was in: a very dark blue with a red tie and an American flag pin up by his shoulder. Ray also noticed that the poor bastard's hair was already starting to show sprouts of white.

Steve looked toward the stage and then saw the president approaching the podium. He quickly turned to Tommy.

"Tommy, he's here!" Steve shouted.

"Yeah I kinda got that when the crowd started to go insane," Tommy said.

Steve shook his head and went back to looking around when he saw a Muslim with a large red turban on top of his head slowly walking through the crowd very suspiciously. Steve quickly put his hand on the radio in his ear.

"Ray, think I got something here."

"Do what you have to," Ray said.

"10-4," Steve confirmed as he started to follow the man.

Ray hit Torque in the arm.

"Heads up. Steve might have something," Ray said to him.

As Steve followed the man he quickly took out his cell phone and dialed a number.

"Come on, come on." Steve muttered to himself.

From the roof top Jasmin's cell phone began to ring again. He answered it immediately.

"Yeah?"

"Jas, it's Steve. I'm following a guy on the right side of the Memorial. He has on a bright red towel. Can you spot him?" Steve asked.

Jasmin quickly looked in his sight and started to look around. It took him a second as he scanned the area.

"Jas!" Steve yelled.

"Got him! He stopped right near a woman with a pink shirt on," Jasmin said.

Steve walked through the crowd; pushing people out of his way until he saw the woman.

"Alright, I see her. Keep your sight on the towel head," Steve ordered.

Steve's eyes finally caught up with him and he started walking faster to the man. Suddenly Jasmin came back over the phone.

"Steve, he's reaching into his pocket!"

Steve suddenly gunned it to the man. Once he was close enough he saw the man digging into his pocket. Steve knew that this was it; he could feel it. And with a sudden rush of energy he body slammed the man onto the ground.

There were so many people around him; no one seemed to notice the two on the ground. Steve quickly rolled the man onto his back and saw blood coming out of the man's nose. Steve quickly dug into the man's pocket and felt a metal object. Steve instantly took out his handgun and aimed it at the man.

"What are you doing?" The man asked in his foreign accent.

"Shut the fuck up!" Steve said as he started to pull the object out of the man's pocket.

It was a small black camera. Steve took a look at it and then placed it back down with a sigh of relief.

"Sorry friend," Steve said as he got up and walked away. "Ray, false alarm."

"Roger that...false alarm," Ray said as he looked at Torque.

"That's a good thing right?" Torque asked.

"Rather have a false one then a real one," Ray said.

The president finally made it to the podium and put his hands in the air with a big smile. The crowd cheered like there was no tomorrow.

"Thank you," The president said into the dozens of microphones in front of him.

The crowd slowly settled down as the president lowered his hands.

"Thank you all for coming out on such short notice..." the president said.

Up on the roof, Bob threw his cigarette off the top of the roof as he began to hear the president's voice echo. Then he walked over to Jasmin and dropped to the ground and looked into his rifle that was next to Jasmin.

"Alright, show time."

"A lot of movement going on," Jasmin said as he looked through the scope.

"I stand here before you today and the nation to address an ongoing concern for our country. While many in my cabinet thought it would be best to leave this unspoken, I'm a firm believer that when you put a face on something, it can be beat," the president said.

The crowd cheered as Tommy and Steve looked all around. Kevin kept his eyes directly on the president as Ray and Torque looked to their sides.

"See anything?" Ray asked.

"Not yet. Would be nice if people could keep still," Torque said.

"That would make it to easy," Ray said.

Tommy looked around for anythin,g but once again got distracted by a young woman in yoga pants.

"Wow look at that ass," Tommy said to himself.

Struck by the beauty of the girl Tommy slowly started to part away from Steve, who was busy looking around, and followed the girl. Ray took out his phone and dialed Jasmin again.

"Jas, tell me what you see."

"Lot of movement. And it looks like you lost Tommy," Jasmin said.

"What do you mean lost Tommy?" Ray asked, almost in a panic.

"Looks like he found a nice young girl he wants to bring home. Guess it was a bad idea to give him that part," Jasmin said.

"I'll deal with that later."

"Today will be a day that will go down in the history of America!" the president shouted, and the people cheered.

Tommy continued to follow the girl and slowly picked up the speed when he realized he was starting to lose her in the crowd.

"Oh no, no, no sweetheart," Tommy said as he started to sprint.

But it was too late; the girl took a sharp turn to the left and she vanished from out of Tommy's sight.

"Shit!" Tommy said.

He started to walk away until he noticed something. He stopped dead in his tracks when he saw it.

"Today is the day America takes a stand that it should've taken years ago!" the president said.

The crowd began to cheer as Ray kept looking around. He suddenly got the old familiar feeling in his gut...like he knew something was off. It was a feeling that he developed a while ago, but only started to listen to it just recently. Torque also looked around. He kinda felt like something was off too, but he wasn't as focused on it as Ray was.

Steve walked to the edge of the crowd and turned around to address Tommy but quickly discovered he was nowhere in sight. Panicking he started to look all around until he was sure that Tommy wasn't near him.

"Ray I lost Tommy," Steve said over the radio.

Ray didn't answer. He kept his eyes on the president. That feeling started to grow heavier inside his gut. It was telling him to open his eyes. The only problem was that he didn't know what he was really looking for.

Tommy slowly started walking toward what had grabbed his eyes. It was a man in an all leather jacket with his hands in his pocket. But it wasn't the man that grabbed his eyes. It was the tip of some medal object hanging at his side. Tommy very slowly took the handgun out of his holster as he walked closer and closer to the man.

"Today the world will see the rebirth of America, and no doubt will be left that America always has, and always will be, the superpower of the world!" the president shouted.

The crowd roared with applause and cheers. As Tommy walked up to the man, the man slowly started to reach to his side. Tommy took the safety off his gun.

"So today I want to address you all to show you that I never have and never will keep any secrets from the nation...the country...and the people I love!" the president shouted one last time.

And as the crowd cheered, Tommy saw the man suddenly pull out a machine gun from his side.

"Gun!" Tommy shouted.

Tommy fired two shots into the man's side. The crowd was going so wild that it muffled the sounds of the gunshot. But Ray quickly looked behind him when he thought he heard shots. Steve did the same thing.

Ray turned to Torque and realized Torque had a look of fear on his face, just like he did. Then Ray quickly turned back to the president and suddenly saw a red dot appear on his forehead, quickly racing down from his face to his heart, the red dot hitting the president's eye for a quick second before he had the chance to react.

Knowing he was about the change the face of history and that the day really would become a part of America's history, Ray suddenly pulled out his gun, lifted it into the air and fired a shot.

Suddenly the president dropped for cover and a bullet flew just over him and hit a Secret Service agent that was right behind him in the head. Blood sprayed out as the back of the agent's head blew off.

"Oh shit!" Bob shouted from the rooftop.

The crowd suddenly panicked and turned into a screaming competition. As dozens of Secret Service agents rushed for the president another shot was fired and struck an agent in the throat. Blood sprayed all over the stage and on the president's expensive suit. Then another shot blew a large hole into the podium.

Suddenly, men all scattered throughout the crowd pulled out machine guns and started firing at the stage. Torque then whipped out his gun and saw a man getting ready to aim his gun at the stage. Torque quickly double tapped the man; firing two shots into his chest.

At the edge of the now panicking crowd Steve saw three men whip out machine guns and start to head to the stage. He quickly fired three shots, hitting one of them in the back. The other two men quickly turned and started firing at Steve. Steve quickly ducked as the bullets sprayed over him; hitting the civilians behind him.

Kevin started firing back at the men who were shooting at Steve, hitting one of them in the leg. Steve took the opportunity to fire one shot at the wounded man and shot him in the head. Kevin then started to fire at some men that were approaching Ray and Torque.

Back on the roof, Bob and Jasmin were busy firing into the crowd. Bob hit one man in the back and Jasmin fired one shot and blew a man's leg off. The man dropped to the ground, blood pouring out of his wound. Jasmin aimed at the man's chest and took the shot. Bob quickly turned to the direction of the sniper who was picking Secret Service agents off.

"Jas! Try and get a shot of the sniper!" Bob shouted.

Jasmin quickly stood up, grabbed his gun and moved it over to where he thought the sniper was shooting from. He placed his rifle at the edge of the building and started to look at the windows all around the building where he was sure the shots were coming from.

Tommy was directly in the middle of the chaos as people ran past him and bumped into him. He saw one man getting ready to aim a machine gun at him and quickly took a shot before the man had a chance. While he did that, another shooter saw Tommy, but before he could take a shot a bullet shot straight through the man's eye and he dropped to the ground. Tommy quickly turned and looked down at the man then looked up to the building where the shot came from.

"Bulls eye," Bob said as he turned his sniper and began shooting at others.

Tommy did the same, thankful that Bob took the shot. Back at the podium multiple agents were down. The remaining few quickly picked up the president and started to move him off the stage. The sniper got another shot and hit the agent on the president's right side. The agent fell to the ground when the bullet hit his back.

Ray quickly moved up to the stage and ducked for cover after shooting two men. He saw a man running towards him with two machine guns in his hands. Ray quickly stood up and fired four shots into the man.

Ray knew he was gonna need a better weapon if he was going to stand a chance. He quickly turned to Torque and saw Torque was taking serious fire. Ray got out of cover and ran over to the dead man's machine guns. He grabbed them and started to run over to Torque.

"Torque!" Ray yelled.

Torque quickly looked after firing at another man and missing. Ray tossed one of the machine guns to him but it fell five feet away from him. Bullets quickly hit the ground all around the gun.

"Really?" Torque asked Ray.

Ray stood up and started to fire back with the machine gun. That bought Torque a small window to grab the gun and he took it. While the battle went on by the stage, Steve was still having trouble getting the last of the three men he first saw. The last man fired again at Steve; hitting four civilians in the process.

"You find the sniper yet, Jas?" Bob asked.

"Not yet!" Jasmin confessed.

"Better do it quick! Down to two agents left!" Bob said as he watched them rush the president to his limo.

The president was only ten feet away from the limo but he knew it was going to be the hardest ten feet he we would ever walk. Suddenly one of the agents behind him took a bullet to the back and dropped.

"One agent left! Come on Jas!" Bob shouted.

In a building directly across from the Memorial, the rifle that was shooting all the agents was smoking from all the use. Once the last shot in the clip was fired, Vincent quickly started to reload it. Suddenly a bullet shot into the window and broke the top of the glass. Vincent quickly ducked.

"Found him!" Jas said.

"Well shoot the fucker!" Bob said, as he fired another shot.

Tommy raced to the front of the stage, but from behind him a man started firing. Tommy ducked to the ground and several bullets hit a civilian. The woman dropped onto Tommy, taking the bullet that would've hit him. Tommy used the dead corpse for cover and then quickly lifted his gun and fired a whole clip into the man. Every bullet hit the man and as he fell to the ground he pulled the trigger to his gun and the bullets hit multiple people trying to run away.

Tommy lowered his head and then moved the corpse off of him and suddenly his eyes filled with fear when he realized the woman that landed on him was the very same girl he was following from before. Tommy sighed and then closed the women's eyes.

"Rest in piece sweetheart," Tommy said before standing back up.

Back at the stage, Ray and Torque were taking fire from all over. Ray quickly stood up and fired, hitting one man in the head. Torque then stood up, fired and hit two men but hit a civilian in the process.

"Watch your fire!" Ray ordered.

Torque's eyes filled with fear as he watched the civilian he just shot fall to the ground almost in slow motion. He couldn't believe what he just did, but he knew now wasn't the time to think about that. That time would come later. Ray quickly stood up and fired back at the men who were shooting at him.

Steve fired one shot into last man of the three he first saw; hitting him in the cheek. But suddenly a shotgun blast hit Steve's chest and blew him off his feet and he landed on the ground.

"Fuck!"

Steve quickly turned to where the shot came from and fired four shots into the man that shot him. Steve then looked down at his chest and saw that there was no blood. He took a second and prayed that he grabbed a bulletproof vest before all this happened. He then slowly started to get up.

Jasmin fired another shot into the window where Vincent was. Then another and another. The last shot he fired struck only inches away from Vincent, knocking him to the ground. Vincent knew it was time to get out while he still could, so he got up and left the room as fast as he could.

The president finally made it to the limo and jumped in. As soon as he did the limo took off, almost hitting people that were trying to run across the street. The president stayed face down in the back until he felt the limo turn onto another road.

Once Ray killed another man that was firing at him, he broke from cover and started to run to where the crowd was. He shot another man and then saw Tommy right in front of him.

"Tommy!" Ray shouted.

Tommy saw Ray and then his eyes filled with fear.

"Behind you!!" Tommy shouted.

But before Ray could turn, the man behind him shot Ray in the back. Torque saw Ray go down.

"Ray!" Torque shouted.

Tommy quickly returned fire at the man, but the man fired the machine gun at Tommy and Tommy quickly took cover behind a trashcan. Ray slowly rolled over onto his back while he dealt with the pain from the vest taking the round. He looked over to his side and realized the machine gun he was using was a few feet away and he had no chance of getting to it in time.

Kevin shot one of the last agressors alive and saw Ray on the ground. He quickly ran to him. The man fired the last of his machine gun at the trash barrel Tommy was behind, and then quickly reloaded his gun. Ray then looked up at the man who was now standing over him. The man slowly smiled and then aimed the gun at Ray's head. Ray closed his eyes and braced for the worst. But just as the man was getting ready to fire, multiple shots from all around started hitting his body. Steve fired three shots, Kevin fired two, Torque fired the last of his clip and Tommy stood up and fired five rounds into the man, all entering into his chest and stomach.

The man dropped his gun as he got ready to fall to the ground when a sniper bullet hit the man, blowing his head clean off and sealing the poor bastards fate; he instantly fell to the ground.

Across the street Roader lifted his eye out of the sniper scope and raised his hand to his radio in his ear as smoke came out of the end of the sniper rifle like there was no tomorrow.

"You okay Ray?" Roader asked over the radio.

Ray put his hand to his ear.

"Yeah...thanks."

"The president is on the move. Heading south east," Roader said.

"Copy that," Ray said as he stood up.

"Bob I think the sniper left!" Jasmin said.

"Alright, let's head down there!" Bob said as he stood up.

Ray slowly stood up as the pain from his vest and knee quickly shot up him. Tommy ran over and helped Ray get all the way up. Kevin, Steve and Torque ran over to him.

"The president is heading south east. We gotta follow him. More than likely there's more of them," Ray said.

"Who the hell are these guys?" Kevin asked.

"We'll worry about that later. Right now we gotta make sure the president stays safe."

The guys started running toward the direction the limo went. Ray quickly took out his phone and dialed Bob. Bob answered as he and Jasmin were walking down a fire exit.

"Tell me what's happening," Bob said as he answered the phone.

"The president is heading southeast, Bob," Ray said.

"Alright we're heading there now."

Bob quickly turned around and saw Jasmin was out of breath.

"Come on, Jas!" Bob shouted.

Ray put his phone back into his pocket and started running to catch up with the guys. As he was running he couldn't help but notice the silence; he looked around and saw all the dead civilians. It instantly reminded him of Vietnam; a memory he never thought he would have to think about again. And as he ran off to the street the blood from all the dead civilians was turning the concrete a horrific red.

III

The president's limo quickly turned onto another street and made the president feel safer. He thought he was in the clear but that would be a thought he would regret. Suddenly a large black truck drove out of an ally and crashed into the front of the limo.

The president got back to ducking in the back seat and the limo swerved and hit a fire hydrant causing water to shoot up in the air. The black truck backed up and then parked sideways in the middle of the road. A dozen men with machine guns got out of the truck, stood in the street, and began firing at the limo.

Just then, past the firing, the president started to hear a loud rumbling and looked out of the sunroof. A large black helicopter appeared in the window and suddenly a bullet hit the window, instantly cracking it.

Up in the helicopter, Dutra fired multiple shots into the limo and shot out the tires with a smile on his face, while the men on the ground continued firing at the limo. The bullets bounced off the ill-fated limo.

As Ray and his team were running they heard the shots off in the distance along with a few screams from up ahead. Ray quickly turned and looked at Steve as they were running.

"Come on guys! We gotta get to that limo!"

"Where the hell is the army?" Kevin shouted.

Back in the helicopter Dutra stopped firing and then turned to look at Street.

"Are all communications on line?" Dutra asked.

"Yes sir," Street said.

"Alright do it!" Dutra said.

Street put on a head set and began the next phase to Dutra's plan.

"All units, all units. The president has made it to the White House! All units are to head there immediately! Repeat all units are to head to the White House!"
Street said.

"Now kill all communication to the city!" Dutra ordered.

Street picked up a laptop from the floor of the helicopter and began to knock out all communication to the city. Dutra quickly looked to the pilot.

"Lower us down behind the truck!"

The pilot began to lower the helicopter down to the street. For a moment he didn't think he was gonna fit but once he got to the street he realized there was plenty of room. As they landed Dutra jumped out, along with Street and seven men in heavy armor and Heckler Koch HK's. They began to walk toward the limo.

A sinister smile grew on Dutra's face as he thought about how close he was to finishing what he had just started. He knew it would be only a matter of time before the president stepped out of the limo, he just had to cut that time as far down as he could. And once he got to the front of the truck he began to.

Instantly he began firing at the limo...and so did everyone else. The bullets from the Heckler seemed to go on and on and the president stayed down. He knew the armor on the car was strong enough but he also knew that it wasn't indestructible. It was only a matter of time before one of the hundreds of bullets made its way into the limo.

Dutra fired every single round his clip could hold into the limo. But once he was out he quickly put his hand up in the air and everyone stopped firing. Silence flooding into the street. Dutra then tossed his Heckler to Street and Street began to reload it as Dutra slowly walked toward the limo.

The president slowly lifted his head up to see the driver of the limo was dead. Then he focused his attention to Dutra as Dutra suddenly stopped only twenty feet away from the limo.

"President Harris!" Dutra began to yell. "Your military isn't coming! The communications are out! No one can help you...so I'll ask only once: please step out of the limo because trust me...you don't want me to come and get you..." Dutra threatened.

Harris looked behind him only to see that Dutra was right; no one was coming. He was going to have to handle this somehow by himself. He knew that if he went outside his fate, along with the rest of the nation, would be clouded to say that least. He was just going to have to ride it out and pray for a miracle.

Once enough time passed that Dutra realized Harris had no intention of coming out, Dutra began to walk back toward his men. Dutra had a feeling this would happen, but he was prepared for it.

"Light it up!" Dutra shouted to his men as he walked to Street.

The men began firing again. Harris quickly ducked again for cover. As Dutra grabbed the Heckler from Street, one of the men in armor loaded a rocket launcher and aimed it at the car. And as Dutra began firing with the rest of his crew, the man fired the rocket launcher at the car.

The rocket sped to the front of the car and blew up. A large fireball went up into the sky as the front of the limo began pouring out thick black smoke. Harris knew the car wouldn't be able to take another hit and started to pray, knowing this was the end for him.

The man with the rocket launcher loaded it again and began to take aim at the back of the car where Harris was. Dutra suddenly ran out of bullets again and started to reload the Heckler as he took his eyes off the limo. The man aimed for the back and got ready to pull the trigger. Harris braced for impact while he kept praying for that miracle he desperately needed.

The man started to squeeze the trigger but before he was able to finish a bullet hit him in the forehead. The man spun around and pulled the trigger to the launcher. The rocket flew out and hit a building dangerously close to Dutra and the rest of the men. From out of the smoke they started to take fire from the end of the street.

Ray, Torque, Steve, Tommy and Kevin all started firing into the men; each of them hitting. Panicking, Dutra quickly dropped the Heckler, pulled out his side arm and began to return fire and once he did the rest of his men joined in.

As the bullets reached the guys they started to duck for cover. Ray quickly stood up and fired a shot and hit the man next to Dutra. Blood squirted onto Dutra's face. The guys quickly used the brief pause to all stand back up and run toward the limo as they returned fire. Steve fired a shot and it hit one of Dutra's men in the chest.

President Harris quickly looked up as he saw Ray and his team running toward the limo. A smile grew on his face but he knew he wasn't out of the woods just yet. He was still going to have to wait until they reached him.

The men in heavy armor were getting hit with bullets but the bullets bounced off them as they returned fire. Dutra wiped the blood of his face and dark sunglasses and reloaded his gun. Ray and his men moved up.

"Tommy! You and Kevin take the left! We'll take the right!" Ray shouted.

"Aim for the truck!" Torque shouted as he gave his first order to the guys without knowing he had.

Once Steve and Tommy went over to the left they began to fire at the truck, taking Torque's first order...without knowing. Ray and Torque started firing at the truck while Kevin focused on the remaining men.

As a bullet passed right over Dutra he quickly ducked back down. Street quickly moved away from the truck as it started to smoke up. Then he ran over to Dutra as Dutra reloaded.

"Boss, I don't think we can take this much longer!" Street said as another one of his men dropped.

Knowing that Street was right, and that it would take time to get back to the helicopter, Dutra had to accept the chance was over. Once he reloaded his gun he quickly turned to his men.

"Fall back!" Dutra shouted as he broke from cover and started to head to the helicopter.

The remaining men began to cover both Dutra and Street until Bob and Jasmin showed up at the end of the street and began sniping the men with heavy armor.

"Aim for the armpit!" Bob instructed Jasmin.

Jasmin aimed and fired one shot and hit one of the men in armpit, instantly causing him to drop to the ground. Ray and Torque began to move up as Tommy and Steve fired at the truck. The smoke coming from the hood of truck was starting to get very black.

On the way to the helicopter Dutra suddenly stopped, turned around, and began firing at the back of the truck where the gas tank was. Once he saw gasoline begin to pour out of it he ran to the helicopter and hopped in.

"Get this thing in the fucking air!" Dutra ordered as he picked up his sniper rifle.

The helicopter slowly started up while Dutra's patience quickly disappeared.

"Hurry up!!" Dutra ordered.

Ray and Torque reached the limo as Steve and Tommy moved up. Kevin took aim at the last man and fired, killing him with one shot.

"Get the president out of there!" Ray shouted to Torque.

Torque quickly ran over to the door and knocked on it.

"Mr. President! You're gonna be okay. I need you to open the door so we can get you outta there!"

Harris quickly opened the door and took Torque's hand as he got out of the car. Steve stopped when he saw Harris get out of the limo. Then he focused his attention to Ray who was running toward the truck.

"Ray!" Steve shouted just before going after him.

Once the helicopter was ready to go it slowly began to lift off of the ground. Dutra reloaded the sniper rifle and then ducked as a bullet hit the helicopter. Dutra quickly turned and looked to see Ray firing at them. Dutra aimed the sniper rifle and began to return fire as the helicopter slowly went up. Steve reached the truck as he saw Ray standing right in the shadow of it.

"Ray!" Steve shouted again.

When Kevin saw the helicopter lift up, he began firing at it too. Dutra quickly ducked as bullets started hitting the helicopter. Ray fired a whole round into the helicopter, quickly reloaded and then started firing again as Steve ran up to him.

Dutra knew he was gonna have to buy the helicopter some time or else they wouldn't make it so he quickly aimed at the ground where gas was by the truck. Steve looked down and saw the gas and then quickly ran to Ray and body slammed him out of the way.

Dutra fired one shot and when the bullet met the gas, it quickly caught on fire and instantly blew the truck up. The blast pushed Steve into Ray as the two went flying and landed on the ground. Torque grabbed Harris and forced him to duck from the blast.

Bob and Jasmin started to run toward the rest of the team, each panicking about the safety of all of them. Ray hit the ground, his face raking the pavement as Steve landed on top of him.

The helicopter rose up past the buildings and began to fly away but a bullet hit the helicopter from a distance. Dutra quickly turned and looked in his scope. He saw both Roader and Jimmy firing at them. Dutra aimed at them and returned fire. Both of them quickly ducked.

"Keep steady!" Dutra yelled as he looked in the scope.

He couldn't see Roader in the scope but he could see a small sliver of Jimmy's face and carefully aimed. And once he had it, Dutra took the shot. The bullet hit Jimmy on the top of the head and he went crashing down. Once Dutra saw Jimmy fall down away from the wall he aimed again and fired one more shot, hitting Jimmy in the lower stomach.

"Let's go! Let's go!!" Dutra shouted to the pilot.

The pilot flew away into the sky as Dutra slowly built up anger from how the whole situation, that he spent months working on, had ended.

Roader quickly looked down at Jimmy.

"Oh my God! Son!" Roader said to his youngest son.

Blood was pouring out of Jimmy. Roader quickly put pressure on the wound, causing his hands to get covered in blood.

"You're gonna be okay! It's gonna be okay!" Roader said, to try and comfort Jimmy.

Back on the ground, Steve slowly started to move and rolled off of Ray. Ray slowly opened his eyes as blood began to drip from his forehead.

"You okay?" Ray asked.

"I got shot, I got blown up and I got pissed on yesterday...oh yeah, I'm great." Steve said.

Ray smiled as he slowly stood up. The guys ran over and helped them up. Ray then looked at the president.

"You okay, Mr. President?"

"...Yeah." He said, shaken up.

Bob and Jasmin reached the guys and joined the circle. Ray looked around.

"Where's Tommy?" Ray asked.

The guys turned around and saw Tommy in the middle on the road on his knees. Most times this would be when Tommy made a joke about the situation, but not this time. This time was alltogether different. Ray was planning on going over to make sure he was okay, but clearly he could tell Tommy needed a moment.

And as the guys and President Harris began to start asking questions about what had just happened, Tommy stayed in the middle of the road crying harder then he ever had before, over the women who saved his life twice, as he tried to contemplate that he would never be able to thank her...or even ask for her name.

Chapter 5: One Last Job...?

As the sun finally set over Washington, damn near every single branch of law enforcement (and news caster of every major network) arrived at the Lincoln Memorial, trying to make sense of what happened. Communications came back on after Dutra was far enough away from the city.

"Not much is being said about the horrific events that took place here at the Lincoln Memorial today but sources have told us that President Harris is unharmed and has been moved to a secure location as the F.B.I. along with Homeland Security and the Secret Service conduct an investigation to try and answer some of the dozens of questions Americans now have..." News Caster Bryan Medeiros told the world as he tried to keep his fear down to a minimum.

While the world focused on the massacre at the Memorial, across the city Ray sat in the E.R. of the George Washington Hospital watching the news as he received stitches for the massive cut on his forehead. Ray was completely drained (and looked it to say the least).

"Okay you're all set, sir," Dr. Leavitt said to Ray just before he walked away.

Ray couldn't stand listening to the news and anymore and decided he needed some fresh air. He started to get up as Torque walked over to him. Toque had a few marks on his face but nothing serious.

"Hey," Torque said.

Ray looked up at him but didn't respond.

"How ya holding up?" Torque asked.

"As good as I'm gonna get kid," Ray said.

"Yeah...some serious shit went down today," Torque said.

"Yeah...serious shit," Ray said as he put his jacket on.

"Just glad everyone is okay...got worried there for a second..." Torque began to say before Ray interrupted him.

"Look Torque...I know you're trying to help and all...but...I just need some alone time. Give me a second will yeah?" Ray asked.

Torque nodded.

"Yeah, you got it. Need anything let me know," Torque said before he started walking away.

As Torque walked away, Steve walked over to Ray.

"How you holding up, Ray?" Steve asked.

"Dumb question, Steve," Ray said quickly.

Steve shook his head as he looked around at all the people in the E.R.

"Yeah...just wanted to give you a heads up that Roader's boy Jimmy was shot by the bastard in the chopper...he's in surgery right now...guess

Roader isn't doing so good..." Steve trailed off.

Ray turned and looked at Steve.

"That's too bad. You know Roader though...he'll replace the kid tomorrow," Ray said.

Steve then took a step closer to Ray once he realized that Ray didn't know.

"Ray...Jimmy is Roader's son..." Steve confessed.

"What?"

"Yeah...I didn't know either. Just found out a few minuets ago. I was gonna go see how he was but I think it would be best if you did that. You've known him a hell of a lot longer then me," Steve said.

Ray nodded in agreement. Yeah it was true that Ray and Roader were always in competition with each other, but he knew that all that had to pause during something like this. It wouldn't be the first time the two had done it either. And Ray knew that if the situation were reversed, Roader would be there for him.

"Where is he?" Ray asked.

"Fourth floor by the surgery wing."

Ray quickly ran out of the E.R. and headed for the nearest staircase as Steve watched him run away. Then Steve focused on the T.V. that was in front of him. The headline on the bottom of the screen said: 'At least twenty dead after shooting.' Steve knew that was a lie. Steve believed without doubt that well more then that were killed during the shooting.

Steve walked away from the T.V. and headed over to Bob, Kevin and Jasmin sitting in the crowed waiting room. Once he walked in, all the guys quickly stood up and walked over to him.

"You alright, Steve?" Kevin asked.

"Fine."

"How's Ray?" Jasmin asked.

"He's fine, he's on his way up to the fourth floor to see Roader."

"Is it true that Jimmy is his son?' Kevin asked, as he remembered punching Jimmy from earlier.

"Yeah it's true, Kevo...where's Tommy?" Steve asked.

The guys looked around.

"No idea," Jasmin said.

"I think I know where he is..." Bob said.

Steve nodded his head at Bob, and Bob quickly turned and started walking away.

"So...now what?" Jasmin asked.

"I don't know on this one yet, Jas." Steve said as he looked around. "You guys head downstairs, grab something to eat and we'll meet up by the van in a half an hour."

Jasmin watched Steve as he walked away.

"This is bad isn't it?" Jasmin asked Kevin.

"Yeah Jas...this is bad," Kevin said as he too started to walk away.

Jasmin took one last look around at all the chaos going on in the E.R. For the first time since he arrived in America with the guys he was scared. Jasmin saw a lot while he was in Bosnia but he never saw anything like he did earlier in the day. Once he had enough of the E.R. he followed Kevin out of the room.

Ray quickly ran up the flight of stairs until he got to a door with a big '4' painted on it. He grabbed the handle and swung it open as he ran into the hall. At the end of the hall he turned and saw that Roader wasn't there. At first he didn't know where else to look until suddenly he heard a helicopter. Ray turned and looked out the window as the chopper flew into his line of sight.

Ray got a feeling in his gut that told him to head up to the roof for some reason. He knew it wasn't the time to question it, so he ran back to the stairwell and began running up the stairs until he got to the top of the last staircase and saw that the door directly in front of him was opened a crack.

Ray slowly opened the door and stepped out onto the roof. The night air was starting to get chilly. Ray got goose bumps as he started walk further out onto the roof. No one was in sight. After looking around for a moment or two he was convinced that no one was up there, so he started to head back to the door when he saw Roader sitting by the edge of the helicopter pad looking at the view of the city.

Even though Ray couldn't see Roader's face he had no doubt that Roader was in great pain. Ray very carefully walked over to the edge of the helicopter pad and slowly sat down next to Roader. He could see Roader's face now, but Roader wasn't crying or sobbing; he was just looking at the view with his face frozen with fear. Roader didn't say anything at first (didn't even acknowledge he was there). For a good while they both just sat looking at the view with distant echoes of police sirens fading in and out.

"I didn't know he was your son..." Ray began, but trailed off.

And finally after a long period Roader broke his silence.

"You know I warned him, when he told me he wanted to join the team. I looked at him straight in the eye and said 'It's not worth it,' but he didn't listen..." Roader softly said without taking his eyes off the horizon.

"Well, he's stubborn...just like his father...and I'm sure he's strong like his father too," Ray said.

"Doctors don't think he'll make it. And I can't just sit in a waiting room until some stranger comes out and tells me the news...you know Ray, we've been doing this for all these years; I know you've seen a lot and I know you know I've seen a lot. I should've been prepared for this...I mean I could get prepared to take down a terrorist who had controls to a nuclear war head...so why can't I prepare myself for this?"

Ray patted Roader on his shoulder.

"Because there're some things that nobody can prepare themselves for...not even guys like us..." Ray said.

"How is your daughter by the way, Ray?" Roader asked.

Ray shrugged her shoulders.

"Last time I saw her was at Diane's funeral. Even there she didn't say two words to me," Ray confessed.

"Why didn't you say something?" Roader asked.

"Cause I didn't know what to say...honestly hardly recognized her...my own daughter...don't even know what color her eyes are..." Ray said, his head lowered down.

"Some days I forget why we decided to do this," Roader said as tears filled his eyes.

Ray thought about that too. He felt the same way on some days. The job was hard when they were young but now that they were getting up there it was starting to take its toll.

"For all this," Ray said as he pointed the view.

"You think it's worth it?" Roader asked.

"I know my daughter is safe every night when I'm out there. I may not be safe but I know she can live life free, and right now your son is downstairs being worked on by the best surgeons in the country. I'd like to think something we've done over the past few decades has made that possible. When I think about it like that...then yes, it's worth it to me," Ray said from the bottom of his scarred heart.

Those words hit close to home for Roader as he wiped the tears from his cheeks.

"You going after that son of a bitch?" Roader asked.

Ray looked at Roader.

"With everything I have left in me. I'm not as young as I use to be...but I still got one fight left in me..." Ray said firmly.

Roader nodded.

"But I'm gonna need help. Whoever these bastards are, they aren't just a couple clowns with access to automatic weapons. They're highly trained and well equipped. I know it's bad timing, but I need you on this one Paul..." Ray said.

Roader thought about it for a moment...and then thought about being miles away from his son if something happened to him.

"I can't. You know I would Ray...I want to be there...but...I don't know, I just can't leave my son alone...if anything happened to him and I wasn't there by his side...it wouldn't be something I'd be able to live with. I haven't been there for him for most of his life...but I'd like to try to be there now...I got enough regret I have to live with. I don't need any more," Roader said with a broken heart.

"I understand. I'd do the same thing if I were in your position." Ray slowly stood up and headed to the door.

"Ray!"

Ray stopped at the door and turned around and looked at Roader.

"Promise me something..."

"Sure," Ray said.

Roader finally took his eyes of the view of the city and met Ray's eyes.

"Put a bullet through that son of a bitches head for me."

Ray nodded his head.

"Promise," Ray said and then walked away.

As soon as the Ray closed the door and Roader knew he had complete privacy, he began to cry not only for his son but also for finally seeing the true effect the job had on the rest of his life.

II

As Ray headed back down the stairs, Bob had finally caught up to Tommy who was standing on the top floor of the parking garage smoking a cigarette.

"Thought you decided to quit," Bob said as he walked over.

Tommy inhaled and then went back to looking up at the stars.

"It's been a tough day, Bob," Tommy said in a pissed off voice.

"Yeah...well I came to check on you. See if everything was okay," Bob said in his gruff voice.

"Well it's not Bob. Besides what do you care anyway? Never gave a shit about anyone besides yourself in your whole miserable fucking life."

Bob knew that nothing he tried to say was going to get through to Tommy, but he knew he had to try.

"I know what you're going through..." Bob began to say.

"Oh like hell you do Bob! I had to watch as some asshole tried to shoot me but ended up hitting a beautiful girl. The very same girl who if I hadn't been looking at, I wouldn't have seen the gun another guy had! You don't know anything about that Bob! So don't try to mind fuck me!" Tommy shouted as loud as he could.

Tommy turned away from Bob and went back to looking up at the sky again. And Tommy was right; Bob had no idea the kind of pain Tommy was going through, mostly due to the fact that Bob never seemed to have any type of feelings. But there was a time when Bob did. There was a time when Bob wasn't this shallow and hollow son of a bitch that he had become.

"Ten years ago, before I joined Ray and Steve...I owned the body shop that we use. Only back then it was a real body shop. I started it up by myself and profited from it...guess you could say I was doing good. One night I walked into a bar, wasn't planning on doing anything but drinking myself to sleep...but all that changed when this girl came in. She caught the corner of my eye and before I knew...I couldn't take my eyes of her. She was the most beautiful woman I've ever laid my eyes on. Back then I was only really out to get pussy, but it was different with this chick. I knew I had to make a move or else I'd regret it for the rest of my life...and so I did. Walked right up to her and handed her a beer. Then we just started talking. One minute it was nine o clock and the next thing I knew the bar tender was calling the final round...we stayed there until the place closed, just talking. And you know the thing that surprised me? It wasn't awkward at all. It just seemed to flow smoothly..." Bob explained.

Tommy slowly lowered his head back down to earth.

"...So we went back to my place. Now normally that would be where we ripped off each other's clothes and got down and dirty...but we didn't. We stayed up all night just talking...hell I even made coffee when I saw the sun coming up. We went onto my balcony and watched as the sun began to come up...I was never happier in my whole rotten life. It was like I had found a piece of Heaven right here on Earth. So we started dating and after less then two months I proposed to her..." Bob continued.

"Talk about moving fast, Bob," Tommy commented.

"Oh I knew she was the one. I knew I wanted to spend the rest of my life with her," Bob said.

"Well then where is she Bob? She fuck your best friend and make you the asshole that you are now?" Tommy asked angrily.

Bob sighed.

"We got married and a month later found out she was pregnant. I couldn't have been happier. We took bets on what the baby would be...I lost; it turned out to be a girl but I was okay with that; even though I really wanted a boy. Everything was going good. Work was great and I felt like the king of the world...until I got a phone call at the shop. I picked it up and found out she had been in a car accident and was rushed into surgery. I quickly left work and floored it to the hospital...ran every red light between the shop and the hospital...but it didn't make a difference. I was too late. Some young prick in a blue outfit told me that my life was over...she was gone...and so was the baby...I didn't believe him. I had to see for myself...and I regret that to this day. When I got into the room and saw all the wires and tubes hanging out of her mouth...I knew right then and there that it was over. The doc asked me if I wanted to see our baby...I regret that too...because once I saw her...and realized...that was the first and last time I would get to see her...a part of me died..."

Tommy slowly turned to Bob and was surprised that Bob wasn't showing any type of emotion as he told the story; proving how damaged his soul had become.

"I shut the machine off myself and walked out of that room with nothing left inside. My piece of Heaven was gone just as fast as it came...I took time off from work to think...and drink. After a few weeks of moping in self-pity and drinking every bottle of alcohol I could get my hands on I finally went back to work. My first day back, Ray and Steve came in as my first customers. We had the place to ourselves and as I heard them talking about their last mission, I asked if I could join them with whatever they did. At first they said no, but I promised them they could work out of the shop. Then they agreed and that's that...I keep everything inside Tommy because I'm a firm believer that the pain of the past is like a knife in the heart; if you pull it out you run the risk of causing more damage, so if you just leave it in, it blocks the wound from bleeding out and all you have to worry about is an infection...but that won't kick in until the next day and since no one is guaranteed to get a tomorrow, you can spend your whole life pushing it off until the next day...so when you go home tonight and realize you won't be able to sleep...maybe it'll help you to know that you wont be the only one up..." Bob said just before he started to walk away.

Tommy watched in awe as Bob walked away. He never thought in all the time they were working together that Bob was carrying a burden as heavy as that. It explained so much about Bob (not to mention that was the most Tommy had ever heard Bob talk) And as Tommy finished his cigarette, he realized that he would never look at Bob the same way again. It was eye opening for Tommy to say the least. After that little talk Tommy started looking at Bob in the same light as Ray and Steve; broken hero's that were like icebergs; not much to look at on the surface but a world of ice just under the surface, struggling to not let the rest get lost in the dark abyss that made up there lives.

III

Tommy kept looking at the sky as Bob's haunting words sank deep into his mind. Meanwhile, Ray walked out of the stairwell and started to walk to the opposite side of the floor to where the elevators were. Ray's mind was all over the place. Anger had begun to mix in with fear as he prayed whatever happened next wouldn't take a large piece of his soul (because he was running out of pieces to lose). Ray was so lost in thought that he almost didn't notice Sullivan sitting by a window in the cafeteria.

Once Ray realized it was Sullivan he veered off course into the cafeteria and walked over to Sullivan.

"How's Paul?" Sullivan asked.

"As you'd expect," Ray said as he sat down.

Sullivan shook his head as he took a sip of coffee.

"How are you and the team holding up?" Sullivan asked.

"How are we holding up or how are we holding up because you want to drop us into another war zone?" Ray asked.

Sullivan sighed as he realized what Ray was getting at.

"Look Ray, we've been doing this for how long?" Sullivan asked.

"Too long," Ray firmly said.

"Yeah, I know. But listen to me Ray, I need you on this one. With Paul out of the picture, the only thing stopping America from going to war is your team."

"You don't have to remind me okay? I know what's a stake. In fact I probably know what's at stake more than you. And I know what you're going to ask me to do. Your gonna ask me to break what's left of my soul...so give me a minute to process everything before you start handing out orders. I mean it's not like you'll be the one pulling the trigger in the end..." Ray said with frustration in his voice.

Sullivan put his coffee without having taken a sip of it.

"Listen to me Ray. Yeah, I may not always be on the ground helping you, but you bet your ass I'm in the situation room watching over you guys every step of the way. You know my heart beats fast when I see you guys are in a jam too," Sullivan said, trying to explain his absence for all these years.

Ray shook his head as he looked out the window.

"Today shouldn't have happened. If you thought there was real danger then you should've done more," Ray said.

"I know. I knew there was danger, but I didn't expect the scale of it."

"How's Harris doing?" Ray asked.

"He's been moved to a safe house up in Seattle. He'll be fine there but he wants answers, and he's looking at me for them and if I come up empty then he's just gonna do it his own way."

"So he's looking at you and you're looking at me. That's how this works?" Ray asked.

"That's how it's always worked."

Ray sighed knowing that even though he didn't want to admit it, inside he knew it was true.

"Yeah..."

"Look Ray I know this is bad timing; you know with you wanting to retire and all but I couldn't live with myself if I let you go and the world turned to shit overnight. I'm sorry old friend but I gotta ask you one more time. I need you and your team for this one because honestly, it doesn't get much worse then this."

"What happens when we finish the job?" Ray asked.

"You get a nice pension and go on to live the rest of your life anyway you want to. All I'm asking for is one last time, and you have my word once it's done, you're good to go." Sullivan promised.

"Okay, but you gotta give me something. You gotta tell me what we're after, Sullivan. Because if we go in blind like every other job you and Joe put us on, we won't make it back home."

Sullivan reached down to his briefcase and unzipped it. At first Ray didn't want to know what he was up against, because he knew that once the truth was out in the open Ray couldn't hide in denial anymore. But it was time to face the truth. And most of all it was time to end this once and for all.

Sullivan took a file out of his brief case and slid it across the table to Ray. Ray quickly grabbed it and opened it and the first thing he saw was a rather poor quality picture of the man that was shooting at him earlier in that day.

"That's the guy from the helicopter," Ray said.

"Yeah, that's the man known as Dutra," Sullivan said.

"That's all you have on him?" Ray quickly asked.

"His whole name is Nicholas 'Dutra' Vacca...C.I.A. just confirmed that about an hour ago."

"What do you know about him?" Ray asked.

"Born in the United States, moved to Russia when he started collage over there but sometime between his junior and senior year he dropped out and went into the drug cartel in Russia. Guess he thought selling cocaine was an easier way to make money then working for a living. Guy's good that's for sure. Went from selling drugs on the streets to becoming a major dealer—one of the best In Russia. Once he reached the top, he quickly got into the weapons business. Got to the top of that and got to where he is today..."

"Which is?"

Sullivan took his eyes off the file and looked at Ray.

"Selling automatic weapons and warheads to some people that really don't like America. Let's leave it at that."

"So what's his deal with America? Must be a reason why he decided to betray his own country," Ray said.

"Just like any other person that hates America: thinks were flawed and need to keep our noses out of other countries business."

Ray looked up at Sullivan.

"Sullivan, that's bullshit. Someone like this just doesn't snap over night; something had to happen to get his attention," Ray said.

Sullivan picked up his coffee and took another sip.

"Sixteen months ago intel came in that Dutra was planning on selling a warhead to Hyun Ki Jung, a leader of a terrorist cell out of North Korea. Obviously we couldn't let that happen, so the president authorized and air strike on the building where it was taking place."

"What happened?"

"We bombed the shit out of it. Jung and a large part of his team were killed and we thought we even got Dutra, but the C.I.A. started getting intel six months later, that Dutra was alive and well, and planning a retaliation on us."

"So, what, you've been sitting on this for ten months?" Ray asked.

"Of course not! Dutra is a whore; would work with anyone to make a quick buck, so we've been monitoring the chatter of our known enemies, thinking he would join alliances with them. We were wrong."

"Yeah, no shit. Tell that to the hundred dead people over at the Lincoln Memorial," Ray said as he shook his head.

"Anyway, so the good news is that Dutra is working by himself on this. You don't have to worry about heat from anyone else," Sullivan began.

"Yeah? And what's the bad news?"

"The man has a small army working for him. He contacted everyone from his drug selling days to his weapon dealing days. Recruited pretty much everyone he's ever met. Intel is still coming in but when it comes down to it...you'll be outnumbered a hundred to one..."

"Great," Ray said as he closed the file and placed it down on the table.

"The President has told me to tell you if you need anything he's just a phone call away, and that this ends with Dutra dead. Whether you get him or the president has to put boots on the ground—he wants Dutra dead, not alive," Sullivan said.

"It's not always that easy, Sullivan," Ray confessed.

"You don't have to tell me that."

"And how do we even know he'll go back to Russia? I mean if he was born here what's stopping him from staying here?"

"Nothing. He might go to Russia; he might stay in the states. We don't know. That's where you and your team will come in," Sullivan said.

"How much time do we have?"

"Not much. More then likely he was planning on taking out the president today, and since we stopped him from that my guess is by now he's already working on what he wants to do next—whatever the hell that is," Sullivan said with fear creeping into his voice.

"Before I decide anything I gotta talk to the guys. I can't speak for them on this," Ray said as he stood up.

"Do what you gotta do, but I need an answer tonight Ray because tomorrow it's all out war."

Ray headed back to the elevator as Sullivan took another sip of coffee and opened the file. He looked again at the picture of Dutra in a baseball cap with dark sunglasses, aiming a handgun.

"God help us all," Sullivan said right before he stood up and threw his coffee in the trash.

IV

As Sullivan headed up to the fourth floor to check on Roader, the guys all met up at the van parked on the lowest floor of the hospital parking garage. From Bob and Tommy to Kevin, Steve, Jasmin and Torque, all had a look of fear in thier eyes. Steve tried to look calm but not even he could do it. But when they saw Ray walking over they all stood up and looked at him.

"Is everyone okay?" Ray asked.

The guys shook their heads (Tommy give Ray the thumbs up sign).

"Hanging in there," Kevin said.

Ray shook his head.

"Good...just finished talking with Sullivan."

"What he say?" Jasmin asked.

"It isn't good guys. I'll be honest with you," Ray confessed.

"So who did this?" Tommy asked.

"The guy, Dutra, that Sullivan mentioned in the situation room today," Ray said.

"What's he want us to do?" Bob asked.

Ray gave Bob a look and then looked at the rest of the guys.

"All of you know what Sullivan wants us to do," Ray said.

"So we doing it?" Kevin asked.

"I am...but I'm not gonna ask you guys to. This time it's different. It's not another ordinary job like the others we've been on," Ray said.

"Why is that? Because this time we know the stakes?" Torque asked.

Ray looked at Torque.

"Guys...there's a real chance that not all of us—or any of us for that matter—will make it back home. You know I've seen a lot in my time, I know the evil mankind is capable of, and I gotta say this guy is nothing like I've ever seen before. Most people have some type of heart or emotion but not this guy. He's empty inside. I have no doubt that he'll be ready to do whatever he has to in order to get his way, and I can't stand here and order you guys to come along for something like this. So if any of you want to stay out of this, I won't blame you." Ray said.

The guys took a minuet to let Ray's words sink in. Torque thought about it the most. And when he realized Ray was scared, he got worried for a moment too. But the silence was quickly cut short.

"I'm in," Jasmin said.

Ray sighed.

"Jas..."

"No Ray! It was you guys that took me out of Bosnia. You guys gave me something to fight for and something to believe in when I thought there wasn't anything else. I owe this to you guys...I owe this to you Ray. I'm in."

"I am too," Kevin said.

"So am I," Tommy said.

Ray shook his head at Tommy and then looked at Bob.

"Oh what the hell I'm in too. I got nothing better to do," Bob said.

Ray chuckled.

"Me too."

Ray quickly looked up at Torque.

"It's better to die on your feet then live a life on your knees right?" Torque asked.

Ray shook his head.

"So count me in too."

Ray turned to Steve. Steve didn't show it but inside he couldn't have been more proud of the guys. And in that brief moment Steve's doubts left his mind and it began to fill up with determination. Steve then met Ray's eyes and nodded his head. Ray returned the gesture and then looked back at all the guys.

"Alright then guys...let's finish this," Ray said.

The guys all smiled.

"Let's move!" Ray shouted.

Bob opened the back of the van and the guys started to jump in. Before Tommy jumped in he turned and looked at Ray.

"I get a shotgun, right?" Tommy asked.

"We'll talk about that later," Ray said.

"Wow, you just won't let that go, huh?" Tommy asked as he hopped in the van.

Ray closed the doors to the van when Torque jumped in, and then slowly turned to Steve.

"You really think you were gonna go at this alone?" Steve asked.

"Well, I was hoping that you'd at least come with me," Ray said as he smiled.

"Who else is gonna save your ass when you do something stupid?"

Steve asked.

"You didn't save my ass!" Ray said as he walked away.

Steve's mouth dropped to the floor.

"I'll remember that Ray," Steve said as he walked to the passenger door to the van.

Ray chuckled as he got into the driver's seat and took out his cell phone.

"Where to first?' Steve asked.

"Back home first," Ray said as he dialed a number.

"I can live with that," Steve said as he leaned his head back and closed his eyes.

The phone rang in Ray's ear until he heard the line pick up on the other end.

"Sullivan...you got your team," Ray said before starting the van.

"Alright Ray, we'll be in touch." Sullivan said. "And Ray, for what it's worth...thank you."

As Ray hung up the guys in the back got comfortable for the long ride home while Ray tried to come up with a game play to deal with the situation that could quite possibly lead him (and a few others) to their graves.

V

Back in New York, Dutra's helicopter landed safely down onto the helipad of the tall skyscraper. As soon as it landed Dutra quickly stepped out into the frigid night air as Street and a couple others followed him inside and then into his office.

Street knew that Dutra was furious about what had happened and he was actually very surprised that Dutra had been able to keep his lid on for as long as he had but he knew it wasn't going to last for long.

And sure enough, the moment Dutra walked into his office he walked over to his desk and slammed his computer onto the floor. Street stopped dead in his tracks as Dutra began trashing the office.

"Goddamn it!!!!!!!!!!!!!!!!!!!" Dutra screamed at the top of his lungs.

Street slowly turned to the men that were standing next to him, and nodded them to leave the room. The men quickly walked out of the office and closed the door behind them as Street very carefully started over to Dutra.

After Dutra picked up the large printer by his desk and slammed it onto the ground he then sat down in his chair, out of breath and filled with anger. Street knew that trying to talk to Dutra when he was like this was dangerous, but leaving Dutra alone like this was ten times worse. because

God only knows what he would do. So Street walked up to the desk and waited for Dutra to say something.

Dutra looked down at the busted computer at his feet and then turned the chair to look out the window at the beautiful skyline that was New York City.

"Sir..." Street carefully began.

Dutra didn't answer. He just kept looking out the window. But once he got bored with the view Dutra finally broke the silence in the room.

"You remember the nuke job, Street?" Dutra asked in a menacing voice.

"Yes sir."

"We had an army there. A fucking army. There must've been thirty of us there," Dutra reminded Street.

"I remember sir."

"We had just gotten the shipment and then suddenly we started taking fire in every direction. You and I left before we got our heads blown off, remember?"

"I do."

"What do you remember when the shooting began?" Dutra asked.

"Came from every direction."

"What else?"

Street taught about it for a moment but couldn't figure out what Dutra wanted him to say.

"Uh..." Street said out loud.

"The shooting! What do you remember?" Dutra shouted.

"Uh it came fast, steady...accurate," Street said under pressure.

"You're damn right it did. Every shot that was taken got one of my guys...and then today I brought the best out to Washington so nothing could fuck this up and what happened today?"

"The same. Fast, steady and accurate," Street said just before he finally realized what Dutra was getting at.

"Now either that's one hell of a coincidence...or we're missing something..." Dutra said as he slowly stood up into the darkness.

"What are you thinking?"

Dutra slowly turned Street.

"I headed back there a few days after the attack...I knew then something was off about it but I didn't really think about it until today," Dutra firmly said.

"So how do you wanna deal with this?" Street asked.

Dutra took his time before he answered. He knew he was going to have to come up with something if he was going to make another move on America.

"You and Vincent, find out who these bastards are. I don't care if you have to move mountains to find them, just do it."

"Just names?" Street asked.

"Names, addresses, family members—every fucking thing! You and Vincent work on getting those, I'll deal with the meeting we have with Radar coming up."

"Sir with all due respect, don't you think we should hold off on the meeting...just until we know who we're dealing with?" Street asked.

Dutra slowly smiled.

"No. Just get me those names. I got an idea."

Even though Street didn't agree with the strategy Dutra wanted to go with, he nodded his head.

"Yes sir."

"They want to play with fire...fine. We burn every fucking thing they have to the ground until they're surrounded by nothing but ash. Think it's time to call back Stone..." Dutra said.

"You got it," Street said.

Dutra shook his head and then went back to looking out the window.

"Every man has a weakness...we just have to find out their's..." Dutra said as he closed his eyes to remember Ray's face as he shot at him from the helicopter.

And as Street left to get to work on figuring out the identity of these very well organized men, Dutra locked himself in his office for the rest of night as the rage began to build up inside him until the only thing on his mind was killing anyone who stood in his way...

Chapter 6: Splitting Up

While the entire nation glued their eyes to Bryan Medeiros as the news about the massacre began unfolding, Ray and his men were hard at work. None of them got any sleep (as to be expected), but by the way each of them were running through the obstacle course you'd never be able to tell. Each of them were finishing at under a minute and fifteen seconds...with the exception of Jasmin (but that was to be expected).

"Again!" Ray yelled from the rooftop as Jasmin joined the rest of them at the end of the obstacle course.

Even though they were out of breath they went at it again, pushing themselves harder then they ever had before. You'd never know it from the sound of Ray's voice, but he was impressed—even by Jasmin. Yeah, he kept coming in dead last, but it was only by a few seconds.

"How long you plan on keeping this up?" Steve asked as he stood next to Ray, eating a jelly donut.

"Another half hour then I'll bring them back in," Ray said. He looked at Steve as he took a huge bite of the donut and jelly fell all over his lips. "Way to be a team player, Steve."

Steve shrugged.

"Hey I could beat these guys any day of the week. Besides, I saved your ass and that entitles me to a pardon," Steve said.

"You're really not gonna let that go are you?" Ray asked.

"Nope."

Ray shook his head as he looked back down at the guys.

"Come on guys! Hustle!" Ray ordered.

"So when we heading back out?" Steve asked as he put the last piece of donut into his mouth.

"Just waiting on Sullivan to get back to me. Probably soon though," Ray said.

"Any news on Roader's kid there?" Steve asked.

"Yeah made it through surgery. Put him in ICU late last night."

"Tough son of a bitch," Steve said.

"That's one way of saying it."

"You get any sleep last night?" Steve asked.

"No...stayed here all night."

"Yeah I didn't much either," Steve said as he dug into his pocket and took out a candy bar.

Ray turned and looked at Steve as he began to unwrap the candy bar. Before Steve could take a bite out of it Ray quickly grabbed it from his hands.

"Hey!" Steve yelled.

"You've been hanging around Jasmin to much," Ray said.

Steve grabbed the candy bar back from Ray.

"When I'm fifty pounds overweight and I need a mirror to see my balls then we'll talk. Besides, I'm carbohydrate loading," Steve said as he took a bite.

"Yeah and so is Jas," Ray said as he chuckled.

Steve softly hit Ray on the shoulder and looked back down at the guys.

"So have you called Emily yet?" Steve suddenly asked.

Ray looked at him.

"What?"

"Emily. Have you called her yet?" Steve asked again.

"Why would I call her Steve?" Ray asked.

"Oh come on Ray. I've been working with you for twenty years..."

"Please don't remind me," Ray added.

"And in those twenty years I've never seen you as nervous as you were last night."

"People get nervous from time to time Steve."

"Ray you know what I'm talking about, so cut the shit. After last night I know you want to call her, maybe even see her."

"Drop it Steve," Ray said firmly.

"I'm just saying you should."

Ray snorted.

"And tell her what? 'Oh sorry I've been a horrible father to you? Sorry I wasn't around for kindergarten, high school and graduation? Sorry I haven't seen you in three years but since I found out I might die on my next job—oh by the way I kill people for a living—and I may not make it back so I just wanted to hi before I go?' Is that what you want me to say Steve?"

Steve shrugged his shoulders.

"Well I wouldn't start there..."

"Like I said Steve just drop it. That time has come and gone already."

Steve took another bite out of his candy bar and looked at Ray.

"You've been saying that for years. When are you gonna wake the fuck up?" Steve asked just before he walked away.

Ray couldn't help but think about all the times he's talked about Emily to Steve. And maybe Steve was right, but now wasn't the time to get caught up in family drama. Now was the time to remain focused.

"Alright guys head on up!" Ray yelled as they finished the course again for the ninth straight time.

As the guys came over it was clear all of them were out of breath. Jasmin looked like he was gonna drop dead if he didn't get any water (or food) in his stomach.

"Not bad guys, but we're gonna be doing a hell of a lot more then running on this next mission. Now it's time to work on your strength..."

While Ray had the guys challenge each other at taking down one another Steve went back into the shop and headed into Ray's office. He took a quick look out the window to see what the guys were doing and then sat down in Ray's desk chair.

For a brief moment Steve got a smile on his face. He fantacised that for just a second he was in charge of the team (which is what he'd always wanted. But he would never want to take the spot unless Ray was sure that he was done. Steve had nothing but respect for Ray and trying to force him out of the job wouldn't be right. It would feel like betraying family in Steve's eyes). Steve looked down at Ray's desk and then carefully picked up a picture of a beautiful young girl with black hair. As he smiled at the picture he started to wonder how could a guy like Ray have a kid that looked as pretty as Emily did in that picture.

Even though Steve was jealous at times that Ray had a kid, he was glad that he had never fathered any. Steve knew what the job had done to Ray and he honestly couldn't imagine having to live with something like that his whole life.

"Busy morning?" A voice quickly shot into the room.

Steve looked up, startled, and saw Joey standing in the entrance in his normal suit and tie with a file tucked underneath his arm.

"Guess you could say that," Steve said as he stood up.

Joey shook his head and then held out the folder.

"Here."

Steve took the folder and opened it.

"That's all you need for your next assignment," Joey said.

"Which is?" Steve asked as he opened the file and began to read.

"Seems like Dutra is continuing on with his plans, despite yesterdays turn out."

"Oh yeah?"

"Yeah. He's meeting up with an American arms dealer named Radar in Florida tomorrow evening."

"Must've worked hard to get a hold of this overnight," Steve said in a sarcastic tone.

"Well that's the NSA for ya. They don't miss a beat. We thought that Dutra would head back to Russia but now it's clear he's staying in the United States for a little longer. Just not sure how much longer."

Steve shook his head as he kept reading on.

"He'll be there in Florida?" Steve asked.

"More then likely. He can't afford not to be. Right now people are probably questioning if he can do his job. He'll want to show that he has what it takes to get it done. The last page in the file is an executive order signed by the president himself. He wants Dutra taken out...by any mean necessary."

"What about this Radar guy?" Steve asked.

"Not your concern. The priority is Dutra. If you can get a shot at both then great, but if not then just go for Dutra."

Steve thought about it for a moment.

"Sounds like it would be easier if only a few of us went instead of the whole team, keep it quiet," Steve said thinking out loud.

"Well that's up to you guys, just make sure you're there when the deal is underway."

Steve nodded his head and he finished reading the executive order.

"Steve for what it's worth, I'm sorry. I just want you to know I did fight to get you," Joey confessed.

"Well too little too late pal." Steve said.

Joey nodded.

"Alright. I gotta head back," Joey said as he started to turn around.

"You're not gonna give this to Ray yourself?" Steve asked.

Joey turned back to Steve.

"No. I gave it to you. I'm sure you can fill him in," Joey said as he looked out the window and saw the guys wrestling on the ground. "Besides, I asked if I could be taken off working with you guys; Ray had some harsh words last time we talked."

Steve turned and looked out the window.

"Yeah. I heard about that."

"Yeah...so from now on Sullivan will be handing you down orders. He just wanted me to drop this off while he stays with Roader," Joey said.

Steve shook his head as he stared at Ray through the window. Nobody else could really see it, but Steve could tell just by the look on Ray's face that he was getting tired; like a car slowly getting consumed by rust, only a matter of time before the check engine light comes on.

"You take it easy, Steve," Joey said as he walked away.

At first Steve wasn't gonna say anything (he honestly felt like he didn't need to) but despite the badass that Steve was, he never liked leaving someone dealing with problems that weren't theirs to begin with.

"Hey Joe!" Steve shouted.

Joey stopped and turned to look at Steve.

"Yeah?"

Steve was going to make a big speech saying that he didn't hold Joey responsible for everything and how he actually kinda liked the guy...but he kept silent. He just lifted up the file and shook it.

"Thanks."

Joey nodded his head and walked away, never to return to the shop again. As he left, Joey couldn't help but think back to all the times that he'd stopped by to give them orders. At first when he came by, when he took the job over, he stayed very professional. But over time as he got to know the guys he finally came out of his shell and ultimately started to enjoy coming by. Sometimes he would just come by to shoot the shit with Ray when the world wasn't in such dire straits.

But Joey was never one to keep looking at the past. He learned very early on that nothing (especially nothing good) lasts forever. Head held high, wondering where life would take him next, he got into his car and drove back to Washington.

After a half hour of the guys nearly beating each other up Ray decided to end it and give the guys a break. Once he gave the orders the guys dropped to the ground to catch their breath. Kevin wiped the blood off his lip while Torque leaned up against the wall and took a sip from his water bottle.

"Alright guys, ten minute break and then back down to the obstacle course, alright?" Ray asked.

The guys were so out of breath they couldn't even acknowledge Ray, let alone say a sentence. Once Ray looked around and realized Steve was nowhere to be found he started to head into the body shop, as Jasmin suddenly threw up right in front of Tommy, getting it all over his shoes.

"Jas! What the hell?" Tommy shouted as Bob and Kevin broke into laughter.

"Oh, sorry Tommy. My bad," Jasmin said as he wiped the chunks off his lips.

"Damn, man," Tommy said as he stood up and started to wipe his shoes off in the dirt.

Bob then took out a cigarette and lit it. As he lit it and put it in his mouth he looked up and saw everyone looking at him.

"Anyone reminds me this is bad for me, I'll shoot you," Bob threatened.

The guys quickly turned away.

"Thought so," Bob said as he inhaled.

Torque turned back to the body shop and saw that Ray was gone. He then took out his cell phone and looked at it as Jasmin took out a candy bar and started opening it.

"Really, Jas?" Tommy asked.

"Don't worry, I feel a little better now. Won't happen again," Jasmin said as he took a huge bite out of the top of the chocolate bar.

"Yeah tell that to my shoes, asshole," Tommy said.

As Tommy finished wiping his shoes in the dirt a soft rumble of thunder rocked in the sky. The guys looked up as they saw dark clouds quickly moving in. Bob threw his cigarette down on the ground and then stood up as another rumble of thunder echoed in the sky—clearly a sigh on things to come.

II

As Ray entered the body shop to grab a bottle of water from the small fridge that was on the body shop floor he saw Steve walk out of his office with the file in his hand.

"Hey, where'd you run off to?" Ray asked before he took a mouthful of water.

"Joe stopped by," Steve confessed.

"Oh yeah? What he want?"

Steve held the file up in the air. Ray looked up at it and then walked over to Steve. Steve lowered it and then tossed the file onto a green Pontiac Grad Prix that was in the middle of the shop.

"Told us where Dutra is gonna be," Steve said.

"And where's that?"

"Down in Walton Beach, Florida."

"Walton Beach? Wasn't that the town that got pretty much wiped out last year by the hurricane?" Ray asked as he looked at the file.

"Yeah. Just looked it up. This time last year twenty thousand people lived there. Now it's a ghost town. Most of the town is still flooded which has prevented people from returning. Perfect place for any number of illegal activities...if you can get to it," Steve explained.

"Well now that we know why Dutra chose this point we just need to know why he's there," Ray said.

"Joe took care of that for us. Seems like Dutra is going back to his old ways, selling weapons and high-tech explosives to a major gun for hire from Mexico named Radar. I guess old habits really do die hard."

"Name doesn't sound familiar," Ray said softly.

"Yeah, well he's not much better then Dutra, in fact might actually be worse. You know about the genocide in Mexico right?" Steve asked.

"Heard about it."

"Well this guy Radar is behind it all. He's got a small army in his pocket too. Sounds like him and his men have been going town-to-town shooting the men, raping the women and enslaving the children, and once they're done, they burn the place to the ground."

"Surprised we're not going after him," Ray said.

"Well Joe made it clear that our mission is to simply take Dutra out."

Ray shook his head as he looked through the file.

"Might be easier for just you and I to go," Ray said.

"I thought the same thing. The less people we have, the less of a chance we'll have of getting caught," Steve explained.

Ray knew that Dutra would be a struggle to get if he had his army with him, and going down to Walton Beach and just shooting up the place would be risky...but if they were able to sneak in they might actually have a better shot of getting Dutra.

"You up for another sneaking around mission?" Ray asked Steve as he looked up at him.

"Always. Nothing like a little suspense to keep you going," Steve said.

"Hmm...well the guys won't be happy with being left behind."

"Well, they may not have too," Steve said.

"How do you figure that?"

Steve grabbed the file and flipped the pages to the back until he found the picture of a log cabin.

"Dutra's got a small place in the sticks of Maine. While you and I deal with Dutra and Radar we'll send the guys up there. Maybe they'll find something that'll give us a better idea of what Dutra is up to, because I don't know about you but I still think something is off about his plan so far."

After giving it some thought Ray realized it was actually a good plan.

"Hit two birds with one stone. Not bad, Steve."

"Well it comes with a risk, but if we split up we might a have a solid chance of ending this before it get any worse."

Ray looked carefully at the picture of the cabin and then turned the page to the executive order President Harris signed.

"Assassination order?" Ray asked to himself as he read the paper.

"Haven't seen on of those in a while, huh?" Steve asked.

"Yeah, it's been a while..."

"So what do you think? I know you don't like everyone being split up but we might not have a choice on this one," Steve asked.

"It's a good plan Steve. I'm impressed," Ray said as he patted Steve on the shoulder.

"The only thing I don't like is not taking out this Radar guy," Steve said.

"Well Dutra comes first. Whether he should or shouldn't isn't up to us," Ray explained.

"But Ray just think about it, if we take them both out we won't have to worry about heading to Mexico one day. Because I gotta say, after everything I read up on this Radar guy, I'm surprised we haven't been asked to go in yet," Steve said.

Ray didn't say it but he was thinking the same thing. The stories coming out of Mexico were awful, and to let the man that was behind all the stories go free didn't make sense, but in the end Ray stayed with the idea that Dutra was worse of the two evils.

"We'll talk about that later when we land in Florida," Ray said just before a loud rumble of thunder echoed in the garage.

Ray and Steve turned to the opened garage door and looked outside as suddenly it started downpouring, and lightening lit up the part of the sky that filtered through the doorway.

"Oh yeah, and it's suppose to rain all day and night down in Florida, too," Steve added.

"That'll help the flooding situation at least," Ray said with sarcasm as he turned and saw all the guys running in.

"Goddamn is it coming down out there!" Kevin said as he wiped the water off his face.

"Over here guys," Ray shouted to them as they came running in.

While Kevin, Tommy, Torque and Jasmin came running in, Bob took his sweet ass time walking in. By the time he got into the garage he was covered in water from head to toe. But once he got inside, he pulled down the garage door and walked over to join the rest of the team.

"Thanks for joining us, Bob." Steve said with a sarcastic smile planted on his face.

Bob flipped him the bird and then focused on Ray.

"Okay guys here's the deal," Ray began as he opened the file and spread out all the papers. "We just got the word that Dutra is heading down to Walton Beach, Florida, for an arms dealing trade."

"Last I heard that place was flooded isn't it?" Kevin asked.

"Wherever there's a will there's a way, Kevo," Tommy said.

Ray looked at the order the president signed and then picked it up to hold up.

"Harris has sighed an assassination order for Dutra," Ray said.

"Guess that's what happens when you try to kill the President of the United States," Jasmin added.

"Cut the jokes guys. This is serious business," Steve ordered.

Ray took his eyes off the guys and then went back to looking at the paperwork on the hood of the car.

"Now, this is without a doubt the best chance—maybe even the only chance—we'll get to take Dutra. He'll be heavily guarded, but Steve and I are going to use stealth to get as close as we can to Dutra. We don't wanna screw this up, so the closer we are the better," Ray said.

The guys shook their heads.

"Okay, so what do you want us to do?" Bob asked.

Ray then picked up the photo of the log cabin.

"Dutra has a safe house up in Maine. Since he's still in the states it's very possible that he's either been up there or is going to be up there before he does whatever he plans on doing and heads back to Russia. You guys are to head up there, find the cabin, take out whoever is up there and find as much intel on Dutra as you can," Ray said.

"Time is sensitive on this one guys. You'll need to be in and out but you also need to make sure the place has been searched properly. If you find anything that even looks like it could be something of value, make sure to grab it before you leave," Steve added.

"Also you are to leave no witnesses; any person even remotely close to the cabin you assume that they work for Dutra. The last thing we need is our cover blown. Let's use it while we still have it."

"Because more then likely, if he's half as good as he is on paper, he will find out who we are," Steve warned.

"Everybody understand?" Ray asked, even though he already knew what the next question would be.

"So, you're saying , we're not going with you to get Dutra?" Torque asked.

Ray gave Torque a glare (almost like he was mad that Torque had asked).

"No," Ray said firmly.

Clearly Tommy wasn't thrilled about the idea (in fact none of them looked happy by the news).

"Since when do we split up?" Tommy asked in a demanding voice.

Ray sighed and looked down as he tried to come up with the words to explain it but as it turned out he didn't have to.

"Normally we don't, but it will be easier to take Dutra down if we do. If it's just Ray and I we're less likely to get caught," Steve explained.

"I don't think it's a good idea," Torque said as he stepped closer to Ray.

"The decision has already been made. Besides, you guys hitting the house in Maine will help us out in case it goes haywire down in Florida," Ray said.

"If it goes haywire down there, wouldn't you want us down there to help you?" Bob asked.

Ray looked at Bob and just before he answered he took another look at the guys. None of them were going to say it, but you could tell they all felt left out. And Ray hated to see that look in there eyes.

"Guys, we're just going to have to do it this way. Besides, what if this Florida thing is a wild goose chase and Dutra is actually in Maine? If you guys don't go it will be a wasted chance, and we can't afford that this time. This is our only shot to get this prick and if we fail, then God only knows what the world will look like when it's over. We have to go at it this way guys, trust me."

And that seemed to hit home. The guys still weren't happy with the whole idea but they started to understand where Ray and Steve were coming from, all expect for Tommy and Torque.

"When we moving out?" Bob asked.

"Tomorrow morning. Nine am," Steve said.

"So everyone get some rest tonight. You're gonna need it for tomorrow, alright?" Ray asked.

As the guys nodded, Tommy walked out of the shop. Ray watched as Tommy slammed the garage door shut.

"I'll talk to him," Bob said as he patted Ray on the shoulder.

"Thanks Bob," Ray whispered to Bob as he and Kevin walked out of the shop and into the rain.

Ray turned and looked back at Steve. Steve looked up at him and gave him a false smile. Ray walked back over to the car as Jasmin picked up the papers and started reading them.

"Sounds like serious shit, Ray," Jasmin said as Ray walked up to him.

"Yeah, listen Jas, you know how to fly a helicopter?" Ray asked.

Jasmin looked up.

"Yeah."

"Good, you're gonna drop Steve and I off down in Florida and pick us up once we give you the confirmation that Dutra is down okay?" Ray asked.

"Yeah, sure. Thank you for the opportunity," Jasmin said.

Over in the corner Torque quickly began to fill with rage from the lack of involvement he was receiving.

"Be here at seven tomorrow alright, Jas." Steve asked.

"I will."

"Alright, go head on home and relax for the rest of night okay?" Ray asked.

"Okay, thanks again Ray. I owe you," Jasmin said.

"Forget it," Ray said with a smile.

Ray patted Jasmin on the back as he walked away. Torque waited for Jasmin to leave the shop and once he did Torque quickly walked over to Ray to make sure Ray knew how he felt about the situation.

"This is bullshit!" Torque spat.

Ray stopped in his track and turned around.

"Excuse me?" Ray asked.

"Oh I know you heard me. I said this is bullshit!" Torque said again even louder.

He stopped only inches away from Ray's face as rage filled his eyes.

"Well, sorry you feel that way but this is what's best for the situation," Ray said calmly.

Torque chuckled.

"Is this your way of punishing me for taking your spot when you leave? Huh? You choose the Russian..."

"He's Bosnian," Steve quickly corrected Torque.

"Whatever! You have him go with you while you make me go with the others on some half-ass trip to nowhere? Is that how this is?" Torque asked.

"Listen kid, you're new to this whole thing so let me spell it out for ya: I choose to do things that work out best for the task on hand, not to make sure you get plenty of time playing field. If you can't understand that then you're gonna have a problem," Ray warned.

"Why don't you just cut the shit Ray? You know I'm the better pick to go with you guys after Dutra...not to go to an open house in Maine!" Torque shouted.

Ray kept his eyes fixed on Torque's eyes.

"I made my choice and I'm standing by it. I've seen Jas in action before, he won't let me down, besides..." Ray started before he got interrupted.

"Besides what? I'm too young? I'm not worthy of it? I haven't proven myself enough yet? Then please tell me how someone is suppose to prove themselves when they can't even be given a chance to do it?" Torque quickly asked.

"The decision is made Torque! If you don't like it, then there's the door!" Ray shouted at the top of his lungs.

Torque stared at Ray for a moment then turned to the door. Suddenly, he started laughing.

"You know what? Fine. I'm done! You think you can handle this yourself...then feel free. I quit!" Torque shouted.

He quickly grabbed his gun and slammed it on the ground and walked away. In that moment Ray looked pissed (and honestly he was. He had been to through too much to be doubted by his own people) but inside he was actually saddened by what Torque had just chosen to do.

Torque walked over to the door, opened it and then slammed it shut as hard as he could. Ray shook his head in disbelief, picked up a wrench and threw it at the wall.

"Goddamn it!" Ray shouted as he stormed into his office.

For a moment Steve was going to try to go in and comfort Ray, but he knew it would be a waste of time. So out of respect Steve walked away and out of the shop to prepare himself for the day coming up tomorrow.

As Ray walked into his office he kicked the water bubbler by his desk, causing water to spill everywhere. Ray then walked over to his desk and fell into his chair as doubts, questions, and fear began to spill out.

Ray didn't want any of this. He always knew that his retirement would be a difficult transition (even if Steve got the spot) but until that moment he had no idea just how hard it was going to be. And in that moment he started hating the fact that he was getting older. He wasn't scared of dying (because let's face it he's seen his fair share of death) but he was always scared of time. Ray looked at time as a type of cancer; it would slowly take it all away and leaving him with nothing.

Tears began to fill Ray's eyes just thinking about everything that he's lost so far on his life's journey. From his best friend in Vietnam, to his family and now it seemed to his team. Ray needed something to remind him why he took on this life, but most importantly he needed something to get him out of the state of mind he was currently in. And since alcohol was out of the question (because of what he was heading into tomorrow), he decided to go with the next best thing. The thing he hadn't done for over a year. The thing that gave him a sliver of hope no matter what type of fucked up situation he was in.

He opened his desk and took out a picture of Emily when she was a baby. The cute grin on her face always put a warm feeling in his heart. And it worked. For a brief moment Ray was able to get away and get lost in the memory of when he first saw her when he came home from Vietnam.

He'd done a lot of things in his life, but seeing his daughter for the first time was the one thing that Ray had never been more proud of doing. Ray's tears in his eyes quickly went from tears of confusion and anger to tears of joy and happiness. Even though he hadn't seen her in years (and didn't know what she was doing in life) he was still proud of her.

As Ray focused on the picture of his young daughter Steve's questions suddenly began racing through his head. And so did Dutra. Ray has dealt with a lot of horrible people in the world but Dutra was quickly proving to be a threat he'd never dealt with before. And finally Ray was able to admit to himself that the chance of him not making it back home was real as the light of day.

And when that thought went through his head Ray suddenly took out his cell phone and dialed a number that Joey had given him a few months ago, when he asked for it. But before he pressed the 'send' button he took a pause, as he questioned if this was a road he wanted to go down, because the road may come to a dead end and Ray didn't know if he wanted to find that out or not. He swallowed hard, and then pressed the send button and waited to see what would happen.

The line rang once. Ray's heart started to race hard, fearing the worst. The line rang a few more times and as it did Ray started to doubt that anyone would pick. He told himself he would wait for one more ring and if nobody picked up after that then he would hang up and do his best to move on, but the line never rang again.

"Hello?" Said a sweet voice.

Ray gasped from the sound of not only her voice, but from how mature it sounded. Ray was damn near paralyzed and couldn't muster up two words.

"Hello?" Emily asked again.

Ray began wiping the tears out of his eyes as he tried to find the strength to respond.

"Hello??" Emily asked again.

"H...hello is this Emily?" Ray asked, despite already knowing the answer.

"Yes it is. Who's this?" Emily asked in her sweet voice.

"This is...your father..."

Silence took over the line for a second. Ray looked around his office, nervous as hell, fearing what would come next. And once the silence got to be too much for him to bear he chose to end it.

"I need to see you," Ray confessed.

Chapter 7: Reconnecting Before Leaving

The thunderstorms lasted through the night. Weather alerts were up for most of the State, warning of damaging winds and power outages. Ray didn't notice any wind, but around one in the morning the body shop lost power. But trying to find light in the darkness was the last thing on Ray's mind.

The conversation he had with Emily was center stage in his mind. It was a mere two minutes long (most of it silence) but Emily finally agreed to meet Ray at Mary Ann's (the local diner just a few miles down the road). Ray had only ever been there once but until last night he didn't know that Emily was the owner of it. If he knew that then he would've made it a priority to go as often as he could.

Ray would never admit it to anyone but over the years he's had Joey looking her up to make sure she'd been doing okay. She'd done a lot of traveling in her young life so far. After she graduated high school she moved out to California to go to college for a Business degree. After she finished up college she moved up to Seattle for a while and then about nine months later moved near Ray (only she just didn't know it). At that point Ray realized what he was having Joey do was an invasion of privacy. He told Joey to stop. The only thing Ray wanted was her phone number in case he needed to call for an emergency. And what he was about to enter was an emergency.

After the phone call, Ray knew for damn sure any type of sleep for the night was out of the question. Around three in the morning he tried to close his eyes but it was a wasted effort. Too many emotions were running through his head for him to get any real rest. Around four, the power came back on. He realized he wasn't getting anywhere, and decided to make a pot of coffee.

Once the caffeine kicked in Ray slowly attempted to stop thinking about Emily and tried to focus on getting the gear ready for the mission. He went into his cabinet in his office and took out the two best rifles he had, cleaned them and locked them up so they were ready to go when the time came. Ray wasn't expecting any company, but around five in the morning he heard the door open to the garage. When the door slammed shut he didn't even look up to see who it was...he already knew.

"Christ I can't believe how hard it's still raining out!" Steve said as he walked into the office, covered in water.

"What are you doing here so early?" Ray asked as he put bullets into his handgun clip.

"I could ask you the same thing," Steve said as he took off his soaked jacket.

"I never left," Ray said.

"Had a feeling you were gonna say that," Steve said as he walked over to the coffee machine and poured a cup of coffee for himself.

"Get any sleep?" Ray asked.

Steve chuckled just before he took a sip of coffee.

"Probably just as much as you," Steve said and then took a sip of coffee. The coffee was strong as it made it's way down Steve's throat.

"You know you really have to learn to make better coffee."

"Yeah, maybe one day," Ray said without taking his eyes off the clip he was loading.

Steve looked at Ray. Ray was always quiet just before they went out but Steve could clearly tell this time was different.

"Everything okay?" Steve asked as he sat down in the chair across from Ray's desk.

"Not really, but it is what it is," Ray confessed.

"You wanna talk about it?"

"Well, took your advice last night..." Ray softly said.

"Oh yeah? And what advice was that?" Steve asked as he waited for the engine oil coffee to sink in and give him a jump-start.

"Emily..."

Steve lowered the cup of coffee away from his mouth.

"Oh...you called her?"

"Yep." Ray loaded the clip into his handgun.

"How'd it go?"

"Just as you'd expect...was like talking to a goddamn stranger."

"What she say?"

"What could she say?"

Steve shook his head as he began to feel bad for Ray. He knew the situation was difficult (he could see that in Ray's eyes).

"Yeah. Sorry Ray," Steve said.

Ray shook his head.

"She finally agreed to meet me for breakfast this morning. Told her there were things I had to talk to her about." Ray said as he picked up the sniper rifle and loaded it with large bullets.

"Well that's a step in the right direction."

"We'll see I guess."

"Any idea on what you plan on telling her?" Steve asked out of curiosity.

"Yeah...everything," Ray quickly said as he finally looked up at Steve.

"Sure that's a good idea?" Steve asked.

"Yeah...I've kept to many things from her throughout the years. It's time she knows the truth...even if she can't understand it."

Steve nodded his head in agreement.

"You need me to go with you, or...?"

"No...this is something I gotta do by myself. It's a long shot that it's gonna change anything but I gotta try...nothing happens if you don't try."

"Tell me about it," Steve said as he finished his cup of coffee. "What time you heading out?"

"Gonna head out now. Don't wanna be out to long...still have a lot of shit I gotta do here."

"No, I'll take care of this. Go out and see your kid Ray...can't always put the job first," Steve said.

Ray chuckled as he loaded the rifle.

"...Yeah...guess I've been doing it for so long it's just become a habit." Ray confessed. He stood up and handed the rifle to Steve.

"We're gonna need three clips for each sniper, three machine guns for the helicopter and two side arms with silencers...then once your done that-"

"Ray! I got this. Go see your kid. I'll have everything ready by the time you get back." Steve said.

Ray shook his head and then walked over to the door, but before he walked out of sight he stopped and turned back to Steve.

"Hey Steve..." Ray began.

"Yeah?"

"Just wanted to say thank you," Ray said.

"That's what friends are for bud." Steve started to load the clips to the sniper rifles.

Ray smiled and then headed out to his truck. As he walked out Steve couldn't help but but watch him. He hated seeing Ray going through so much. It was like seeing a brother in pain and there wasn't anything he could do. He just wanted Ray to find some type of redemption while he still could, and he hoped that seeing Emily would be a step in the right direction...

II

All the way to the diner all Ray thought about was how he was gonna start the conversation. Honestly, how do you start talking to a stranger that's actually your daughter? Not even a man like Ray knew how to go into something like that. Over the years Ray had been in dozens of situations that made him nervous, but this one topped those any day of the week. He had never been more nervous in his life (not even when he and Steve were taking enemy fire from all directions in Bosnia).

Emily had told Ray to be at the diner by six but Ray made sure that he was there earlier (the man will be early to his own funeral). He arrived at the diner around five thirty. It was dark inside as Ray slowly drove by it and parked his truck in front of it. When he shut the pickup off he started to look around.

He realized he was the only one on the rain-covered street. He looked down at the clock radio and watched the time slowly go by. As he stared at the clock he kept thinking about that little girl in the picture, he started to wonder what she would look like now. Ray hoped that she ended up looking like her mother (the only thing Ray wanted her to inherit from him was his eyes. Nothing more.).

As Ray looked at the clock he tried to remember the last time he saw Emily...and realized he couldn't. It had been that long. Time has the tendency to move fast when you're not looking. Ray had learned that as the years passed, and regretted that it took him so long to finally understand that. But his train of thought was cut short when he saw a white car pull onto the street and then park just off to the side of the diner.

Ray focused on the car as the headlights shut off and the driver came out. As the person walked closer to the diner Ray tried to get a good look, but the rather thick fog and drizzle on his windshield made it difficult to do so. But once the person got to the front door of the diner Ray clearly saw that it was Emily. And with a deep breath, Ray opened his truck door and walked out.

Emily was in a brown jacket with her long black hair flowing down to her shoulders. She stuck the key to the diner into the locked entrance. Ray closed his truck door and then slowly walked up to her with his hands in his pocket. Emily still didn't seem to notice that she had company as she struggled to unlock the door. Ray cleared his throat and then walked up to her.

"Hey," Ray said softly.

Emily quickly looked up and saw Ray, for the first time in years. She looked back at the door and then opened it.

"Come on in..." she said as she walked into the dark diner.

Ray slowly followed as Emily walked behind the counter and turned the lights on. When the lights came on Ray started to look around and a smile grew on his face.

The place was clearly a tribute to the 1960's. Pictures of old cars and trucks from that era were hanging up all over the walls and there was even an old gas pump that was all lit up in the dead center of the room.

As Emily headed into the kitchen Ray walked over to the counter and slowly sat down and started to take off his jacket. Emily then walked out of the kitchen and back behind the counter.

"You want coffee? Something to eat?" Emily asked.

"Uh...just coffee please," Ray said.

Emily walked back into the kitchen as Ray looked at her; he could not believe just how beautiful she had grown up to be. She really did look just like her mother. It was spooky for a moment. For a brief second it almost looked like she was still alive. Then Emily came back out with a mug and a pot of coffee in her hand. She placed it down in front of Ray and then poured him some coffee.

"Thank you," Ray said as he picked up a packet of sugar.

Emily shook her head and then put the coffee pot down on the counter. Ray put in his sugar, mixed it and then took a sip.

"Oh wow, that's good. Better then what I'm use to drinking," Ray confessed.

Emily gave him a quick smile as she looked at the man that was suppose to be her father. Ray took another sip and then looked around.

"Like the setup you have going on here. Brings back a lot of memories," Ray said.

"Yeah. A lot of customers tell me that...we even play oldies music when the place is open."

"Oh yeah? What time do you normally open?" Ray asked.

"Seven most days but recently I've been opening it up around six. Can't sleep so I just come here."

"Yeah...I know the feeling," Ray said.

The two of them looked at each other as silence once again took over. It got to the point where Ray thought he was gonna have to speak to end it but suddenly Emily decided to end it...by asking about the elephant in the room.

"So...why'd you come?" Emily asked.

Ray put his coffee mug down and then looked up at Emily.

"Figured we had a lot to talk about stuff..."

Emily looked down.

"Kinda hard to talk about stuff to someone who's never there..."

Ray shook his head as that sentenced echoed in his mind.

"Yeah...I came here to try and explain that...better late then never, right?" Ray asked in an awful attempt to make a joke.

"Not really..."

Ray quickly lost the smirk off his face and then looked down in regret.

"Listen Emily...I know there's a lot I haven't been there for...a lot I haven't told you but I can explain it."

Emily turned to the kitchen so the man that was her father wouldn't see her eyes beginning to fill up with tears.

"Kind of a lot to explain..." Emily said as she tried her best to make sure her voice didn't crack.

"I know but if you just give me a second..." Ray began.

Emily quickly turned around.

"No, I've given you more then a second. I've given you years. My whole life Mom has told me that one day you would come home for good and we could be a family...she said that all the way up to her deathbed. Even then she defended you...and even then you weren't there..."

Ray started to get tears in his eyes as he looked at Emily.

"The last thing Mom said to me before she died was to not lose faith in you. She promised me that one day you would be around...and I believed her. When you didn't even bother to come visit her when she was dying...I told myself you'd be around for the funeral...and when you didn't show up to that...I still gave you the benefit of the doubt, so I still held on to the hope. But when days turned to years...and I realized I was wasting my life for something that was never gonna happen...I moved on...and Mom should've done the same. But every time we talked about you she always said how much of a hero you were and I never understood why or how she could stay with a man that was never around for us..." Emily said as she began to cry.

Ray shook his head with tears running down his cheeks as he finally realized what the job has truly taken from him.

"I don't know why she stayed either..." Ray said with a broken heart.

Emily then turned and looked at Ray as her tears began causing her eyeliner to run.

"You have a lot of explaining to do after all these years...but all I wanna know...is...why did you allow Mom to hold onto false hope her whole life? Why didn't you just let her go?" Emily asked.

Ray lowered his head in pain and realized nothing he said could be a good enough reason for allowing his daughter to be in this much distress. But he had to try...even if it would ruin the very last piece of untainted soul he had left in him.

"I tried to tell her to move on Emily...believe me. I told her she deserved better but every time I said that she would stop me dead in my tracks and tell me never to think like that..." Ray said. He stood up and looked out the window. "Your mother was the most amazing woman I've ever met. She was stubborn too to say the least..."

Emily chuckled for a brief second before the tears came back in her eyes.

"I knew she deserved more then what I was providing her but I couldn't be the one to leave...she had to make that call on her own...but she never did...no matter what job I took," Ray said in amazement.

Emily wiped her eyes as Ray turned to her slowly.

"I never meant for any of this to happen. I know you probably don't believe that, but even though I wasn't there for you...I always kept you close to my heart. I did the same with your mother...the both of you kept me going when I was lost in the dark..."

Emily tried to believe the words her father was saying but the years of having no father were difficult to let go of.

"I'm sorry Emily. I wish I could change the past...but I can't. There's so much I need to tell you...but I still can't...not yet. And I'm sorry for that," Ray pleaded with his heart in his hand.

Emily sniffled and then looked up at Ray with a disappointed look on her face.

"I'm sorry too."

Ray shook his head up and down trying to hold back his tears.

"You should go," Emily said.

Ray nodded and took one last look at Emily (knowing this would be the last time he would ever see her). He gave her a quick smile, placed a five dollar bill down onto the counter and headed for the door. Emily then closed her eyes as a river of tears ran down her cheek.

As Ray headed to the door he gave some serious thought to finally telling the truth about why he was never around. The truth about the other life he's lived...the truth about the job...but it was obvious Emily wasn't ready to know yet. If Dutra wasn't out there then maybe that thought could be seriously considered but not until Dutra was in the ground with a bullet in his head. But Ray knew if he didn't say something he would regret it for the rest of his days on this brutal planet. So he stopped at the door and slowly turned around.

"On the day of your graduation you were in an all white gown. Your hair was shorter back then and you had contact lenses in your eyes that made them look green...and on the day of your Mom's funeral you had on a black dress with a white rose on your chest...your Mom's favorite."

Emily slowly opened her eyes and looked up at Ray in disbelief.

"How could you possibly know that?"

Ray slowly pried his eyes off the view of the street and looked at Emily.

"There's a side of history that hasn't been written," Ray said.

And with that Ray walked out of the diner and headed for his truck as Emily dropped to the floor and began to sob. Ray unlocked his truck and got into the driver side when a sudden pain from his leg began to sink in. He grabbed his leg for a moment and rubbed it as he took one last look at the diner. For a split second he was hoping that Emily would come running out, but he knew it was a long shot. Ray was always right when it came to bad things.

Once the pain in his leg was tolerable he started his truck and drove off, heading back to the shop, sobbing the whole ride back as he finally realized there was a price for mistakes of the past that not even time can heal.

III

Back in New York, high up in his skyscraper Dutra was in the process of finishing up a thousand pushups in his office. His office was still a disaster after his breakdown but he had made room to exercise (which was part of his everyday routine). He had just finished his last one before the door to his office opened and Street walked in.

"Excuse me boss?" Street asked.

"What?" Dutra asked as he slowly stood up.

"Just wanted to let you know the chopper is ready when you are."

Dutra wiped the sweat from his face and grabbed his shirt off his desk (despite Dutra being a very dangerous, almost certifiably insane man, when it came to staying in shape he did it well. The ropes of muscle along his arms and six-pack clearly proved it).

"Alright. Tell him I'll be up in ten."

"You want any company for your meeting with Radar?" Street asked.

Dutra thought about it for a moment and realized that probably wouldn't be such a bad idea. Better safe then sorry (even Dutra's ego wasn't big enough to forget that).

"Yeah...get me Josh, Dave and Scott. Tell them to head up to the helipad to give Vincent a hand with the merchandise," Dutra said.

"You won't need me?" Street asked.

"No. I need you to finish up finding out the names of those fuckers that attacked us yesterday...any progress on that yet?" Dutra asked.

"Still looking. So far nothing in the F.B.I. computer records. Gonna hack the C.I.A. computers today. Hopefully something will turn up there."

"Do what you have to: C.I.A. the N.S.A., hack them all. I want those fucking names!" Dutra shouted.

"Oh I'll find them; just a matter of time. What do you want me to do once I get them?" Street asked.

"Kill them all except for whoever is in charge of them...that fucker is mine. Understood?" Dutra asked, still almost shouting.

"Yes sir. I'll go get the guys now."

Dutra put his shirt on and then brushed his hair with his hands. He wanted to focus all his attention of finding the guys, but he knew missing this chance with Radar would be a grave mistake. Besides Dutra knew one day he might need an alibi just across the border. He opened the gun cabinet in his office and took out his sidearm, got his bullet proof vest and dark jacket on and then headed to the roof. Meanwhile Street grabbed the three guys so they could give Vincent a hand on the roof to help him load the warhead into the helicopter.

IV

While Dutra and his men got ready to head down to Florida, Kevin arrived at the shop. Steve had just finished laying out all the gear when Kevin opened the door with a big yawn.

"Morning," Steve said.

"If you say so, Steve," Kevin said as he walked in, trying to get the crud out of the corner of his eyes.

"You get any rest?" Steve asked.

"Sort of."

Steve looked up at Kevin in confusion.

"Sort of? Most times people just answer it with a yes or a no," Steve said.

"Well...I got laid last night..." Kevin said with a smile.

Steve then shook his head.

"Okay then...sort of," Steve said as he went back to putting down the rest of the gear.

"Jas, I don't think that's what you call them you sick bastard," Tommy was saying.

"Tommy, I'm not saying it to sound gross, but I'm pretty sure that's what you call them," Jasmin said.

"Both of you are fucked up, you know that right?" Bob asked as he took off his sunglasses.

"Okay then what would you call it Bob?" Tommy asked.

"Nothing, I do what I can to avoid it!"

As the guys walked over to Kevin he decided to get in on the conversation.

"What would you call what?" Kevin asked.

Bob shook his head.

"You don't wanna know."

"I do, really," Kevin said.

Tommy sighed. "We're trying to figure out what you call the stomach part of a fat chick where her pussy would be," he explained.

"Okay maybe I didn't wanna know," Kevin said as he took a step back.

"No, I'm serious guys. There's a name for it but I can't remember what it is!" Tommy shouted. "What the fuck do people call it?"

"Horrifying?" Kevin asked.

"Besides that, Kevo."

Jasmin shook his head.

"Tommy, I'm telling you that's what they call it!" Jasmin said.

Tommy rolled his eyes and then crossed his arms.

"Jas they don't call it a bottom pussy!" Tommy shouted as Steve walked over to Kevin.

"What are they talking about?" Steve asked.

"Bottom pussy," Kevin said.

Steve looked at the guys and then back at Kevin.

"What?"

"That large piece of stomach on a fat chick that hangs where her pussy should be?" Kevin said to Steve to try and ring a bell.

"Oh yeah. My mother had one of those," Steve said.

Kevin looked at Steve and shook his head.

"You're a sick man, Steve," Kevin said.

While the guys tried to come to an agreement on 'bottom pussy' Ray pulled up to the shop and got out of his truck, slamming the door as he exited. Clearly he had passed the sad stage and was entering the angry part. As soon as he walked in Steve could tell just by the pissed off look on Ray's face that it hadn't gone well.

"Alright guys cut the talking and let's move!" Ray shouted at the top of his lungs.

The guys quickly stopped their conversation and then walked over to the gear and started to put it on. Ray walked past them without even looking at them. Kevin was getting ready to also put his gear on when he noticed someone was missing.

"Ray...where's Torque?" Kevin asked as Ray walked past him.

"Don't worry about it kid. Just get your shit on. We're already late as it is," Ray said.

Kevin shrugged his shoulders and then started to get into gear. As Ray walked closer to Steve, Steve could tell something had happened during Ray's visit.

"How'd it go?" Steve asked.

"Take one goddamn guess," Ray said as he walked into his office and slammed the door.

Steve took a deep breath and then walked over to the guys. Clearly the guys were a little nervous and down in the dumps now.

"Hey guys...he's not pissed at you. He's just dealing with a lot alright?" Steve asked.

The guys shook their heads. Steve shook his and started to walk away when a train of thought suddenly popped into his head that he thought he would share with the guys.

"Oh and guys?" Steve asked as he turned back around. "I gotta agree with Jasmin. It should be called bottom pussy."

Jasmin slammed his hands on the table.

"I knew it!" Jasmin shouted.

"Shhh!!!!!!!!!!" All the guys yelled at him.

Jasmin slowly lifted his hands off the table.

"Oh, sorry."

The guys shook there heads at Jasmin and smiled as they got ready for their run, while Steve decided to head into the wolf's den: Ray's office. When he walked in Ray was putting on his bulletproof vest.

"Everything all set?" Ray asked.

"Yeah, the guys are just suiting up now." Steve said.

"Good I want to get this done and over with," Ray firmly said.

Steve shook his head and then walked over to Ray's desk and picked up his handgun to put in his holster. As he did so he couldn't help but keep his eyes on Ray. Steve had never seen Ray look they way he did: broken and empty; as if he didn't have anything left inside of him (like the last part of his soul was gone). Before Steve had a chance to speak Ray quickly picked up the sniper rifle and walked out of the office. Steve just shook his head, knowing it was going to be a long night.

"Damn it," He said to himself.

As Ray walked out the guys all looked up as he walked over to them.

"Alright, everybody set?" Ray asked.

"Ready when you are," Jasmin said.

Ray nodded. "Alright let's do this then," he said as he walked away.

Bob carefully watched Ray as he headed for the door. Steve walked over and Bob turned to him.

"What's up with him?"

"Nothing he can't handle," Steve said as he followed Ray.

"Hope your right," Bob said.

"Yeah," Steve whispered to himself. "Me too."

Steve walked out with Ray and Jasmin followed them as Bob looked at Tommy and Kevin.

"Okay guys, let's get this over with," Bob said.

Chapter 8: American Chernobyl

The rain was starting to pick up as Jasmin flew the helicopter across the gloomy night sky. As the rain hit the windshield it made a horrible, eerie sound over the engine running. With visibility down to less then a quarter mile Jasmin paid attention to what was in front of him (which was very little). Normally Jasmin was the first one to talk but not in this case.

And with Jasmin focusing on not crashing, that left Ray and Steve in the back to carry on a conversation, but since Ray was still sore about how he ended things with Emily, Steve knew it was going to be a long and rather boring ride. So he dug into his jacket pocket and took out a large cigar and lit it as Ray looked out the side of the chopper, staring down at the fog beneath him.

Steve wanted to say or do something to get Ray's sprit up, but it was kinda hard to do so on a helicopter ride that could ultimately lead to the death of everyone on board. So Steve kept quiet and double checked his weapons. After damn near thirty minuets of silence, and with the sky as dark as the deepest parts of space, Ray stood up and walked over to Jasmin.

"How much further?" Ray asked.

"Not too far. Maybe about another ten miles!" Jasmin shouted over the roar of the chopper.

"Alright, where you dropping us off at?" Ray asked.

"Well I did some research last night. Most of the city is still in water so most likely the meeting will take place at the far end of the city by the amusement park. That part of the city is a little higher up so it isn't as prone to flooding as the rest of the city. I'll drop you guys a few miles away from there. My best guess for you guys to head is to a parking garage that overlooks the amusement park. More than likely the lower levels will have water in them but if you head further up to the top you should be able to see down below just fine! When you take the shot, you'll radio me and I'll land at the top level of the parking garage and pick you guys up before anyone even knows we were there!" Jasmin explained.

"Alright, sounds good. Nice work Jas!" Ray said as he patted him on the arm.

Ray slowly turned around and then headed back to the door and looked at Steve.

"Everything okay?" Steve asked.

"Yeah. About ten minuets out!" Ray said.

"About bloody time! Starting to go stir crazy in here."

"Yeah you and me both," Ray softly said to himself.

"You heard from Bob yet?" Steve asked.

"Not yet. I'll give him a call when we land!" Ray shouted as the helicopter began to rock back and forth.

"Hold on guys! It's gonna get bumpy for a moment!" Jasmin shouted out.

Ray quickly grabbed the seat then sat down and put on the seatbelt while Steve stayed sitting down on the floor smoking his cigar. Ray was surprised as to how calm Steve looked (even Ray knew he didn't look that calm; that was mostly due to what happened between him and Emily, but nevertheless).

"So how ya holding up?" Steve asked Ray.

"Never better!" Ray shouted back.

Steve chuckled.

"You know you never were a good lair."

Ray smiled for a moment and then looked back out the side of the chopper. He still couldn't see anything as rain hit the chopper from every direction. But despite the near zero visibility, the wind hadn't kicked up yet, which was a good thing for them. Ray just hoped that it wouldn't until they landed on the ground. Jasmin thought that same thing as his stomach began to rumble.

"So you think he'll be there?" Steve asked Ray.

"Yeah, he'll be there," Ray said.

Steve shook his head as he slowly stood up.

"Hope so. It would suck if this was all for nothing." He walked over to the seat and sat down next to Ray.

"He'll be there. Trust me," Ray said again.

"How can you be so sure?" Steve asked.

"Because I would be there," Ray said.

Steve shook his head and then took another puff of his cigar as the helicopter pushed further into the darkness of the night.

II

As Jasmin, Steve and Ray began to close in on the deserted town of Walton Beach, back at home Torque sat in a bar and finished his second beer. As music and people's voices filled the air he started to think maybe he should've just stayed home for the rest of the day (hell he didn't wake up until quarter past one in the afternoon).

As Torque waved the bartender down to bring him another beer, he started thinking about how he left things with Ray. Even though he felt like he had wasted a lot of time for nothing, he couldn't help but wonder what the guys were doing at this very moment. But as he started to question if he made the right decision or not, he quickly picked up his fresh beer and began to drink the doubt away.

It seemed to work for a while but once the beer was gone those questions quickly came rushing back in, only this time they were questions about where he was going to go next. More then likely he would have to head to Washington to tell Sullivan that he left, and Sullivan would end up putting him back on the front lines overseas. It wasn't something Torque wanted to do but he convinced himself it was better then working an eight to five job for five days a week. Besides Torque wasn't the type to live a life like most other people. He would never admit it to anyone (or even himself) but Torque enjoyed the feeling of waking up in the morning and not knowing what the end of the day would bring.

But in that moment in the bar the only thing Torque wanted to do was drink until he passed out. He told himself he would deal with the rest of the world tomorrow. It wasn't the smartest way to use the day but right then and there Torque thought it was a great idea.

The bar was beginning to fill up faster as the music got louder. It got to the point where the music was almost giving Torque a bit of a headache. When the bartender handed him his fourth beer of the night he told himself that after that beer he would head back home to try and rest up for his trip to Washington tomorrow. But just as he finished downing his ice-cold beer his eyes stopped dead in their tracks when he noticed a girl.

Now Torque had been to a lot of places, met a lot of people (fucked a lot of girls) but this girl was without a doubt the most beautiful girl his eyes had ever come across. From her straight long hair to the way her ass looked in the tight jeans she was in, Torque was left in awe.

As the girl turned toward the bar and Torque got a good look at her face he was struck by not only how gorgeous this girl was but also by how familiar she seemed to look even though Torque knew for a fact that he'd never seen or met her before. But boy did he want too all right.

As the bartender handed her some fruity little drink with a small umbrella in it her eyes glanced across the bar and met Torque's. Torque instantly gave her a half smile (the very same smile that he's been told by girls before makes them weak at the knees) and she returned the smile.

As they looked at each other Torque couldn't stop trying to figure out why this girl looked so damn familiar. Even her eyes looked familiar. As the two of them kept their eyes glued to one another Torque couldn't help but start to think that he might get lucky if he played his cards right, but something inside told him there might be something more to this if he walked over and started talking to her.

As the girl picked up her drink and began sucking on the straw, Torque's half smile quickly turned to a full on smile and at that point he knew if he didn't go over there and say something it would be something he would regret. So after he finished what was left of his beer he slowly got up and headed down to the opposite end of the bar, keeping his eyes on the girl to make sure she didn't disappear suddenly (like most promising girls do).

"Hey." Torque said as he stood over the girl.

The girl smiled and she looked Torque up and down.

"Hey yourself," she said as she smiled.

"Is this seat taken?" Torque asked.

"It is now."

Torque smiled and sat down as he kept his eyes on the girl.

"So...what brings you to a place like this?" Torque asked.

The girl pushed her long black hair over her ears.

"Been a long day. Just needed a break...so what better way then to get drunk and make an ass out of myself, right?" She asked.

Torque chuckled.

"Yeah, I've been there myself," Torque said as he looked around the bar.

"So where you from?" The girl asked.

Torque shrugged his shoulders.

"All over. My job takes me to many different places," Torque confessed but made sure he didn't say what he really did.

"What are you, a soldier or something?" The girl asked.

"...Yeah..." Torque said.

The girl slowly lost the smile on her face for a moment. She was happy to hear that Torque was a soldier but the military was a weak spot for her to talk about. She had lost her father to the military a while back when she was very young.

"Wow. Good for you, nice to see some guys my age have a good head on their shoulders," the girl said.

Torque smiled. "Well I don't know about that..."

"No I'm serious. It takes a lot of guts to sign your life over to defend people you've never met before. It's nothing less then brave. My father was the same way from what I'm told..." The girl said as she went back to sipping her drink.

"Never really looked at it like that before...it's just a job really. I'm no better then anyone else here," Torque said.

The girl smiled as she finished her drink.

"So, you gonna buy me a beer or what?" She asked with a smile.

"Hmm...I don't know if I should be talking to a stranger. I was brought up to get to know someone before I started really talking with them," Torque said.

The girl looked at Torque.

"Oh yeah? Funny, I didn't hear you introduce yourself yet..." She said. Suddenly they both started to chuckle. Then Torque put his hand out.

"My name is Johnny..."

"Well nice to meet you, Johnny. My name is Emily..."

"Well Emily, can I buy you a beer?"

"I don't know. It's gonna cost yeah..." Emily said.

"I think I can handle it," Torque said boldly.

Emily smiled, and as Torque got her a beer and they began talking and getting to know one another, Emily was quickly able to forget about everything that happened with her and her father from earlier in the morning...in the diner she owned ...

III

While Torque hit on Ray's daughter in the bar (without knowing she was), all the way up in the beautiful state of Maine Bob, Kevin and Tommy were driving into the woods. As Bob drove over a large rock on the dirt road Kevin banged his head on the passenger side window and Tommy went bouncing in the back.

"Jesus Christ Bob! You think you could maybe *try* to miss a bump once in a while?" Tommy asked.

"Tommy it's pitch black out here! How the hell am I suppose to try and miss something that's on the road?" Bob yelled from the front.

"Maybe if you slowed down a little!" Tommy shouted.

"Why, so we can miss Dutra if he's there?" Bob shouted even louder.

"Guys, guys! Take a chill pill both of you. Bitching to each other isn't gonna make this night go any smoother." Kevin rested his hand on the side of his head that hit the glass.

"Easy for you to say, you didn't just squish your nuts," Tommy said as he reached and started to massage his balls.

"Oh grow a set and be quiet," Bob said to Tommy.

"Keep this up Bob and so help me God I'll piss all over you," Tommy threatened.

"Ooh I'm shaking," Bob said in a girly voice as he shook his head and focused on the road.

Kevin took out his side arm and loaded a clip into it.

"How much further?" Kevin asked Bob.

"Probably about another half mile...maybe less. I'm gonna pull off to the side here when we get a little closer. We're gonna have to walk it from there. Don't want to take a risk of someone spotting the truck," Bob explained.

"Great. Nothing like walking in the woods in the middle of the night."

Kevin said looked out the window to see nothing but darkness.

"Yeah, just think: maybe if we're lucky we'll get eaten by a bear instead of getting shot," Bob said trying to look on the bright side.

"Yeah Bob, because being ripped apart but a five thousand pound animal is so much better than taking a bullet," Kevin said in sarcasm.

"Exactly, right?" Bob said in a serious voice (clearly not picking up on the sarcasm).

As they hit another bump the truck lurched violently and Kevin groaned at the roughness of the landing. Bob, keeping his eyes on the road to make sure he was able to see something if anything suddenly popped out, slowly started to feel something warm trickling down his arm. At first he didn't notice it but once he did, he quickly reached down under the steering wheel and turned the lights on inside the truck.

"What the hell?" Bob muttered to himself.

As the lights came on, Bob turned and realized he was staring directly at Tommy's penis as Tommy pissed all over his arm.

"What the fuck?!" Bob shouted.

"Tommy?" Kevin asked as he hugged the passenger door.

"Thought I was bluffing, huh Bob?" Tommy shouted.

"Oh you son of a bitch!" Bob shouted as he took his hands off the steering wheel and pushed Tommy violently. Kevin quickly grabbed the steering wheel.

"Bob?" Kevin asked.

The truck hit another bump and went soaring up again and Tommy lost his balance, causing piss to go all over the front of the truck, and onto Bob's chest.

"You fucking son of a bitch! Come here!" Bob shouted as he reached for Tommy and took his eyes of the road.

"Fuck you, Bob!" Tommy shouted as he started to put his penis away.

As Bob reached for Tommy, he began to press down on the accelerator. When Kevin realized that the truck was going faster he started to tap Bob on the leg.

"Uh, Bob?"

"Come here you fucking little shit!" Bob shouted to Tommy.

"Bob?" Kevin asked again when he realized they were starting to go a dangerous speed.

"Not now Kevin. I'm a little busy here!" Bob said reaching for Tommy.

"How ya feeling Bob?" Tommy asked with a smile.

Suddenly Bob took out his side arm and aimed it at Tommy.

"Take a guess!" Bob shouted.

Tommy quickly lost the smile on his face.

"Oh shit," Tommy said.

As Bob cocked his gun Kevin realized he needed to do something to get Bob's attention before he lost control of the truck, so he looked down and then grabbed Bob's nuts.

"Whoa!" Bob shouted.

Bob quickly turned back to Kevin, grabbed his shoulder and looked right at him. Kevin's eyes then met Bob's eyes.

"You in on this too?" Bob asked.

But just before Kevin could answer, Bob looked out the windshield and saw a large moose standing in the middle of the road.

"Oh shit!" Bob shouted as he took his foot off the gas and slammed on the brakes.

But it was too late. The truck slammed into the moose at a solid forty-five miles an hour. Blood splattered on the windshield and Kevin and Tommy screamed for their lives.

Finally, after what seemed like a lifetime to the guys, the truck came to a dead stop. As the guys breathed heavily they stared at the large animal as it made one long groan and flopped onto the ground.

Kevin quickly lowered his head back and sighed and then suddenly opened the passenger side door.

"My fucking truck!" Kevin shouted as he ran to the front of the truck, braced for what he was going to see, but nothing could prepare him for what he discovered. When his eyes saw the front of the truck, his jaw hit the ground...and Tommy and Bob fell out of the back door and onto the ground as they wrestled each other.

"What the fuck!" Kevin shouted.

The front of the truck was totaled. From the huge dent in the hood to one of the headlights swinging by its wires, clearly Kevin's pride and joy was no more. Once he was able to pry his eyes off his belved truck (that he'd had it for years) he turned and looked at Bob and Tommy as they punched one another.

"Really guys?" Kevin asked, throwing his hands in the air in disbelief.

As Bob punched Tommy in the face Kevin's cell phone started to vibrate inside his pocket. He knew for a fact that it would be Ray checking on things, so he reached into his pocket as he tried to make it sound like everything was good.

"Yeah?" Kevin asked as he answered the phone.

"Kev it's me. How you guys doing?" Ray quickly asked.

"Uh...were almost at the cabin," Kevin said.

"Alright, perfect timing; we just landed. If you need anything just call, alright?" Ray asked.

"Alright...sounds good boss..."

"How's Tommy?" Ray asked.

Kevin slowly turned and looked at the two of them as Bob elbowed Tommy in the gut.

"Ow!" Tommy shouted.

"Like normal..." Kevin admitted.

"Okay, just keep an eye on him for me will ya?" Ray asked.

"Will do."

"And how's Bob holding up?" Ray asked.

As Bob punched Tommy in the face one last time Kevin turned around and looked at the dead moose carcass in front of his truck.

"He's a little on the pissy side you could say..." Kevin said.

"Alright, like I said just keep an eye on them. I'll give you a call once we finish up here," Ray said.

"Okay Ray. Later." Kevin quickly hung up as Bob walked over to the front of the truck and took off his jacket, which was covered in piss.

Tommy got up from off the ground and wiped his bloody nose as he walked over to join the other two.

"Wow, that's a big fucking deer." Tommy said, almost as if nothing had just happened between him and Bob.

"Really, that's all you have to say?" Kevin asked as he crossed his arms.

Tommy shrugged his shoulders in confusion.

"Uh...it's a really big fucking deer?" Tommy asked, thinking that's what Kevin wanted to hear.

Kevin shook his head and then headed for the passenger door.

Tommy looked down at the dead moose as blood poured out from its neck wound.

"Sorry about the truck, Kevo." Bob said as he put his sidearm back in it's holster.

"Fuck yourself, Bob." Kevin.

"Hey! He started it!" Bob said as he pointed to Tommy.

"Oh don't worry, I'm mad at him too," Kevin said firmly as he took out the three rifles and headed back to the front of the truck.

"So now what, Bob?" Tommy asked.

Bob looked around.

"Well...we'll just have to walk it from here. Can't be too much further up the road." Bob grabbed one of the machine guns from Kevin.

"What about my truck? I'm not gonna just leave it here!" Kevin shouted.

"We're in the middle of fucking nowhere. Nobody is gonna touch it out here," Bob said as he took out the clip to his gun and checked to make sure bullets were in it.

"Yeah and on our way back we can grab the deer," Tommy said thinking it would be a good idea.

"It's a fucking moose, Tommy," Bob said.

"No I'm pretty sure it's a deer Bob," Tommy said.

And suddenly Kevin lost it.

"Guys, who gives a shit what it is! Let's just get to that cabin and get back home! And your not putting a fucking deer in the back of my truck!" Kevin said.

"It's a moose Kevin," Bob softly said.

"WHO CARES?!" Kevin shouted, his voice echoing in the dark forest.

Bob cocked his gun and then headed for the driver's side door to shut off the engine, while Tommy loaded up his gun. Suddenly, Tommy felt like someone (or something rather close) was watching his every move. Very slowly he looked up and realized it was Kevin, giving him a look of death. Tommy sighed.

"Oh come on Kevo, I was just messing around. Besides how was I suppose to let Bob get away with saying that?" Tommy asked.

"You pissed in my truck!" Kevin firmly reminded him.

"Don't worry, I'll clean it up and it'll be just as good as new," Tommy said with a smile.

As the headlight finally detached and landed on the ground Bob closed the door and walked over to them.

"Alright. Let's go hunting," Bob ordered.

The guys then started to head down the dark road, darkness slowly pushing them further away from the truck and the dead moose.

"Way to go Tommy, the whole truck smells like piss," Bob said.

"Funny I thought the smell was coming from you," Tommy quickly shot back.

Suddenly from out of the darkness Tommy felt a sudden pain across his face as Bob slapped him.

"Ow!" Tommy said.

"Whoops. Didn't see you there." Bob said.

"Really Bob? Really?" Tommy shouted.

"I knew I should've gone with Ray and Steve," Kevin said as he rolled his eyes in the pitch-blackness of the forest.

IV

While Kevin tried to stay calm (and not shoot the both of them), back in Florida Ray and Steve watched as Jasmin took the helicopter back up into the dark, cloudy night sky. As it began to rain harder they quickly ran out of the deserted street and headed into what looked like an old corner store.

As they entered, Ray looked around to make sure no one was there, while Steve slowly closed the door to the once nice store. Ray couldn't help but be amazemed by the destruction all the water had done to the place. Windows were broken, glass was everywhere, shelving was on the ground and mold was on the walls.

"How far to the parking garage?" Ray asked.

"About a mile. Think we'll run into anyone?" Steve asked.

"Doubt it. Doesn't look like much is around here anymore," Ray said as he put a radio into his ear. "Jas...you there?"

"Yeah I'm here."

"You see anything as you headed up?" Ray asked.

"No man. Place looks like a ghost town."

"Were you able to spot the parking garage?" Ray asked.

"Yeah, it's southeast of your location."

"Copy that," Ray said to Jasmin. "Alright Steve...let's move."

Steve nodded his head and the two of them headed to the back of the store and slowly opened the back door. As lightning lit up the sky it was clear that they were the only two around so they quickly ran across the street and down a dark ally.

"Haven't done this for a while, huh?" Ray asked.

"You can say that again. As much fun as it is to just start shooting I prefer the sneaking around. Nothing like a little suspense at work," Steve replied as they reached the end of the ally.

Ray agreed. He never admitted it to anyone but he loved running around in the enemy's backyard. It gave him a rush that was indescribable. And running around in the abandoned town brought back a lot of memories of his glory days when he would go on a mission like this every other week with Steve.

"Bob and the guys reach the cabin?" Steve asked as he stuck his head out of the ally and looked down the street.

"Just about," Ray said.

"Okay, time to make these next few minutes count...you ready old timer?" Steve asked.

"Ready as I'll ever be," Ray said as he began to feel the tingles of pain in his knee slowly creeping up on him.

"Okay...go!" Steve shouted.

The two of them raced across the street and took cover behind a car that had been flooded from the hurricane. Once they got down Steve quickly looked up to check the street and once he knew it was safe they ran onto the sidewalk and started to head up the opposite side of the street.

Ray could already tell that his knee was going to give him problems; it was just a matter of time, but he did his best to stay focused. Once they reached the end of the street they quickly turned onto another. Suddenly thunder rumbled across the sky, ending the rather creepy silence that filled up the street.

More lightning shot through the sky like a bad special effect, lighting the street well enough for Ray to see a large building that was directly in front of them. It was hard to make out what the building was at first, but as they ran closer and closer it became clear that the large building was some type of college.

"Let's head in there," Ray ordered as the two ran to the college.

"You sure about that?" Steve asked.

"No...but it beats running around in the street," Ray said.

"Not as much fun running around in our home country than in a different one, huh?" Steve asked as they crossed the street.

"Little to close for comfort for me," Ray confessed.

As they reached the front entrance of the once beautiful college, Ray took out his silenced pistol and shot the lock on the door. Once the lock dropped onto the wet ground Steve quickly kicked opened the door and the both of them headed inside.

The interior brought a new meaning to the word darkness. It was darker then any place Steve or Ray had entered in their lives. As Ray closed the entrance door Steve took out a flashlight and turned it on. The ray of light was a blip on the radar compared to the blackness inside.

It looked just as bad as the store had, actually even worse. From books and papers to shoes and broken glass, the place looked like a bomb had gone off. It was a very chilling sight for Steve as he looked around, almost as if he could hear echoes of the last voices that had been in the building at the time of the storm.

"Jesus Christ, Ray," Steve softly said as Ray turned away from the door and looked at the end of the flashlight beam.

"Yeah, scary stuff huh? It's amazing what Mother Nature can do when we piss her off."

"Never thought about that until now," Steve confessed.

Suddenly the silence was broken by a noise coming from Ray's radio in his ear. He quickly reached his hand up to it.

"Jas, is that you?" Ray asked.

"Ray! Where are you guys?" Jasmin asked in a panic.

"Just entered what used to be a college at the far end of town."

"Well stay there! Looks like you're about to have company! I'm seeing multiple targets coming down the street. Get to cover...now!"

"Shit! Come on Steve!" Ray grabbed Steve and started to head to what appeared to be the main office of the building.

"What?" Steve asked.

"We got company."

The two quickly ran over to the office and took cover behind the reception desk as both their hearts began to race. Once they were down Steve took out a knife from his back pocket as Ray kept his silenced pistol at his side. Once they both were ready, Steve shut the flashlight off and darkness suddenly surrounded them once again.

At first nothing happened. All they could hear was rain hitting the ceiling of the school. It took some time for Ray's eyes to adjust to the dark but once they did a ray of light started to come down from the street and quickly raced toward the school. Then before either one of them knew it the entire front of the school was lit up by SUV lights.

The three large SUVs stopped in front of the school, each carrying several men. A man sitting in one of the passenger seats got out and looked around as thunder clapped overhead.

Ray and Steve peered carefully above the reception desk, silently watching. Once the man spoke it was , but Ray and Steve were able to hear what the man said.

"You two cover the perimeter. Once you've checked it meet us back at the fairgrounds," the man ordered.

Two men hopped from one of the vehicles as the guy who gave the order headed back into his SUV.

"Is that Dutra?" Steve asked quietly.

"I don't think so."

"So what's the plan? You wanna sneak past them or take them out?" Steve asked.

Ray looked at Steve.

"Right, dumb question." Steve said as the SUVs drove away from the entrance.

"Let's wait, see what they do first," Ray said before going back down for cover.

A part of Ray really just wanted the guys to walk past the college. It would make the situation so much easier, because Ray knew (just as Steve knew) that once they started taking out guys it would only be a matter of time before someone from Dutra's camp (or Radar's camp) realized they were missing some people...and then the countdown would begin. But that idea didn't last long once Ray and Steve heard the front doors to the college open.

For the briefest moment Ray thought about just letting them pass but deep down he knew it wasn't the right way to go. If they were patrolling the street then that was one thing (by the time they circled around to the other side Ray and Steve would've been long gone), but Ray knew it wasn't worth the risk of getting caught.

As their footsteps started getting louder and coming closer Steve got into his attack position, while Ray carefully started to get his gun ready. But just before Ray and Steve sealed the deal the men started talking in Spanish (quickly proving that Radar's men had arrived).

That was gonna complicate things. Ray was hoping that by the time everyone started arriving to the site, he would be all locked and ready to go. But now that Radar's men were here it was only a matter of time before Dutra and his group arrived.

Just as the men were about to walk past the reception desk, Ray suddenly stood up. despite the aching pain in his knee. He quickly aimed his gun at one of the men and fired a shot right into his head, killing him instantly.

Steve leaped the counter, grabbed the second man by the shoulder and stuck the long knife right into the man's neck. Instantly blood started to gush out and the man started struggling, but Steve stuck the knife in harder and deeper until he finally stopped moving. Steve pushed him to the ground and Ray hopped over the desk.

"Okay, we gotta move," Ray ordered.

Steve quickly turned on his flashlight and shined it on the dead bodies.

"These must be Radar's guys. No way Dutra has people like this in his group," Steve said.

"So why would this Radar guy have his men moving all around way the hell out here?" Ray asked.

"I don't know...maybe checking to make sure it's clear out this way?" Steve asked.

"Or he's trying to make sure no one can leave," Ray speculated.

Steve shook his head.

"No I don't think so. Dutra is a crazy son of a bitch but he isn't stupid. He wouldn't get into bed with someone that would retaliate. Like it or not, the man does have half a brain," Steve said.

"Yeah well let's just hope he doesn't use it. Come on let's go. No time to hide the bodies."

Ray and Steve quickly headed down the long dark hall while blood continued to pour out of the bastards they just killed. Normally Ray liked to keep things neat but now that he knew people were arriving, it was time to put it in high gear or else he would lose the opportunity to get Dutra.

"Jas?" Ray asked into the radio and the two of them started heading down a staircase.

"Yeah go ahead Ray? You guys okay?" Jasmin asked from the sky.

"Yeah we're fine. We took care of the guards but can you see anything down in the streets?" Ray asked.

"Oh, damn it, no I can't. The wind starting to pick up. And the rain is making it hard to even see in front of me," Jasmin confessed.

"Roger that, just stay on alert until I call you. We'll be at the parking garage in about five minuets," Ray said.

"Copy that."

Ray and Steve went down the flight of stairs. Ray took out his flashlight and shined it down the long windowless hall. Watermarks were about half way up the wall (once again proving Mother Nature has a mind of her own). But as they started walking down the hall a smell got there attention. A truly horrible smell. A smell that Ray and Steve smelt once, a very long time ago, a smell that they had hoped they would never have to smell again.

"Do you smell that?" Steve asked.

Ray swallowed hard knowing that what he was about to see wouldn't be enjoyable.

"Where's it coming from?" Ray asked.

They continued down the hall. Even with the flashlights it was tough to see all the way down toward the end of it. With each step they took the smell was getting worse and worse. Once they reached two red double doors it was obvious the smell was coming from inside.

Ray took a quick glance up at Steve and then slowly grabbed the handle to the door and began opening it. As the door opened the smell multiplied in intensity. It was so strong that Steve began to gag. Ray pulled the door opened and Steve quickly ran in and hoped the smell wasn't what he thought it would be while Ray closed the door behind him.

"Oh my unholy God," Steve said as his jaw dropped and his eyes widened.

Ray turned around and walked over to beside Steve.

"Oh Jesus..." Ray softly said to himself.

Steve and Ray were looking at an in ground swimming pool. The far back wall had high windows, so some type of light was able to filter through, but in that moment the two would've much rather kept the darkness compared to what they were looking at.

Clearly the water from the ocean had made It all the way up to the college and the swimming pool, but it must've rushed out just as fast as it rushed in, leaving a path of destruction like nothing they had ever seen before.

But the pool wasn't filled with water (in fact there was hardly any water in it at all)...it was filled with bodies. Dozens and dozens of bodies: black, whites, young, old. It was a view that could turn even the brightest soul pitch black. Not to mention the smell was the most horrid thing to ever lift into the air.

Steve and Ray couldn't help but take a moment of silence as both of their hearts sank. Steve had never seen anything like it before. He knew that mankind always had a dark side but until that moment he never realized just how black it could get.

Ray, on the other hand, had known all along, but over the years he'd tried his best to make sure he forgot about what he saw when he was overseas (and promised himself he would do everything in his power to make sure nothing like what he saw last time would ever again happen on his watch. He quickly he realized that he had once again failed in his mission).

"How could someone do this, Ray?" Steve asked as his eyes fixed on a very young child near the top of the human pile of death.

"I'll be damned if I know," Ray said.

Ray tried desperately to take his eyes off the pool but every time he came close he had to double check to be sure of what he was looking at.

"What do we do?" Steve asked.

"Nothing we can do...we just have to move on," Ray said.

"Christ man," Steve said.

Ray finally pried his eyes off the bodies and looked at Steve.

"This just got a whole lot bigger then Dutra, Steve...this changes everything." Ray said as his eyes locked on Steve's.

"You saying what I think you're saying?" Steve asked.

Ray nodded his head.

"We can't let anyone leave here tonight. If we do, God only knows what will happen to the world...come on."

Ray started to walk away from the pool, heading toward a door at the far side of the deep end, but Steve couldn't just leave, not without doing something. Steve took another look at the pool and his eyes locked back onto the dead child at the top. Once Steve saw that the boys eyes were open, and looking into them he knew they would haunt him forever.

Steve then lowered his flashlight and took the necklace off of his neck. It had been given to him by an old woman who's life he had saved, a priceless gift that Steve had always held onto and sought hope in whenever times got tough on the front lines. Steve loved the necklace but he knew the lost souls of the pool needed it more. And with a deep breath he tossed it into the human pit. When he saw it land on the little boy's chest Steve wiped a few tears out of his eyes and then headed to the door to catch up with Ray.

V

While Ray and Steve closed in on the meeting spot, back closer to home Torque was about to close the deal with Emily. When he first saw Emily, the last thing on his mind had been bringing her home, but as they started talking (and she kept drinking) it was clear she was way too drunk to drive herself home.

The whole ride to Emily's apartment, Emily talked Torque's ear off. Normally Torque hated when people talked a lot when they would drink but he actually enjoyed listening to Emily. She wasn't wild and crazy either. She was calm and alert but very open.

"It's the white building on the left," Emily said as she pointed to the building as Torque drove up to it.

Torque looked at the place. It was a little run down but nothing compared to what Torque lived in when he was younger (Torque's mother was a hopeless drug user and alcoholic, and had spent most of the weekends bringing home men like the world was ending. It was hard for Torque to get use to that when he was just a kid. From an early age he told himself once he was old enough, he would leave one day and never look back. He had kept his word; he hadn't seen his mother in years).

"Nice place," Torque said.

"You don't have to lie...even I admit it's a shithole," Emily replied as the car came to a stop.

As Torque put the car in park Emily looked around the rather empty street. She then looked back at Torque.

"So, thank you for the ride," Emily said.

Torque shook his head.

"No problem."

Emily gave Torque a quick smile before she grabbed the door handle and opened the door. She was able to get one leg out of the car but when she went to get the other foot out she lost her footing and almost fell out of the car. Torque quickly opened the driver side door, got out and walked over to her.

"You alright?" He asked as he gently grabbed her arm and helped out of the car.

"Yeah I'm okay," Emily said trying to prove that she was able to take care of herself.

"Well let me help you to the door," Torque said.

"No that's fine. You've done enough."

"I insist." Torque said.

Emily looked in Torque's brown eyes and then decided to give in.

"Okay, solider boy."

Torque closed the door to the car and put his arm around Emily as they walked to the front of the building and up the staircase. Normally Emily liked to do things herself (and this time was no different) but she wanted to remain respectful to the man that had just brought her home. Besides she got the feeling that Torque was a pretty all right guy. When they got to the top of the staircase Emily lost her footing again.

"Whoa! Careful." Torque said.

Emily smiled as her face turned red from embarrassment. She started regretting having that last drink, even though she knew she needed it after what happened back at the diner. Once she got to the door, she put the key into the lock and then opened the door.

Torque was a little confused at this point. Normally this would be the time when he would go in and make love to whichever chick he picked up but he could tell that Emily wasn't like most other girls...so he waited to see what she said next before he decided to do anything.

Emily opened the door all the way and stepped into the dark apartment. The street lights filtered in that orange looking glow into the apartment, but it still wasn't light enough to just walk in, so she reached over to the wall and turned on one of the living room lights.

For a moment Torque actually thought that Emily was just going to close the door without saying a word. She definitely wasn't acting like she wanted to get any action (which was fine by Torque; that only made him admire her more). He started to look around the street while Emily turned on the light to her apartment but he quickly turned back to her direction when he saw her pop her head back out.

"Come in if you'd like, I'll make you some coffee," Emily said with a smile.

Torque returned the smile and was just about to step inside when he remembered the long drive he was going to have to make in the morning. He knew he was gonna need a good nights sleep to explain to Sullivan what had happened between him and Ray.

"Thanks for the offer but I got to head back. Busy day tomorrow," Torque said.

Emily shook her head.

"Well...what if I said I insist?" Emily said with a cute smile as she brushed her long black hair over her ears.

Torque looked at her and suddenly realized she had just used the same excuse as he had just used to make sure she got into the apartment safely.

"Then I guess I would have no choice then would I?" Torque asked.

Emily chuckled.

"Come on in," she said.

Torque took his hands out of his pockets and then walked into the apartment. The building on the outside looked like a shithole (as Emily put it) but the apartment was beautiful to say the least. From the gorgeous furniture to the neatness of the overall place; Torque quickly forgot about what the place looked like on the outside.

"It's not much, but it's home." Emily said.

Torque looked at Emily.

"It's nice, it's...cozy," Torque said.

Emily shook her head and then crossed her arms as she stood in the entrance to the living room. She then started to really check out Torque hard core. She knew he was good looking back at the bar, but the lighting in there was beyond poor so she wasn't able to get a good look; but now that the lighting was much better she could look at the whole picture...and she liked it.

"I have to say that this is the moment when most of the guys I've been with decide to make a move on me," Emily said as she looked down.

Torque took his eyes off the beautiful painting that was behind the T.V. and looked at Emily. He didn't really know how to respond. He knew he had to say something but he didn't know what answer Emily wanted to hear. So instead of making a move (like he normally would), he decided to take another direction.

"Well, you seem like a classer girl then that," Torque said just before he cleared his throat.

Emily shook her head and then looked down at Torque's legs.

"Hmm," she softly said.

Torque wanted to say more but he didn't know what Emily was exactly thinking. His bladder started give off that feeling like he had to take a piss so he decided to lead with that next.

"Well, you mind if I use your bathroom before I head out?" He asked.

"Um...sure. Down the hall, first door on the right," Emily said, pointing the way.

Torque nodded his head.

"Thanks," He gave a smile and headed down the hall.

"Anytime, soldier boy," Emily said with a smile.

Torque headed down the hall and stepped into the bathroom. It was dark in there for sure. He began feeling around the wall to find the light switch. It took him a moment but once he did, he flipped on the light and then closed the door behind him.

It was clear that a woman used the bathroom; the place was fucking spotless. The bathtub and sink were the purest form of clean white and the walls were a deep purple. He headed to the toilet and made sure that he lifted up the seat (something he learned to do a very long time ago).

As be began doing his business he began thinking about what the guys were doing. He might have been pissed at Ray for going after Dutra by himself, but that didn't mean that Torque didn't want to be there. It was in that moment where he started regretting making the choice to quit. When the words came out of his mouth he knew one day he would regret it, but he didn't realize that day would come so soon.

Torque knew the ride to Washington was gonna be long now that he was able to admit to himself that he made the wrong call. A part of him wanted to drive back to the body shop and wait for Ray to come back, beg for another chance, but Torque was positive that Ray wouldn't take him back.

For a brief moment he completely forgot about where he was and who he was with. In fact, he even started to feel depressed, but all that would quickly change once he flushed the toilet and went back into the living room.

Torque opened the bathroom door, shut the light off and then began to walk back down the hall. He really liked Emily's company but he knew he needed some time to be by himself to rethink everything.

"I think I'm gonna get going. Thanks for the coffee offer, but I got a long day tomorrow." Torque said as he walked down the hall.

He was going to say more, but when he walked into the living room he stopped dead in his tracks. Emily was standing in front of the couch, dressed in only black panties and a black bra. The bra was just light enough for Torque to make out Emily's nipples as they damn near pierced out of the bra.

He tried to take his eyes off her breasts, but they then made there way down to her magazine looking legs. The shine off her skin sent chills down Torque as he looked at her in amazement.

"Oh, okay. You can go if you want," Emily said, slowly walking over to Torque.

Torque stood motionless as Emily walked up to him and began putting her hands on his stomach.

"Or you can stay..." Emily said.

Suddenly, without warning (or even thinking it over) Torque grabbed Emily by the back of the neck and they began to kiss passionately while Emily began to undo Torques belt.

Torque normally tried not to sleep with a date on the first night (Or at least that's what he would tell himself before going out. Wouldn't always work but he did try.) and neither did Emily. But in that moment both of them were lonely after the day each had had. Inside, they both knew what they were doing wasn't right (and would make them feel even emptier in the morning) but not even that thought was going to stop them from ripping of each other's clothes.

As Emily roughly took off Torque's shirt so she could put her hands all over his muscular body, Torque took off Emily's black bra and began to carress her breasts. Their tongues entered each other's throats. As the kissing grew more intense, Emily unbuttoned Torque's rather dirty looking jeans and reach into his underwear.

But before she got the chance to grab anything, Torque suddenly picked her up and brought her over to the couch. Once he gently put her down, Emily pulled down Torque's pants all the way to his ankles. They eventually would go down on each other before taking the rest to Emily's bedroom all the way down the hall. And in those briefest moments both forgot about the troubles the day had brought them.

VI

While Torque was having sex with Ray's daughter, back in Maine Bob, Kevin and Tommy had finally reached the cabin. For a brief moment it looked like no one was home, but as the trio made there way closer to the back entrance it was clear they were not alone in the thick woods of Maine.

The front of the house was crawling with armed men. While three of them were sitting on the front porch, three others were patrolling the house. Each one carrying a fully loaded automatic weapon. The guys quickly knew that it was going to be a lot harder then each of them thought it would be.

"I count six guys outside," Kevin said as looked through binoculars from a good distance away.

"Awful lot of people guarding one place. Maybe Ray was right about something being here," Tommy said as he looked down at Kevin.

"What are they packing?" Bob asked.

"Uh...looks like automatic weapons...extended clips...and possibly side arms," Kevin answered.

Bob sighed as he reached down and grabbed the binoculars from Kevin to look for himself.

"Think this Dutra guy is in there?" Kevin asked.

"No idea," Bob shrugged. "Probably not but not gonna find out from over here."

"So how you wanna do this?" Tommy asked.

Bob slowly lowered the binoculars as he began to think about the best way to approach the cabin.

"I'd say snipe them from here," Kevin said.

"Fuck that Kevo, let's just walk right up there and start shooting. It'll be the last thing they suspect," Tommy said.

"Yeah, what about the people inside? What if Dutra's not in there and they alert him? That will put Steve and Ray in danger," Kevin shot back.

"Well if you got a better idea, by all means..."

"I do! I say we snipe them from here. Were you not listening to me, Tommy? God, pull your head out of your ass," Kevin said.

"Wow, what crawled up your ass and planted a seed?" Tommy asked.

Kevin took his eyes off the cabin to quickly look at Tommy.

"Really Tommy? You have no idea why I'm pissed at you?" Kevin asked.

Tommy sighed.

"Dude just let it go! It's a damn truck!" Tommy shouted rather loudly.

"Hey, both of you shut the hell up!" Bob ordered.

They listened to Bob and got focused on the task at hand (even though Kevin couldn't truly let the whole situation about the truck go). Bob then turned away from the cabin and looked at them.

"Okay here's what we're gonna do. Tommy you take the left, Kevin you take the right. All of us will take out the patrols, regroup by the front of the house and then breach the place. Be swift and keep it quiet. Understood?" Bob asked.

The two nodded their heads.

"Alright lets move," Bob ordered.

The guys broke off and headed in the directions that Bob had ordered them to go. Kevin seemed fine about the idea (hell, before he even became part of the group, all he did was solo missions) but Tommy was a whole different story. Tommy was a firm believer that they work at their best side by side. He was still pretty sore about Ray deciding to take off and deal with Dutra on his own. So when he heard the words come out of Bob's mouth to split up he was far from pleased. But in spite of not agreeing, he continued on as he ducked and started to head toward the patrol.

The patrol was in all black clothing with an automatic weapon resting at his hip. Tommy first thought about just quickly standing up but remembered what Bob said about saving ammo. Tommy was never one to prefer knifing over shooting but he was gonna have to do it this time to be on the safe side. As Tommy creeped up on the man he slowly reached down to his hip and quietly took out the large knife holstered on his right side.

As Tommy got into position from the left; Kevin carefully made his way to the patrol on the right. Like Tommy's, the patrolman also carried an automatic weapon. Only instead of just walking around he was looking all over. Kevin knew that if he was going to be able to take him out quietly he was gonna need to get closer so he carefully dropped to the ground and began crawling through the thick high grass.

Bob watched from the binoculars. Once he saw Tommy and Kevin getting ready to close in, he quickly dropped the binoculars and picked up his sniper rifle and aimed for the three men on the porch. Bob couldn't hear what they were saying but it sounded like they were cracking jokes. Bob then closed his left eye and looked into his scope.

Tommy made it about a foot away from his target. He held his position as he turned and looked back into the direction where Bob was. It had been a while since Tommy had taken anyone out in cold blood with a knife, so long that in fact he was nervous as hell about doing it. He could feel the adrenaline running through his body but did his best to breathe calmly and wait for the order.

Kevin crawled closer and closer to the man. He couldn't see two feet in front of him but he was sure that he was close. He thought about stopping but had second guesses; thinking maybe he wasn't close enough, he decided to move up just a little bit closer. But as he moved his leg, it got stuck on a small stick and before he could shake it off, he put down the full weight of his leg and the twig snapped.

The patrolman quickly turned and aimed his gun where the sound came from. The noise didn't sound like much but it was enough to grab his attention. The darkness of the forest made it impossible to see anything, so the man reached into his pocket and took out a flashlight.

Kevin remained still as his heartbeat pulsated in his ear. He knew for certain that his target had heard the noise (how could he not? It was the only sound around). As Kevin began to slowly lift his eyes up he quickly lowered them when he saw the flashlight beam suddenly filter through the thick grass.

Bob noticed the flashlight beam from the corner of the scope and quickly turned the gun and aimed it at the patrolman. As the patrolman started to walk into the thick grass Bob turned his scope more to the right and saw Kevin was laying in the grass only feet away from the target.

"Don't know what you did, but you got his attention," Bob said into the radio in his ear to Kevin.

Kevin lowered his head.

"Thanks for the heads up," Kevin sarcastically whispered back.

Bob knew that the patrolman would only need to step another couple of feet before he spotted Kevin so Bob quickly turned back to the front porch of the cabin. Bob took the safety off on the rifle and aimed for the man standing up. He was just about to pull the trigger when the man suddenly started heading into the cabin. Bob watched as the man entered the cabin.

"Bob, hurry up!" Kevin whispered louder as the patrolman took another step toward Kevin.

Bob kept his eye on the man and once he closed the door to the cabin Bob quickly turned the gun back to the two remaining men on the porch.

"Engage," Bob said as he locked the scope onto the head of the man who was sitting on the porch.

He quickly pulled the trigger and the silenced bullet shot out and hit the man directly in the forehead. A red of mist sprayed out of the bullet wound and landed all over the other man on the porch, but before he even had the chance to react Bob fired a bullet into his neck. The man quickly dropped his gun, clenching his throat with his hands as blood poured out.

The patrolman took another step closer to Kevin and shined his flashlight beam directly onto Kevin's back. His eyes quickly lit up once he realized that a man was literally right in front of him. The flashlight beam lit up Kevin's face as Kevin jumped up and knifed the man in the stomach.

The man began to groan loudly as Kevin twisted the sharp blade into the man's abdomen. As the groaning got louder Kevin put his hand over the man's mouth, ripped out the blade and then shoved it up the top of the man's jaw. As blood gushed out Kevin grabbed the man and then slowly lowered him onto the ground.

Tommy's patrolman quickly looked into the direction of Kevin when he saw the flashlight beam suddenly go out. He was getting ready to walk back over when Tommy suddenly got out of cover and shoved the knife into the man's back. Instant pain shot through the man's body as he tried to turn around and face his attacker but Tommy grabbed the man's neck and slowly began to twist until he heard a loud snap.

Once he saw Tommy take out his patrol, Bob quickly stood up and ran to the house. Tommy pushed the man onto the ground and ran to the front to meet up with Bob and Kevin. Kevin ran over to the front of the cabin as he put his knife away and pulled out his silenced machine gun.

Once Bob reached the porch he quickly went up the stairs and pushed one of the bodies off the edge. Kevin did the same thing once he got up the stairs. Tommy wiped off the blade of his knife before pulling out his sidearm. As Kevin began to pick up the last body he struggled trying to get the man over the railing. Tommy started to walk over but before he could get to Kevin, Bob had picked up the man's legs and helped Kevin throw the body into the bushes right below the porch.

"There's at least one more inside. Possibly more. Kevin, you head down to the basement, Tommy you clear the first floor and I'll sweep the second floor," Bob said.

Tommy and Kevin nodded and Bob slowly walked over to the door and then very slowly opened it. It was quiet inside the cabin. The place was lit up like a Christmas tree but when Bob stuck his head into the doorway no one was in sight. Once he was sure no one was near the front door he quickly opened it all way and they went rushing in. Tommy headed to the right, Kevin headed for the back of the house and Bob began to walk up the staircase in front of the front door.

Kevin made his way into the kitchen as he check all around. The kitchen was a real mess. It was clear that the guys that were there had been there for a while. Kevin made his way to the far back wall of the kitchen and still didn't hear anything. He got to the wall and noticed a light switch. After taking one last look around he quickly flipped the switch and the kitchen went dark. It took a moment for his eyes to adjust but once they did he noticed a glow at the end of the kitchen. He aimed his gun to the light and slowly walked over. As he turned to the direction of the light he noticed a staircase that headed down. He stopped for a moment and focused his attention to his hearing to see if he could hear anything. For a brief moment he didn't but suddenly he heard what sounded like glass breaking on the floor. After a moment he started down the stairs and put his hand on the trigger.

Tommy entered the living room and began shutting the lights off all throughout the room. When he shut the last light off out of the corner of his eye he saw a shadow enter the room.

"Hey!" The man shouted.

Tommy quickly turned and fired three silenced shots into the shadow. The man dropped and fell into the darkness. Tommy then began to walk in the direction that the man had come from, shutting off every light in his path as he made his way to the back of the house.

Bob reached the top of the staircase and began looking around. He didn't see anything at first, but he knew he wasn't alone. It was like he could feel it. Then suddenly a door right behind him opened. Bob put his back to the wall as a man stepped out and started toward the staircase. Just as the man stepped down one step, Bob grabbed him by the shoulder and plunged a knife into the back of the his neck.

The man squirmed around in Bob's grip for a moment until death finally took over. Once Bob pulled out the knife he grabbed the man by the lower back and carefully placed him down onto the now blood covered floor.

Kevin slowly reached the bottom of the stairs and got ready. He was just about to enter the next room when suddenly a man popped in front of the staircase. Before the man had a chance to react, Kevin fired multiple bullets into the man. As the bullets flew out of the man's body they impacted the wooden walls of the cabin's basement, making a loud noise upon impact.

"What the fuck?" A voice shouted from the other room.

Kevin rushed in and started firing multiple rounds into the two men standing outside a doorway to what looked like some type of workshop.

Even though Kevin was firing from the hip his aim was dead accurate. The men quickly dropped to the floor. Kevin kept his eyes on them as he walked over to the large flat screen T.V. When he reached the T.V. he quickly turned and fired one shot into the screen. Suddenly the T.V. sparked and the screen went black as Kevin made his way to the workshop.

The muffled shots in the basement grabbed Tommy's attention as he made his way into the back entrance of the kitchen. He turned and quickly aimed down the staircase. He decided that since he was positive the first floor was clear he was going to go down and help Kevin but that quickly changed when suddenly a man body slammed Tommy right off his feet and onto the ground.

Tommy hit the ground hard, sending his gun flying into the darkness of the kitchen. He started to get up but suddenly he was kneed in the face and plummeted back down to the cold hard floor. Tommy slowly rolled over onto his back and got to see the shadow of the man for the first time. Just judging from the shadow the guy must've been over two hundred and fifty pounds and well over six feet.

Tommy knew that he had no time to go and look for his gun; he was just gonna have to improvise. The man started walking over to him and Tommy began looking around for anything he could use as a weapon. The man walked closer before reaching to his side and pulling out a gun.

Knowing that the element of surprise would soon be lost if that gun was fired, Tommy to his feet and body slammed the man against the kitchen stove. Tommy used all his might to make sure it was an effective blow (and it was) but, the man quickly grabbed Tommy and pistol-whipped him in the face.

Tommy groaned in pain as he fell back and put his hand over the side of his face. With rage in his eyes the man then violently kicked Tommy in the privates. Pain shot through Tommy's body as he groaned and dropped to his knees. He slowly lowered his hand from his face. He could tell by the feeling of his hand that he was bleeding.

Tommy tried to get himself together but the pain from the kick was still too much for him to get over. Every time he tried standing up his legs felt like jelly. From the darkness he could hear the man chuckling to himself as he walked over to Tommy. He still needed more time to get back up but that didn't stop Tommy from taking out his knife.

The man walked up to Tommy and began to aim at him but before he shot, Tommy lifted his blade up and suddenly brought it soaring down, sticking it right into the man's foot. The six-foot man screamed in pain then quickly lifted up his other foot and kicked Tommy in the chest.

The kick knocked the wind out of Tommy and sent him flying backward until he landed on his back. When he landed he felt a metal object underneath his back. He didn't know what it was at first but he knew he needed to get his hands on it, so he quickly rolled over and picked it up. Much to his surprise it was his gun. He quickly turned back to the man (who was already aiming at him) and fired five silenced shots at the man. The first two shots missed, striking the wall off to the side of the man, but the last three hit. Two bullets hit somewhere around his stomach and the last hit in his upper chest.

The man yelled as loud as he could as the bullets entered his body. But even with bullets in him that still didn't stop him from trying to shoot at Tommy. It took a bullet to the head for him to finally collapse.

Tommy watched as the bullet hit the top of the man's head. But just when Tommy thought he was in the clear the man began pulling the trigger as he went soaring down to the floor.

"Oh shit," Tommy said to himself.

The gunshots echoed throughout the house. Kevin heard it from downstairs and Bob heard it from upstairs. Bob let out a big sigh when he heard the shots as he reached the last unchecked room on the second floor.

Then from inside the room Bob heard men start shouting and heading to the door. But before they could open the door, Bob kicked it in and began firing at the three men. He kept firing at them until they had all fallen to the ground and once he was done he raced back downstairs. Kevin also ran for the staircase to find out where the gunshots were coming from.

As soon as Kevin got to the top of the stairs he clicked on the lights to the kitchen and saw Tommy still on his back with half of his face covered in blood from his head wound.

"Tommy!" Kevin shouted as he quickly ran over to Tommy.

Tommy slowly started to get up.

"You okay?" Kevin asked.

"Course not! I got my ass kicked!" Tommy shouted as Kevin helped him up to his feet. "First floor is clear."

Kevin shook his head. "So is the basement."

Tommy got to his feet and then holstered his weapon as Bob came running into the kitchen.

"What happened?" Bob asked in a panic.

"Everything's fine, Bob." Tommy said as he wiped the blood running down his cheek.

Bob looked around and once he saw that everything was good he rolled his eyes.

"What part of keep it quiet do you not understand, Tommy?" Bob asked.

"The guy is the size of a goddamn Buick. I'd like to see you take him out quietly!" Tommy shouted as he pointed to the dead man on the floor.

"We're clear down here Bob," Kevin said to change the subject.

"Okay so is the second floor," Bob said as he looked at his watch. "We probably bought ourselves five minutes. Let's check this place fast and just get the hell out of here."

"Alright." Kevin said.

"You sure you're okay, Tommy?" Bob asked.

"I'm wonderful, Bob," Tommy said with a sarcastic smile.

Bob shook his head and then started back for the stairs.

"Meet at the front door in five!" Bob shouted.

"Copy!" Tommy said as he walked over to the refrigerator and opened it.

While Tommy looked for something to help him with the pain (most likely alcohol) Kevin took a hard look at Tommy's forehead as blood leaked out of it.

"Damn that looks deep. You sure you're alright?" Kevin asked.

"Would you quit worrying about me! Go and check the basement. Just wanna get the hell out of here," Tommy said.

Kevin patted Tommy on the shoulder and then headed back down to the basement. Inside the fridge there wasn't a lot of food so it made it easier for Tommy to look through all the drawers. He didn't find anything on the top ones but when he opened the bottom drawer he quickly saw cans of beer inside.

"Oh thank God." Tommy said as he grabbed one.

He cracked it open and drank the whole thing (Tommy hadn't had a drink in months, mostly due to Ray saying he drank too much but at this point Tommy just didn't give a fuck). Once Tommy finished it he threw the empty can down onto the ground and then reached back in the fridge and grabbed another one. He cracked it open and then looked down at the dead man next to him.

"Here's to you, asshole," Tommy said as he raised the can, cracked it open and then began swigging from it.

VII

As the guys searched the cabin (well, as Kevin and Bob searched the cabin) Ray and Steve made their way into the abandon parking garage. The rain was starting to come down at a much faster clip by the time they ran into the entrance.

"Just in time," Steve said as he looked back outside and saw how heavy it was raining.

Ray slid his hand through his hair to ring out the water in it as he looked down to the lower level of the parking garage and saw rain running into the already flooded underground level. As Steve looked around to make sure no one was following them, Ray put his hand to the radio piece in his ear.

"Jas, we made it to the parking garage." Ray said.

"Okay. You're gonna wanna get to the third level facing the south side. You should be able to see the meeting from there," Jasmin said.

"Copy that," Ray said as he walked toward Steve.

"We're gonna need to move fast. Place is already starting to flood again," Steve said as he pointed to to the water filling up the undreground level.

"We should be alright on the third floor," Ray said as they began running over to a staircase.

Ray turned on his flashlight as they made their way to the door that led to the staircase. As Ray slowly opened the door, Steve kept an eye behind them for any stragglers. Ray stuck his flashlight into the staircase and made sure it was clear. Besides water leaking in from a crack in the ceiling they were still alone.

"Alright,come on Steve." Ray entered the staircase and ran up the stairs. Steve shut the stairwell door, and quickly followed up the stairs. As Ray reached the top he put his hand on the doorknob and then slowly pulled it open and stuck his head through the doorway.

"Okay, we're good." Ray said back to Steve.

They both walked out of the stairwell and headed over to the opposite side of the third level. Aside from a lone piece of shit silver car the level was completely deserted. Scattered all around the floor were pieces of debris and puddles of water slowly adding up with the rain that was coming in through the sidewalls. Lightning lit up the sky again as Ray and Steve approached the edge of the south side wall.

"Don't think it's gonna stop anytime soon," Steve said in amazement as he watched Mother Earth roar.

"Seems like every time we go on one of these it rains. You ever notice that?" Ray asked.

"It wasn't raining when we did that job in Somalia," Steve pointed out.

"True...but we did have to swim though, so can't win for losing."

"Have to say after last time I never wanted to go on another one of these again," Steve said as he turned away from the view of the sky.

"You and me both."

Once Ray and Steve made it to the edge they walked over to the wall and looked at the view and were amazed. They were looking down at the old abandon fairground that was surrounded by water on all four sides. Jasmin was right though: the fairground was just high enough that the water did not reach it, but Ray was sure that before the storm was over it would be.

Thunder rumbled across the sky as Ray took his eyes off of the fairground and looked at the ocean. The waves were roaring in and were massive in size. Neither one of them had seen anything like it before.

"Would you look at that," Steve said as he put his gun down.

"Yeah, it's something," Ray said.

"Always had to go into another country to see a view like this," Steve said.

"It's amazing what you can find in your backyard if you look hard enough," Ray said as he put his gun down.

Steve began setting up his sniper rifle while Ray radioed Jasmin again.

"Jas?" Ray asked into his headset.

"Yeah?" Jasmin said through the static.

"Hey, we're on the third floor," Ray said.

"Okay. I'll loop around and be standing by for your orders," Jasmin said again.

"Okay and Jas...make sure to let us know when you see something."

"Copy that Ray. Will do."

Ray then started setting up his gun. He mounted it onto the wall and made sure it was loaded as Steve did the same thing.

"Think we're too far away?" Steve asked.

"Naw should be alright. At this distance the bullet will probably take a second or two to reach. It's the wind that's got me worried," Ray confessed.

"So how you wanna do this?" Steve asked.

"We'll shoot on my mark. I'll take Dutra and you take Radar," Ray explained.

Steve stopped working on his gun and looked up at Ray.

"You positive you wanna go for both? I mean, if we both aim at one there's a better chance to hit..." Steve began to say before Ray suddenly interrupted him.

"You saw the college," Ray said.

"Yeah but..."

"But nothing. It's my call and I say were gonna go for both," Ray said in a pissed voice.

Steve shook his head.

"Understood boss." Steve went back to working on his gun.

Ray finished setting up and was just getting ready to load a large bullet into the rifle when he stopped and took a deep breath and then exhaled.

"What?" Steve asked as he looked up for a moment.

Ray slowly took his eyes off the gun and then looked down at the fairgrounds.

"Nothing. Just the sight of that...brought back a lot of memories that's all," Ray said.

"No offense, but I'm glad I can't say that." Steve said.

Ray shook his head and wished he could say the same.

"Back in Nam I was dropped into the jungle about two miles away from a village that we were told was an ally to us. My platoon leader said we would be able to rest there, get food and shelter and use the place as a base while we conducted operations around the area...it was suppose to be a walk in the park as he said. Well about half a mile away from the village we started to smell something in the air. At first we thought it was just nothing, maybe a rotting animal or animals somewhere nearby. But we quickly stopped being naive when we got to the village."

Steve shook his head, knowing that what Ray was about to tell him was the very reason why Ray never talked about what he did over in Vietnam.

"Ray, you don't have to tell me. I can figure the rest out for myself," Steve offered to try and save Ray from going down his bloody memory lane.

Ray shook his head as he moved his eyes to the violent waves of the ocean reaching the shore. "When we got to the village it was quiet. Nobody said anything, but the moment we got that village in our eyes we knew something was wrong. It didn't long to find the first sets of bodies: a young women and three young children. One of the kids was about four years old if I had to guess. I didn't realize until I got deeper in the village but they were the lucky ones, they were only shot. Everyone else...was a different story."

Steve closed his eyes as the image of that young boy on the top of the pool entered his mind.

"Not one single body was intact. Hands were missing, heads were gone, women were clearly raped and strangled and the men were cut into pieces. I knew right then and there that if I made it home I was never going to be the same...I knew that whoever had done that to those people were an evil that the world had never known before. You know, nowadays we hear about shit like that all time in Iraq and Afghanistan, but back in 1968...nobody knew how dark the soul of a man could get. As we walked through the village we quickly started to get an idea of how dark, but it wouldn't be until we reached the middle of the village...there was a fire pit in the dead center of the village. The villagers probably used it to cook their food on it...but that wasn't the case when we got there. Right in the middle was a pile of bodies, a large pile of bodies that had been burnt. I stepped closer because at first I couldn't tell what the hell it was, it just looked like one big pile of ash...but it didn't take me long to stop, drop to my knees and vomit."

Steve closed his eyes and shook his head. "Jesus," he murmered.

Ray began to tremble for a moment (almost as if he was right back there in Vietnam).

"They had gathered up all the children they could find when they slaughtered the villagers, put them together, and set each and every one of them on fire," Ray said, remembering the sight as clear as day. "We buried them all. Each of them,every single piece we could collect. I didn't eat for days after that...I couldn't stomach anything."

Steve shook his head, no he knew why Ray never wanted to talk about Vietnam.

"What happened next?" Steve asked.

"Next day we got our orders in to track down a man by the name of Chao Guozhi and his small army he had with him. We were told that it was him and his men that were responsible for the massacre. Intel indicated they headed west after they burned the children, so that's where we headed. All night and day we just kept marching on until we found them. Must've followed them for a solid month, but never got close to them. All we found were other villages and people who had come across them. After about a month and a half we were told to give up and head back for a new assignment. Never got the chance to face Guozhi or his men..."

Steve patted Ray on the shoulder.

"Sorry Ray...don't really know what else I could say," Steve confessed.

Ray shrugged his shoulders.

"It was a long time ago. Bastards probably dead by now anyway...just would've been nice to help speed up the process."

Steve forced out a smile and then went back to loading his gun. Thunder rumbled in the distance but it was not loud enough to drown out the sound of Ray's cell phone ringing. Ray quickly dug into his pocket and answered it.

"Yeah?" Ray asked.

"It's me," Bob said on the other end of the line.

"Talk to me, Bob."

"Got to the cabin, took out a few people and Tommy got his ass kicked," Bob said.

"Hey fuck you, Bob." Tommy said in the background.

"Did you find anything?" Ray asked.

"Not sure yet. Found a lot of guns and computers. Kevin's currently working on those. Said there was some type of shop downstairs. Tommy and I are gonna look there but so far it seems to be a dead end, and no sign of Dutra," Bob said.

Ray sighed.

"Shit. All right. We'll call you on our way back," Ray said.

"Alright. After we take a look in the basement we're gonna take off. You just want the place left alone?" Bob asked.

Ray thought about it for a moment.

"No. Burn the place to the ground. And everything in it," Ray ordered.

"Copy," Bob said before he hung up.

Ray closed his cell phone and put it back into his pocket.

"Shit," Ray muttered.

"What?" Steve asked.

"Sounds like a dead end on the cabin," Ray said.

"No sign of Dutra?" Steve asked.

"No. That means he has to show up here," Ray said.

Ray picked the large bullet back up and loaded it into the gun.

"So you never told me how it went with Emily," Steve began.

"Dead end Steve. Just leave it at that," Ray pretty much ordered.

Steve sighed and then went back to looking into his scope. After seeing how Ray reacted when he got back, Steve had an idea of how things went, but he wanted to ask to make sure. Ray not wanting to talk about it made it clear that things didn't go well. That bothered Steve, but he knew that when something was bothering Ray it was best to give him space.

Even though Ray didn't show it at all he did want to talk about it with Steve (Steve was always good at telling people to never stop going after something and Ray really needed to hear that), but he knew it wasn't the right time. Ray dismissed the idea, but not totally. Just until they got back (or if they got back). The silence of the garage was interrupted by the static coming through the radio in his ear.

"Ray! Ray!" Jasmin said in a panic.

"Jas, what's going on?"

"You got a helicopter heading to your position from the north," Jasmin shouted.

Steve looked into his scope and saw several vehicles pulling into the fairgrounds.

"Heads up Ray," Steve quickly said.

Ray looked down at the fairgrounds. He saw the headlights of the vehicles moving toward the middle of the fairgrounds.

"Alright, Jas this is it. Get into position. Can you make out what type of helicopter it is?" Ray asked.

"Can't see it all that great, but it looks like the one from the shooting," Jasmin said in very heavy static.

"Alright, stay clear of it. If we lose communication, keep an eye out for our sign okay?" Ray said.

"Yes sir," Jasmin said.

"Fuck. The radio frequency is getting worse by the second," Ray confessed to Steve.

"No surprise there," Steve said.

"We got a chopper heading this way. Should be flying over us any second," Ray said to Steve.

"Alright...let's do this." Steve closed his eyes and then looked in the scope.

Ray took a deep breath and did the same and his heart began to pound. He felt around his sniper rifle until he found the safety and once he did he clicked it off.

"Safety's off," Ray announced.

"Right behind you," Steve said.

"Alright you son of a bitch. Come on..." Ray softly said to himself.

VIII

The wind was picking up and fast, but that didn't stop the people in the vehicles down at the fairgrounds from putting the cars in park and getting out. The doors to all the vehicles opened and a dozen men with automatic weapons came out and stood outside in the rain. All the doors slammed shut with the exception of one passenger side door in the middle that never opened in the first place.

"Alright, I'm counting thirteen assholes," Steve said.

"Same here. The vehicle on the right—did you see the passenger door open?" Ray asked.

"Negative."

"Okay make that fourteen. Radar must be in that one," Ray mused.

"Good call, Ray. Is our boy late?" Steve asked.

"He's never late," Ray muttered to himself.

As Ray and Steve locked on to the men in the fairgrounds, just above them a large helicopter came rushing down from overhead and began heading in the direction of the fairground. Ray quickly lifted up his gun and looked through the scope to see if he could get a better look at the incoming chopper. Not surprisingly, it looked very familiar. A rush of adrenaline quickly went punding through Ray.

"That's him!" Ray shouted.

"Copy," Steve responded.

Ray lowered his gun and aimed it at the helicopter as it descended onto the fairgrounds. It was starting to rain even heavier, making it damn near impossible to see very well through the scope.

As the chopper met the ground the men standing outside held onto the cars as the force of the helicopter blades intensified the wind. Once the chopper landed on the ground the side door slid open and multiple men began coming out.

"Stay sharp Steve. This is it," Ray said.

The men exited the chopper and headed toward the cars as the passenger door to the vehicle began to open. Once it opened all the way a bald man in a dark jacket stepped out.

"I have Radar in my scope, he just stepped out of the car," Steve quickly said once he was sure.

Ray kept his scope focused on the door to the helicopter. He was so busy looking at that, he didn't even notice the passenger door to the helicopter open. As it swung open Dutra quickly jumped out of the chopper and made his way over to the parked vehicles. Dutra also had on a dark jacket that matched with his dark sunglasses he had on. As he walked around the chopper he took a look at Radar's men as they aimed their guns. Dutra grew a sinister smile as excitement began to grow in his tainted black soul.

Dutra remained alert as he looked around to get a head count of how many men Radar brought in case shit starts to go down. Once he made a tally and told himself he was good to go, he began to walk over to Radar. Radar kept his eyes of Dutra as he walked over to him.

"That's far enough," Radar said.

Dutra suddenly stopped and shook his head.

"Really needed to bring your whole group for a simple exchange?" Dutra asked.

"I could ask you the same," Radar shouted back as thunder rumbled across the sky.

Dutra suddenly smiled; clearly it was a smile that tried to ease the friction between the two men but it didn't do much good; Radar could clearly see the darkness that truly lived inside of Dutra (takes one to know one).

"You bring it?" Radar asked.

"You bring the money?" Dutra quickly shot back.

"I wanna see the product first."

"Cash first...product after," Dutra said as he wiped the rain off his face.

"That wasn't the deal!" Radar shouted.

Dutra started to step closer but Radar's men were quick enough to aim their guns, forcing Dutra to stop. Dutra's men quickly aimed their guns up at Radar's men.

"Looks like it's getting tense," Steve said as he fixed his scope onto Radar.

"Maybe with any luck they'll shoot one another," Ray said.

"I got the target in my sight. Just say the word Ray," Steve firmly said.

"Hold until they make the exchange. We need to see what were up against," Ray quickly said.

Ray and Steve kept their sights locked on as Dutra took a small step towards Radar.

"Listen...I know you do this your way down in Mexico with your army of river niggers but this is America. We do things my way...if you got a problem with that then by all means...let me know...so I can put a bullet through your fucking head, throw your corpse over the border and get on with the rest of my day," Dutra said in his menacing voice.

A trickle of fear began to run down inside of Radar; clearly Dutra was as menacing as his reputation said he was...but so was Radar. And the last thing Radar was going to do was show fear in front of his men.

Radar began to chuckle as he stepped toward Dutra. As Radar walked up to his face Dutra began to chuckle himself (Dutra had heard the stories of Radar and his pack of 'river niggers' but he never took them seriously. A bald but foolish way to think.). Radar did not stop walking until he was in Dutra's face. Dutra could smell the horrible breath of Radar as he finished laughing.

"You Americans are all the same...think the world revolves around you. But little do you know the truth. Each day that passes America is getting closer and closer to falling from its grace. And I have every intention to be a part of that. I don't care if I have to go around you or through you...I will do what I have too. You're a fearless man, Mr. Vacca, but you forget there are other fearless men in the world," Radar said.

As the words trickled out of Radar, Dutra could tell from Radar's eyes that he was just like himself: willing to do what is necessary to be the bigger fish. And for once in Dutra's life, he realized that he might be barking up the wrong tree.

The men kept eye contact for a while before the next move was made. But finally after a long enough silence Dutra broke eye contact from Radar and slowly turned to his men, who were still aiming at Radar's men.

"Get the product," He ordered.

And right when Dutra gave the order, Radar did the same thing.

"Grab the money," Radar shouted to his men.

The men from each camp lowered their guns and began to carry out the order while Dutra and Radar went back to staring each other down.

"Maybe I underestimated you," Dutra confessed.

"Maybe I overestimated you," Radar suddenly said.

The tension remained tight between the two, but back up on the third floor of the garage a different kind of tension was building up.

"Okay Radar's men have the money, and they're walking over with it. Ready to go?" Steve asked.

"Dutra's guys still haven't gotten out of the chopper yet," Ray said.

Steve sighed.

"Ray, they're in a perfect spot."

"Not yet goddamn it! We wait until those men get out of the chopper!"

Ray shouted in anger.

Steve exhaled deeply and went back to looking at through his sight. For a moment he lost Radar. His heart quickly began to beat, fearing the worst, but he was able to find him and lock back on to his forehead.

Dutra finally broke his eye contact when his phone began to ring in his jacket. He dug into it and looked at the screen. Once he saw it was Street, he quickly swiped his thumb across the screen.

"What?" Dutra answered.

"It wasn't easy and it's only a matter of time before the C.I.A. finds out there servers have been hacked..." Street began to say before he got interrupted.

"Cut to the fucking chase! Do you have the names or not?" Dutra shouted.

Radar watched Dutra as he shouted into the phone. He quickly decided that once this deal was over, he would never do business with Dutra again, not because he was threatened by him, which he was, but because he could clearly tell Dutra had a few screws loose where they should've been securely tightened.

"Raymond Gagnon, Stephen Brown, Kevin Bear, Bob Tiggs, Thomas Sitrenella and Jasmin Gagareacka. Hired by the C.I.A., F.B.I., and Secret Service throughout the years. Gagnon is the leader...the man that shot at you in the helicopter."

A dark and sinister smile grew onto Dutra's face.

"You get addresses?" Dutra suddenly asked.

"Yes sir."

"Do it," Dutra said.

"Already on it, oh and sir!" Street shouted knowing that Dutra was about to hang up the phone.

"What?"

"You were right by the way," Street said to boost Dutra's ego.

"Bout what?"

"Bosnia...files said that they were sent there to 'investigate and take out a potently harmful and dangerous situation'," Street said.

Quickly Dutra put the pieces to together and realized his hunch was right. The anger began to boil inside of Dutra as he slowly forgot his surroundings and started to think about Ray's face as he shot at him back in Washington. Dutra knew right then and there what he had to do next and was willing to do it, wipe out Ray and everyone involved with him.

As Dutra finished up his conversation with Street, one of Radar's men walked over to him and slowly bent down to his Radar's ear. Radar felt the breath on the back of his neck and quickly took his eyes off Dutra.

"Sir, Abran and Bertoldo haven't check in yet...they should've been here by now," the man said.

It took a moment for the information to sink in, but once it did Radar quickly looked back at Dutra and suddenly pulled out his gun.

"Mother fucker!" Radar shouted.

Dutra quickly looked up.

"What?" Dutra shouted.

"Radar just pulled a gun on Dutra..." Steve confirmed through his scope.

"Hold, I can see Dutra's men getting ready to come out of the helicopter," Ray said as he struggled with getting a good sight through his scope. "Goddamn it! I can't fucking see shit!"

Dutra put the phone back into his pocket.

"Who else is here with you?" Radar shouted at Dutra.

"The fuck you talking about?" Dutra quickly asked.

"They're coming out," Ray said.

"You see what they're holding?" Steve quickly asked.

"I'm trying..."

Steve moved his scope to Dutra.

"Come on Ray," Steve said.

"Two of my men are missing!" Radar shouted as he cocked the gun in Dutra's face.

That quickly got Dutra's attention.

"What?"

The men on the helicopter began to pull out a large metal object but Ray still was having trouble trying to see it.

"Fuck," Ray said. He lifted his head away from the scope, grabbed the binoculars that were next to him and looked into those. He quickly locked onto the men getting out of the chopper and finally got a look at what they were holding. Ray's eyes widened with paralyzing fear as he took the first glimpse at what the men were carrying...a B61 warhead.

"Oh my God," Ray said with panic.

Steve quickly turned to the helicopter and saw the tip of the nuke.

"No way..."

"Aim for the target!" Ray quickly said as he dropped the binoculars on the ground; shattering the glass tips.

Steve quickly turned back and locked onto Radar as Ray went back to looking into his scope. His heart pumped like crazy as he looked all around to find Dutra.

"I said two of my men are missing, so tell me, who else did you bring?" Radar said again.

"Nobody," Dutra confessed as he began to turn and look at the helicopter.

His turning was able to grab Ray's attention as he looked through the scope.

"Got him!" Ray shouted.

"Me too!" Steve shouted back.

"Do it!!" Ray shouted.

Both of them fired one shot each at the same time (like they always do when they have to play hide and seek), their eyes locked onto their targets.

As Dutra looked around he noticed two flashes come from the upper floor of the garage and ducked to the ground as fast as he could. He had only just moved when Steve's shot hit Radar in the upper shoulder, while Ray's shot missed and hit the man right beside Radar in the head.

Radar cried out in pain as blood instantly began to flow out of his left shoulder. Suddenly Dutra rose back up with his handgun and took aim in the direction of the shot. He wasn't sure exactly where it went but he didn't fire to shoot back, he fired to get everyone at the fairgrounds into a panic. The shot echoed throughout then entire fairground. Instantly his men dropped the warhead and began firing in the same direction that Dutra was firing in.

"Fuck!" Ray shouted as he took cover.

Steve fired back one shot but quickly ducked when the bullets started to get a little to close for comfort.

"I got Radar!" Steve shouted.

"I missed Dutra! Fuck!" Ray said again.

Dutra fired all the rounds that were in his gun before reloading, grabbing the two suitcases of money and running back to the helicopter.

"Let's move! Now!" Dutra shouted as he quickly ran into the helicopter.

The pilot of the helicopter turned it on and suddenly the roar of the engine revved up as the propellers began to slowly spin. While the helicopter prepared to leave Dutra's men continued to fire into the darkness of the city.

A few bullets hit the wall just in front of Ray and Steve. Ray quickly ducked as Steve suddenly stood back up and began returning fire. Even though Steve couldn't see much, he was still dead accurate as he took down three of Dutra's guys. Ray then quickly stood up and began firing back, shooting one man in the chest and blowing another man's head off.

"Jas! We've been compromised! Come pick us up!" Ray shouted into his radio.

"Roger that. On my way."

"It's gonna be hot Jas!" Ray shouted.

Up in the sky Jasmin quickly turned his helicopter around and started to head back to the fairgrounds as the wind howled into the cabin of the chopper.

"Jesus Christ," Jasmin said to himself as the helicopter rocked around in the sky.

As another bullet, fired by Steve, shot another one of Dutra's men in the head, Dutra quickly turned to the pilot.

"Let's go!" Dutra shouted.

"Roger," The pilot said as he slowly began to lift the helicopter into the air.

Ray quickly fired again and hit a man who had just gotten onto the helicopter. Once he realized the helicopter was about to take off he quickly tapped Steve on the shoulder.

"Dutra's taking off!" Ray shouted.

"Yeah, I see it!" Steve said as he turned his gun and aimed for the helicopter.

Suddenly both of them began firing on the helicopter, shooting as fast as they could. Steve focused on shooting at the propellers and Ray tried to hit Dutra through the window of the passenger door.

Ray's bullets began spraying all over Dutra's door; causing Dutra to duck as the glass was shot out. Dutra grabbed the lever of the helicopter and yanked it up, sending the chopper soaring into the darkness of the sky. Ray fired until his sniper rifle ran dry.

"Shit!" Ray shouted.

"Now what?" Steve asked.

"Dutra's gone but we can't let Radar escape!" Ray said.

"Where the hell is Jas?" Steve shouted as he fired his rifle.

Suddenly a huge explosion lit up the fairgrounds, instantly blowing up one of Radar's vehicles and killing the rest of Dutra's men who were running for cover. The explosion lit up the night sky as Ray looked up and saw Jasmin flying over and shooting the machine guns that were mounted on the front of the helicopter.

"Come on we gotta get to the roof!" Ray ordered.

Steve quickly began to dismount his sniper rifle but Ray stopped him.

"Leave that! We gotta get to the roof now Steve!" Ray shouted.

Steve dropped the rifle and began running toward Ray as Ray made his way up to the top of the garage. Ray could feel the discomfort in his knee beginning to act up again but he kept running as fast as he could despite knowing he was gonna pay later for pushing himself.

Jasmin kept firing down onto the fairgrounds. Bullets cut through the metal of the other SUV like warm butter. All of Dutra's men were clearly down or had taken cover from the air assault. Jasmin fired a few more times and then concentrated on reaching the garage.

Down on the fairgrounds Radar's men quickly helped him into the last usable SUV as blood poured out of his bullet wound. Once Radar was in, he slammed shut the door and turned to the driver.

"Get us out of here! Let's go!" Radar shouted.

The driver of the SUV put it in drive and then sped off the fairgrounds.

"Sir, you okay?" The driver asked Radar.

"Fine, just get us the fuck out of here!" Radar ordered, clearly in pain.

As Ray and Steve climbed the stairs, Jasmin descended down onto the pavement of the top level. Ray and Steve quickly ran to him. The rain came down like bullets, each drop stinging there hands and face, but that didn't stop them. Both knew this was their only chance to take out Radar since Dutra was already gone. As soon as Jasmin set the helicopter down, Ray jumped into the cabin and then helped Steve get up. Once Steve was in Ray quickly turned to Jasmin.

"You alright?" Jasmin shouted.

"Did you hit all the vehicles?" Ray shouted back.

"No! One was driving off the fair grounds as I was landing!" Jasmin said.

"Radar must be in that one!" Steve said.

"You see where it went?" Ray asked Jasmin.

"Yeah! It was heading west!"

"Alright head that way!" Ray quickly ordered.

"Copy!" Jasmin said as he began to lift the helicopter back up into the air.

Ray looked around to try to see if Dutra was still in the area, but it was a wasted effort; darkness surrounded everything but the fires burning down below at the fairgrounds. Ray was pissed, Dutra had once again slipped through his fingertips, but he had to accept the fact that it was too late to do anything about it. All he could do was focus on getting Radar, before he escaped as well.

When the helicopter was high enough off the ground, Jasmin turned it to the west. Quickly Ray and Steve began looking out of the cabin to see if they could see any type of movement or headlights, but the rain made make either one difficult to spot.

"See anything?" Ray asked in a panic.

"No!" Steve shouted back.

"Jas, can you see anything?" Ray shouted to Jasmin.

Jasmin didn't answer right away. He didn't want to let Ray down or get his hopes up, so he very carefully began analyzing the streets. Nothing popped out of the darkness right away until he flew over another street and saw the SUV below. Jasmin double-checked to make sure his eyes weren't deceiving him.

"There! On the street below us!" Jasmin shouted back.

Ray stuck his head out of the cabin and looked. From the corner of his eye he saw the SUV racing down the street.

"Got him!" Ray said as he stood up and took hold of the mounted gun that was hanging in the entrance to the cabin.

Steve looked down and right away saw the neon headlights racing down the street and toward a very familiar place.

"Looks like he's heading to the college!" Steve shouted.

"Jas! Hold us in this position!" Ray shouted.

Jasmin quickly let go of the accelerator and right when the chopper was steady, Ray began firing the machine gun down at the SUV. As soon as Ray began to fire, Steve blocked his ears with his fingers due to the extreme loudness of the gun.

Ray's ears quickly started to ring with every shot he took. He tried to ignore it but the sound was so intense, even Jasmin was trying to block his ears. It was hard to see where the bullets were going but Ray did his best to aim not only where the SUV was but where it was heading.

Back down on the ground you'd never know Ray was struggling to aim, the bullets quickly started hitting the SUV all over. The men inside ducked down as Radar applied pressure to his gunshot wound, but it wasn't helping with the blood flow. When a bullet hit the windshield and cracked it Radar turned to the driver with anger.

"Come on! Get us to the fucking school!" Radar shouted.

The driver floored it and the SUV quickly began to pick up speed. Radar rolled up his window as they approached the college. He knew that the headlights were giving their position away but knew he couldn't shut them off. If he did most likely they would crash into one of the abandon cars scattered throughout the road.

Ray kept firing the gun until the gun ran dry. Once it did, Steve slowly took his fingers out of his ears and then looked down and saw that the SUV was still driving on down the road and picking up speed fast.

"I'm out! Jas! Anyway you can get a shot?" Ray quickly asked.

Jasmin turned the helicopter to the position of the SUV and began to slowly descend back down to the flooded city. Once he was in position it took him a moment to find the SUV.

"Hurry Jas! We gotta stop them from reaching the collage!" Steve shouted.

In a panic Jasmin shook his head all around until he finally saw the lights to the vehicle, and not a moment to soon. They were only moments away from the college.

Jasmin put his finger down on the red button of the controls and began firing at the SUV. Ray got up and moved into the passenger seat of the helicopter as the chopper nose-dived to the street. Ray quickly grabbed the seat belt and put it on.

"Steve, strap in!" Ray shouted.

Steve quickly rushed over to the seat in the back of the cabin and put the seatbelt over his waist as he looked out and saw the buildings getting bigger and bigger.

"Oh shit," Steve whispered under his breath.

Jasmin kept his finger on the red button as bullets shot out of the helicopter and sprayed all over the SUV. Ray was able to see bullets bouncing off the SUV like pinballs. He was sure that the SUV couldn't take much more.

And he was right. Inside the SUV the men were shouting in a panic. Radar was just about to roll the window back down and return fire when a bullet shot through the ceiling and hit the driver on the top of the head. Blood splattered all over Radar's face and the driver suddenly dropped his head, causing the steering wheel to turn sharply to the right. Radar saw that the SUV was about to drive off the road and hit a car that was on the side, so he quickly reached over to take hold of the wheel as more bullets shot through the top and killed two of the three men in the back.

But it was too late. By the time Radar was able to firmly grab the wheel, the SUV suddenly drove onto the curb and slammed head on into the parked car, sending the SUV up in the air and violently landing on the roof. Radar braced for impact and the roof of the vehicle met the tar of the street, instantly crushing the enite top in.

Once Jasmin saw the SUV land, he quickly took his hand off the red button and pulled out of his nosedive. Ray reached to his side and pulled out his sidearm.

"Put us down!" Ray ordered as he began to twist off the silencer of his handgun.

Jasmin slowly began to bring the helicopter back down. Ray looked all over to make sure that Dutra's helicopter wasn't somewhere off in the distance watching and waiting to strike when the time was ready. The helicopter softly landed on the street, kicking up all kind of debris with the wind from the propellers. Once it landed Ray turned and looked at Steve, who was also taking the silencer off of his handgun.

"Let's make this fast Steve!" Ray shouted.

Quickly both Steve and Ray got out of the helicopter and rushed toward the SUV as Jasmin watched, fearing that something was going to happen to one of them. He knew that Ray would want him to stay in the chopper to be ready in case they had to make a quick get away, but something inside told Jasmin to do more then sit there with his stomach grumbling, so he quickly opened the door to the helicopter, picked up his assault rifle and got out.

Knowing at any moment Dutra could suddenly appear in the sky and begin firing, Ray hightailed it to the SUV, running as fast as he could even though he could feel his knee beginning to give way. He did his best to keep going but the pain was getting worse, worse than it ever had been. In the end Ray had no choice but to slow down or else he would be limping for the rest of the foreseeable future.

Smoke rose out of the capsized SUV as Radar slowly opened the passenger side door and began crawling out. Once his head was out he felt a sharp stinging pain on the top of his forehead as the rain pounded on it. He raised his hand and it was suddenly met with blood gushing out of a large cut on his forehead. By the amount of blood alone, Radar knew it was deep. But that was the least of his worries.

Once his eyes began to focus he could clearly see both Ray and Steve running toward him holding guns in there hands. Refusing to go out like a wimp Radar lifted his head back in the SUV and looked around for his weapon that was in his hand before the crash.

"I see movement!" Steve shouted, as he got closer.

Ray put his finger on the trigger, ready to finish what he started when the time came. He thought about just walking up to Radar and blowing a hole through his head but he knew that despite knowing what he already knew about Dutra, Dutra's intentions were still unclear. But if anyone had an idea about what he was planning, it would be Radar.

Ray and Steve were so focused on making sure Radar didn't lift up a weapon at them, that they didn't even see the passenger door on the driver side swing open. As it violently swung wide, the last surviving man quickly stood up, holding a machine gun in his hand. He could hear Ray and Steve running over so he ducked down and waited for them to get close enough to take a shot. And after a brief pause the time came.

The man suddenly stood up from cover and aimed at Steve, who still didn't see the danger that was right in front of him. The man took aim at Steve's head and began to pull the trigger. But before he could push the trigger all the way down, a shot from nowhere met the lower part of his jaw, blowing it off.

The gunshot startled both Ray and Steve. They whirled around to see the man standing up with a gun aimed them. Suddenly they also began firing at the man multiple times until he fell back behind the SUV. Ray turned back for a moment and noticed Jasmin aiming his gun at the man. Ray nodded his head.

"Thanks, Jas," Ray said over the radio.

Ray turned back to Radar and saw him on his knees aiming up his handgun he had found, but before he could get a shot, Steve quickly double tapped his trigger, sending two bullets into Radar's stomach.

The bullets blew large bloody holes into his gut, sending Radar tumbling to ground along with his gun. Once Radar was down Ray ran over to him while Steve stayed where he was and looked around for any type of reinforcements.

Blood began filling up Radar's mouth as his body slowly went into shock. He had been shot before but this time it felt different to him. The pressure from the impact of the bullets began to paralyze not only his body but also his mind as the thought of death began to take over. Suddenly Ray appeared in Radar's now blurry and watery vision and he felt Ray violently grab him and lift him off of the ground.

"Look at me!" Ray shouted before punching Radar in the face.

Radar's head bobbed around like a bobble head.

"Look at me!" Ray shouted again before punching him in the face again.

Giving in to the pain of Ray's punches, Radar slowly turned his head and his eyes met Ray's, whose were clearly filled with rage.

"You tell me right now, what's Dutra up to? Huh? What is he planning to do next?" Ray shouted with all his might.

Radar spit the mouthful of blood onto the ground and slowly a smile grew on his face. Ray knew what he was doing was a waste of time, Radar wasn't anymore afraid of death than Ray was. And talking to a man that isn't afraid of death is a waste of time on everyone's part. But in order to take down Dutra, Ray needed to prepare for what he was planning next.

Ray aimed his gun at Radar's head and cocked it, hoping the coldness of the gun would suddenly make him aware that once Ray pulled that trigger it was all over for him, but it never came. The only thing that came out of it was confirmation that Radar was truly no better then Dutra.

"You...think...it ends here...old man?" Radar was able to muster up.

"Why don't you tell me? You're the one on the wrong end of the gun," Ray firmly said as lightning lit up the fury in his eyes.

"You kill me...and you spend the rest of your life looking over your shoulder...wondering who from my camp will end up blowing your head off..." Radar threatened.

Ray shook his head...then suddenly lowered the gun away from Radar's face, aimed for the sky and fired two shots. He then pushed the tip of the gun back to Radar's face, burning the flesh it met. Radar screamed in pain.

"I can kill you fast, or I can kill you slow. Either way works for me," Ray said.

"Fuck you..." Radar said as he spit in Ray's face.

Ray lowered the gun off of Radar's face again, grabbed Radar's hand and aimed at his middle finger. Ray looked up at Radar to see if Radar was going to fold but Radar kept that smirk on his face. Ray slowly grew a smile on his face and then squeezed the trigger.

The bullet blew off the tip of Radar's middle finger, causing blood to burst out as the tip of the finger fell somewhere on the street. Radar screamed again but even louder.

"Alright! Alright!" Radar shouted.

Ray quickly grabbed Radar by the throat and slammed him onto the SUV tire and leaned into his face.

"Talk," Ray said.

"He's planning on bombing a city in the U.S. I don't know which one!" Radar shouted into the sky.

"Is he working with anyone?" Ray asked.

Radar began to cough as death slowly crept into his central nervous system. Ray began to squeeze tighter on Radar's neck.

"Who's helping him?!" Ray shouted one last time.

Radar spit out more blood and then looked at Ray.

"Everyone..." Radar said with his dying breath.

Ray kept his eye contact with Radar until he saw the light leave his eyes and felt his body loosing up. After letting what Radar said sink in, Ray threw Radar down onto the pavement and fired one shot into the back of his head, sealing Radar's fate forever.

Steve slowly holstered his gun when he saw Ray fire the shot and start to walk back over to him. As Ray got closer Steve could tell that Ray looked worried. He wanted to ask what Radar had said but decided to leave it be as they both walked back to the helicopter and left Radar's body in the quickly rising rainwater.

"Get us out of here!" Ray shouted to Jasmin as they all got back into the helicopter.

Once Steve got inside, Ray slide the door to the helicopter cabin shut as Jasmin began to lift off from the ground.

"Ray...you alright?" Steve asked trying to be supportive.

But Ray didn't answer. He was too busy in deep thought as he tried to figure out what Radar meant by 'everyone'. Ray went into this with just a rough idea of what Dutra was planning to do...but now he was back to square one. At this point Ray didn't know much, but one thing was clear: Dutra was quickly proving to be the most dangerous man Ray's ever been after in all of his years on the job. With each passing moment it was becoming more obvious that the chance of Ray not making it to see his retirement was increasing with every second Dutra remained on the run. That thought haunted him for the rest of the ride back home.

Chapter 9: The Upper Hand

As the team made their way back home, Joey was in Washington, speeding toward the F.B.I. headquarters. He had received a phone call from Sullivan, telling him a serious situation was taking place. Joey asked what was going on but Sullivan hung up before giving Joey any type of answer.

The traffic was damn near in gridlock when Joey got the call. He flipped on the red and blue lights in his gray undercover car but it didn't do much good. It took him a while to be able to find a spot to drive over the curb, but once he did he quickly took the opportunity and floored it.

Judging by Sullivan's voice alone, Joey knew something big must've been going on or else Sullivan would've just waited for the morning to get in touch with him. As he drove back onto the road and ran a red light he started to wonder what it could be.

After his already twelve-hour day, Joey had been looking forward to going home and attempting to relax, but by now Joey was getting use to the fact that the job comes before anything else in his life (that's why he was still single as he approached his thirtieth birthday). It was at moments like this that he hated the job.

As he made it to the front of F.B.I. headquarters he quickly parked in a fire zone, ran out of his car and rushed in, hoping that whatever was happening inside wouldn't be as demanding as the past few days had been. However, he was wrong; what lay ahead would truly test Joey to the point of desperation.

Walking into the main computer floor of headquarters he stopped dead in his tracks when saw what was going on. People were franticly talking and running around everywhere.

From computer workers to dozens of Secret Service and F.B.I. agents, it was clear that everyone was there. It got to the point that so much was happening right before his eyes that Joey didn't know where to turn. It would take Sullivan walking right up to him and hitting his shoulders to truly get back his attention.

"Took you long enough," Sullivan said as he began walking over to a computer terminal.

"Sorry, got here as fast as I could. What the hell is going on?"

"One of the C.I.A. computers got hacked about two hours ago," Sullivan confessed as he looked down.

"We're just finding out about this now?" Joey shot back.

"Yeah. Hell, I just found out thirty minuets ago," Sullivan said.

"Any idea on what got hacked?"

"Still trying to figure that out. Anything yet?" Sullivan asked Jamir, the computer software technician who was working on the computer that Sullivan was looking at.

"Give me a second," Jamir said without looking up.

Joey looked down at the computer monitor (Honestly, Joey wasn't the best when it came to knowing about computers. He gave up working on them when he got a virus on his home computer after looking up porn. He wished he could figure out how to really use a computer, because honestly that's where the money was, but he just never had the patience to do so.).

"You hear back from Ray yet?" Joey asked.

"Nothing yet," Sullivan said without breaking focus of the computer screen.

Joey nodded as he suddenly began worrying about Ray.

"What about Steve or Bob?" Joey asked.

"Joe, relax. We'll hear something when we hear something. Right now let's try and focus on who just breached the national security data base," Sullivan ordered.

Joey took his eyes off of Sullivan and looked down at Jamir as Jamir began shaking his head in amazement.

"I don't know who was able to do this, but whoever it was has access to some very serious software. They got past all five firewalls." He typed away on the keyboard.

"Is there a way to reroute the breach and trace it back to where it came from?" Sullivan asked.

"Nope. It's a clean in and out. Probably the only thing I can do is search around and maybe access the audit trail of what the hackers looked up," Jamir said in a panic.

"How long will that take?" Sullivan demanded.

"Ten, fifteen minutes," Jamir quickly said.

Sullivan looked as his wrist watch, confirming he was as pressed for time as he thought he was.

"Make it five and I'll buy you a beer," Sullivan barked.

"Alright, I'll try."

Sullivan took a deep breath and walked away from Jamir as he tried to calm his racing mind. Joey followed.

"How's Roader?" Joey asked.

Sullivan cleared his throat.

"Same. His kid is still in ICU. He must be a fucking wreck. Gonna take a miracle for that kid to recover." Sullivan took out his cell phone and looked at the screen.

"Any ideas on who this was?" Joey asked.

"Got an idea but can't really say for sure," Sullivan softly said.

"Dutra?" Joey asked as he leaned closer to Sullivan.

Sullivan nodded his head.

"Yeah...but I have no idea how he was able to do it. Should've been in Florida at that meeting with Radar. You need lots of computer power to do this; you can't get that kind of access just from an average laptop," Sullivan said, thinking out loud.

"Think he had help?"

"How the hell else could he have gotten in?" Sullivan asked.

Joey nodded. "No idea. This situation is getting more complicated by the second."

Sullivan shook his head in agreement, thinking about how they could find out who could've breached their database. It took him a moment but he finally got an idea; the only one that he could.

"Alright, head back to the office and start pulling reports on agents that have either retired or been fired. Go as far back as ten years. Try finding anyone with connections to the Dutra camp," Sullivan ordered.

"That'll take hours!"

"Just do it. Right now it's the only thing we can do. Let's just pray that this leads to nothing. Last thing we need right now is a conspiracy theory rumor circling around here," Sullivan said.

But as Joey turned to go, Jamir quickly got both of their attentions.

"Sullivan. You're gonna want to take a look at this!" Jamir said.

Both Sullivan and Joey quickly hustled back to Jamir's workstation, and once they saw what he was able to pull up, their hearts sank to the floor. Fear suddenly set into Sullivan as he stared at the screen containing the names of all undercover United States agents throughout the world.

"Scroll down," Sullivan said to Jamir.

Jamir took a hold of his computer mouse and began sliding down until he reached the bottom. Right at the bottom of the audit trail was a picture of Ray and the entire team. Sullivan quickly grabbed Jamir and pushed him off the chair.

"Are we looking at what I think we're looking at?" Jamir asked.

Joey quickly turned to him.

"Give us a second."

Jamir shook his head and then walked away while Joey looked back at the screen and watched Sullivan click on the picture of Ray.

"Are they compromised?" Joey asked.

"Not just them, Joe, there's hundreds of names on here," Sullivan said with mortal fear in his voice.

Joey shook his head in disbelief.

"Yep Ray, Steve, Bob—the entire team is compromised, goddamn it!" Sullivan said as he looked through the trail.

Joey was in a panic but was trying to remain calm and think what Dutra would do with the information on Ray and his team. He was sure that Dutra would now go after them but it seemed too easy; all Joey had to do was call Ray and tell him to keep an eye out. Something was off; Dutra was smarter than that. Joey began thinking about all the times him and Ray talked to try and figure out how Dutra would go after Ray, and suddenly it clicked.

"Oh my God," Joey said.

Sullivan kept his eyes on the screen but acknowledged Joey.

"What?"

"Ray's daughter..." Joey said.

Sullivan quickly lifted his eyes of the computer screen and looked up at Joey. That's all Joey needed to say and suddenly it made sense. If Dutra was going to go after Ray, that's how he would do it. Sullivan quickly stood up and the both of them ran out of the chaotic situation room and headed out to their cars, hoping they could reach Emily before it was too late.

II

As Joey and Sullivan got into their undercover cruisers and drove away from headquarters as fast as they could, back at Emily's apartment Torque was trying to fall asleep but all he seemed able to do was watch the ceiling fan go round and round over Emily's bed. Sweat was still on his chest from the sex they had just had. He rolled over and tucked his hands under the purple pillowcase his head was resting on and made another attempt to fall back asleep (it wasn't that Torque was uncomfortable, it was just that he was still nervous about how Sullivan would react about him quitting Ray's team).

The blanket that he was under was made out of a cloth like material that Torque always thought made him get too warm, making it hard to fall asleep, so he began pushing off the blanket, trying not to bother Emily. But Emily could feel the bed moving, causing her to fall out of sleep mode.

"Everything okay?" Emily asked.

"Yeah, fine. Just a little warm," Torque said before leaning in and kissing Emily's soft arm.

Emily smiled.

"I don't normally do this..." Emily began to say.

Torque shook his head.

"I don't either," Torque said, even though that was a bit of a lie.

"Just been a long day," Emily said.

Torque softly nodded his head and put his arm over Emily.

"You wanna talk about it?" Torque asked.

"Not really...saw my father for the first time in I don't know how many years...and it was just tough to do," Emily said.

Torque sighed. He felt bad, not just for Emily but anyone who had to deal with having a father that was anything but around. It was something Torque knew all to well.

"Yeah, I know the feeling," Torque confessed.

Emily looked at him.

"You do?" She asked softly.

"Yeah I do. My old man took off when I was two. Don't even know if he's still alive anymore to be honest," Torque said as he rubbed Emily's soft skin.

"Not fun to live with is it?" She asked with a chuckle.

"No, it's not."

Emily leaned into Torque and gave him a kiss, a long passionate kiss. When she broke away she looked into his eyes with a smile. Torque returned the smile and then got up and put his underwear, pants and shirt on.

"You're not leaving are you?" Emily asked as she yawned.

Torque smiled. "No, just going to use the bathroom," he said.

"Well hurry back, I'm cold," Emily said with a smile.

Torque nodded and walked over to the bedroom door. He opened it and made his way to the bathroom. While he started taking a leak he began to really think about everything that was going on and everything that had just happened.

Torque knew it was way too early to have true feelings about Emily, but he couldn't help but focus on that idea when it suddenly popped in. At first he did his best to deny the idea but when he realized that if this was just like one of the other countless one night stands he had during his high school and college years, he would've already left by now.

Torque had been with a lot of girls, from wild and crazy to wannabee rednecks, but Emily was different. He didn't get the feeling that Emily slept with random guys often; he felt like she just did it to clear her head, maybe for the first time in her life. Torque could see Emily's vulnerability and that wasn't something many girls show right away, and Torque liked that. He felt that if she could trust him enough to express those kinds of emotions, then maybe Torque could finally do it too, instead of keeping everything bottled in.

Torque flushed the toilet once he was done and started heading out of the bathroom with a smile on his face and a feeling inside like everything might be all right. Christ knows he hadn't felt that in a while. He was still nervous about what tomorrow would bring, but in that moment he just wanted to get back to Emily.

But once he exited the bathroom and got into the hall he quickly stopped as he looked at the bedroom door. He began to retrace his footsteps leading to when he left the bedroom and once he did he couldn't help be feel a little bit confused.

The bedroom door was closed all the way, which seemed very odd because when Torque left he kept it open a crack; he was positive he did. He started wondering if Emily got up and closed it but quickly dismissed the idea after realizing that if she had, he would've heard her close it (or even get up).

Letting his guard down he thought he was just overthinking the whole thing and began to walk back down to the bedroom. He was reaching for the door knob when suddenly out of nowhere, the spare bedroom door opened and Vincent suddenly body slammed Torque to the floor.

Torque violently landed on his back with no type of breath left in him from the massive hit Vincent gave him. Torque began to slowly get up but by the time he was able to get to his knees, Vincent was already up and kneed Torque in the face, knocking Torque down to the floor again.

Suddenly the bedroom door swung open and four men dressed all in black came out. They were holding machine guns, with the last man holding Emily in a chokehold, his other hand over her mouth. Dazed and confused, Torque once again tried to get up.

"Emily!" Torque shouted.

Emily struggled in the man's arms and was able to bite the man's finger as hard as she could. In pain the man screamed and quickly retracted his hand from her mouth.

"Johnny!" Emily screamed.

"You fucking bitch!" The man who had just gotten his finger bit shouted.

Torque bounded to his feet and rushed over to Vincent, intending to elbow him in the back. But before his elbow impacted, Vincent quickly turned around, blocked it and then began punching Torque in the face.

Torque blocked a few but when Vincent brought his fist up and punched Torque in the jaw, Torque instantly fell back and down to his knees. With a smile on his face, Vincent grabbed Torque, stood him up and pushed him all the way down the hall and into the living room as the men walked past him with Emily and started heading out of the apartment.

Torque wiped the blood from his lip looked at Vincent. Vincent gave him a smile and then pulled out a gun from his hip holster and aimed it at Torque.

Fear trickled down Torque's spine, sending a shockwave through his body. Vincent cocked the hammer of his pistol and kept his eye on Torque. Torque looked at him for a moment and then looked into the dark barrel of the handgun.

"Tough motherfucker, I'll give you that," Vincent said.

Torque looked back up into Vincent's eyes.

"Normally this would be the point where I would aim for your head and pull the trigger, but not this time," Vincent said just before throwing the gun onto the floor.

Once Torque saw the gun get thrown from Vincent's hand he lunged at Vincent, body slamming him onto the kitchen counter. When he felt Vincent's back hit the counter, he stood up and began punching Vincent in the face as hard as he possibly could.

On the fourth punch, Vincent blocked and brought up his right hand and punched Torque in the throat. Torque fell back and began coughing from the pain in his throat. Knowing he was wounded, Vincent walked over to Torque and began punching him in the stomach and then the face.

After two heavy and brutal punches to the face Vincent grabbed Torque by the back of the head and slammed his head onto the counter. The blow knocked the wind out of Torque, instantly dropping him to the ground.

Once Torque was down, Vincent walked over to Torque, grabbed both his arms and slid him back into the living room. At this point Torque couldn't even shake the stars from his eyes, let alone try to fight back. When Vincent dropped him into the middle of the living room he remained still and prayed that Vincent wouldn't do anything else. It was almost a relief when one of the armed men walked into the house with a gallon of gasoline.

"She in the car?" Vincent asked the man.

"Yeah, but we gotta move. One of the neighbors saw us," the man said.

"Fuck, get in the car. I'll be right there."

Vincent snatched the container of gas from the man, opened the top and started pouring it all over the kitchen and then living room. The place quickly began to fill up with the smell of gasoline.

As Vincent walked into the living room from the kitchen he started pouring gas all over the furniture and the entertainment system but he didn't use all of it; there was still some left when he walked over to Torque and knelt down next to him.

"Like I said your tough kid, just not enough," Vincent said before he started pouring gas all over Torque.

Torque quickly shut his eyes to avoid getting any gas in them. Vincent poured the gas all over Torque's body until nothing was left in the container. Once it was gone, Vincent threw the container down the hall and then walked over to pick up his gun. Torque knew he was in trouble as he struggled to try and stay awake. He could feel blood running down his face as he lay on the floor in pain. He kept still as he tried to look for a way out. When he saw Vincent move toward the door he quickly shut his eyes.

Vincent cocked his gun and then looked back down at Torque.

"Mr. Dutra Vacca sends his warmest regards," Vincent said.

Torque inhaled softly as he braced for the flames.

Vincent aimed for the floor of the kitchen and fired one shot. The moment the bullet hit the floor, fire instantly appeared and quickly began to spread. Vincent lowered his gun and then ran out of the apartment and down to the van.

The moment he heard Vincent take off, Torque leaped to his feet and ran down the hall as fire quickly engulfed the kitchen and then spread into the living room. Torque rushed into Emily's bedroom and closed the door in a panic. Smoke was already starting to come through the bottom of the door when Torque grabbed his clothes from the bed.

Torque began coughing as the smoke intensified in the room. He knew there was no way he was going to be leaving through the living room. He was going to have to improvise if he was going to survive.

He rushed to the window at the far end of the room and threw it open. Once he opened it all the way he stuck his head out and saw it wasn't that far down (if you don't call two stories far). Torque took one last look at the door. The smoke had become so thick he couldn't even see it anymore. He took a deep breath and then pushed his feet through the window.

Torque had always been afraid of heights (another part of the job he hated), but he tried to keep focus on his feet. As he got both his feet out, he started to push his legs and midsection out. He was just about half way out when an explosion from the kitchen rocked the place, sending a ball of fire rushing through the hallway and into the bedroom. Not knowing what else to do, Torque let go of the window frame and began falling.

Fearing the worst, Torque closed his eyes and put his hands over his head as he fell. The heat from the fireball warmed up his back just before the coldness of the ground cooled it down. When he met the ground, whatever air he was able to get back quickly left as pain shot through his back.

He slowly opened his eyes to fire burning through the bedroom window. And once he knew—besides a few cuts and bruises—that he was okay, he took a moment trying to get back his strength, wondering what had just happened. But little did Torque know that Dutra had just gained the upper hand.

III

Ray, Steve and the rest of the guys made it back to the body shop just before dawn. As each of them walked in, it was clear that they were exhausted, tired and drained. Ray slammed his sniper rifle onto the ground, causing Bob, Kevin and Tommy to jump. Ray then walked into his office and slammed the door as hard as he could.

"So I take it you didn't get Dutra," Tommy said.

Steve took a deep breath and then looked at Bob.

"What did you guys find at the cabin?" Steve asked.

Bob exhaled. "Just what I thought we would find...nothing. It was a complete waste of time," He looked at Kevin, who had a worried look on his face. "Oh and we owe Kevin a new truck."

"You make sure everything was taken care of before you left?" Steve asked.

"Yeah, burned that fucking place to the ground," Tommy said.

Steve shook his head. "Good."

While Steve, Bob and Tommy talked, Jasmin focused his attention to Kevin, who was clearly worried about something.

"You okay?" Jasmin asked as he walked over to him.

"Yeah...fine. Heard you guys missed Dutra," Kevin said.

"Oh man it was crazy shit. Fun, but crazy. Any luck at the cabin?" Jasmin asked.

"No...dead end," Kevin said, lying through his teeth.

"That sucks. Wish you guys were there...we could've use yeah," Jasmin said.

"There's always next time," Kevin said as he patted Jasmin on the back. "How was flying the helicopter?"

"Horrible. Now I remember why I stopped doing it," Jasmin said as he took a candy bar from his pocket.

"My God Jasmin! You're like a vending machine!" Tommy shouted from across the room when he saw Jasmin take a huge bite of the chocolate bar.

"Give me a break Tommy. I haven't eaten all day!"

Tommy chuckled as he looked back at Steve and Bob.

"So now what?" Bob asked Steve.

"Not much we can do now. Let's all just head home for a while. Hopefully either Sullivan or Joey come up with something," Steve said as he shook his head.

"Okay. Jas, Tommy, Kevo, let's go home!" Bob shouted as he walked away.

Steve turned and looked at Ray's door. He gave some serious thought to going in and at least letting Ray know that he was going home, but decided it was best for Ray to be left alone, so he started to follow the guys out.

"You're leaving too?" Bob asked.

"Yeah. Ray needs some time to himself," Steve confessed.

Bob knew what that meant so decided to keep any other questions to himself for the time being. Bob opened the door and the guys started walking out, all except for Kevin. As Tommy walked out Steve walked out behind him and began closing the door but suddenly stopped when he saw Kevin was still in the room.

"Kevo! Let's go," Steve said.

Kevin exhaled deeply and then looked at Steve.

"I gotta talk to Ray really quick," Kevin said.

Steve shook his head in disbelief.

"Don't say I didn't warn you," Steve said before shutting the door and heading home with the rest of the guys.

Kevin nodded and when the door closed all the way he walked over to Ray's office. He knew that bothering Ray when he was like this wasn't the wisest thing to do, but Kevin had to...this couldn't wait.

Kevin got to the door and got ready to knock when he realized that even if he knocked, Ray wouldn't acknowledge it anyway, so he very slowly opened the door and walked in. The office was dark, not even the light on Ray's desk was on, but somewhere in the darkness he knew Ray was there.

"What do you want Kevo?" Ray asked as he looked out the window.

"How'd you know it was me?" Kevin asked.

"Because everyone else is smart enough not to bother me when I'm in here thinking," Ray quickly shot back.

"Sorry." The only thing Kevin could come up with.

"What's up?" Ray asked as he opened the drawer to his desk and took out his bottle of scotch.

"We found something...or rather I found something at the cabin," Kevin began to say.

"A million dollars? Cause if you found that, just give me half. I can live off of half a million dollars for the rest of my days," Ray said.

"Ha...I wish."

"What did you find Kevo?" Ray asked.

Kevin inhaled deeply.

"We all found guns..."

"No surprise there," Ray said.

"But while Tommy and Bob searched the cabin, I was able to hack into one of the computers I found in the basement," Kevin said.

"What was on it?"

"Powerful software...I mean stuff only the F.B.I. and other government agencies would be able to get their hands on...so I looked through it and..."

"Come on spill it out Kevin," Ray said in a rather angry voice.

"Ray it looks like they're trying to hack into the F.B.I. server...and with the programs on that computer alone, I'm sure they'll be able to...it's only a matter of time...if they haven't already," Kevin finished.

Ray shook his head in the darkness.

"Jesus Christ," Ray said softly but loud enough for Kevin to hear it.

Kevin shook his head in agreement.

"I don't know why they are though, couldn't figure that out," Kevin started saying.

"Yeah you can..." Ray interrupted.

"Sir?"

"You can figure it out..."

Kevin thought about it; really thought about it, and an idea slowly popped into his mind.

"He's looking for us?" Kevin asked.

"Yeah, he's looking for us. He knows just from our brush together at the Lincoln Memorial that we weren't just some Secret Service agents in civilian clothes, and by now he's probably gotten a plan in place to hunt us all down."

Kevin's eyes widened with fear.

"You really think it would come to that?" He asked.

Ray turned and gave him a serious look, the answer lying directly in Ray's dark eyes.

"Shit," Kevin said.

"Have you told the others about the software at the cabin?" Ray asked.

"Uh no. I wanted to let you know first. Figured it was best for them to hear this coming from you."

Ray shook his head as he rocked in his chair.

"This guy Dutra is good Kevin. I knew just from hearing about him that he wasn't going to be easy for us, but I never would've guessed it was going to be this tough to get him. Maybe I'm losing my touch after all these years," Ray confessed in the darkness.

"Come on Ray, don't say that. Age is just a number," Kevin said.

Ray chuckled for a moment.

"Yeah, I remember when I use to think that too. But you hit a certain point where it stops being just a number and it starts to be a lifestyle. It happens over time so you don't notice it until one day, and once you do, you realize it's been happening right before your very eyes for years. I should've retired years ago. Too stubborn for my own damn good I guess," Ray said as he took his first sip of alcohol of the night.

Kevin moved closer and sat down on the chair in front of Ray's desk. Kevin still couldn't see his face, but could at least see the outline of Ray now.

"You know we go all over the world, get put into places that are hell on earth, and there's days where it feels like I'm not cut out for this," Kevin began.

"Some people aren't."

"Which is my point: some people aren't. They don't have the strength and energy to do what we do on a regular basis. And all this time I've been here, I've never heard you complain about anything once. You don't sit behind a desk and give orders to us, Ray. You're right there next to us, every time. When we're out there getting shot at by God knows who, I know that I can always count of you to be right there with us, trying to come up with a plan to get us back home. I've never doubted that you could keep up with us. Hell, most of the time it's us having to keep up with you. We're all bound to get older, hell that's life. But you've kept up with the times. You're the best of the best Ray. You're a legend. Don't let age take that away from you."

Ray grew a smile on his face in the darkness, and for the first time in a while, a part of Ray briefly started thinking that maybe age *still* was just a number.

"Thanks Kevo...means a lot," Ray said.

"Anytime Ray," Kevin said firmly.

Ray smiled as Kevin got up and started for the door.

Ray said, "You know I've never been afraid of anything in my life, until I sat down and really started to think about time. Knowing that it takes everything and nothing can stop it just scares the shit out of me. Guess with everything going on, I still can't seem to stop thinking about that."

Kevin stopped opening the door and looked back at Ray.

"Time doesn't take memories Ray," Kevin said.

Ray shook his head. "Hope you're right Kevo."

"Take it easy Ray, I'll see you tomorrow."

"You too, Kevo, you too," Ray whispered to himself.

It was in that moment that Ray regretted having disliked Kevin when he first started out. Back then, he thought Kevin was just a hothead looking for quick money and the chance to fire a gun. But over time Kevin really proved Ray wrong. In Ray's opinion, Kevin was right up there with Steve: not just a loyal worker, but also a person he could call a friend at the end of the day.

As Kevin walked out he couldn't help but feel bad for Ray. Kevin knew getting older was no picnic (he learned that the hard way when he saw his grandmother die from cancer, which haunted him for years), but Kevin had never really thought about getting older until after he talked to Ray. He was so busy trying to live now that he never thought about thirty, forty years down the road.

Kevin walked out of the body shop and headed over to his wrecked truck. When he looked up at it he started to think back to Bob and Tommy fighting, and he couldn't help but laugh about it. He was honestly still surprised by what happened. He wasn't worried about the damage to it though (despite babying it for all these years). He knew eventually Tommy or Bob would end up fixing it for him.

Kevin was so deep in thought as he crossed the road to get into his truck that he didn't even notice an all-black car slowly approaching him from the north. Kevin unlocked his truck and opened the door. Once he opened it the headlights of the car got his attention from the side mirror of his door. Kevin turned and looked as the car stopped and the passenger window rolled down.

"Hi I'm sorry to bother you, but I was wondering if you could help me out," the driver said in a very pleasant voice.

"Yeah, sure," Kevin said with a smile (the smile mostly coming from thinking about Tommy pissing all over Bob).

"I'm looking for a guy by the name of Kevin Bear. I was told he's around here," the man said.

"You're looking at him my friend," Kevin said.

"Uh, you're Kevin Bear, huh?"

"I am."

"Excellent," Street said from the driver side of the car.

Kevin leaned down and looked into the car, suddenly losing the smile on his face when he saw Street was aiming a black 9mm at him. His heart began to race.

"Give Ray a message for me will yeah? Tell him this is from Dutra Vacca," Street said in an ice-cold voice.

Kevin's eyes grew wide and before he even had the chance to react, Street fired one shot. The bullet struck Kevin's neck, creating a red mist that sprayed all over the passenger side door.

Back in the office Ray jumped out of his seat and, grabbing his handgun from off his desk, bolted out of the body shop.

As soon as Kevin fell to the ground, Street got out of the car and walked around to Kevin. Blood was leaking out of Kevin as he jerked around on the ground. Street smiled, and then suddenly fired three more shots into Kevin's chest.

Ray looked around to figure out where the shots came from. He looked until he saw Street getting back into his black car and quickly taking off. He didn't see Kevin on the ground until the black car drove out of the way, but once he did, Ray's heart sank.

"Kevin!" Ray shouted.

Ray turned and fired multiple shots at the car. He fired until his clip was out. He quickly reloaded it and aimed at it again but the car was too far out of sight. Once he realized that, he went running across the street and dropped to his knees when he reached Kevin.

"Kevin!" Ray shouted as he looked down at the bullet holes in Kevin's body.

Kevin gagged as blood flowed out of his mouth. Ray quickly dropped the gun on the ground and then gently picked up Kevin's head.

"Kevin! You're gonna be all right! You hear me?" Ray asked.

Kevin opened his mouth but only blood was able to come out at first as Ray reached into his pocket, took out his cell phone and dialed for help.

"Yeah, I have a gunshot victim at Ray's Auto Body...please hurry!" Ray said as he hung up the phone. "Kevin...it's gonna be okay...you're gonna be okay..."

Kevin slowly lifted his left hand, grabbed Ray's arm and started to pull. Ray lowered his down to Kevin's mouth. He waited for Kevin to say something, but more blood suddenly gushed out and sprayed all over Ray's face and shirt. Ray began to tremble in fear.

"Kevin...who did this...?" Ray asked.

"...D....Du...Dut..." Kevin was only able to muster up.

But that's all Ray needed to hear. He knew who it was. Rage began to build in Ray's eyes, behind his tears.

"We'll get him you hear? You're gonna be fine and then we're gonna go out and get him. I promise," Ray said to Kevin as he looked into his eyes.

But even though Ray was trying to be optimistic, he could tell just by the look in Kevin's eyes that he wasn't going to make it. More tears began to fill up Ray's face when he saw a tear run from the corner of Kevin's eye.

"I love you, kid," Ray said as his voice broke.

Kevin gave Ray one last nod and then took his eyes off Ray and looked up into the starry night sky above him. And with one final breath, Kevin dropped his head as Ray felt the energy leave Kevin's body.

With tears in his eyes and the sound of distant police sirens down the road, Ray leaned down, turned Kevin's head to shut his eyes and said his final goodbye as he began sobbing into Kevin's shirt.

Chapter 10: Vengeful Sins

While Ray impatiently waited for the ambulance, so he could follow it to the hospital, Sullivan and Joey raced for Emily's apartment. It didn't take too long for them to reach it, maybe about a half an hour, but to them it felt like an eternity. During the ride both had a bad feeling rumbling around in their gut but neither one of them spoke up about it at first. It took seeing the smoke and flames rising up from her apartment to break the silence in the car.

"Oh Jesus," Sullivan said as he turned onto the street and saw dozens of police cars and fire trucks.

The sight struck Joey to his core as he began to fear the worst for Emily. He knew Ray was still pissed from before, but if anything happened to Emily, all bets were off to get the friendship they had back.

As they pulled up to the burnt down apartment building Ray's words about doing what he could to protect his daughter kept playing in his mind. He almost starting getting tears just thinking about having to tell Ray that Emily was hurt, or worse. He started telling himself that if he had to tell Ray the news he would have to do it face to face. Telling him about it over the phone wouldn't cut it this trip.

Sullivan quickly put the car in park and they both stepped out. Police and fire fighters filled the area as water from a fire hose continued to spray what was left of the now ruined building. It was a site that neither one of them could contemplate, but in order to get to the bottom of it, they knew they were going to have to try and keep focus. Sullivan ran over to the police officer in charge.

"Hey," Sullivan shouted as he walked over.

"Sir you'll have to step back! This is a closed scene," The chief shouted back.

Sullivan quickly took out his badge and held it up in the air.

"Agent Sullivan, F.B.I. and this is my partner, Agent Selerno," Sullivan said as he pointed to Joey.

"F.B.I.? The hell are you guys doing here?" The chief asked.

"We're looking for a women who lived here, did you get anyone out?" Sullivan asked and Joey walked closer to the chief.

"So far we only got one person out, afraid he might be our only survivor," the chief said in a cold, emotionless voice.

As soon as Joey heard the chief say 'he', both Joey and Sullivan knew that the worst had come true.

"Fuck," Joey said putting his hands in the air.

"Can we talk to him?" Sullivan asked.

"You think it can wait? The guy fell out of a three-story building. Not sure he's up to talking about it," The chief said.

"No it can't wait. Now where is he?" Sullivan shouted.

The chief rolled his eyes and then pointed to the line of ambulances.

"Back of the second ambulance."

Sullivan quickly headed to the ambulance while the chief shook his head at him.

"Fucking F.B.I.," The chief muttered under his breath, before walking away and over to some of the other officers on site.

Joey stayed put and looked at the building in horror. He knew he should've stayed with Sullivan but he couldn't stop himself from walking over to it as a firefighter walked out.

"Excuse me, are there any other survivors?" Joey asked the firefighter as he walked out.

The firefighter took off his helmet.

"No. Place is a complete mess. It'll take us a while to go through everything, guess about ten families lived here. Why?" The fire fighter asked.

"I'm looking for someone," Joey said softly.

The fire fighter shook his head and then patted Joey on the arm.

"Sorry for you loss," the firefighter said before walking away.

What was left of Joey's heart sank to the bottom of his foot. He was heartbroken for Ray. Joey knew that Ray wouldn't be able to handle this (honestly how do you tell a father that his child is gone?). After Joey took in the view until he couldn't bear to look at it anymore he returned to the car.

Sullivan quickly ran to the ambulance. He started running faster when he saw it start up. Once he got to the side of it he began banging on the side, causing the driver to quickly put his foot on the brake. As soon as it stopped, Sullivan walked over to the driver side door.

"Hey what the hell are you doing? We're trying to get to the hospital here!" The driver shouted.

Sullivan lifted up his badge again.

"I'm Agent Sullivan. I need to talk to the guy," Sullivan quickly said.

The driver exhaled deeply and then looked back at Sullivan.

"Alright. Make it fast."

Sullivan shook his head and then ran to the back door.

"Fucking F.B.I." The driver said as he put the ambulance in park.

Sullivan got to the door and knocked twice. As he waited for the door to open he started thinking that there was a real chance that this would be just one big dead end but in that moment the survivor was the only lead they had. But little did Sullivan know who the survivor was.

The door quickly opened. As it opened Sullivan grabbed it, opened it all the way, and jumped inside. The paramedic in the back looked up and then stood up and stopped Sullivan in his tracks.

"Hey you can't be back here!" The paramedic said.

"Easy, F.B.I.," Sullivan said.

Sullivan lifted up his badge again as he looked the paramedic in the eye, but suddenly his eyes began moving off of the paramedic and then focused on the survivor, who looked very familiar.

"Torque?" Sullivan asked in confusion.

Torque looked up at Sullivan.

"Sullivan?"

"What are you doing here??" Both of them asked at the same time.

"You're supposed to be with Ray and his team," Sullivan said firmly.

"Yeah, long story, but I quit," Torque said as he dropped his head.

"You what?" Sullivan asked with anger.

"Never mind that, why the hell are you here?" Torque shot back.

"I'm here for Ray's daughter," Sullivan said.

"What?" Torque asked.

"I don't have time to explain but Ray and his team's identity have been compromised. I came here to get his daughter," Sullivan briefly explained.

Torque was beyond confused. He knew Ray had a daughter but the way Ray talked, he made it seem like she was living on the other side of the world.

"Wait a minute...back up...what's his daughter's name?" Torque asked.

"Emily."

Torque's eyes grew with fear.

"Oh my God," Torque said.

"What?" Sullivan asked.

"Dutra's men have her," Torque said in a panic as he tried to grasp the fact that Emily was really Ray's Emily.

"What? How could you possibly," Sullivan began to say before he answered his own question.

Sullivan looked down for a moment and then looked back up at Torque in anger. Torque shrugged his shoulders.

"Sullivan, I had no idea. I met her at a bar and..." Torque started to say.

But Sullivan didn't want to listen to it. He quickly slammed the ambulance door shut and then started back to the car. Sullivan paid no attention to Torque quickly opening back up the ambulance door.

"Sullivan wait!" Torque shouted as he ran to catch up to Sullivan.

But Sullivan didn't stop. He had other things he had to deal with, but Torque was persistent.

"Sullivan!" Torque said again as he grabbed Sullivan's shoulder.

Sullivan quickly pushed Torque's hand off of him then turned around and looked at Torque.

"Get your fucking hands off me!" Sullivan shouted.

"Let me explain," Torque began to say.

"No! Even if I had time to listen, which I don't, I still wouldn't. You fucked up, Torque! Instead of thinking with the head that's above your shoulders, you were too busy thinking with the one in your pants!" Sullivan said.

Torque couldn't do anything but look down in shame knowing that Sullivan was right, Torque had let his guard down.

"Do you have any idea what this will do to Ray when he finds out? Do you care? Do you give a shit at all that Dutra will probably end up killing the poor girl?" Sullivan asked.

"I didn't know she was his daughter! Okay? It just happened. What else do you want me to fucking say?" Torque asked in frustration.

Sullivan shook his head as he looked around.

"Nothing. Just get the fuck out of here. I'll deal with this now. You've done enough. I should've listened to Ray when I had the chance, he was right: you really are just another disappointment, and I was a fool to think differently. Trust me though, it won't happen again."

Torque tried to come up with something, anything to try and make sense of the situation, but he couldn't. Sullivan's words were just too difficult to top. All Torque could do was stand there with the mistake on his shoulders.

Sullivan gave Torque one last look and then walked away from him as another ambulance pulled up to the scene. Torque didn't know what to do. He knew he couldn't just walk away from this now. Not because he wanted to prove to Sullivan that he was wrong, but because Torque realized that even though he had only known Emily for a few very short hours, he was sure that if he had the chance to spend more time with her, there was a strong chance that she might be the girl he's spent most of his adult life looking for. Torque never believed in love at first sight until his eyes met hers. In the end he knew what he had to do, he had to face Ray again and prove that he wasn't like everyone else from his generation.

As Sullivan walked back to the car he started to wish he could go back and listen to what Ray had to say when Ray mentioned to him that he was planning on retiring. It was in that moment when Sullivan realized that Ray had been right all along. He just hoped there was still time fix his mistake and win back Ray's trust. But he knew before he could do that he was going to have to somehow tell Ray that Dutra now had the upper hand. Sullivan began trying to come up with a way of telling Ray when his cell phone began vibrating in his pants pocket. He quickly stopped his train of thought and took out his cell phone.

"Sullivan."

"He's been shot," Ray said, shaken up.

"Ray?" Sullivan asked loud enough for Torque to hear.

Torque quickly ran over to Sullivan.

"They got him," Ray was barley able to say.

"Ray, Ray! Slow down. What's happening? Who's been shot?" Sullivan asked in a panic.

"..."

Just before Sullivan was able to ask again the line went dead.

"Ray? Ray!" Sullivan shouted before he lowered his cell phone away from his ear. "Fuck."

Torque quickly looked at Sullivan.

"What's going on with Ray?" Torque quickly asked.

"Nothing you need to know about," Sullivan said as he began to walk away.

But Torque wasn't going to just get pushed to the side, not again. Too much was already at stake and Torque knew that whatever Dutra was planning on doing next, Sullivan was going to need all hands on deck. Torque ran in front of Sullivan, stopping him dead in his tracks.

"No! You're not going to just push me aside on this one. I've fought for years to get to where I am now! I've been shot at and I've lost my friends. I know I fucked up here, I get that. But please Sullivan, let me try and make this right. You can fire me when this is all said and done, but even you can't deny that right now you need my help to stop this asshole. So please, I'm asking you...give me a chance to make this right," Torque pleaded with his heart in his hand.

Sullivan kept his serious face up, but inside he knew; no matter how pissed off he was at Torque, that he was right: Sullivan was going to need a small army if he was going to try and stop Dutra.

"Get in the car," Sullivan exhaled.

Torque nodded and then went into the car. Sullivan took one last look at the burned down apartment before heading back into the car with Joey and Torque.

"What's going on? What's he doing here?" Joey asked as Sullivan opened the driver side door and got into the car.

"I'll explain on the way," Sullivan said.

"Where we going?" Torque asked.

"We gotta find Ray," Sullivan said.

"The dealership?" Joey asked.

"No. Torque what's the closest hospital to the dealership?" Sullivan asked as he handed Torque his cell phone.

"Hold on," Torque said.

"Why is he looking up the closest hospital to the dealership? Did something happen?" Joey asked in a panic.

Sullivan started the car as he continued to process everything from the breach at headquarters to Emily being kidnapped.

"Yeah Joey...something happened...I just don't know what."

"The Elliot Hospital at River's Edge is about five miles away from the dealership," Torque said from the backseat.

Sullivan quickly put the car into gear and sped off as each of them wondered what the rest of the night was going to bring for them. Torque worried about Emily, Joey worried about Ray, and Sullivan worried about everything from Emily and Ray to what Dutra had waiting for them just over the horizon. They had more questions than answers but one thing was clear: the only way to stop Dutra was to engage him in an all out war. That answer was clear, it was just a question of who would be left standing when it was all said and done.

II

As Joey, Torque and Sullivan raced to catch up with Ray, Emily wept in the back of the SUV as she felt it come to a complete stop. The blindfold over her eyes felt rough across her face but that was the least of her worries. All she could think about was the look on Torque's face as she was taken out of the apartment.

When she was being put in the van she saw smoke coming from her apartment but wasn't able to see the actual fire. They only thing she knew about it was from what she overheard Vincent and the others in the SUV talking about as they drove.

As soon as the SUV stopped, Vincent quickly opened the passenger door, causing Emily to jump out of her skin. But that jump was nothing compared to the jump she had when she heard the door next to her suddenly swing open.

"Welcome to your new home sweetheart," Vincent said just before grabbing her arm and pulling her out of the SUV.

Emily did her best to not make it seem like she was scared or even crying but she couldn't help it when a few sniffles squeaked out. As they began walking she thought about trying to make a break for it, but she could tell just by Vincent's grip on her arm that it would be a wasted effort. Besides she had no idea why she was even there. For all she knew, they would kill her any second.

"Is Vacca back yet?" Vincent asked one of the guards by the elevator.

"Yes sir. He just arrived a few minuets ago."

"Good," Vincent said as he pushed Emily into an elevator.

Emily went soaring into the elevator from Vincent's rough push but quickly stopped when her head banged against the back of the elevator wall, causing her to fall to the ground.

She began to feel dizzy, almost thinking all this was a bad dream she couldn't wake up from. That changed when Vincent's ice-cold hands reminded her this was anything but. She was in this for the long haul.

The elevator rumbled as it began shooting up into the skyscraper. If Emily didn't have her blindfold on, she would've been able to see a beautiful view of the New York City skyline at night, but since the blindfold was darker then parts of space, only Vincent was able to admire the beauty of the view.

The elevator seemed to go on for an eternity as Emily waited for it to stop. For a while she almost thought it was never going to stop. She began thinking maybe this was some fucked up way to get into heaven. At least that's what was able to keep her calm through the long ride up.

Suddenly the elevator came to a dead stop as the brakes squeaked and the doors opened. As the doors opened all the way, two men stepped in and grabbed Emily by her arms and pulled her out of the elevator. Even though it was a longshot to get some answers Emily felt it was the right time to start asking.

"Where are you taking me?" Emily asked.

The men said nothing.

"Why are you doing this?" She asked in a panic.

Tired of her voice already, Vincent pushed her roughly.

"I wouldn't talk if I were you," Vincent threatened.

And Emily took the threat to heart. She didn't muster another word. She kept her mouth shut as she walked down the hall to Dutra's office. She kept taking steps closer until she felt the men stop.

Vincent pushed Emily out of the way and then knocked on the door. Emily waited to hear a voice acknowledge it but that voice never came. Instead, Vincent opened the door and pushed Emily in.

Emily did her best to keep her balance but Vincent's push was too much for her and she went tumbling down onto the cold hard floor of Dutra's office. Thinking it would be best if she just stayed put, she decided not to even bother trying to get back up to her feet, but when Vincent grabbed her by her long beautiful black hair, she couldn't help but force herself back up. Once she was back on her feet she stood frozen still, waiting with fear of what was about to happen.

Filling up with disgust Dutra slowly began to walk over to Emily as he inspected her from head to toe. With each second his eyes were locked on her Dutra got more engaged. And as he walked up to her, Dutra couldn't help but realize that taking her was the best way to get Ray's attention, but also the most dangerous.

Underneath the blindfold Emily closed her eyes, panicking with thoughts about what was going to happen next. Just as she started to relax a little (or as much as she could) she suddenly jumped when a hand grabbed her blindfold and ripped it off her face.

Dutra threw the blindfold down onto the floor of his office as he took a good look at Emily. He actually thought Emily was rather attractive; she was someone Dutra could easily see himself with.

"Leave us," Dutra ordered to Vincent and the rest of the men who had followed him in.

Vincent nodded his head and walked out of the office with the guys as Dutra grew a horrific and rather sinister smile on his face.

"Open your eyes," Dutra softly said to Emily.

But being just as stubborn as her father, Emily ignored the demand and kept her eyes closed. Quickly losing his patience, Dutra suddenly grabbed Emily by the hair and gave it one good yank.

"Open your eyes, or I'll cut off your eye lids," Dutra threatened in a soft voice.

Emily could tell just by Dutra's voice that he was serious; he clearly didn't sound like one of those guys who just made threats. And in the end Emily's gut told her to do what he says, and so she did.

Emily very slowly opened her eyes to Dutra looking directly at her face. The look on Dutra's face frightened her like something out of a horror movie. If she thought running away would've done any good, she would've quickly turned around and started running, but she knew she wouldn't get very far.

The two of them stared into each other's eyes for what seemed to be a lifetime. Dutra could see Emily's eyes were full of life while Emily stared into the darkest set of eyes she's ever come across...even darker then her own fathers.

Enough time had passed where Emily was on the verge of getting ready to say something, when all of a sudden Dutra raised his fist and punched Emily right in the face, causing her to fall instantly. Once Dutra saw her fall to the ground, he turned his back on her and walked back over to the window to look out at the amazing view of the city.

Blood began to run down Emily's cheek as she tried to shake the stars out of her eyes from Dutra's massive and devastating blow. As she opened her eyes again the room felt like it was spinning, like something out of a bad dream.

Knowing that the more she stayed on the ground, the more vulnerable she would be, Emily slowly began to get back up to her feet. She used all the strength she could muster but in the end was only able to long enough to fall into the chair the sat in front of Dutra's desk.

"You must feel like a real man," Emily said as she whiped the blood off of her lip.

"Shut up!" Dutra snapped as he kept his face to the window. "Don't you dare talk to me about a real man."

Emily began to tremble in fear from the dryness and lack of emotion in Dutra's voice. Any thoughts of trying to stay and act strong quickly shot out of the room, leaving Emily feeling like just another helpless victim.

"Why...are you...doing this?" Emily asked as tears of fear began running down her cheeks.

"Oh I'm sure you can figure that much out for yourself," Dutra said as he finally took his eyes off the view and pointed them at Emily.

Dutra watched her for a moment. Once he realized that she was actually having a bit of trouble putting it all together Dutra quickly reached down and opened the top drawer of his desk. Inside was a yellow folder sitting right on top. He picked it up and slid it across his desk.

Emily watched the folder as it slid over to her. She looked back up at Dutra in confusion but she could clearly tell from Dutra's eyes that he wanted her to pick it up and open it...and she did.

As she slowly opened the folder a couple papers fell out and landed on her lap. She quickly grabbed them and started looking at the pictures, but it still didn't answer her question. The men in the pictures were complete strangers. It wouldn't be until she got to the last one in the folder that she would start understanding what this was all about.

When she flipped over the last picture in the folder her heart began to beat rapidly. Suddenly everything she had assumed proved to be wrong. The picture she was looking at was a picture of Ray in his armor.

"Dad...?" Emily asked softly under her breath as she heard Dutra chuckling evilly.

"The sins of our fathers," Dutra said and turned back to the window.

Emily's jaw dropped to the floor in confusion as she tried to piece together what Dutra was saying exactly.

"I don't understand," Emily confessed.

"You can pretend all you want...but I can see right through you. You think Daddy is going to come save you? Oh he'll come all right but he's not leaving the moment he sets foot in this building. Every man has to pay for his sins, and his time has come," Dutra said.

Emily kept trying to figure out what Dutra was saying, but there was still a very large piece missing. Her father was a mechanic, at least that's what she had always thought. She wanted to tell Dutra that he must have the wrong person but when she took another look down at the picture, she knew for sure that Ray was the man in the picture...and that confused the hell out of her.

Before she had time to even try to come up with something to say, Dutra quickly turned and rushed over to her. She jumped but that didn't stop Dutra from grabbing her by the hair and pulling her head up. She looked back into Dutra's lifeless eyes as fear rushed through her.

"And I'll tell you this much. When he gets here, I don't plan on throwing down my gun and killing him with my bear hands. As soon as I get a shot, I'm pulling that fucking trigger until the gun runs dry. Then I'll put it down, just so I can kill you with my bare hands," Dutra firmly said, pulling harder on Emily's hair.

Emily groaned in pain from Dutra's fist pulling her hair, but just before she was forced to let out a painful cry, Dutra released his fist and Emily's hair dropped back down to her shoulders. She caught her breath but it was quickly taken away again when Dutra punched her in the face again.

Emily's face shot to the side as blood dripped out of her bloody lip and landed on her white pants. She started seeing stars again as her head dropped to the floor. She could feel the pressure from Dutra's punch on her cheek as the pain began to sink in.

Dutra watched with a menacing smile on his face, as he got ready to hit her again as soon as she lifted her head back up. And when he saw her slowly trying to lift her head Dutra clenched his fist and got ready to punch again but was interrupted when the cell phone in his pocket began to ring.

Emily sighed in relief when she heard the cell phone start ringing; she knew it had bought her some time, but only very little. As she lifted her head back up she watched as Dutra took out his cell phone and swiped the screen before putting the phone to his ear.

"What?" Dutra asked.

"It's done, Kevin Bear is out of the picture," Street said over the phone.

Dutra looked at Emily as she looked back at him and blood ran down her cheek.

"Good. That should rattle their cages enough to get their attention. How far out are you?" Dutra asked.

"About halfway there," Street said.

"Okay, hurry up. I need everyone here for when our guest arrives," Dutra said.

"Copy that, sir," Street said before he hung up.

Dutra hung up his phone and put it back into his pocket, but he kept his eyes on Emily.

"Well, you might get to be seeing your father a lot sooner then I expected," Dutra sinisterly said.

Even though Emily was still a little out of it from Dutra's hard punches she knew exactly what Dutra had meant.

"Please tell me this isn't happening," Emily whispered to herself, thinking Dutra couldn't hear her.

"Oh it's happening, believe it," Dutra quickly shot back. "Just think: this time tomorrow, you'll be dead...scary isn't it? Guess some things really are better left unknown."

Emily dropped her head again and began to quietly sob as Dutra looked out the window and started to wonder how Ray was holding up. He assumed Ray was in pieces right about now and that's exactly how Dutra wanted him to be: broken, feeling uneasy and most importantly...angry. Because when people get angry, they make mistakes. Dutra learned that the hard way a while back.

It had been a tough thing for Dutra to have to go through, but in the end it made him more careful and most of all, it made him sharper then he ever was before. After he learned how to deal with his own anger he was able to shift it off to whatever poor bastard landed on his radar. And this time that poor bastard was Ray...and Ray was just slowly starting to realize that.

Ray had followed right behind the ambulance as it drove down the road to the hospital. Ray knew even before the paramedics got to the shop that Kevin was long gone, but the paramedics kept working on him as they lifted him up and put him in the back of the ambulance. Ray was never one to think positive, but he tried his best to believe that Kevin would somehow make it.

As the ambulance pulled up to the busy hospital, they stopped in front of the Emergency Room doors and quickly started to bring the gurney Kevin was on to the ground as doctors rushed over to assist.

Ray parked right in front of the hospital, quickly got out of his truck and rushed inside. But by the time he made it inside (after stopping because of the pain in his knee) Kevin was already well on his way to surgery. With nothing else to do but wait, Ray took out his cell phone and called Steve, and only Steve.

The conversation was short but Steve was able to grasp that Ray was in no shape to call the other guys and tell them what had happened, hell he was lucky he had enough strength to call Steve. Once Steve said he would let the others knows, Ray hung up and did the only thing he could do: sit and wait.

Ray felt powerless as he watched the clock hanging on the wall slowly tick away. He wished he could've somehow done something different so this never would've happened. He began believing that if he and Kevin kept talking in his office just for another minute or so maybe this never would've happened (or at least happened differently).

The job was able to squash Ray's fears of death in the beginning but nothing could take away his fear of having those around him die before him. He learned about that fear way back in Vietnam. Some things just stand the test of time, whether you want them to or not.

After a half hour of waiting Ray just couldn't stay in that waiting room any longer, if he did he was going to go insane. He got up and walked out of the waiting area and over to the elevator. He pressed the button a dozen times (thinking maybe it would go faster) and once the doors opened he walked in and pressed the button to the top floor. He wasn't sure where exactly he was going, all he knew was that he needed to be somewhere else.

Ray decided to do what Roader did while Roader was waiting to hear about his son: go up to the roof. He knew nothing could completely take his mind off of Kevin's clouded fate, but sitting in that waiting room wasn't doing any good. Ray just needed some time to think, collect his thoughts and most of all, keep thinking about what he was going to do with Dutra.

As soon as the elevator doors opened, Ray rushed out of it and walked over to a door labeled 'Stairs'. He opened the door and began walking all the way up. As he reached the top of the stairs he noticed a door at the end of the last staircase and once he got to it, he grabbed the doorknob and opened it.

Cold night air swept through the stairwell as Ray walked out and closed the door behind him. Just judging by the smell in the air, Ray could tell the end of summer was rapidly approaching. Another summer gone too soon as far as he was concerned.

But the summer being just about over was the last thing on his mind. Kevin's fate had taken center stage and was quickly stealing the show. Not even the thought of breaking Dutra's neck with his bare hands was playing in his mind, it was all focused on Kevin.

Over the years Ray had seen more then his fair share of death. At this point in his life Ray knew more about death then any scientist or medical examiner could ever possible understand. Getting to live a life among the dead was nothing short of a nightmare as far as Ray was concerned. Because when you're around death for so long, not only do you get to see it up close, you're also made aware of the warning signs that come right before it. And when Ray was holding Kevin, Ray couldn't help but notice that Kevin looked like one big black label warning.

Holding Kevin in his arms not only kept playing back in his head but it also got Ray thinking about his fallen brother in arms: Sergeant Praft from Vietnam. On the plane back home from the jungle, Ray told himself he would do whatever it took to forget the emptiness of his eyes when he died. And he was able to keep that promise to himself for years but he couldn't help but acknowledge that Kevin had that same look in his eyes as he watched the paramedics pick him up and put him in the ambulance.

Ray shook his head when he felt tears building up under his eyelids. He knew it wasn't the right time to grieve but grief has a way of coming whether you want it to or not. That was something Ray learned a long time ago. He started to get angry with himself when he felt the first tear roll down his cheek.

"Goddamn it," Ray whispered to himself in shame.

But to his luck (if you can call it luck) his mind quickly stopped thinking about the fate of Kevin when his pocket began to vibrate. He dug into his pocket and took out his phone to look at the screen. To his surprise it was Roader giving him a call, clearly Steve was in the process of letting everyone know about what was going on. Ray took a deep breath and swiped his finger across the screen.

"Yeah," Ray said out of breath.

"Is it true?" Roader asked.

"Yeah," Ray said just before bursting into tears.

Normally, Ray would go out of his way to try and impress Roader and most of all keep any type of emotions at bay, but in this case he couldn't. Ray was a mess inside and out. And Roader knew that.

"I'm sorry, Ray," Roader said.

Ray wiped his eyes with his hand as his knee gave way and caused him to collapse onto the ground. The pain from his knee jolted through his body, worse than anything it'd ever done before, but that pain was nothing compared to the pain that was taking over Ray's heart.

Ray wanted to talk; he wanted to ask for advice, but he just couldn't find the words or the strength to pull himself together. Grief is messy. Roader knew that, but he also knew that just having someone to talk to could really make a difference. Roader could hear Ray over the phone trying to put words together but knew he was in no shape to talk, so Roader decided that for once he would put their bitter rivalry aside.

"I know nothing I can say will help, but I want you to know Ray that I've always admired you. Most guys in our line of work don't give a shit about their team members. But you always have, and that's something I've always admired about you Ray, you care, even when you don't have to," Roader said from the bottom of his heart.

"Thank you," Ray was barley able to say.

"You think he'll pull through?" Roader asked.

"It doesn't look good," Ray confessed.

"Damn. Sorry Ray, I know you cared for the kid."

"Yeah...how's your boy doing?" Ray asked to try and change the subject.

Roader sighed. "Well he's out of ICU. Just waiting for him to wake up...never been much for waiting."

"None of us are," Ray said as he sniffled.

"Yeah. Anything I can do?" Roader asked.

"Naw...you calling is enough. I know you have your own trouble to deal with," Ray said.

"Alright brother, you need anything just let me know," Roader said.

"Thanks Paul. I mean that."

"What else are friends for?" Roader asked.

Ray was able to get a smile on his face as he hung up the phone and put it back in his pocket. In a way he was actually surprised that Roader gave him a call to see how he was. Of course when he started really thinking about it, Ray stopped being so surprised. Yeah, sure, the two of them were always at each other's throats (especially when they were younger and just starting out) but age seemed to have mellowed both of their egos. And in that process you could say that they even became friends (they both just didn't realize it).

II

While Ray tried to pull himself together on the roof, back down in the Emergency Room the guys were starting to filter in. Jasmin was the first to arrive. He wasn't exactly sure what was going on; Steve just told him to get to the hospital ASAP. Jasmin, just like Ray, was amazed as to how busy the hospital was for how late it was. It was so busy that for a brief second Jasmin thought something on a large scale was taking place. He kept looking around for a good while until he heard a familiar voice shout from across the room.

"Jas!" Tommy shouted as he quickly walked over.

Jasmin turned and looked up at Tommy, who was clearly worried (and a little drunk).

"Dude what the fuck is going on here?" Tommy shouted in a panic.

"No idea, Steve called me about twenty minuets ago," Jasmin said.

"Yeah same here. What'd he say?" Tommy asked.

"All he said was get here, and prepare yourself. What he say to you?" Jasmin asked.

"Same fucking thing. Have you seen anyone else yet?" Tommy asked.

"Naw, just got here."

While Jasmin did his best to remain calm, Tommy was another story. His head was roaming around like a child at a toyshop, trying to make sense of what was going on. Tommy's eyes looked all around, trying to see if any of the faces in the room looked familiar. At first no one seemed to stand out, until he saw Bob walk in.

"Bob!" Tommy shouted.

Bob looked up when he heard his name and saw Tommy waving his hand in the air. Bob began to walk over, weaving in and out of people as he made his way to the other side of the waiting room.

Jasmin hadn't really had the chance to work one on one with Bob like most of the other guys had, so he didn't notice anything different about Bob. Tommy, however was a whole different story. Tommy was really the one that Bob had chosen to work with ever since Ray hired Tommy, and over that period of time, Tommy hadn't really gotten to *really* know Bob (don't even think Ray had either) but if anyone could tell something was bothering Bob, it was Tommy.

"Something's wrong..." Tommy said as he looked at Bob's rather pale face.

As Tommy watched Bob get closer and closer it almost looked like Bob had been crying due to the redness in his eyes. And if whatever happened was strong enough to get to even Bob, Tommy knew that it was serious.

"Bob, you know what's going on?" Jasmin asked as Bob walked up to them.

Bob kept his face to the ground and cleared his throat. In that moment Tommy knew that Bob was told something that he and Jasmin weren't.

"Bob...?" Tommy said as he tried to lower his head and make eye contact with Bob.

Bob cleared his throat again and finally looked up at them.

"How long have you been here?" Bob said.

"Just got here. What's going on?" Tommy asked.

"Are Ray and Steve already here?" Jasmin asked.

Bob ignored Tommy's question and decided to answer Jasmin's.

"Ray's here somewhere, and Steve should be here any second, I gotta sit down," Bob said before looking for an empty seat to sit in.

Tommy followed Bob to a seat by a window overlooking the entrance. Bob quickly sat down and put his hands over his face as Tommy patted him on the back. Jasmin began walking over to them until he saw Steve quickly walk in and look around.

"Steve!" Jasmin shouted.

Jasmin's voice grabbed Steve's attention and he started walking over when he heard a door from behind him slam shut. Steve quickly looked at where the loud slam came from and saw Ray walking over to him. Steve stopped walking over to Jasmin and waited for Ray to walk over to him.

"Any news yet?" Steve asked.

"I don't know," Ray said in pain.

Once Ray was in reach, Steve patted him on the back as Ray looked around the crowded waiting room.

"The guys are here," Steve said.

Ray shook his head as he wiped away the last remaining tears in his eyes.

"Did you tell them?" Ray asked.

"Told Bob, didn't have the stomach to tell the others, couldn't do it," Steve said.

Ray shook his head and then walked over to Bob and Tommy. Steve took a deep breath and then followed right behind Ray. In a way he felt like he had let Ray down for not telling the guys, but when Steve said he just couldn't stomach it, he was being honest. It took Steve by storm when Ray muttered the sentence to him over the phone.

Jasmin kept his eyes fixed on Ray as he walked closer and closer. Just like Tommy knew something was wrong when he saw Bob, Jasmin instantly knew when he saw Ray's face that something terrible was happening. When Ray reached Tommy and Bob, Ray put his hand on Bob's shoulder while Bob continued to stare at the floor. As soon as Ray put his hand on Bob's shoulder, Tommy looked up with worry covering his normally wild and excited face.

"You heard anything yet?" Bob asked.

"Still waiting, Bob." Ray said.

Steve put his hand over his mouth and exhaled deeply.

"How the fuck could this happen?" Steve shouted in anger.

"Think he'll be okay?" Bob asked, raising his head up from the floor.

Ray kept silent. It was hard enough to make eye contact with Bob let alone answer. But when Bob saw the look in Ray's eyes, he got his answer.

"Damn it..." Bob whispered.

While Ray, Steve, Bob and Tommy kept silent, Jasmin couldn't help but notice that a part of the gang was missing.

"Hey, did anybody call Kevin?" Jasmin asked.

The guys' hearts sank, Steve even closed his eyes and looked the other way while Ray slowly turned to Jasmin. Ray could see that Jasmin was honestly wondering.

"Is he on his way?" Jasmin asked.

Ray knew what he had to do next, whether he was ready to or not. He opened his mouth and was just getting ready to say it when a young doctor in blue scrubs walked over to the guys.

"Excuse me? I'm Doctor Peacock, are you who came in with Kevin Bear?" he asked.

Jasmin quickly turned to Doctor Peacock as Bob lifted his head off the ground. Ray quickly stepped forward.

"Yeah, we are..." Ray said with bloodshot eyes.

Doctor Peacock could see the pain already in Ray's eyes. He knew what he had to tell Ray and the guys, but he also knew that Ray was clearly the kind of guy who knew what was coming next.

"Is...uh...is he..." Ray said as his voice broke.

Doctor Peacock gave that infamous smile and softly shook his head.

"When he arrived, he had lost a lot of blood. We were able to control it, however, it was too late. His heart gave out from the loss of blood," Doctor Peacock said.

Ray shook his head as he looked into Doctor Peacock's eyes. Doctor Peacock inhaled very softly as he looked at Ray.

"I'm sorry," Doctor Peacock said with a heavy heart.

Ray closed his eyes, Bob lowered his head back down, Steve turned and left the room, Tommy's jaw hit the floor and Jasmin was left in a fog.

"What?!" Jasmin quickly asked as he looked at Tommy.

Even with his eyes closed, Ray could feel the tears building up as Doctor Peacock patted Ray on the shoulder. Ray opened his eyes and tried to control his emotions as he looked back up at the doctor.

"Would you like to see him?" Peacock asked.

Before Ray answered, he thought about it. And as he thought about it, he started thinking back to Vietnam and watching his friend die. He thought about the pain he has had to carry from seeing that, but he also started to think about his mission to keep the world from ever having to see what he saw.

"Yeah," Ray said as he shook his head.

Peacock gave Ray a sympathy smile.

"Okay, right down this way," Peacock said as he started walking down the hall with Ray.

III

While Ray headed down the hall to see Kevin, outside in the parking lot, Sullivan, Joey and Torque pulled up to the busy entrance. Sullivan didn't even look for an open parking spot, he parked right in front without even thinking.

As soon as the car was in park, Sullivan and Torque quickly opened their doors, but Joey didn't. He didn't even move. As Sullivan was getting ready to close his door he realized that Joey hadn't gotten out yet, so he bent down to see why.

"Hey, you coming in?" Sullivan asked Joey.

A depressed looking Joey shook his head softly.

"No, gonna get some fresh air." Joey said.

Sullivan nodded and then shut the door and walked briskly into the hospital with Torque. Joey watched as they went in. For a moment Joey thought about going in with them, even started to open the door, but again hesitated. Ray's words were still playing in his mind and Joey didn't want to be anywhere near Ray once he learned that Dutra had his daughter.

The thought of Ray finding out that his daughter was taken frightened Joey to the point where he quickly got out of the car and began walking away from the hospital. He wasn't quite sure where exactly he was heading, but all Joey knew was that he needed to be alone with his thoughts.

Sullivan and Torque entered the waiting room and began looking around. The room was slowly starting to lose some of it's people, so it made it a little easier for Sullivan and Torque to find the guys. Sullivan looked around for a moment and then saw Bob, Tommy and Jasmin sitting down.

"Over here," Sullivan said to Torque.

Torque turned his head and looked toward them. Then he followed Sullivan over to them. As Sullivan was walking over he could clearly tell that something was off. The guys looked completely drained. Tommy and Bob were so focused on the floor, they didn't even see Sullivan and Torque walking over. It was Jasmin that noticed them but only from the corner of his eye. As soon as he saw them, he bumped Bob on the arm. Bob looked at Jasmin, who then pointed up.

"Hey," Sullivan said to the guys.

Bob went back to looking at the floor.

"The hell are you doing here Sullivan?" Bob asked.

Sullivan looked at Bob then shrugged his shoulders.

"Ray gave me call earlier. Sounded serious..."

Jasmin stood up from his chair and then walked over to Torque. He quickly noticed the marks on his face from the fall out of Emily's window.

"Damn, what happened to you?" Jasmin asked.

Torque shook his head. "Long story."

"Clearly," Jasmin said.

While Jasmin and Torque were talking, Steve walked back in the room and saw Sullivan talking with Tommy and Bob.

"Sullivan!" Steve shouted.

Sullivan quickly turned and looked at Steve.

"Steve, thank God," he began as he walked over to him. "We need to talk."

Steve shook his head.

"Yeah we do," Steve said just before he turned and started walking back out of the room so they could talk privately.

Sullivan followed Steve out of the room and into the hallway. Aside from a few people and doctors walking around the hallway was rather empty.

"Alright Steve, we have a serious situation here," Sullivan began.

Steve looked up at Sullivan.

"You damn right we do! Dutra just made a move against us, I don't know how the hell he and his fucking guys found us but they did."

Sullivan shook his head. "Bob just told me, is Kevin gonna make it?" he asked.

Steve sighed deeply and looked down. Sullivan instantly knew what that meant.

"I'm sorry, Steve," Sullivan said.

Steve turned around and looked out the window into the parking lot.

"Not half as sorry as Dutra will be when we get his hands on him," Steve promised.

Sullivan sympathized with Steve. He knew where Steve was coming from, but Sullivan also knew the position Dutra had on all of them and it was time for Sullivan to share that information.

"Steve, the F.B.I. server was compromised earlier today," Sullivan began.

Steve quickly turned around and looked at Sullivan.

"What are you saying, Sullivan?"

"Steve...Dutra knows everything. He knows your names, where you live, what you do for us, everything."

Steve shook his head.

"How in the fuck is that possible?" Steve shouted.

Sullivan shook his head.

"We're still trying to figure all that out, but right now the only thing you need to concern yourself with is that Dutra knows who you are."

Steve took a moment to process it all in, and then slammed his hand into the wall before he turned back to Sullivan.

"Was just Ray and myself compromised, or the whole team?" Steve asked suddenly.

Sullivan tried to answer, but he realized in that moment just how much he had failed the team. And all Sullivan could do was lower his head in shame. Steve threw his hands up in the air.

"Jesus fucking Christ! Do you have any idea what this means now?" Steve shouted as loud as he could.

"Yes, I..." Sullivan began to say before Steve interrupted him.

"Oh like hell you do! When we first started this, both Ray and I specifically asked you if there was any chance there was a way for our identity's to be known! Do you remember what you said?"

Sullivan didn't answer right away, which sent Steve into a rage.

"DO YOU?!" Steve shouted again.

"Yes," Sullivan softly said.

"Uh huh. You said there was no possible way. You said everything was off the books. No record of anything. Should've known better then to trust someone like you. Now were all in fucking danger from that maniac! Have you told Ray about this yet? Have you told him he's going to have to tell his daughter about everything?"

Sullivan exhaled deeply and then looked down as Steve shook his head in disgust and started to walk over to the window.

"Son of a bitch." Steve mumbled to himself.

But Sullivan knew he couldn't just leave it at that. He knew Steve (and the rest of the guys) were going to have to know one last thing. So Sullivan swallowed hard and braced for Steve's reaction.

"Steve..." Sullivan said.

Steve quickly turned away from the window and looked at Sullivan.

"What? What the fuck do you wanna say to me?"

"When we found out that headquarters was compromised, the first place Joey and I went to was Emily's place. Steve, Dutra has her..." Sullivan admitted.

The words sank into Steve like a knife into his heart. His eyes got big and his heart began thumping. Steve couldn't say anything at first. Hell, he couldn't even think straight. The only thing that he was sure of was that this changed everything. Dutra had the upper hand.

"I'm sorry Steve," Sullivan said.

Steve shook his head and then turned back to Sullivan.

"No, you don't get to say sorry to me. You want to say sorry to someone then you say it to Ray. This was your fuck up, so you get to be the one to tell Ray about his daughter," Steve said and walked away.

Sullivan watched Steve walk away, then headed back into the waiting room. Deep down Sullivan knew all along that it was going to be him that had to tell Ray the news, but up until that point he tried to avoid thinking about it. But there was no more time to put it off.

"Damn it," Sullivan said to himself.

IV

As Doctor Peacock lead Ray down the hall, Ray kept trying to prepare himself for what he was about to see. Before the ambulance came to pick up Kevin, Ray knew then that Kevin was in rough shape, but inside Ray knew the state he was about to see Kevin in would haunt him until the day he died.

The hallway was filled with a lot of activity, which was a good thing for Ray. All the nurses running around and a few patients vomiting were able to distract Ray for a moment or two. In the long run, it wouldn't help, but at least it was able to keep my calm as he walked down the hall. Of course all that changed the moment he set foot into the room where Kevin was.

With wires running out of his arms and chest and white bandages wrapped around his throat, Kevin laid peacefully on the bed. Ray was only able to look at him for a brief second or else he was going to start bawling right then and there, so he turned away and looked at Doctor Peacock.

"Could you give me a second?" Ray asked.

"Of course. Take all the time you need," Doctor Peacock said before walking out of the room.

When Doctor Peacock was out of the doorway, Ray slowly began shutting the door. The door wasn't even halfway shut when tears started running down Ray's cheeks. Ray leaned his head on the door and wiped the tears off his cheek.

In that moment Ray not only felt like a coward, but he also felt like it was his fault for what happened. He knew that Dutra was a serious threat, but Ray couldn't help but wonder what the circumstances would be if he had taken the threat more seriously. He turned around and looked at Kevin.

With the tube in Kevin's mouth and the heartbeat monitor slowly beeping away, Ray couldn't help but feel like he had seen this before. The whole situation began to cast a haunting feeling over him. As he walked over and sat down in the chair next to Kevin, Ray couldn't help but remember his late wife in the same situation.

"You were my brother Kevin," Ray began as his lifted his head up. "This shouldn't have happened to you, it shouldn't be you in this room. This bastard put you here, and I'm sorry. But I give you my word, I'll do the same to him. This ends with him dead."

Ray took his eyes off of Kevin in shame as he lowered his head. And with the thoughts of his late wife sinking in more and more, Ray stood up and took one last look at Kevin.

"I'll see you on the other side brother," Ray whispered and began walking away.

As he made his way out of the room Ray's feelings quickly changed from sadness to rage. The thought of Dutra still breathing in that moment began to fuel the beast inside of him. But those thoughts were interrupted when his cell phone began ringing in his pocket. Ray closed the door to Kevin's tomb and then dug into his pocket and took out his phone.

"Yeah?" Ray said as he cleared his throat.

At first the person the other end of the line didn't say anything. But even though Ray's mind was branching out in all directions he could clearly hear the person on the other end of the line breathing.

"Hello?" Ray said as he looked at his phone.

Then suddenly a voice, a familiar yet dark and deep voice broke the silence.

"Now I figured a man with a reputation such as yours would have a much deeper tone," Dutra said.

It took a moment for it to sink in, but as soon as Ray realized the voice was the very same voice he heard back in Washington, his eyes quickly grew wide.

"You motherfucker," Ray said as deep as his voice could get.

"Now that's more like it. How are you Ray? How's the team holding up?" Dutra asked with pure sarcasm.

"You listen to me you son of a bitch, I don't care what it takes. I don't care if I have to follow you to the gates of hell myself, I will find you, and when I do, I'm gonna snap every single bone in your goddamn body," Ray promised.

"A man that's been in the business as long as you should know threats don't mean shit to guys like us," Dutra said.

"It's no threat. You're dead," Ray said.

"Spoken like a true killer, huh? Let me ask you this Ray: do you really think that you'll be able to walk through hell to get to me?" Dutra asked in all seriousness.

"Just give me the chance," Ray said.

"Are you sure? Answer me this: when it comes down to it, when it's just you and me and a loaded gun, will you be able to head into that situation without any hesitation?" Dutra asked.

"You bet your ass I will. I've dealt with asshole like you for decades. And it always ends the same...with me putting a bullet in there heads. So yeah...when the time comes, nothing will be holding me back from doing it...only I wont be using a gun on you. I want you to feel your neck break just before you die. And don't think for even a second that I'll think twice about it," Ray said.

Dutra chuckled.

"Tell me something Ray, you're getting a little older now aren't ya?" Dutra asked.

Ray didn't answer.

"Yeah, you are, aren't yeah? And you're probably now wondering what's gonna happen to you, because you know just as much as I do, when we leave this business we're never the same person as when we started out, are we? I know I'm not, and I'm pretty sure you aren't either," Dutra said.

"I'm not the one with the heavy conscience," Ray firmly said.

"Oh you most certainly are. What, you think having a different point of view somehow shields you of any wrongdoing? Well, let me tell you something that you should've learned a long time ago Ray: it doesn't matter if you kill for the right reason or the wrong reason, the outcome is the same, the soul gets stained regardless. If God isn't on my side, what makes you think he'll be on yours?"

Ray was getting ready to tell Dutra he was just grasping at straws, just trying to get under his skin...but he wasn't. What Dutra just said defined the greatest battle Ray had been facing for years.

"You don't know shit," Ray grumbled.

"I'm sure most of the time when someone says something to you and it actually hits home you dismiss it like it's nothing, but right now...we both know better don't we?" Dutra asked, even though he knew he wasn't going to get an answer for that question.

Ray shook his head.

"Like I said, I'm coming for you and nothing and no one will stop me. You hear me? I'm not hesitating for anything," Ray firmly said

"Oh don't worry...I don't think that you'll hesitate. I know for a certain fact that you will," Dutra said with a chuckle.

"Grave mistake on your part. But I'm sure you'll find that out soon enough," Ray said.

"Before you start going all macho on me let me ask you this: do you feel the same way now as you did when you lost your wife? Does your heart race? Does it hurt every time it beats, now? Does knowing the fact that instead of killing you I chose one of your own haunt you?" Dutra asked.

"Why don't you tell me where you're at so I can tell you face to face? Come on Dutra, grow a pair and prove to me you're more than the low life piece of shit that I think you are."

"I would, but I'm a little tied up at the moment. You see I'm entertaining a very close friend, and wasting the time I have with her would be a shame. Would you like to say hello to her? I think you'll find you have a lot in common...hold on..." Dutra said.

Blindsided by Dutra's rather clever choice of words, Ray waited, trying to figure out what part of the puzzle he was missing, because clearly there was something that he wasn't seeing. But before he could put the answer together himself, the answer emerged.

"Hello?" Emily asked in pain.

In that moment Ray felt the ground underneath him drop. His eyes widened with fear as his heart began pumping in a way that rivaled how it was when he was getting shot at back in Vietnam. And it was clear that Dutra was truly in control.

"Emily..." Ray began to say.

"Dad!" Emily said as she began crying.

Trembling with fear, Ray quickly put his hands on his head, in a desperate attempt thinking that would somehow calm his strung out mind. It was a wasted effort, Ray himself could feel that he was quickly approaching his breaking point.

He wanted to say so much, needed to say so much. He knew that Emily must've been more confused than she had ever been in her twenty-three year old life. Ray wanted to explain, needed to explain, but the opportunity never came. Just before he was able to provide comforting words to his daughter he heard Dutra's breathing on the other end of the line, indicating that would be the only conversation Dutra would allow.

"I'm gonna fucking kill you! You hear me? I'm gonna rip out your fucking heart!" Ray screamed as his voice echoed throughout the hallway of the hospital.

"Hey get your head out of your ass! Pull it the fuck out and listen to me!" Dutra screamed back.

Ray slowly calmed his breathing.

"Now, let me explain the situation to you: your daughter is dead Ray. You understand? She's not leaving here alive. Call it the price of doing business. But I'll make you a deal: you and your team of retarded assholes step the fuck back and stop getting in my way, then I'll make sure it's quick. I promise she won't have to find out what my balls taste like. It'll be quick and painless," Dutra explained.

Dutra's words echoed in Ray's ears as he tried his best to take in Dutra's twisted ultimatum.

"If you and your team back the fuck off she'll die in peace, that's the deal. But make no mistake about it: if I so much as smell you sticking your nose in my business, I will make sure every single one of my guys gets a taste of her ass...and then I'll pull her apart myself...piece by fucking piece," Dutra threatened.

"Now you listen to me..." Ray began to say before being interrupted.

"No, you listen to me motherfucker! I'm giving you the choice on how your daughter will die! Don't make me take it back! I'll blow a hole through her fucking skull right now and don't you dare think I fucking wont! Now do we have a deal or not?" Dutra shouted.

Ray was never one to give in but not even he could deny that he knew Dutra would do it. It was in that moment when Ray finally saw just how far Dutra was willing to go. In the end Ray had no choice but to give in. And with tears in his eyes, Ray cleared his throat as he heard Dutra cock a gun.

"Yes...but please...let me talk to her one more time," Ray begged.

Dutra rolled his eyes as he thought about just hanging up, but then he thought that if he at least gave Ray the chance to say goodbye, Ray might actually stay out of the way.

Dutra lowered the phone from his ear and walked over to Emily, who was finally able to control her breathing. Dutra poked her in the arm to get her attention and when she looked up Dutra handed her the phone.

"You got twenty seconds," Dutra said.

Emily took the phone from Dutra's hand and then put it up to her ear.

"Dad?" Emily asked.

Ray closed his eyes as tears ran down his cheek.

"Sweetheart..."

"Dad...what's going on?" Emily asked.

"Em, listen to me: I promise you...I'm coming to get you. Do you believe me?" Ray asked.

Emily sniffled and shook her head.

"Yes."

"Good," Ray said as he wiped his eyes.

"Dad?" Emily asked.

"Yeah baby?"

"I'm scared," Emily said as she began crying.

Once Emily said those words, any type of stability in Ray's heart gave way.

"I know sweetheart, but I'm coming. I love you..."

"I love you too," Emily said.

And the moment Emily said those words, Dutra snatched the cell phone out of Emily's hand and ended the call. Silence filled Ray's ear as he closed his eyes, praying all this was just a hellish nightmare.

Ray lowered the phone from his ear as Dutra's words sank in deep. Ray was in such a state of shock that he didn't even feel the cell phone slide out of his hands or even hear it smash onto the floor.

Emily's voice echoed through his mind as he began to think about what Dutra could be doing to her in that exact moment. But Ray knew that he needed to pull himself together because if he had any chance of saving his daughter, it was going to have to be soon.

As Ray slowly started to get his mind back together he quickly turned and headed for the end of the hall but stopped when he saw Sullivan standing a few feet away from him. Sullivan's face looked like that of a broken man, almost matching Ray's. Instantly Ray knew why Sullivan was there; Sullivan didn't even have to say a word.

"Ray..." Sullivan began.

"How long have you known?" Ray quickly asked.

"Just found out a little while ago," Sullivan admitted.

Ray shook his head in disgust.

"I truly am sorry Ray." Sullivan admitted.

It was a wasted effort on Sullivan's part. Ray had hit the point where he was done. He didn't even bother to let Sullivan get another word in. Ray just through up his hands and walked away and Sullivan sighed as he shook his head.

Sullivan knew he fucked up, there was no denying that. He also knew that the situation was escalating to something big. Sullivan knew he was going to have to somehow try and fix this, but it wasn't going to be easy.

Dutra was clearly preparing for something big, but the full picture still wasn't clear. However, Sullivan had an idea of someone who might know more about it. He dug into his pocket and dialed Joey's number.

"Joe, meet me at the car now," Sullivan ordered.

"I'll be right there."

Sullivan hung up and quickly began running toward to car. His idea was a bit of a long shot, but in that moment it was the only idea he had.

Sullivan knew that if he was going to try and redeem himself and make this right, he was going to have to do it quickly because time was running out, and fast. While he raced to the car all he could think about was the look on Ray's face the moment he saw him hang up that cell phone.

V

While the guys were leaving the hospital to figure out what their next move would be, back in New York Dutra was busy making plans himself. After punching Emily one more time, damn near knocking her out, Dutra picked up the phone on his desk and dialed a number.

"Get in here," he ordered.

Instantly both Street and Vince walked in as Dutra hung the phone up and looked down at his desk.

"Everything alright?" Vincent asked.

Dutra took a moment to go over the plan in his head one last time. Once he did though, he was beyond confident that the plan was flawless.

"Lock down the building, seal all the entrances, put a guy at every doorway. Seal this place up like a fortress," Dutra ordered.

"Yes sir." Vincent said right away and ran out of the office.

"There a problem sir?" Street asked.

"Yeah, that bastard is gonna be coming for us," Dutra said.

"I thought you were gonna make him an offer," Street asked.

"I did."

"And he didn't agree?"

"No he did...but he's not gonna listen. I could tell just by the sound of his voice. Man thinks just because he's been around the block, he knows everything about it; well, times change. He thinks the players change but the game stays the same. We're just going to have to show him how the game really is nowadays," Dutra said.

"I understand boss."

"Oh and I'm moving the deadline up to tomorrow night, so make sure you tell your boys about it," Dutra added.

"Will do," Street said, and started out of the office.

Street wasn't too thrilled about Dutra moving up the job, but he was confident that Dutra knew best. There was one thing that Street couldn't figure out and just needed to know.

"Hey boss," Street said as he turned back to Dutra.

Dutra looked up.

"Just curious...you're locking down the building...what makes you think this guy will come looking for you here?" Street asked.

Dutra slowly smiled.

"Glad you asked," Dutra said menacingly.

Chapter 12: Revelation

Joey didn't muster a word for damn near half the ride as Sullivan drove them down the highway. For a while Joey wasn't quite sure where he was at, it took him seeing signs on the highway that read 'New York' to figure it out. Joey looked over at Sullivan a few times—a blank, emotionless face plastered on him—and decided he would stay quite a little while longer. But finally Joey decided to end that silence.

"Sullivan...you okay?"

"No, but thanks for asking," Sullivan quickly said.

Joey shook his head and was getting ready to speak but Sullivan beat him to it.

"Twenty seven years I've worked with Ray. Did you know that?" Sullivan asked.

Joey shook his head.

"No I did not...long time."

"Yeah. Very long time. When Ray started out, I was in your position, going to him every couple of days and sending him to another piece of hell on Earth. Always felt bad doing it but Ray never complained, not once. You see, Ray started out solo. Guess he was told he could either stay a lone wolf or turn it into something else..." Sullivan explained.

Joey shook his head as he processed in all the new information about Ray. Joey didn't know all that much about Ray's past way back when, but he did know the man and how he worked.

"So how long did he stay solo?" Joey asked.

"Close to ten years. Yeah, he worked with military troops quite a bit but when it came to assassinations and doing wet work, Ray did it all himself. Brilliant fucking man I gotta say. His shots: always dead accurate. Never missed a beat; we told him where to go, that's where he went. Didn't think twice about it. He then reached out to Steve for a job in Somalia; they've been partners ever since," Sullivan explained as he drove down the dark highway.

To Joey's surprise he wasn't bored with the conversation; in fact he actually really liked getting to know more about Ray. He always wanted to anyway, but it was kinda hard for Joey to ask any personal questions when the person you want to ask is assigned to attempt to save the world from the evil of the human race.

"So how did it go from Steve and Ray to everyone there is now?" Joey asked as he kept his eyes out the window.

"More than likely it was Steve's idea," Sullivan said.

"What makes you think that?"

"Ray's the kind of guy who likes to do things himself; why bother settling for second best when you can be the best, right? Ray knows that, Steve knows that; hell everyone knows that. But we all know Ray's age, too. Now don't get me wrong, Ray has a lot of years left in him. I would never take that away from him. But at some point you do have to have a serious talk about how late in the game you want to be. I have no doubt that Ray could still do this well into his seventies, but I also know he's been wanting a way out since his mid forties, so I would imagine while Ray and Steve were on one of their adventures, the subject came up and Steve got him to consider getting more hands. Don't know how the fuck he did it but whatever Steve said, it worked," Sullivan explained.

Joey started to finally understand. It was all making sense; everything that Ray had talked about with his daughter and always wanting a way out; it was clear that once Ray put together a team that he was sure could carry it all on, he could retire with ease. So it was no wonder Ray flipped when he found out that it would be Torque taking over and not Steve.

"Didn't realize how long you've known him," Joey said.

Sullivan sighed.

"Yep. Some days it feels like a lifetime ago," Sullivan confessed while he started to think about his own age.

"So where we heading to?" Joey asked as he watched Sullivan begin to get off at an exit labeled 'Exit 5'.

"Going to meet an old asset of mine," Sullivan said very cryptically.

"Old asset?"

Sullivan shrugged his shoulders.

"Okay, well not really an asset, more of like a professional criminal," Sullivan confessed.

"Who?" Joey quickly asked.

"Peter Labossiere."

The name instantly rang a bell in Joey's head and it wasn't a good ring either.

"Wait a second, Peter Labossiere, as in mob boss Peter Labossiere?" Joey quickly shot back in a panic.

"Yep, that's him," Sullivan said as he pulled off of the exit ramp and started to head into the city lights.

"Jesus Christ, Sullivan, are you sure about this? I mean the man has been in more interrogation rooms then I have," Joey shot back trying to desperately change Sullivan's mind.

Sullivan knew in order to shut Joey up, he was going to have to explain himself, and the real reason why they were on there way to see one of the most dangerous criminals in the country. Sullivan honestly didn't really want to go through the whole story, but after he gave it a quick thought, he told himself that Joey had earned at least that.

Sullivan saw an open parking spot on the street and quickly pulled into it. He paid no attention to the car honking at him as it drove past, he just pulled into the spot and shut the car off as Joey tried to figure out what he was doing.

"What are you doing?" Joey asked.

Sullivan exhaled very deeply and then looked at Joey.

"Okay, so what I'm about to tell you is way past your pay level, but since you're coming on this with me I guess I have no choice but to tell you. But I'm warning you, this stays between us," Sullivan demanded.

"Fair enough," Joey said.

"Okay. Now yes, Peter Labossiere is one level below being considered a mass murderer. In his years of being in charge, he's ordered the kills of dozens of people," Sullivan began.

"Okay, so I'll ask again: why the hell are we on our way to see a bastard like that?!"

Sullivan took in a deep breath as he got ready to tell the story again (it had been quite a few years since the last time he told it and even longer since he had seen Labossiere in person).

"Before I transferred over to the F.B.I. I use to work here in city homicide. I had been with the department for close to two and a half years before a spot in homicide opened up. Once I finally nabbed the job I wanted to get people talking, didn't want them thinking I was just another young hot shot prick; I wanted the guys in the department to respect me. Now even when I was just patrolling in the streets I heard rumors about the Labossiere family. From them smuggling in tens of thousands of pounds of cocaine every week to executing rivals with buckets filled with cement," Sullivan started of.

"Oh shit.".

"Oh yeah, Joey. Even thirty years ago, no one fucked with the Labossiere's, and if they did, they must've been shit stupid; I was that stupid," Sullivan confessed.

Joey shook his head. "What happened?" he asked.

Sullivan chuckled as he shook his head.

"I got a tip from one of my informants that Labossiere was bringing in a shipment and that he was personally going to be at the exchange to make sure nothing went wrong. Guess he was having problems with a few of his guys, so he decided to go himself. I didn't even call for back up, didn't even think about it. All I thought about was the look on everyone's face when I dragged him into the station," Sullivan began.

"Did you get him?"

"When I got to the exchange he and a few of his guys were already there. I told myself if I had to take down his guys I would. Nothing was stopping me from getting that son of a bitch. As I got closer to him, one of his guys got out of the car parked by the dock and took out Daniel Irving."

"Who was that?"

"Daniel Irving was a low life piece of shit who shot a patrol officers in the face when he pulled him over. Damn near everyone at the police department was trying to find him but he suddenly disappeared, no one could find him. Anyway, the guy walked Irving up to Labossiere; Irving's face was so swollen he probably couldn't even see out his eyes. Then Labossiere grabbed Irving by the neck and dragged him to the edge of the dock, and pulled out a gun. I took aim at Labossiere, ready to blow his head off...but I stopped when I heard him say something to Irving"

"What he say?"

"He said: 'Captain Anderson says goodbye...' then he blew Irving's brains out. And then suddenly it all made sense as to why he was never arrested or charged with anything. I knew I had to get the hell out of there but one of his guys caught me and quickly dragged me over."

"Jesus."

"When he brought me over to Labossiere, my heart was pounding. I thought for sure I was a dead man, but to my surprise Labossiere had other plans for me. Right then and there he told me everything. He said he and Captain Anderson were sharing information with one another for close to three years. Labossiere told Caption Anderson when shipments were coming in, so he could send us down there and arrest Labossiere's rivals, while Caption Anderson protected him from any type of charges. But that was all going to change, because Caption Anderson was retiring at the end of the year, and Labossiere would lose his life line in the department. So he told me I was going to be Anderson's replacement."

Joey shook his head.

"You did It, didn't you?" Joey asked.

Sullivan looked down in disgrace for a moment before lifting his head back up.

"I knew that if I said no, he would've shot me right then and there on the spot. I didn't have a choice back then," Sullivan said as he looked at Joey.

"So what happened?"

"I did that for almost ten years. Labossiere used his money and power to have me promoted and take Anderson's job when he retired. I gotta say, even back then Labossiere always had good contacts. So anyway, during those ten years, Labossiere gave me info to make me look good while I supplied him with information about other known mob families in the state and kept the police off his back when he...did what he did. For the longest time I was so damn sure I was gonna get caught. I mean Christ, some days it just got crazy, but I never did. Not one person realized. Labossiere's info throughout those years was flawless. I looked like an American hero on paper and that's why the F.B.I. showed up one day in my office and made me an offer to join them."

"Jesus Christ, Sullivan! You do realize that you just confessed to breaking dozens of laws? So what, when you transferred to the Bureau did you stay in contact with him?" Joey quickly asked with anger and disbelief.

"No! Of course not! He tried to remain in contact but I never responded," Sullivan quickly said.

"Then why in the name of Christ are we meeting him?" Joey asked yet again.

Sullivan shook his head, then put the car in drive and started to drive down the street.

"After I broke contact with him, Labossiere started to do business with a big timer that was from the Middle East. The guys name was Abdul Bari; he was on Interpol's watch list. When I got the news that the Bureau was going to take him down, I was put in charge to lead the task force. I didn't realize Labossiere was going to be at the arms deal. So the team and I swept right in. The guys took care of Bari's men, got the drugs, Bari shot himself in the head, and I dealt with Labossiere. I could've arrested him right there. I should've, but I couldn't," Sullivan confessed.

"And why the hell not?" Joey asked.

"Because I thought back to when he had the chance to kill me that night on the dock. He spared me...and I had to do the same to him."

Joey rolled his eyes in disgust and he turned his head to look out the passenger window.

"I don't expect you to understand but I didn't have a choice."

"There's always a choice Sullivan. People only say there was no choice when they know they didn't make the right one," Joey said.

Sullivan knew that there was no changing Joey's mind. Joey was that type that once he had an idea of what he thought you were, there was no changing it. Sullivan knew that him telling Joey about Labossiere wasn't the best idea, but Sullivan needed Joey to be caught up because the last thing Sullivan was going to do was meet Labossiere alone.

II

The rest of the car ride was quiet. It was only when Sullivan pulled into the back of an abandon warehouse that Sullivan heard Joey. Joey didn't say anything, all he did was exhale deeply and Sullivan knew exactly what that meant because he was thinking the same thing: this probably wasn't the best idea he's had. He knew meeting Labossiere after all these years was a dangerous idea; Labossiere was already slowly losing it when Sullivan left for the Bureau, he could only imagine what the man was like now.

Over and over Sullivan told himself, yeah this wasn't a good idea...but it was the only idea he could think of. And even though it was far from the safest idea, it was an idea that had real potential and brought real hope for Sullivan and the rest of the guys to take down Dutra before it was too late.

Sullivan pulled up to the back door and shut the car off as Joey looked all around to see if anyone was around. The place was deserted, and the broken windows and rust covered walls proved the warehouse had seen better days.

Suddenly out of nowhere, a tingling feeling shot right up Joeys back and sent shivers down his body, like he had just stepped into a bathtub filled with cold water. It was a feeling he was never a big fan of. That feeling, along with his nervousness, caused him to slowly reach down to his sidearm and pull it out.

"Don't take that out," Sullivan ordered.

"Why the hell not?" Joey asked.

"Because you're just gonna get us killed. The moment we step foot in there, we'll be outnumbered ten to one," Sullivan firmly said, almost as if he had been in this situation before.

Joey shook his head and then put his sidearm back into it's holster.

"Sullivan, how do you even know that Labossiere will even have any idea about what this Dutra guy is doing?" Joey boldly asked.

"Because Labossiere knows everything. Yeah, he may be well past his glory days but the man still has connections," Sullivan said as he took out his cell phone and looked at the time.

"What do you mean past his glory days?"

"He was diagnosed with Alzheimer's and cancer about a year or so back, and from the sounds of it, he's losing both fights fast," Sullivan said.

Joey rolled his eyes.

"Great..."

Sullivan's face agreed with Joey's last sarcastic statement as he honked the horn of the undercover vehicle twice. In a way Sullivan was probably more nervous meeting Labossiere this time then any other time. Sullivan lost his father to Alzheimer's only a little while back. Sullivan had seen first hand what the sickness does to the body and mind, and Sullivan wouldn't wish it on anybody...not even someone like Labossiere.

It took a second or two after Sullivan honked the horn for the warehouse door to open, but once it did, three heavily armed men came rushing out, aiming automatic weapons at the car. Sullivan quickly put up his hands and Joey followed his lead.

"Just relax and do everything they say," Sullivan ordered from under his breath.

Sullivan looked at the men holding the guns and then locked on to a face that looked familiar. It took him a moment to place the face in his head, but once he did, a small rush of fear crept down his spin.

The man holding the gun on him was none other then Bobby Eric, Labossiere's son. Labossiere always told Sullivan back in the day that he had a good feeling about the kid and how he planned on having Eric take over the business when the time was right.

"Out of the car, slowly!" Eric ordered.

Joey looked at Sullivan as they began to slowly lower their hands to open the car doors. Joey looked down at his sidearm as he got out, just to make sure it hadn't fallen out or anything while Sullivan kept his eyes locked on Eric as he closed the car door.

Eric slowly checked out Joey and then turned to Sullivan. His eyes grew rather large. Sullivan swallowed as he started to really think going there was a big mistake.

"I'll be goddamned. Caption Sullivan," Eric said as he kept his gun up.

"Bobby Eric," Sullivan said in a very flat voice.

Eric chuckled and then slowly began walking over to Sullivan.

"Well, well. You actually remember me, I'm impressed," Eric said as Sullivan tried to figure out what angle Eric was coming from.

"I could say the same."

Eric walked up to Sullivan and checked him out, removing Sullivan's sidearm from the holster on his left hip.

"I gotta say Sullivan, you look the same as you always did. Guess some things don't change."

"I'll take that as a compliment," Sullivan said.

"Don't," Eric quickly shot back in a pissed off voice.

Sullivan stayed calm and hoped that Joey would do the same.

"So what the fuck brings you back after all these years?" Eric asked.

Sullivan exhaled.

"I need to see him."

Eric processed that for a moment before he broke out into laughter with the other two guys that were with him. One of them grabbed Joey's sidearm, removing it quickly from his hip.

"Well I hate to be the bearer of bad news, but my father is no longer running much of anything anymore. I am...and you know what? I should kill you right now," Eric said.

Sullivan had a bad feeling about the situation but wasn't sure until he heard Eric say it from his own mouth. But Sullivan still needed to talk with

Labossiere, even if not much was there.

"Eric. I need to talk to Pete...there are bigger things happening here between your father and I," Sullivan said.

Eric kept a straight face even though he knew Sullivan was right.

"So, are we gonna get this over with or what?" Sullivan asked.

Eric shook his head for a moment before suddenly turning around and opening the warehouse door to let Sullivan in. But just as Joey was getting ready to follow Sullivan, the two men that came out with Eric quickly grabbed Joey and stopped him dead in his tracks.

"Hey, what the fuck?" Joey shouted.

Sullivan quickly stopped and turned to Joey as the men grabbed him by his arms. Sullivan turned back to Eric.

"He stays outside," Eric said.

"I'll be back, Joey." Sullivan said.

Joey watched Sullivan walk deeper into the warehouse before suddenly shaking free of the men's grasp.

"Get the fuck off me!" He shouted at them.

III

Sullivan played detective as he followed Eric into the warehouse; his head was moving all around and watching the activity. As Sullivan watched Labossiere's men unload pounds and pounds of cocaine from several big rigs parked inside the large warehouse, he knew all he had to do was make one phone call and Labossiere and his guys would go to prison and probably never see the light of day again.

The warehouse had changed since the last time Sullivan had been in it, but the awful smell still lingered throughout the air—a crossover between body odor and grandma's basement kind of smell. Even way back when, Sullivan hated the smell. But he tried to focus on just getting the meeting with Labossiere over with.

"So Eric...how's he been?" Sullivan asked.

"Why the fuck do you care?" Eric quickly shot back as he turned his head at Sullivan.

"Come on, just humor me."

Eric exhaled.

"He has Alzheimer's...how do you think he is? He still remembers to wipe his ass most days, but those days are rapidly coming to a close. Course it's your lucky day though, Sullivan."

"Oh yeah?" Sullivan asked, wishing he still had his gun on him.

"Yeah, today is one of his good days. Woke up and remembered everything...fucking miracle...even had the energy to come on down here," Eric said.

"Imagine that," Sullivan said.

"So I heard D.C. is a war zone..."

"Yeah."

"Shouldn't you be there instead of wandering around here?" Eric asked.

"Trust me, I'd rather be here."

"You know I don't doubt that. I may have been little back then but I remember how much time you and my father spent together. Hell I remember he use to have you over the house for dinner and we would play baseball," Eric said as he began to walk up a staircase.

"Yeah. Well that was a long time ago, Eric"

"Not as long as you'd think, Sullivan," Eric mysteriously said as they both reached Labossiere's office.

Sullivan took his eyes off Eric and then looked at the door.

"Good luck Sullivan. With any luck maybe he won't put a bullet in your head," Eric said as he patted Sullivan on the shoulder.

Sullivan watched as Eric headed back down the stairs. As soon as Eric was far enough way, Sullivan slowly grasped the door knob, turned it and then opened the door and stepped inside, wishing he had something to use as a weapon.

The office was on the dark side, nothing but a small light on the desk. The windows that overlooked the harbor had been blocked out years ago along with the walls, the walls were covered with papers.

It took a moment for Sullivan's eyes to adjust to the dim light. For a second he was afraid that Labossiere would pop out of the shadows and grab him, but Sullivan quickly overcame the fear when Labossiere's face slowly leaned into the light from behind his desk and a different type of fear ran down Sullivan's spine.

"Well. Look what the wind fucking blew in," Labossiere said in an awful growl.

Sullivan knew this was when he had to be at tiptop shape. He had seen a lot of shit and met a lot of evil people ever since he took his job with the F.B.I., but Labossiere still was near the top of the list.

"How are you, Pete?" Sullivan said as he slowly walked over to Labossiere.

"Living the dream," Labossiere said before he started to cough.

Sullivan shook his head as he approached the desk. Labossiere dug into his pocket, took out some pills, opened the cap of the bottle and popped a few in his mouth, washing them down with what appeared to be a glass of Scotch.

"Good to be here, you're looking well," Sullivan said as he sat himself down in the seat in front of Labossiere's desk.

Labossiere finished coughing and then went back to making eye contact with Sullivan. The lighting situation wasn't on Sullivan's side, but he could tell just by the outline of Labossiere's face that he was slowly slipping away with his old age. The bags under his eyes and the double neck proved to Sullivan that Labossiere must've looked a lot older then he really was. He had a hard time believing that Labossiere was only seven years older then he was.

"Yeah. Why don't we skip past the small talk bullshit and get to the reason why you're here," Labossiere suggested.

Sullivan shook his head.

"I need your help, Pete," Sullivan admitted.

It took a moment for Labossiere to understand what Sullivan just said but once he did, he quickly broke into laughter.

"You...need...my help?" Labossiere asked as he laughed menacingly. "Wow. Guess time really does change things. Years ago we'd be in this exact office but the conversation would be switched, if I remember..." Labossiere said as a few more chuckles fell out of him.

Sullivan shook his head as he tried to stay on subject.

"A group with overseas connections tried to assassinate the president," Sullivan began.

"Oh yeah...Eric mentioned that to me earlier...damn shame," Labossiere said even though he honestly couldn't give a shit.

"Anyway. I came here because I need information about the leader of the group..." Sullivan confessed.

Labossiere smiled.

"Oh yeah? And what makes you think I have any idea who that is?" Labossiere shot back.

"I don't. I'm just hoping you do and you'll help me out."

Labossiere chuckled.

"Well, I guess you could say that I've been out of the business for so long..." Labossiere began to say before Sullivan interrupted him.

"Trust me, with a man like this I'm sure you've at least heard of him."

"And who is this man, then, Sullivan?" Labossiere asked, thinking it was someone he worked with before.

"Dutra Vacca."

Sullivan kept his eyes on Labossiere as he witnessed Labossiere's face slowly change, confirming he'd heard of the name before. Labossiere slowly shook his head before slowly looking down and leaning back in the desk chair.

"Mr. Vacca, huh?"

"Yep. He and his team were the ones that made the hit on the president."

"Was he successful?" Labossiere asked.

"Almost, but we were able to stop him."

"Interesting."

"What is?"

"The fact that he didn't get his target. He normally does."

"So you do know him?"

"Only the word that was on the street. Course it's been a while so a different kind of word could be out there today."

"Look Pete, just humor me, will ya? I need to know what he's up to."

Labossiere shook his head, knowing deep down that Vacca was a threat to not only Sullivan but to himself as well.

"At first we heard that a man named Dutra had just come from overseas and was beginning to buy large amounts of guns and ammunition. He was buying so much, that I heard about it all the way up here. He was also recruiting a large number of people, close to thirty. The rumor was any money they came across, he gave it all to them and he didn't take a penny. And somehow he stumbled across a large amount of cash, and he was able to get a large building to work out of. Course nobody ever had proof such a building existed. It's kinda hard to break into a skyscraper. He got my attention when we heard that the building was close by. With the amount of weapons he had, he could've started World War Three. But then he vanished." Labossiere continued, "But as soon as he disappeared, we heard about another man who was going around with another large group of men. They had killed George Argondizza and wiped out his organization—all forty of his guys...dead...except for one. He kept one alive, saying he was to deliver a message to my business partners..."

"And what message was that?"

"He told the poor bastard to tell everyone his name...Vacca. And just like that a mob war was started. Everyone on the pacific coast ripped through one another to try and figure out who Vacca was working for," Labossiere said.

"So you were on edge, too..." Sullivan said as he nodded his head, thinking he had an idea of what Labossiere was talking about.

Labossiere quickly looked up to Sullivan from the darkness.

"What are you fucking kidding me? Hell no! I was happier then a pig in shit when those clown across the country started killing each other off! There loss was my gain. I said that then and I'll say it now."

"So you weren't worried of Vacca?"

"Naw. I told my guys that if the time came, we would protect what we had to, but that was it. Besides I was more interested in this Dutra character. If anything, he was my biggest worry. Anyway, the mob war raged on until damn near most of the original families were wiped out.

Only myself and Paul Costigan from Boston were the last ones on the entire East coast...West coast sounded like a war zone...fast forward about nine months, I was heading down to a business meeting with Costigan and some of the last bosses down in Florida for a gun shipment. We all decided we needed to prepare and be ready for the shit storm on the horizon. When I got there, the crates were gone and everyone that I was supposed to be at the meeting with was dead, except for Costigan. He took one to the knee cap and two to the stomach. By the time I got there he had damn near bled out. So I walked over to him, tried to keep him calm as the bastard died but instead of remaining calm, he grabbed my shirt...pulled me down to him and whispered... 'Dutra Vacca'... and right then and there is how I found out they were the same person..." Labossiere said, lowering his head as he began to miss his once close business partner and friend.

Very slowly Sullivan was starting to understand a little more about Dutra, but he still couldn't quite shake off the feeling inside telling him that he was still missing something—something big.

"So how did Dutra...Vacca, go from being at war with the mob to where he is now?" Sullivan asked.

Labossiere laughed before the laugh turned into a cough.

"You still don't get it do you? You see in that moment, he had just signal handedly wiped out more then two thirds of the mob. A guy like that doesn't just vanish into thin air, he moves onto a bigger target. And in this case it was business overseas, but that didn't last all that long."

"And why was that?"

"Dutra disappeared off the radar...went underground..."

"Why?"

"Word was that he had taken some serious heat during his last trip outside the country. Said he put everything on hold and had begun to use his resources to track down everyone behind the ambush."

"And what was he trying to get at the ambush?"

"Rumor was that he was trying to get his hands on nuclear material. Shitty part of the world to be doing business in if you ask me."

"Why, where was he at?"

"Bosnia."

And then suddenly it clicked...now finally Sullivan began to see the bigger picture as his face began to drop. Labossiere clearly saw that he had stumbled onto something.

"Looks like I rang a bell. I take it, it was your boys, your dogs were the ones who ambushed him, weren't they?" Labossiere asked with a large grin on his face.

"There's no way he could possible know it was us..." Sullivan began before Labossiere interrupted him.

"Vacca knows everything! You understand? Every fucking thing. If it was you that attacked him in Bosnia...I'm sorry pal...but you and your friends are dead. Dutra will stop at nothing, you can count on that. Dutra was at the top of the list when he entered Bosnia; everyone feared him because he was reliable. Anything he set his mind to, he got. Dutra lost everything when he lost the shipment in Bosnia. His name, his reputation was broken because of that. I don't think I need to remind you what a man is capable of when he loses everything."

Sullivan wiped the sweat from his forehead and he inhaled deeply.

"All this because we intercepted one of his weapon shipments?" Sullivan asked out loud to himself.

"You kidding me? He doesn't give a shit about the shipment anymore, it's what your dogs took from him while they were there," Labossiere said as he leaned back into his chair.

Sullivan quickly looked up.

"What the hell does that mean?" Sullivan asked.

"Oh I'm sure if you look hard enough within, you'll figure it out...you don't expect me to give you all the answers, do you?"

Sullivan was starting to get frustrated. He knew that Labossiere was leaving something out—something that could change the big picture—but he knew that Labossiere wasn't going to finish what he started quietly.

"Come on Pete. I wouldn't ask if it wasn't this important," Sullivan said.

Labossiere could see the desperation in Sullivan's eyes, and he enjoyed seeing it. He even began to think about telling Sullivan he was happy to see him in the situation he was in, but Labossiere knew that if Dutra was out of the picture, everyone would benefit from it, including Eric.

"Last I heard, Dutra had been in business with a man by the name of Jonathan Street, a good software hacker even back in the day. The guys also has money...but he also has a history. I'm willing to bet that if you find him, you'll find Dutra..." Labossiere said.

Sullivan burnt the name into his mind before he quickly stood up and headed to the door.

"Thanks Pete," Sullivan said.

"Not so fast, Sullivan," Labossiere said, causing Sullivan to stop at the doorway, "I gave you something...now you give me something..."

Sullivan softly shook his head, thinking he should've known there was going to be a catch, there always was when it came to working with Labossiere.

"Okay Pete, name it."

Sullivan prepared for either an absolutely horrific demand or an impossible one; Labossiere liked to go back and forth with his type of demands, so Sullivan figured this time would be no different...but to his amazement, it was.

"I'm dying Sully...I can't deny that anymore. And when I'm gone, Eric will be on his own," Labossiere began to say as his voice started to crack, causing him to clear his throat.

"What are you saying to me, Pete?"

"I'm not asking you to look out for him, but when the time comes—cause we both know it will—promise me it will be you who takes him down," Labossiere asked as he looked at Sullivan.

Sullivan swallowed hard as he began to see for the very first time that behind the wall of evil and death Labossiere built up, lay a trace of a caring father...and that shocked Sullivan to the core.

"You have my word, Pete," Sullivan said as he nodded.

Labossiere shook his head up and down as he looked away from the dim light coming from his desk.

"Thank you," Labossiere softly said as he opened the top drawer of his desk and pulled out a silver handgun. "I'd rather take my chances with the Devil then lose my memory waiting for God. Course guys like us don't get into Heaven, do we?"

The light shined off the gun and got Sullivan's attention rather quickly, but Sullivan wasn't worried; he could tell just by the look on Labossiere's face what was gonna happen next.

Sullivan took one last look at the man before he slowly walked out of the office and closed the door behind him. As Sullivan walked out of the warehouse he started to forget about everything that was happening with Ray and Dutra and just took a moment and said a prayer for Labossiere; he figured it was the least he could do after everything.

Sullivan took one last look at Eric as he walked past him and Eric also made eye contact, until the sound of a gunshot rang through the warehouse, instantly ending the eerie silence of the place. And as Eric, along with everyone else, began to run up to the office of Peter Labossiere, Sullivan quickly ran outside and regrouped with Joey.

Sullivan and Joey raced back to the car. They needed to meet up with Ray so they all could try and make sense of the whole situation. For a brief second, as Sullivan was explaining to Joey everything that Labossiere had said, he actually thought with complete certainty that after all this time, they had finally gotten the upper hand on Dutra. But that thought would only last briefly.

IV

While Sullivan and Joey high-tailed it back to headquaters, back in the big apple, high up in his penthouse suit, just below his office, over looking the city, Dutra sat patiently in his living room, holding a glass of eighteen-year-old scotch in his hands and his cell phone and a handheld radio resting peacefully on the coffee table before him.

All the lights in the penthouse were off, but the lights from the city buildings gave the apartment a rather brilliant rage of ambient lighting throughout, offering a peaceful and comforting resting space

But that was the last thing Dutra was thinking about, In fact, the lighting only reminded him that his plan still wasn't in effect, which quite frankly pissed him off to a certain extent. But while half of him was waiting for his phone call from Vincent, to let him know the explosives were in place, the other half of him was jumping for joy inside, like a child at an amusement park, because he knew the time of waiting was soon coming to a close. This was it, this was where all of Dutra's work was about to pay off.

During those last final moments of calmness, Dutra took one last moment to reflect back on the whole idea and how he believed it would end. A smile grew on his face and he confirmed the plan would work. It had too, as far as Dutra was concerned.

He was able to finish his second glass of scotch and pour his third before his black cell phone started to vibrate on the coffee table. He topped off the third glass and then walked over to the coffee table and picked up his phone. It was Vincent.

"Are we set?" Dutra asked as he answered the phone.

"We are boss. Explosives are in place," Vincent said.

Dutra nodded his head.

"Good. Bring the boat back to the harbor, torch it, then you and the guys get back here ASAP understood?" Dutra quickly said in a rather soft yet deep voice.

"Copy that, we're on our way," Vincent said.

Dutra hung up the phone and then carefully placed it in his pocket before turning around and walking over to the window. The lights from the city lit up Dutra's face as he reached the window and looked all the way down at the poor unsuspecting city. Dutra began to grin as he cracked his knuckles a few times. He kept watching until he could no longer fight the urge, and then briskly walked back over to the coffee table and picked up the radio.

"Street," Dutra said.

"Yeah boss?" Street quickly responded back.

"Vincent is set...are you?" Dutra asked.

"Just about..."

"What do you mean, just about? What's taking so fucking long?" Dutra asked beginning to lose what little patience he had.

"It's a little more difficult that I thought, just give me a minute..."

Just imagining Street thinking that Dutra was gonna wait made Dutra chuckle for a moment, before he brought the radio back up to his mouth.

"I'll give you thirty seconds, how's that? And then at the end of that thirty seconds..." Dutra began to say as his voice got louder before Street suddenly interrupted what was going to be a pretty serious threat.

"Got it! Got it! I got it," Street said as he raised his hands in the air from his laptop.

Dutra exhaled softly and then shook his head.

"Good," Dutra said before he turned the channel on the radio. "Everyone check in."

It took a moment for Dutra's men to respond, but one by one they all checked in. The first that responded was Vincent, who had just gotten to the harbor and was currently looking up at the Manhattan Bridge, just across the city from Dutra.

"Manhattan reporting," Vincent said.

After Vincent checked in, it was three of his guys standing in front of the Sears Tower in Chicago.

"Chicago reporting."

Then another...

"Boston reporting."

And more...

"Philadelphia reporting."

"D.C. reporting."

Dutra shook his head and took a brief pause. In that moment everything stopped for Dutra. He knew that once he made the call to start the final piece of his plan, there would be no turning back...*everyone* would be looking for him. And in that last moment he exhaled and then put the radio back up to his mouth.

"Begin..."

Chapter 13: Prepping For War

The full moon lit up Ray's dark office as Ray sat at his desk with a cigar in one hand and a glass of whisky in the other. As the fifth hour of him sitting in his office approached, he finished his drink and then looked down at his lap and picked up the picture of Emily from when she graduated high school (another family moment Ray missed due to his profession).

He kept his eyes on the photo for a while as he began to think back to the very few times he was with both Emily and his wife, Diane. For the longest time the only moments he could remember about his wife was when he saw her at the hospital for the last time, a moment that's haunted him more than anything he's seen in the profession, but this time was different.

Ray was remembering when he had come home from Vietnam, with the promise that he never had to go back. Ray arrived at the airport late in the night all those years ago, and was greeted by Diane holding eight month old Emily in her arms. Ray quickly ran over, dropped his bags and picked up his daughter for the first time, and in that moment almost forgot the horrific images that scarred his mind.

Ray began filling up with tears as he remembered picking up his daughter and holding her up into the sky. It might have been years ago, but Ray still got the feeling in his gut just like he did back then, and he wished he could somehow go back.

But the loaded weapons on his desk reminded him just how much everything had changed in his life, and just like that, the pleasant feeling disappeared into the shadows of his office, leaving him with nothing but a broken heart and tainted moonlight from his office window.

As Ray finished his glass and started to load the weapons that were scattered all over his desk, he still was in the process of trying to figure out a way to get his daughter back. He had made the deal with Dutra, but Ray knew as much as Dutra did, that he wasn't going to give up that easy. Ray was going to do everything in his power to get his daughter back, even if the cost was his own life.

Ray had loaded about half of the weapons when he heard his office door slowly open. Ray didn't notice at first, it took the door closing to get his attention. Once Ray focused on the face in the shadow, he quickly lowered his head and then returned to loading the weapons.

"What are you doing here?" Ray asked Torque without looking back up at him.

"Just checking to see how you're doing," Torque softly said.

"I'm sure you can figure that out yourself."

Torque took a moment to respond back, even thought about leaving, but told himself Ray needed to be with someone.

"Anything I can do to help?"

Ray cocked the large machine gun and then dropped it on his desk.

"Yeah. You can tell me why in the fuck you were at my daughter's house," Ray said.

Torque froze in place and the sweat began to pour off him like no tomorrow; Torque knew he was fucked, because he could already see the anger in Ray's eyes. He took a brief moment but he knew he couldn't take a long one, cause Ray would quickly pick up on it.

Torque knew without any doubt that if he told Ray the truth (that he had just met her in a bar and they just went back to her place to fuck around), Ray would shoot him; hell if Torque had a daughter and he was told that, he would probably do the same.

Torque knew that lying to someone like Ray could spell major trouble down the road, but he knew that Ray didn't (and couldn't) have time to deal with this, he needed to focus on today.

"She's my girlfriend."

Ray shook his head and then slowly stood up and began walking over to Torque.

"Your girlfriend?" Ray asked as they stood face to face.

Torque lowered his head for a moment and then quickly brought it back up.

"Yeah. If I had any idea that she was your daughter..." Torque began but was interrupted by Ray's fist.

Ray's left hand to the face knocked Torque to the ground as his lip started to bleed. At first Torque didn't even move; the punch not only completely took him by surprise, but it also caused him to black out for a second or two. Torque rolled over onto his back and started to cough.

"What the fuck was that?" Torque shouted as he wiped the blood off his lip and spit the rest that was in his mouth onto the floor of Ray's office.

"What do you think it was for?! Why the fuck didn't you protect her?" Ray shouted as he stomped back over to his desk, picked up his glass of booze and then threw it as hard as he could against the wall.

Torque put his hand on his bloody lip as he slowly started to get to his knees.

"I didn't know she was your daughter, Ray!" Torque said as he groaned in pain.

Ray wiped the sweat off his forehead and then exhaled deeply.

"I know...I know...motherfucker!" Ray began to say softly before he screamed out loud, then suddenly picked up his computer and smashed it on the ground.

Torque protected his face when he heard the computer smash on the floor and then he looked back up at Ray.

"Goddamn it!" Ray said, before sitting back down in his chair, trying to relax even though he knew he wasn't going to be able to.

As Torque finally got back to his feet he kept his eyes focused on Ray. Torque let a rather long moment of silence pass by before he tried to say anything to Ray.

"Look Ray..." Torque began to say but got interrupted.

"Don't. Listen...uh..." Ray began to say.

"You don't have to apologize Ray...I understand," Torque said as he slowly walked over to Ray.

Ray chuckled for a moment.

"At least someone does, because I sure as hell don't," Ray confessed.

Torque patted him on the shoulder. Ray quickly looked down at Torque's hand on his shoulder but then went right back to looking at the picture of Emily that was on his desk and then slowly he began shaking his head.

"This isn't how I pictured my life would be at this stage. Now I finally understand what Dutra was saying," Ray said in disgust.

Torque felt horrible for Ray; it was like he could see that Ray just had nothing left in him to lose and that chilled Torque to his core.

"Hey!" Torque said as he knelt down and looked up at Ray, "I'm not giving up Ray. And if I'm not then you're not either," Torque said.

Ray forced a smile on his face and then stood up and patted Torque on the cheek. Torque nodded his head as he clearly saw the gratitude in Ray's eyes.

"Thank you, Johnny," Ray said.

"Like I said: whatever you gotta do...I'm in."

Ray nodded and then looked down at all the weapons on his desk when a voice called out from the office entrance.

"I'm in too," Steve said as he stood in doorway.

Ray looked up. Torque turned and when he saw it was Steve he smiled. Ray walked over to Steve and gave him a hug. Steve returned the hug by patting Ray on the back. Ray then slowly let go and looked at his old friend.

"Steve, you didn't have to come," Ray said.

Steve gave Ray a weird look.

"You kidding me of course I had too...we all had too," Steve said.

Ray raised his eyebrow at him.

"We?"

Steve nodded his head out to the floor and Ray walked out. As he did he started to get a good feeling, a feeling like maybe there was still a chance to end this right. Ray never said anything, but he knew he could always count on Steve to make him feel a little better about a situation.

On the body shop floor, Ray stopped dead in his tracks. It took him a moment to realize exactly what he was looking at. Ray was never one to cry over being happy about anything, but if he ever came close, it was then.

Standing in a large circle was Bob, Tommy, Jasmin and about a dozen more people that he didn't know. Ray made eye contact with Bob, Tommy, and Jasmin.

"We got your back, Ray," Jasmin quickly said.

Tommy shook his head in agreement.

"You didn't really think I was gonna sit this one out, did ya?" Tommy asked.

Ray chuckled as Bob shrugged his shoulders and look at Ray.

"You know me, Ray...I'm down for whatever," Bob said in his usual blank personality.

He gave his three guys a nod before he looked at all the other guys he didn't know. He was getting ready to ask who they were right before a familiar voice began talking to him from his right side.

"You've met some of my guys, but I figured now is probably the best time to meet the rest of them," the voice said.

Ray quickly turned to the direction of the familiar voice, and from the shadows Roader emerged, smoking a cigarette.

"Paul?" Ray asked in complete surprise. "What are you doing here?"

Roader walked over and the two leaders shook hands with one another.

"Where else would I be?" Roader quickly asked.

Ray nodded and then shook his hand even harder.

"I thought they hated each other," Jasmin said, as he leaned into Tommy.

Tommy looked at Jasmin.

"It's more of a love-hate relationship," Tommy tried to explain.

Jasmin had absolutely no idea what that meant.

"Okay, that still doesn't help," Jasmin said.

Tommy rolled his eyes and then went back to looking at Ray and Roader.

"Well your Bosnian...some of the shit you people do doesn't make sense either," Tommy said.

"Wow way to be racist, Tommy," Jasmin said.

"I wasn't being racist...if you and your country of towel heads feel the need to decapitate a chicken every now and then, more power to you...I don't judge," Tommy said with a smile.

Jasmin gave a sarcastic smile back.

"Thank you Tommy...I feel so much better about my myself."

Steve chuckled under his breath from Tommy's bluntness, one of the things he always loved about Tommy. But he took his attention off Tommy and Jasmin when his cell phone started to vibrate in his pocket. Steve quickly and quietly took the phone out and looked at the screen to see it was Sullivan.

"What is it Sullivan? Wait...what?" Steve said.

Steve turned away from Ray and Roader as the two of them finished up talking.

"You sure your up for this?" Ray asked Roader.

"If you are, than so am I. Besides, docs think Jimmy will pull through so it's a step in the right direction," Roader said.

"Glad to hear that, Paul," Ray said happily.

Roader shook his head.

"Now what about Emily? Do you have any idea where Dutra—or Vacca—would take her?" Roader asked.

Ray looked up at Roader.

"I was hoping maybe you might have an idea..." Ray said in desperation.

Roader didn't even have to think about it, he knew right away that he had not one single idea as to where Dutra was...not even a clue.

"Oh...oh dear," Roader said.

But before Ray could even respond, Steve got off his cell phone and got Ray's attention.

"Ray!" Steve shouted as he walked back over to everyone.

Both Ray and Roader turned and looked at Steve as the rest of the conversations suddenly stopped.

"Yeah, what's up Steve?" Roader asked.

"I just got a call from Sullivan, he says he might know where Dutra is."

Instantly Ray's head snapped back up and looked at Steve.

"How far out is Sullivan?" Ray asked.

"About two hours."

Ray shook his head and then turned to look at everyone on the floor. Then he focused all his attention to Tommy.

"Tommy, go get your shotgun," Ray said.

Tommy suddenly got a smile on his face.

"Ray, are you saying what I think you're saying?" Jasmin asked.

Ray shook his head.

"Let's mount up!!" Ray shouted to everyone.

"Yes, sir!" Shouted everyone.

II

Even though Ray had a lot of the weapons locked and loaded, he hadn't gotten to loading up spare clips or even grabb any grenades, so Jasmin and a few of Roader's guys worked on that while Bob smoked a cigar and loaded up the sniper rifles.

Tommy, on the other hand was to busy loading up and polishing his shotgun to even ask if anyone needed any help. It had been years since Tommy was allowed to use his pride and joy, and now that he finally was able to get it back, he was going to do whatever it took to prove he could be trusted with it...even though he really couldn't be.

"You sure it was a wise idea to let Tommy use his shotgun?" Steve asked Ray as he loaded his sidearm.

"Probably not but hey it can't hurt anything right?" Ray said as he put on his black boots.

"Well if anyone knew if it would hurt, it would be you, Ray." Steve said just before he laughed.

Ray didn't catch that zinger at first but once he did, he quickly grabbed his right shoe and chucked it at Steve.

"Shut up, Steve!" Ray said.

Steve kept laughing, which caused Ray to give in and start laughing too.

"You know what Steve? I really don't like you," Ray said as Roader walked in.

"Why do you hate him? He's not the one who shot you in the ass," Roader said as he finished putting on his bulletproof vest.

Ray quickly stood up from tying his shoe and looked at Roader.

"How the hell do you know about that?" Ray asked.

Roader very slowly took his eyes off Ray and then looked at Steve.

"Sorry, Ray," Steve said.

"I'll remember that one day, Steve," Ray warned.

"Looking forward to it pal," Steve said with a big smile.

"I'm sure you are," Ray said as he sat down and finished tying his shoes.

Steve put his sidearm into the holster on his hip and then looked at Ray.

"Alright, Jas and Roader's boys are working on supplies, Bob is on snipers and Tommy is...well two steps away from taking out his dick and fucking that shotgun," Steve began.

"Good let him. I heard karma is a bitch." Ray said.

"So who do you want me with?" Steve asked.

"Jas and Paul's boys should be good. Give Bob a hand but keep an eye on Tommy, though...I don't need a hole in my roof," Ray said.

Steve smiled.

"You got it Ray," Steve said and then walked out of Ray's office.

Once Ray finished tying up his boots, he took out his sidearm from the holster on his hip and then loaded a clip into it. As Ray loaded up his gun, Roader couldn't help but think back to the last time both him and Ray had worked side by side. Roader had a tough time believing that it had been close to ten years, but in the end it wasn't that hard to believe; Roader had been noticing things going by faster and faster ever since he turned fifty.

"Long time since you and I have worked together, huh?" Roader asked.

Ray shook his head.

"Yeah, long time," Ray said as he cocked his handgun.

"Listen Ray, I know that normally there's a little bit of a rivalry between us..." Roader began.

"A little?" Ray asked with a smile.

Roader chuckled.

"Okay maybe not so little, but I just want you to know that I've always looked up to you...you know how you treat your team and how well you get the job done is just amazing...the world really is a safer place because of you," Roader said.

Ray nodded.

"If it were safe, Emily would be home safe...not with him," Ray softly said.

Roader lowered his head as he saw the pain that was infecting Ray begin to reach the surface.

"Paul, can I ask you something?" Ray asked.

"Sure."

"You believe in Heaven?" Ray asked.

Roader looked at Ray and then slowly sat down next time him.

"From time to time, why?" Roader asked.

"What happens to guys like us?"

"What do you mean?" Roader asked.

"I had to go to church every Sunday when I was growing up because of my folks. I went even when I didn't want to. I went every weekend until my eighteenth birthday. As soon as I turned eighteen I got sent to Nam and when I came back I never went again...I just stopped believing altogether," Ray said.

Roader shook his head.

"War has a way of doing that, Ray. We see things in war that we never thought were possible. Mankind has many faces; some of them aren't that pretty," Roader said.

"Yeah ...I told myself that if a higher power existed, he would never allow half of what I saw back then, and that's how I've been living my life for the past forty years. But now that I'm getting older..." Ray began.

"You're starting to second guess yourself..." Roader finished.

Ray lowered his head and exhaled.

"Murder is the ultimate sin. I know that, but...is there any chance that...I don't know, maybe there's time to find redemption for what's left inside, Paul?" Ray asked.

Roader shook his head for a moment and really tried to think but there was just no way of answering that for Ray directly, even though he really wanted to.

"It's never to late to start Ray. I don't believe in much but I do believe in that, and I'll tell you one more thing I believe in: our job forces us to do things. Nobody knows that better then you and I, but it's not the amount of lives you take, it's the amount you save...and we save a lot Ray. And to me that's the only number that counts. Its not who you fight...its what you leave behind," Roader said.

Ray took Roader's wise words to heart; it still didn't make everything suddenly all better, but it was just that right pick me up that Ray desperately needed.

"Thank you, Paul," Ray said.

Roader nodded and then patted Ray on the arm.

"Anytime Ray, just don't go thinking were friends now," Roader quickly said with a smile.

"Wouldn't dream of it," Ray shot back.

Ray and Roader chuckled at each other until Steve quickly walked up to them. Ray looked up at Steve and just by Steve's expression, Ray knew it was serious.

"What?" Ray asked.

"You guys have to come see this," Steve said in disbelief.

Ray and Roader both looked at each other and then quickly got up and followed Steve out of Ray's office.

"Now what?" Roader whispered under his breath.

Ray was so tired and emotionally drained he honestly wasn't even really thinking about what Steve was bringing him to, but Roader on the other hand knew just by seeing everyone standing all around up ahead that it was something that got everyone's attention.

"What's everyone standing around f—" Ray began to say before he stopped himself when he looked at the T.V. screen.

On the screen was Erin Dinsmore, a young female news anchor in a red dress. But it wasn't the low cut dress that had everyone's attention, it was the text scrolling under her that had everyone in a state of shock: 'America Under Attack: Bombings all around the nation.'

"—As we try to get more information as to what is happening there in Boston. Meanwhile we want to turn it over to Joni Caines who's live in New York...Joni?"

The screen instantly changed from the news anchor to Joni, a young women who had been working for the station for close to two years. Her long dark hair waved all around as smoke lifted up into the view from behind her.

"Yes, we're here just overlooking Manhattan and this is how far we are allowed to get. From what we all are hearing, it is believed that a bomb exploded right in the middle of Times Square a few hours ago. Those who have been watching since we went on air know that we originally came on to report about an explosion of some kind that took down the Manhattan Bridge. Right where that smoke is rising up into the sky is where the Manhattan Bridge is. Originally we believed it was some type of major car accident that sent flames into the air, but now it's believed that it was indeed an explosion that happened not only in the middle of Times Square but also the Manhattan Bridge..." Joni said before she got cut off.

"And right now we are just getting word that there was an explosion at the White House moments ago..." Erin said before she suddenly got cut off.

The T.V. screen went black, leaving everyone in complete and total silence.

"Holy shit," Tommy said into the eerie silence.

It took Jasmin, Tommy and the rest of the young guys no time at all to react. The older guys, however—Ray, Roader, Steve and Bob—couldn't believe what they just saw. In a way Jasmin, Tommy and the others had only a rough idea about what these attacks meant, but Ray and the rest could see the big picture clear as day.

"So that's what he had up his sleeve the whole time," Roader said.

"Yeah but there's no way in hell he was able to do all that on his own," Bob said.

"Wherever there's a will there's a way...looks like he found his way," Roader said.

Bob nodded his head an agreement.

"He just changed the game," Bob said.

"Bob's right. This changes everything; we gotta move," Ray began. "Steve, call Sullivan and find out where the hell he is..."

"I'm right here!" Sullivan shouted as he closed the door to the body shop.

Ray and the rest of the guys quickly turned and walked over to Sullivan as he and Joey entered the room. As Sullivan and Joey looked down at the files in their hands, Ray could clearly see that both Sullivan and Joey looked exhausted, even from a distance.

"Sullivan...is it true about New York?" Roader asked.

"What about the White House?" Steve asked.

"The news also mentioned Boston," Bob said.

"Aright, listen up everyone. Yes, it's true about New York...the Manhattan Bridge is gone and a bomb went off at Times Square...there was also a shooting at the JFK international airport," Sullivan explained.

"What?" Steve quickly asked.

"The news didn't say anything about that," Jasmin said.

"We're trying to keep a lid on as much as we can. If the public were to know what was going on all at once...an even greater panic would break out. As of right now all internet connections were shut down as well as every cell phone five miles outside of Washington and a mile outside of New York," Joey explained as he turned and looked at the now blank T.V.

"And you don't think that'll cause a panic?" Tommy asked with sarcasm.

"Right now, it's the only plan we got," Sullivan confessed.

"What about the White House?" Ray asked.

"It was shot at by a rocket launcher. The president wasn't inside at the time; he's currently on Air Force One and will remain there until we figure out what the hell is going on," Sullivan said.

"We already know what's going on Sullivan," Steve said.

Sullivan turned and looked at Steve.

"No you really don't, Steve. In fact, I didn't fully understand what was going on until about ten minuets ago, after my conversation with the Vice President. The Chinese Embassy in Chicago was also attacked. Now I don't need to remind you about how fragile our relationship with China already is," Sullivan began.

"Son of a bitch," Ray said as he shook his head.

"What? Who gives a shit about a small ass embassy?" Tommy asked.

"Yeah, what's an attack on the embassy have to do with our relationship with China?" Jasmin asked.

"It means that even though the embassy is on American soil, it's still a part of China, and any attack on the embassy would be considered an attack on the country itself. Ask yourself how we would react if we found out someone attacked one of ours?" Roader asked.

Ray shook his head.

"We have to deal with this fast," Sullivan said before looking down at the rather thick file in his hand and then handing it to Ray.

Ray grabbed it from Sullivan and quickly opened it. Inside right at the top was a large picture of Dutra with a rather evil looking grin on his face. The picture alone made Ray's blood boil.

"One of my old informants was able to provide information on one of Dutra's last known associates, a man named Jonathan Street. A brilliant computer hacker, rivals damn near anyone we have over to the Bureau," Sullivan said as Ray flipped the page of Dutra and then saw the picture of Street (the photo of Street was a little on the aged side, but even with dark sunglasses on and the picture being taken rather far from the target, Ray could clearly identify Street).

"This guy was in the helicopter with Dutra back in Washington," Ray said.

"Not surprised, the two of them have been close friends ever since they first started working together. Now we ran his name through every single data base and so far only came up with one known address," Sullivan began.

"431 Berkley Street, third floor, apartment 307, New York City, less than a quarter of a mile away from Times Square," Joey finished.

Ray looked up when he heard the address. He was about to ask a question but Steve beat him to it.

"Wait a second, if this guy is really in bed with Dutra, why would he help blow up a bomb that close to his place?" Steve asked.

"Hopefully you guys can figure that out when get there," Sullivan said.

"Isn't the city on lockdown?" Bob asked.

"Yes, but once the president found out about the situation, he authorized one helicopter to fly into the no fly zone, and you guys are gonna be on the helicopter."

Joey stepped in. "You'll land in Time Square; there will be heavy police presence when you land. There will also be a command post set up," he told them. "when you guys get there, ask for Chief Burke; he'll be the one in charge. However once you guys take off and start to head to Street's apartment, you'll be on your own. Most that live there have either fled or are holed up in their homes. The streets will most likely be deserted."

Ray looked at Steve. Ray could tell just by the look on Steve's face that Steve was ready for action...and so was Ray.

"Have you given any serious thought that Dutra might actually be in New York?" Roader asked.

Sullivan quickly turned and looked to Roader.

"We haven't confirmed anything yet, but we believe he very well could be. In fact, I personally think he is," Sullivan said.

"But?" Roader asked.

"But Home Land Security believes Dutra is somewhere in Washington. They haven't been specific, but they say they're working on a few leads," Sullivan said.

"Oh give me a break, they don't know their elbow from there asshole,"

Steve said as he shook his head.

"Well at least while they're working in Washington, all of us can focus on New York," Ray said as he looked to Roader.

Sullivan looked down for a moment and cleared his throat. He knew the next bit of news wasn't going to make anyone in the room happy but in the end he had no choice, just another perk of his job.

"Yeah, there's a problem to that..." Sullivan said.

"What do you mean there's a problem?" Steve asked.

"The president wants to be sure he has a team in Washington ready to go in case something goes down there, I tried to explain that you guys work better together but Harris was insistent," Sullivan explained.

"Insistent about what?" Roader asked.

Sullivan exhaled as he prepared for that look in Ray's eyes again.

"The president wants myself, Joey, Roader and his team back in Washington," Sullivan said.

As soon as the sentence fell out of Sullivan's mouth, the guys lost it. Tommy through his hands in the air, Roader shook his head and Steve rolled his eyes.

"This is horseshit," Jasmin said in his Bosnian accent.

"You gotta be fucking kidding me!" Bob shouted.

"Why in the hell does he need me back in Washington?" Roader asked.

The guys quieted down as Roader asked the question.

"It's not my call...I tried my best to explain the situation but...it's out of my hands," Sullivan confessed.

Roader shook his head. "Always is," he muttered quietly.

"So what are we suppose to do in New York then with no backup?" Steve asked.

"Do what you normally do," Sullivan said as he frowned.

Normally Ray would've been right on Sullivan, telling him what complete bullshit this was, but Ray didn't have to. He could clearly tell just by Sullivan's face that he didn't like the situation either.

"I know that's not the answer you want to hear, but until the president gives the K.O. to move on from this lead in Washington, there's nothing I can do," Sullivan further explained.

Most everyone in the room was beginning to have second thoughts, especially Sullivan, but the only one that didn't have any second thoughts was Ray. He was going to do this with or without his team.

"What if we move the assault back to later tonight?" Ray asked as he crossed his arms.

Sullivan and Joey looked up at him.

"What?" Sullivan asked.

"If we held off until tonight, would that be enough time for you, Roader and everyone else to clear Washington so that way we all went into New York together?" Ray asked.

Sullivan thought on it for a moment, so did Joey; hell so did everyone else in the room, and the more they thought about it, the more they realized it was a good idea—or at least better then splitting up.

"That's not a bad idea at all if you ask me," Roader said.

"I'll second that," Steve said right after.

"We'd have more time to prepare," Jasmin added.

"And we would have the cover of darkness," Torque added.

"And we all would be together, strength in numbers," Joey said as he turned and looked at Sullivan.

Sullivan thought out the idea in his head. He slowly looked up and without warning was looking directly into Ray's eyes.

"It could work. No guarantees, but I'll do what I can," Sullivan said.

"Good, because if all of us hit him at the same time, we might have a chance of stopping him; but if we go after him alone, I'm not sure we can stop him. You know, don't get me wrong guys, you all are the best at what you do, but this guy—he's nothing like what we've dealt with in the past," Ray said.

Sullivan shook his head and then looked at Roader.

"I'll go, but my team stays here with Ray and his team," Roader said.

Ray quickly looked at Roader. Before Ray could say anything Roader nodded at him and then looked back at Sullivan.

"Done," Joey said.

"When do they want me there?" Roader asked Joey.

"ASAP," Joey said.

"Well, let's get moving then..."

III

As Sullivan, Joey and Roader took off to get back to Washington as fast as they could, Ray's team—along with Roader's team—went back to loading up, only now it was much different, especially for Tommy. Before, Tommy was a little nervous about the whole situation, but now after hearing what Sullivan had to say and just by looking at Ray, he knew this was going to be a hell of a fight. In fact everyone knew it was going to be, especially Ray.

Ray (and possibly Steve and Bob) knew that there was a real chance that not everyone would come back from this, but that was a chance Ray promised he would deal with when the time came. No use in worrying about something that hadn't happened yet. Ray's main focus was trying to find the best way to get to Street's apartment.

He didn't say anything at first, but it was clear that with Roader's team tagging along they were going to have to split up; the threat of staying together in such a large group was too extreme; Ray knew that and so did Bob and Steve.

"You really think splitting up is the better idea?" Bob asked Ray.

Ray looked down at the map of New York that Sullivan had put in the folder.

"If we stay together, we'll be spotted," Ray said.

Steve nodded in agreement.

"I think so too. What are you thinking?" Steve asked.

Ray kept his eyes on the map.

"Roader and I planned on splitting the team up anyway. I think we should stick with that if he doesn't make it back from Washington in time." Ray said.

"You sure?" Bob asked.

Ray nodded.

"Okay, so who would take Roader's team?" Bob asked.

Ray kept his eyes on the map as he tried to figure out the best way to pull this off. Even though he would be the better choice, Ray didn't want to give up Steve. If things were gonna get messy Ray wanted Steve right at his side, and he had planned to put Bob up in a sniping position.

"I don't mind taking them," Steve offered.

Ray shot that down.

"Naw, you stick with me on this one."

Steve then shrugged his shoulders. "Okay, so who then?"

Steve had an idea even before he asked. Under any other circumstances Ray would be a little more cautious with picking a choice, so no one was being looked upon as a favorite. And Ray did give it some thought, serious thought, but at the end of that train he ended up with the same name.

"Bob. Go grab Torque, tell him to get his ass in here," Ray said.

Bob nodded and then walked out of Ray's office. Steve looked up at Ray.

"Think it'll work?" Steve asked.

"It has to...we won't make it out of New York if it doesn't. Let's just pray Sullivan gets back in time," Ray said as Bob walked back into the office with Torque right behind him.

Torque walked in and looked down at the large map covering Ray's desk. He then looked up at Ray and Steve.

"Bob said you wanted to see me," Torque said in a rather soft voice, sounding like he was emotionally drained.

"Yeah. Listen, we're sticking with the same plan even if Sullivan and

Roader can't get back..." Ray started.

"And what's that?" Torque asked.

"We're splitting the teams up: Our guys will be with us, Roader's guys will be with him," Steve said.

"Only problem to that would be if Roader doesn't make it back, then we would need someone to be in charge of his team," Ray said.

"Okay, so what do you need from me?" Torque asked.

"You're going to be leading Roader's team if he doesn't get back," Ray said.

Torque quickly looked up. A slight grin suddenly appeared on his face.

"Really?" Torque asked.

"Hey, hey, hey, don't let this get to your head! It's a big responsibility. You take this seriously. We don't have time to be acting like a school girls in heat," Steve said.

"Steve's right. You fuck up on your end, we're all fucked. Same goes for us—we can't afford to screw this up. Can you deal with that?" Ray asked.

Torque turned back to Ray and looked him dead in the eye.

"You bet I can," Torque firmly said.

Ray nodded.

"Alright. We're out of here as soon as we get the call," Ray said.

Torque nodded. "You got it, boss."

Torque headed back into the body shop.

"Think you gave the kid a hard on, Ray," Bob chuckled.

Ray raised his eyebrows.

"Well, hopefully he doesn't fuck us with it," Ray said.

Steve lit a cigar as he looked back down at the map.

"Think they'll make it back in time?" Steve asked Ray.

"I hope so Steve, I really hope so," Ray said.

And in that moment that's all Ray had to hold onto...hope.

Chapter 14: Destruction On The Horizon

"Well, here's to hoping," Steve said to Ray as they shook around in the helicopter on their way to New York.

"Yeah," Ray said as he held onto his machine gun and looked out into the sunny sky through the helicopter door.

"Told you Sullivan and them weren't going to make it," Bob said as he leaned into Ray.

Ray shook his head in frustration as Bob then turned and looked across the helicopter and saw Tommy and Jasmin talking. Bob didn't say anything, but he was (in his own way) glad that he was able to have had that talk with Tommy back at the hospital, even if Tommy was only half listening.

Bob had been bottling everything up for so long that he forgot what it was like to actually talk about things to someone. It was one of the things he wished he could change about himself, but couldn't. Bob was a firm believer that you really can't teach an old dog new tricks.

"Hey, Ray!" Jasmin shouted over the roar of the helicopter engine.

"Yeah?"

"Not that I'm in a rush to get shot at, but how much longer on this damn thing? My ass is falling asleep!" Jasmin shouted.

Steve chuckled at the way Jasmin's voice sounded as he yelled.

"Maybe another half hour!" Ray shouted back.

"The sun should be down by then right?" Steve asked.

"Hopefully it will be. Wouldn't want to start shooting up the streets of New York in broad daylight!" Tommy shouted.

"Yeah, it should be down by the time we land!" Ray said.

Turnng back from Jasmin and Tommy, Ray looked back out at the sunshine filtering in through the window. As he looked at the great ball of fire through his sunglasses, he couldn't help but fear that he wouldn't see it again. All this time he had been trying to block that thought out of his mind and stay positive, but right then and there it all came out, and it honestly frightened Ray. It took Torque tapping him on the shoulder for Ray to pull his head out of wherever it went.

"Hey, you alright?" Torque asked.

"Yeah, just thinking," Ray said.

"Rides like these bring back a lot of memories, huh?" Steve asked as he leaned in close to Ray.

"Just a little bit," Ray said as he tried to stop thinking about Emily and focus. But it was a waste of time; Ray couldn't stop thinking about her, and he didn't want to either. It was almost like he told himself that if he kept thinking about her, she would feel his presence, wherever she was.

"I got a question," said Tim Clement, the main gunner on Roader's team.

Tim was one of the youngest on Roader's team and had the baby face to go along with it. The military style haircut didn't even make him look older, if anything it just made him look younger.

"Yeah, what's up kid?" Ray asked.

"You ever heard of a group of guys they use to call 'the dogs'?" Tim asked.

Ray kept his eyes on Tim as a few of the guys in the helicopter chuckled.

"Who hasn't heard of them and their gas masks? A classic urban legend right there," Tommy said.

"Naw Tommy, it's no urban legend man," Jasmin said.

Tommy quickly took his eyes off his shotgun and looked at Jasmin.

"Don't tell me you believe in them? There's no possible way," Tommy said.

"Yeah. Isn't there a story about them being dropped into Northern Pakistan and they were surrounded by fifty men and all they had were knives?" Bob asked.

"I heard it was a hundred," Tim said.

"What about that story in Cuba?" Jasmin asked.

"What about it?" Tommy asked.

"I know for a fact that happened," Jasmin insisted.

Tommy blew raspberries as he shook his head at Jasmin.

"What happened in Cuba?" Tim asked.

"Rumor has it the 'dogs' took down a major terrorist site off the shores of Cuba back in the early nineties...supposedly they prevented a truckload of nuclear weapons from falling into hands that were associated with terror cells in the middle east," Bob explained.

"Really?" Tim asked.

"Oh, don't tell us you believe that shit now," Tommy said.

"Yeah, I have to go with Tommy on this. We couldn't even do half the shit they supposedly did, and we have twice as many guys," Bob said.

"What about you Ray? Any thoughts?" Tim asked.

"Yeah Ray, you must've heard about them; you've been around forever," Jasmin said quickly without thinking.

Ray turned and looked at Jasmin. Suddenly Jasmin realized he really did just say what he said, and quickly grew a smile on his face and turned red.

"Sorry, but you know what I mean," Jasmin added.

Ray didn't say anything at first, almost as if he was still trying to process the fact that Jasmin just called him old. Or maybe he was trying to process that...well...he really was starting to get old.

"Ray, you know anything about them?" Tommy asked.

"Yeah, I've heard the stories," Ray said, nodding.

"What's your take on them? Think they really existed?" Torque asked.

Ray cleared his throat. "In some way, I believe they do, or did." Ray said.

"What do you mean by that?" Jasmin said.

"Not a lot is known about them. In fact, no one is sure how many of them there were...some say it was all done by one man, some say it was by two or three," Ray shouted back to Jasmin over the roar of the helicopter.

"So what's the story on how the dogs formed?" Tim asked.

Ray looked over at Tim.

"Supposedly, it was sometime back in the early eighties. Rumor has it the F.B.I., N.S.A and the C.I.A. were given orders by the president to recruit and train three men—men that would be dropped into the worst area's of the world, area's that could change the face of the world if disaster headed their way. Now by in the late eighties we were having trouble with Iraq, tension was high with Russia—much like today—and of course we were all still in awe after the Chernobyl disaster. The men were never to be working on the same mission together."

"What does that mean?" Tim asked.

"It meant that if the F.B.I. sent their guy into Russia for intel, the other two had to keep there guy out. It seemed to work; we made it out of the eighties without any type of nuclear detonation, everything seemed to be going fine... "

"So if it was working so great, why the hell did they suddenly stop?" Tommy asked.

"In the mid nineties U.S. intel received information that major activity was taking place in the outskirts of Chernobyl. A wealthy warlord had been attempting to get his hands on nuclear reactor fuel to sell to the highest bitter. President Clinton knew the seriousness of the threat, so he authorized a meeting with all three men just outside of Washington. It was the first time all three men had been together in one room. Clinton told them of the situation and ordered all three of them to go in and take out all targets," Ray said.

"If they had never worked together and they were never meant to, why put them on this one?" Torque asked.

"Because the F.B.I., C.I.A., N.S.A and the President all agreed that the situation was that serious," Ray explained.

"Why not send in troops?" Bob asked.

"Because the last thing we needed was another war. We were still recovering from the Gulf War and Clinton was in no way going to authorize a military operation of that scale. He said right then and there: 'It's all on you guys'."

Jasmin threw back his head. "Damn. I didn't know that," he confessed.

"Actually, in a way you did Jas. You see it wasn't Northern Pakistan that they were outnumbered in, it was Chernobyl," Ray said.

"Wait, wait, wait...so you're saying the rest of that story is true? They were really outnumbered, and all they had was knives?" Tommy shouted.

"Course they had guns Tommy, until they ran out of ammo, then they used knives. And then their fists, until every single target was eliminated," Ray explained.

"So how did they get into Chernobyl? I mean come on...place would've been covered in radiation...there's no way they could survive that," Bob quickly said to remind everyone that there's no way the story could be true.

"They could if they were wearing gas masks," Ray began, "and that's what they did. In fact, many people believe that Chernobyl was the first time they ever put on gas masks."

Jasmin smiled as he pictured what the battle looked like. He felt a trickle of fear as he imagined one of those gas masks running up to him with a knife.

"That's awesome. I always wanted to know why they went with a gas mask," Jasmin confessed.

"Well, that's the reason," Ray said.

"So what happened next?" Tim asked.

"Well they got the job done, killed the target and then headed back home. Everone was so impressed that they decided to have them go back on one more mission...off the shores of Cuba," Ray said.

"No shit," Torque said shaking his head in amazement.

"No shit. They put on their gas masks and went after twenty five targets, without firing a single shot," Ray said.

Tommy chuckled. "Yeah...right."

Ray nodded. "A lot of people have a hard time believing that," Ray said.

"Yeah, cause there's no proof," Bob said as he inhaled his cigarette.

"Oh there's proof, Bob," Ray said.

"Oh yeah and what's that?" Bob asked right back.

"If they didn't stop that deal from happening, none of us would be here today. You see, the buyer was the leader of a terrorist cell just outside of Northern Afghanistan," Ray revealed.

Bob thought about that for a moment and eventually it kinda started to make sense. He still didn't believe it, but even he couldn't deny it did make sense.

"So what happened to them after?" Tim asked.

"Well, after the President was told how it went he started to grow concerns about the three of them, said that it was too much power for three men to have. Too much responsibility, too, so he put a stop to it...and the dogs were officially released, so to speak," Ray said.

Jasmin shook his head. "Stupid, stupid way to end," he said.

"Not really, Jas. You see, once the Cuba situation was taken care of, the world became quiet. There wasn't a need for them anymore, they had done what they were created for," Ray said.

Torque chuckled. "Well, we could really use them now couldn't we?" He asked Ray.

Ray lifted his eyebrow and then patted Torque on the shoulder.

"Alright. Now that we've taken care of that, let's get back to focusing on the task at hand, alright?" Ray asked.

"Yes, sir." Roader's men all said together.

Now that the story was over, everyone on the helicopter took the last of the ride to relax and prepare for the wickedness that was just on the horizon. The quietness of the helicopter took over as Tommy and Jasmin checked their ammunition. Torque loaded up his sidearm and Bob finished up his cigarette. The only two that didn't check their weapons were Ray and Steve.

Steve couldn't help but smile as he looked at Ray; same thing with Ray. Steve always enjoyed listening to Ray tell the story of 'The Dogs of War'; Steve could never build up the tension like Ray could. The story was able to get a smile on Steve's face before he slowly dropped his head and started to question where he had placed that old gas mask...

II

Over at Dutra's skyscraper, the building was on lockdown. A large number of people were patroling inside the building, and an even larger crowd was just outside the main entrance to the building.

The shut down of the city was working perfectly, just like Dutra knew it would. It got people off the streets and gave Dutra's men a clear path to block the street with dozens of SUV's and large trucks, not to mention the thirty or so guys with enough automatic weapons to stop a tank from coming through the blockade. And with the police focused on the Manhattan Bridge and Times Square, Dutra could rest easy knowing that even if shots were fired, nobody would be around to respond.

He smiled as he looked down at the blockade from his penthouse. He was excited; he knew the plan was working perfectly, and it was only a matter of time before Ray and his team were dead and he could continue on with his business.

The death of Radar was a bit of a blow to Dutra's ultimate goal, but with eight billion people in the world Dutra was sure that he could find someone else to replace him. Besides Dutra didn't really care for Radar anyway, in fact he was kinda glad the bastard was dead.

"Everything's in place sir," Vincent said, stepping forward.

Dutra didn't acknowledge him; he was too much in thought to answer back...one of the things Vincent always hated about Dutra.

"Sir?" Vincent asked again.

"Yeah, I heard you. Building is secure?" Dutra quickly asked.

"The entire building is on lockdown. I have guards on every floor," Vincent confirmed.

"Where's Street?"

"He's on his way back from the apartment," Vincent said.

Dutra nodded his head as he slowly looked up. Then he began cracking his neck.

"And is the apartment..." Dutra began before Vincent interrupted.

"It is..."

Dutra cracked his neck one more time and then smiled.

"Excellent."

"You still want me outside?" Vincent asked, hoping Dutra would change his mind.

Before Dutra answered, he began thinking if Vincent could be of any more use to him...and the answer was clear.

"Yes, I want you outside, but take Keith and Bobby with you. Let's keep this outside," Dutra said.

"Yes, sir."

Vincent was far from happy that he had to go outside, but Bobby and Keith were animals; they wouldn't stop for nothing, so that made him feel a little better about the situation, just like Dutra thought it would.

Even though Dutra honestly didn't care what happened to Vincent, he knew that Vincent could take care of himself and wouldn't go down without a fight. And that was going to come in handy later on, so it was best to keep Vincent's emotions at bay. And Dutra just needed to put one last nail in the coffin.

"Hey Vin..." Dutra said as he turned his head.

Vincent stopped and then turned back around and looked at Dutra.

"Yeah, boss?"

Dutra then turned his whole body and looked at Vincent.

"What do you think happens to men like us when we die?" Dutra asked.

Vincent was confused, almost dumbstruck. It was like he not only didn't understand the question, but also wasn't sure if that's what Dutra said because after all the time that he'd known Dutra, he would never ask a question like that.

"I'm sorry, sir...?"

"When we die...what happens to us?" Dutra asked.

"Are you asking me if I believe in an afterlife?" Vincent.

"In a way," Dutra said, his eyes on Vincent.

"Dunno. Never really gave it any thought, I guess," he said even though that was a complete lie.

"Huh. Well, you should. It's always good to think about the future. You know why?" Dutra asked.

Vincent shrugged his shoulders.

"It's good to think about the future because it helps shape the present," Dutra said as he slowly walked over to Vincent.

Vincent nodded his head as Dutra came walking over.

"I'll remember that, sir," Vincent said.

Dutra stepped closer and closer until he was literally right in Vincent's face. Vincent started to fill up with a bit of fear; the look on Dutra's face was impossible to read, or even attempt to figure out what he was thinking. But suddenly, just when Vincent started to think he had to worry about his life, Dutra quickly lifted up his hand and softly patted Vincent on the cheek.

"I'm sure you will," Dutra said and quickly turned away, walking back to the window. "Get a helicopter on stand by, in case Stone fails on his part. Tell them to meet us on the roof when the time comes."

"You got it."

Dutra smiled and then looked back down at the blockade in the road. When he heard the door close to his penthouse, he exhaled very deeply and began to once again relax in silence...until his cell phone rang.

Annoyed by the ring, Dutra dug into his pocket and took it out. He looked down at the screen with the intent to ignore the call when he realized it was Street. Even though he wanted to relax for a little longer, he knew the phone call was important and after the fourth ring, he picked it up.

"Where are you?" Dutra snapped.

"Less then two blocks away," Street said.

"Good, and everything is ready to go?" Dutra asked.

"Oh yeah. It's quite the scene over there," Street said.

Dutra cleared his throat.

"Good, when you get here, tell the guys with you to head outside and then you head up to my office," Dutra ordered.

"Alright. I'll be there in five," Street said.

Dutra hung up and then placed his cell phone back in his pocket. He felt more excited then he ever had been, for he knew that the opportunity to show his skill to the rest of the world was approaching fast, and that provided Dutra with nothing but enthusiasm. Nothing was going to get in his way.

III

As the blazing sun slowly set over the far horizon, the hazy, dense smoke lifted into the air and blocked out most of the remaining daytime light above the New York skyline. The deep shades of red, orange, and purple shot across the sky in beautiful fashion, but due to the thickness of the smoke, the colors of the sunset were not visible anywhere near Times Square.

The chopper carrying Ray and the whole gang flew in from the west so the guys were able to get a quick glance at the sunset just before heading over to the promised land. It was Tommy who noticed the sunset first and one by one they all turned their heads and witnessed the amazing view.

The guys didn't say anything; they didn't need to. Each one of them knew that was that moment: that last quiet, almost peaceful moment before the storm. Danger lurked on the visible horizon, but in a way the guys didn't want to pry their eyes away from the view. It was like the light from the sky was washing them clean of all past sins and no one wanted to break from that. Nobody said anything to one another, but in that moment every last man on the chopper had a sliver of hope reborn inside of them.

"Alright, guys here we go," the pilot of the helicopter announced.

As soon as Ray heard the words he slowly stood up and exhaled deeply from the pain shooting through his arthritis-filled knee. Ray knew the five seconds of freedom were over, it was time to play in the mud.

He remembered that awful feeling he got in his gut when he was listening to Sullivan as he briefly described the situation in New York, but that feeling amplified into something he never could've imagined when the large clouds of smoke came into view.

"Jesus," Ray whispered under his breath.

The blooms of smoke quickly grew larger as the helicopter rushed straight towards them. Ray wished he could some way spare the rest of the guys from seeing what the country they've been fighting for had turned into, but not even Ray could change that.

"Holy fucking shit!" Tommy said as he looked out the window and saw the smoke.

Everyone in the helicopter remained silent, frozen with disbelief and a trace of fear. Not because it was a sight they never saw before (in fact a war stricken city was a rather normal thing to see), but because never in a million years did they think they would ever see something like that on American soil.

As the chopper began crossing the city skyline more and more fires could be seen burning in and out of the smoke clouds. Clearly the damage from the bomb, or bombs, was extensive. Sullivan had made it seem like everything was under control back at the body shop. He'd left out the part about it being a complete disaster zone.

Ray could hear his heart beginning to beat in his ears as the helicopter pushed him and the entire team deeper and deeper into the war zone. He closed his eyes a couple of times to make sure he was seeing exactly what he thought he was, and he was.

For the briefest second a sudden shock of fear raced down his body because for a moment he thought he was back on the helicopter in Vietnam. That war was many years ago, and Ray had seen plenty more between then and now, but like they say: you always remember your first, and this was no different. The fear exited as fast as it came, leaving the rest of the team unaware of what Ray just went through, and that was fine with him. Because the last thing he wanted the guys to know was that inside he was scared as fuck. He knew that if he was that nervous, then the guys must be too.

And sure enough he was right; Ray turned his head away from the disaster and turned back into the helicopter only to see each and every face on that chopper looking down with the same look plastered on it...fear. Even Steve had a look of disbelief stitched on his face.

"Ever seen anything like this?" Torque said as he leaned into Ray so he wouldn't have to shout.

"Yeah, just never thought I'd see it here," Ray confessed.

Steve couldn't take looking at the view sitting down anymore and quickly got up and stood next to Ray and Torque, still in a state of shock.

"Ray?" Steve asked.

"Yeah, Steve?"

"How? How could one man do all this?" Steve asked as he took his eyes off the city and locked onto Ray's face.

Ray did the same and looked into Steve's eyes. Ray could tell that Steve wanted a real answer and not some smart-ass answer, but Ray had either.

"I don't know, Steve, I don't know anymore."

Steve shook his head and looked back down as the helicopter passed a burning skyscraper.

"How do we come back from something like this?" Steve asked.

Ray shook his head."We'll think of something. We always do."

Steve inhaled deeply as Ray lifted up his wrist and checked the time. He then turned and walked over to the pilot.

"How much longer?" Ray asked.

"We should be coming up to Time Square any second," the pilot said.

Ray shook his head as he looked out the windshield of the helicopter.

"Great," he muttered to himself.

It took a moment to see but once the helicopter made its way through another thick cloud of rising smoke, suddenly Ray and the pilot were looking at Times Square (or what use to be Times Square).

"Sweet Jesus," The pilot said as Ray's jaw damn near hit the floor of the helicopter.

With fire spreading all around the ground, buildings and cars burning and dozens of police car sirens flashing all and in between, it was clear that whatever type of Hell Dutra wanted to unleash for New York, he had suceeded.

The helicopter was too high up to see any bodies, but Ray and the rest of the guys knew that they were down there and most likely in numbers; thousands possibly even in tens of thousands.

Tommy and Jasmin looked down in horror as they began to hear muffled police sirens lifting into the air like a bad sound effect for a movie. Tommy was having difficulty taking it all in, but Jasmin was moments away from crying. This was the reason why he left Bosnia in the first place, so he wouldn't have to worry about war destroying his home or taking away people that he cared about.

You would never know by looking at Bob but the view was ripping him apart, too. Before he signed on to be with Ray, Bob use to live in New York before his life went to shit and he turned into the careless prick everyone thought he was. He didn't have much, but the few moments that he looked back at and made him smile were mostly all when he was living in New York; the view was a tough pill for him to digest.

But out of everyone on the helicopter, it was Steve who just couldn't believe his eyes. Normally it would be Ray who would be a wreck, but since Ray was more concerned about getting to Emily, it was Steve who was the one questioning it all and wondering how he could have let something like this happen. The sight of the burning city didn't build up rage in Steve like it did for Torque, Tommy, and the rest of the younger guys. The sight, if anything, broke his heart, like it was proof that no matter how hard they fight, they'll never truly stop the evil ways of mankind...and Steve began to think they were all fools for trying to think they could.

While Steve was struggling to get his head out of negativity, Ray was so focused and worried about getting to Emily in time, it took him a while to notice the helicopter was getting ready to land, but once he got his mind back into the game, he lifted up his machine gun and loaded the clip inside and then the rest of the guys followed suit. Bob loaded up his sniper rifle as

Torque cocked his machine gun and double-checked his side arm. Each one of them knew it was time.

"Twenty seconds to drop!" The pilot shouted out to the guys.

"Show time," Bob said as he cocked his sniper rifle and then looked up at Tim.

Tim swallowed hard as he looked into the serious expression that covered Bob's face.

"Think we'll make it out of this one?" Jasmin asked.

"Only one way to find out," Tommy said as he lightly elbowed Jasmin in the arm.

Jasmin shook his head as sweat began dripping down his forehead.

"Yeah," Jasmin said as he exhaled.

"Ten seconds to drop!"

"Alright, everyone ready to go?" Ray shouted as the helicopter began to make it's decent into the darkened city.

The guys nodded and lifted their thumbs up.

"Yes, sir," Tim said.

Ray nodded.

"Alright...let's do this..."

Even though there wasn't much time, Ray took a moment to look at everyone. From Tommy to Torque, each had the same expression: locked, loaded, and ready to go. A part of Ray felt proud, because he not only was he able to take these guys and make an ass kicking team, but also that he looked at all of them—even Torque—as friends. Thoughts of retirement were wearing Ray down, due to the fact that he was afraid he would be all alone, but that brief moment on the helicopter was able to push those thoughts right out and give Ray the encouragement he had been looking for every since this whole situation with Dutra started, maybe even before that.

But just as one part of Ray was at an all time high, another part was darker then the city they were slowly lowering down to. He knew that the guys were tough as nails and capable of just about anything, there was no denying that. But he also knew the threat Dutra posed to not only him but to the rest of the team. Ray would've never admit it to the team, but the voice inside his mind spoke before he could even deny it: there was a very strong possibility that this would be the last time everyone on the team would be together...alive.

Chapter 15: City Of Silence

Smoke whipped all around from the propellers as the chopper landed right in the middle of the abandoned Times Square. As soon as Ray felt the helicopter meet the pavement, he quickly grabbed the door and slid it open.

"Alright let's move!" Ray shouted as smoke began pouring into the helicopter.

Just like every other time, Ray was the first person to set foot on the ground followed quickly by Steve, then Bob and then the rest of the guys.

"Holy fucking shit," Steve shouted as he lifted his hand over his face to try and block the powerful wind coming from the helicopter.

The damage was worse then anyone thought. From up in the sky it just looked like a couple buildings on fire and smoke blowing around, nothing major. But one by one, each team member quickly realized the extent of the damage. The burning skyscrapers were the first things to grab everyone's attention, followed by the dust and ash that was falling all around; Dutra had painted an apocalyptic masterpiece.

"Always wanted to see New York, but not like this," Tim said to Torque as he looked up into the smoke filled sky.

The blades of the helicopter roared like thunder overhead as the rest of the guys jumped off and onto Dutra's playground. It was tough at first but once the helicopter began pulling back up into the sky, the guys were then able to hear police sirens that were clearly coming from all directions. The thick smoke blowing all around made it damn near impossible to see even ten feet in front of them but the guys knew the police cruisers were out there.

"Hey, Steve?" Ray shouted as the helicopter began to slowly lift back into the air.

"Yeah?" Steve asked Ray, before shouting to everyone, "Everyone get your radios on!"

"How far is the apartment?" Ray asked.

"About a mile away...give or take," Steve answered as Bob and Torque walked over.

Ray shook his head.

"Alright, so how you do you want to do this?" Torque asked.

"Joey said a police command post would be close by, so let's stick together until we get there! No sense in splitting up now!" Ray shouted.

Bob, Steve, and Torque nodded their heads.

"Works for me," Torque said.

"Alright, let's move out! Stay close to one another!" Ray shouted so the rest of the team could hear him.

Once Ray made sure everyone heard him, he turned forward, only to see nothing but smoke and fire in front of him. He started to march forward, and the rest of the guys followed right behind.

"Alright everyone stay close to each other!" Steve shouted from over his left shoulder.

Bob quickly turned and looked as Jasmin.

"You guys hear that back there?" Bob shouted at the rest of the guys toward at the end.

"What?" Torque shouted from the last of the line.

"Stay close!" Bob shouted back.

"Yeah!"

Once Bob made sure everyone was set, he turned forward again, but not before quickly looking at Jasmin, who was literally inches away from him.

"Jas, I said stay close, not try and grab ass me," Bob said.

Jasmin pushed back a little as he looked at Bob.

"Sorry, just nervous," Jasmin confessed.

"Well have Tommy hold your hand then," Bob said.

Jasmin rolled his eyes before wiping his forehead (Jasmin was always sweating like no tomorrow, but with all the gear and hot smoke blowing all around he was burning up something awful). He began wishing he had packed something to drink instead of the two chocolate bars that were in his ass pocket, probably melting away into his pants.

Ray tried to cover his face from the extreme heat and the smoke. Even though his left arm was no match for the heat, it worked just well enough for him to make it out and get into an area that wasn't completely filled with smoke: the heart of Time Square. Once he cleared his eyes, he finally got to see the destruction in full...and it was just as bad as he thought it would be—hell, even worse.

One by one the guys emerged from the smoke like a special effect, and took a moment to look up and see the evil that Dutra had unleashed on the city of New York. While most of the younger guys were so focused on what was right before them, the older, more experienced ones not only feared what was before their eyes, but also what else Dutra had done in the other cities he'd attacked.

"Ray, over there," Steve said as he pointed.

Ray quickly turned and way off in the distance he could see multiple police cars with flashing lights.

"This way!" Ray shouted and started to sprint in the direction of the police cars.

As soon as the guys saw Ray take off, they followed, sprinting past burning cars and piles of debris that appeared to be pieces of concrete that had fallen from the skyscrapers above.

"Never thought I'd be happy to see cop cars, let alone be running toward them," Tommy said to Jasmin.

"Good thing Ray's up front, if they saw me running toward them, they'd probably end up shooting me before I got there," Jasmin said as his man boobs started bouncing.

Tommy chuckled.

"Oh and by the way Jas...nice tits," Tommy quickly said just before scooping Jasmin's left boob with his right hand.

"Oh fuck yourself Tommy!" Jasmin replied.

"After seeing those chest baskets bounce, I just might...gotta do it when the memory is fresh, you know?" Tommy said.

"Tommy, seek professional help," Jasmin suggested.

Tommy chuckled as he playfully whacked Jasmin in the arm.

"Jas, Tommy! Cut the shit and focus will yeah?" Bob shouted at them.

As Ray ran toward the police cars, he didn't notice anyone, which caused him to panic at first. The last thing he needed was to run into officers while they were trying to get to Street's apartment. But just as Ray reached the end of the first police car, he turned and saw a large group of police officers and S.W.A.T. members, all lying in large pools of dark blood.

The sight snatched up the very little breath Ray had left in him; he was not expecting it at all, none of the guys were as they all walked up to the grisly sight of thirteen men in a bloody pile.

When Steve saw it, he thought immediately about the pool of bodies back down in the flooded city of Walton Beach; a sight that he had hoped to eventually forget.

"Walton Beach," Ray said as he looked at Steve briefly before turning back to the bodies.

"You can say that again," Steve said as he shook his head in disgust.

The rest of the guys made there way up to Ray and stopped when they saw the sight. All except for Tim, who as soon as he saw the human pile walked straight over to it.

"Careful," Ray ordered.

Tim nodded as he kept his eyes on the bodies and then slowly kneeled down next to them and began to examine them.

"That from the blast?" Jasmin asked.

"Not unless that blast could fire bullets. Each one of them has multiple bullet wounds, and all have head shots," Tim said as he stood back up and looked at Ray.

"Execution style...terrific..." Bob said.

"So what does that mean?" Torque asked as he stood next to Ray's shoulder.

Ray kept his eyes on the bodies as he began to explain.

"It means that Dutra's here, or at least people that work for him are," Ray carefully said.

Torque instantly got confused from Ray's rather bland answer.

"That doesn't make sense. He just blew up half the goddamn city! Why the hell would he come back?" Torques asked.

Ray muttered to himself for a moment as he put the pieces together in his head, trying to get an idea of what was going through Dutra's head...when suddenly it hit.

"It was a cover," Ray said.

Steve turned to Ray.

"What was a cover?" Steve asked.

"The bomb, the bridge, everything," Ray said.

"What are you saying, Ray?" Jasmin asked.

"Whatever Dutra is after, whatever his endgame is, it's in that apartment!" Ray replied..

"The perfect cover," Torque said, as what Ray was saying began to click.

"We gotta get to that apartment," Ray firmly said.

"Ready when you are," Steve said.

"Let's do what we do," Ray firmly said.

And once he said that, all the guys gave him back a smile, each just as ready as the next to start retaliating at a moments notice.

II

Once the entire gang got down past the intersection, Ray gave the order for Torque to take Tim and the rest of Roader's team and head down the opposite side of the street.

"Stay sharp and keep your head down," Ray's voice echoed inside Torque's head as he and Roader's team quickly went sprinting down a dark ally.

"Stop at the end," Torque ordered to the six guys.

Once Scotty Robidoux, Roader's newest member in the group, got to the end of the street he stopped and then turned and looked at Torque.

"What street is it?"

Torque quickly pressed down on the radio in his eardrum.

"Ray, what's the address again?" Torque asked.

"431 Berkley," Ray said.

"Berkley," Torque said to the men.

Scotty and Tim then turned from Torque and slowly stuck their head out onto the empty and dark street. It was Tim who noticed the name of the street.

"This street is Hanover," Tim announced.

"Ray, we're on Hanover..." Torque said into his radio.

"Alright, Steve is saying Berkley should be two streets up from you," Ray said.

"Alright, copy that," Torque said to Ray before walking over to Roader's guys. "Ok guys, Berkley should be two streets away from here."

"So, how you want to do this?" Scotty asked.

Torque carefully stuck his head out of the dark shadows of the ally and then looked up and down the street. He knew that going all the way down the street would be faster and would be easier to spot someone, but he also knew that taking the street would mean they would all be out in the open, and Torque didn't want to risk that.

"We'll shoot across the street and into the alley in front of us," Torque said as he pointed.

"Why not take the street?" Scotty asked.

"Alley will give us cover of darkness," Torque explained.

"From what?" Scotty asked quickly, clearly not happy with Torque's decision or answer.

But before Torque could answer, four large trucks suddenly turned onto the street, engines roaring up into the smoky night sky.

"From that," Tim quickly said.

The guys quickly looked toward the roar of the engines. The power outage across the city made it difficult to see, but the trucks clearly had the outline of American muscle and obviously had after market white/blue neon headlights on high beams and heading right in their direction.

"Oh shit, back in the alley now...now!" Torque demanded.

The guys may not have thought Torque's idea to head into the alley across the street was a good idea, but all of them jumped at the chance to listen to him when it came to running back into the alley.

"Shit," Tim said.

Torque quickly searched for an area all of them could not only hide in, but also fit, and came up with nothing, not because he wasn't clever, that wasn't the case at all, it was just too damn dark for him to really be able to see all of his surroundings. But he knew he was going to have to come up with something fast.

"Six hundred feet and closing," Tim shouted to Torque as he carefully stuck his head out of the ally.

Torque's heart began to pump and beat like nobody's business. He could literally hear every beat of his heart in his ear, but as the roar of the trucks grew louder and nearer, it only made the beating faster and faster.

"Shit," Torque said to himself.

He wiped the sweat from his forehead and then suddenly noticed a door literally right in front of him.

"Really?" Torque sarcastically asked himself before reaching for the doorknob, only to find that it was locked. "What a surprise..."

"Four hundred," Tim said.

Torque knew it was now or never; it was either get that door open, or be spotted, and Torque wasn't going to fuck up everything and let Ray down any more then he felt like he already had.

"Two hundred," Tim shouted.

Very quickly Torque lifted up his machine gun and aimed for the doorknob...and then waited...waited for the right moment...that loud moment...that loud enough roar moment...and once it came, Torque double tapped the trigger to his machine gun and shot the lock on the door.

"Everyone get in, now!" Torque shouted as he pulled the door open.

The guys rushed into the door and started pushing each other in as the sound of the truck grew deafening. Once Tim made it to the door, Torque quickly pushed him in, ran in himself and shut the door just as the first truck made it's way past the alley, and drove right by.

As soon as Torque heard the first truck drive by he let out an overwhelmingly large sigh of relief. He wasn't sure for a moment there, came close to shitting his pants, but once he saw the neon headlights continue on down the road, he was able to keep calm and push the shit back up into his puckered rectum...until suddenly what Torque thought was the last of the four trucks turned into the alley, the headlights lighting up the cracks of the door frame.

"Oh, shit! Everyone get down!" Torque whispered.

The guys quickly rushed down the flight of stairs and ran over to the wall of what appeared to be the basement of a shithole apartment building. Torque was the last one down the stairs and as soon as the headlights lit up the small window near the top of the basement wall, he ducked and hid behind a washing machine with Tim.

"Think they saw us?" Tim whispered.

"Guess we'll find out," Torque said.

"You did lock that door, right?" Tim slowly asked.

Suddenly a chill ran down Torque's spine.

"Oh, fuck!" Torque said.

Tim exhaled deeply and then slowly lifted his head back up and looked into the window, only to see the large tire of the truck stop right in front of it. The screeching tire made an awful sound as it came to a dead stop, sending waves of panic through Torque and everyone else, but the sound did nothing compared to when they all heard the truck doors open.

"Oh, shit," Torque said as he looked down and slowly took the safety off of his gun.

It was no sooner after that when they begin to hear what they assumed were Dutra's men, walking around, with one guy giving orders.

"We'll sweep this area again. You two take the east and we'll cover the north. Now let's make this fast! Stone wants us out ASAP!" the man ordered.

Torque waited until he heard the men starting to move out before he got up and darted for the staircase. As he made it to the stairs, the truck outside suddenly revved and started to pull away from the building and head down the alley.

Tim watched through the window as the light from the taillights began to grow dimmer and dimmer until the view from the window was completely black. And as soon as it was, Tim quickly looked up at Torque and then lifted up his thumb. Torque saw it and he nodded his head.

"Alright guys, let's move out...nice and quiet," Torque said as he began walking up the stairs.

Scotty and the guys quickly got up and followed up the staircase as Tim made his way to the stairs but kept a close eye on the window. Once Torque made it to the top of the stairs, he very slowly reached for the doorknob. He paused for a moment, just to make sure he couldn't hear anything outside, and once a long enough time went by that he felt comfortable enough, he cracked open the door, confirming that he hadn't locked it.

"Unlocked?" Tim asked.

"Little bit," Torque quickly said.

Torque flung open the door and stuck his head out into the alley. Darkness once again took hold. A light wind was the only sound that Torque could hear. And after a wave of his arm, he stepped back into the alley.

"Alright, let's keep it quiet," Torque said as he started in the opposite direction of the truck, his machine gun whipping around in front of him as he looked around.

"Nothing like a quick heart attack to get the blood pumping," Scotty said sarcastically.

Torque was too busy looking around and pressing down on the radio in his ear to hear the sarcastic remark.

"Ray," Torque said.

"Yeah?" Ray asked over static.

"Keep an eye out, there's four trucks with neon headlights driving around...sounds like three are heading your way," Torque warned.

"Of course...you guys all right?" Ray asked.

"Yeah, we're good."

"Good...keep making your way to the apartment complex...we'll deal with the guys in the trucks," Ray said.

"Copy that. Over and out," Torque said before lifting his hand away from his radio and turning back to the guys. "Okay guys...let's get to the apartment building."

The guys nodded their heads and jetted across the street. They entered the alley across the way and dissolved back into the darkness...just before ten more trucks with only fog lights running pulled onto the street and then began to slowly drive down.

III

"Alright guys, we got company coming," Ray said to Steve, Bob, Jasmin and Tommy.

Instantly the guys sprung into action, quickly taking off in different directions and trying to find a place to hide.

"Get off the street!" Steve shouted as he turned and saw what appeared to be headlights heading down the street.

Bob quickly ran into a dark alley while Ray and Steve ducked behind a large dumpster that was across from the alley where Bob hid in the shadows. But it was Jasmin and Tommy who decided the go for the more obvious hiding spot. Jasmin quickly ran over to a piece of shit rusted out car, smashing the back passenger side window with the butt of his gun. As Jasmin put his hand through the opening to unlock the door, Tommy looked up and saw the vehicles heading their way...and fast.

"Hurry up, Jas!" Tommy cried as he watched the trucks get closer and the headlights get brighter.

"Hold on," Jasmin said, still reaching for the lock. "Got it!"

Once Jasmin unlocked the door, he quickly opened it and was about to jump in when he saw that the back of the car was a disaster: food and garbage covered the floor and seats.

"Get in Jas!" Tommy shouted.

"No, it's filthy!" Jasmin quickly shot back.

Tommy rolled his eyes.

"Oh, don't be a baby!" Tommy said lifting up his right foot and pushing it firmly on Jasmin's left ass cheek, causing him to belly flop onto the seat. Jasmin hit the seat with a low groan as Tommy suddenly belly flopped right onto his back, causing Jasmin to groan even louder.

"Quiet!" Tommy said as he rested his head on Jasmin's back.

Steve and Ray looked at each other and shook their heads in frustration as they watched Jasmin and Tommy get in the car.

"Idiots," Steve said.

Bob thought the same thing as he slowly lowered himself to his knees and waited for the trucks to pass.

"Alright, everyone stay down," Ray said over the radio.

Ray finished his sentence as the roar of the trucks grew closer and closer. Unlike Torque, Ray was able to keep his calm and not panic to the same extent, though his heart did begin to race a little faster as the glare of the neon headlights grew brighter.

"How you want to handle this boss?" Bob asked over the radio.

"Keep it quiet and just let the trucks pass," Ray ordered.

"What if they don't pass and they end up staying here?" Jasmin said in a muffled voice, due to his face being smooshed into the seat from the weight of Tommy on him.

"Be positive, Jas," Ray said.

"Yeah, but what if they don't?" Jasmin asked again in his muffled voice.

"Then, we'll cross that bridge when we get there!" Ray quickly said back to shut him up.

A moment later, the first truck sped on by, shooting past them like a bat out of hell.

"Damn," Steve said as he and Ray lifted their heads up from the dumpster.

"Torque, how many trucks did you say there are?" Ray asked over the radio.

"There should be three heading your way. All are American made and have those asshole neon headlights," Torque answered.

"Copy that, That's one," Ray said as he turned and looked at Steve.

Steve nodded and then another drove past, not as fast as the first vehicle but not all that slow either.

"That's two," Steve said.

"What's going on?" Jasmin said as he turned his head so he was facing the side instead of with his whole face down.

"Quiet, just stay down," Tommy said as he watched the truck pass the car they were in.

Jasmin exhaled deeply and then stayed quiet, and then began to focus on the clear, rubbery object that was literally right in front of his face. The object looked familiar but at that moment, Jasmin couldn't place what the strange looking thing with some type of brown coating at the end was.

"Okay guys, should be one more truck," Ray said.

"Copy that, think I see another set of lights heading this way," Bob began. "Yeah those are definitely headlights, only these ones are moving a hell of a lot slower then those last two."

"This one must be the search party. Tommy!" Ray said over the radio.

Tommy slowly lifted his hand up to his ear.

"Yeah."

"Do you two boneheads have enough time get the hell out of the car and make it over to Bob or me?" Ray asked.

Tommy slowly looked up, only to quickly drop his head again when he saw the neon lights lighting up the street.

"Doubtful, Ray," Tommy said.

Ray shook his head as he saw the lights starting to come up the street.

"Shit," Ray said to himself before putting his hand back on his radio in his ear. "Just keep your heads down, the both of you and keep quiet...understood?"

"Roger," Tommy said back.

Ray looked back at the car Tommy and Jasmin were in and then looked across the street to where he saw Bob's head.

"Bob?" Ray asked.

"Yeah?"

"You in a position to cover the two of them?" Ray asked.

Bob chuckled briefly for a moment.

"Yeah, I am," Bob responded as he lifted up his sniper rifle.

"Just keep ready and wait to see what they do. No need to make noises that we don't have to," Ray said.

"Copy that," Bob shot back as the headlights began to appear in his scope.

The lights began lighting up the inside of the car as Tommy quickly dropped back down, landing hard on Jasmin and then covering his head.

"Quiet, Jas," Tommy said, as Jasmin continued to lightly groan from Tommy falling on him.

"Sure," Jasmin said, out of breath, as he continued to examine the clear, rubbery object that was on the tip of his nose.

The truck made it's way close enough to the guys that Ray and Steve ducked, dropped to their knees, and then popped their heads out from near the bottom of the dumpster. Ray groaned in pain as he kneeled down; he quickly learned that the arthritis that was slowly taking away his knee no longer allowed him to move down quickly without horrific pain. Steve saw Ray bite his lower lip, but didn't say anything; it wasn't the time or the place to tell Ray for the hundredth time to get surgery on it.

As the truck moved slowly and steadily Ray tried to make out how many people were inside, but the windows had been tinted out, making it impossible to see anything from where he was.

"Bob, you see how many people are inside the truck?" Ray asked.

Bob carefully looked through his scope, and realized that even the windshield had been tinted.

"Windshield is tinted. No way I can tell," Bob said.

Ray sighed.

"Shit...alright, I'll think of something," Ray said.

"Better do it fast, Ray..." Bob began as he looked through the scope, "looks like they're stopping."

Ray quickly lifted his head back up only to see that Bob was right, the truck was coming to a complete stop. And once it did, it stopped right in front of the car that Tommy and Jasmin had decided to hide in.

"Of course," Ray said.

"Well, what are the odds of that?" Steve asked.

The idling of the truck echoed in Tommy's ear as he tried to keep low in the back seat of the filthy car. Even though he knew he had to keep still, Tommy began to slowly shift his head down and look down onto the floor of the back seat, only to see that his shotgun was too far out of reach for him to get without moving.

Ray shook his head, then lifted up his gun and began to dig into his pocket. He felt around until he was able to grab a hold of the metal tube cylinder and pull it out. Then he quickly began to screw on the silencer to the end of his gun.

"Bob, we're going silent," Ray quickly whispered into the radio as Steve also began to screw the silencer on his gun.

Bob briefly chuckled and then took his eye out of the scope only to look at the silencer that was already on his sniper rifle.

"Way ahead of you," Bob said.

Ray exhaled and then looked at Steve.

"On my mark," Ray said.

Steve threw up his thumb and then they both turned back to the truck and aimed down in their sights to get ready for a shot.

"Here goes nothing," Steve whispered to himself.

As Ray, Steve and Bob aimed at the truck, suddenly another truck drove up to the idling truck.

"Shit," Ray said, turning and aiming at the other truck as it violently slammed on its breaks when it approached the first truck.

Suddenly the driver of the first truck flung open the door and hopped out of the truck, entering the light of the other trucks headlights, revealing the murder and rapist only known as Stone—a muscular man in a dark black jacket and long black hair.

"Out of the truck you fuckers!" Stone shouted as he banged on the back end of the truck he had just gotten out of.

The passenger side door and the two back doors quickly opened and three men, all dressed in black ski masks and holding large machine guns, exited the truck and turned as the truck shut off it's engine.

"Ray, I'm counting four that have just gotten out of the first truck," Bob said over the radio.

Then just as Bob finished his sentence, all four doors to the truck that had just pulled up behind Stone's truck quickly flung open and four more men got out. Each man, including the driver, were in ski masks and holding large machine guns also.

"All together I'm counting eight," Steve said to Ray.

Ray then quickly lifted his hand to his ear radio.

"Everybody hold, let's see where this is going," Ray ordered.

"What about Jas and Tommy?" Steve asked.

Ray sighed.

"Hopefully they don't make a sound."

Once the last of the guys came out of the second truck and closed the door, Stone then approached the driver.

"You must be the new guys Vacca hired," Stone said.

Even though Stone was *attempting* to be civil, the driver of the other truck made absolutely no effort to even engage, proving the type of person Dutra enjoys hiring. Once Stone realized he wasn't getting an answer, he quickly decided to stop be polite.

"Dutra said he wants you cocksuckers to cover this area. Think you can do that?" Stone quickly asked.

Once again the men said nothing. Stone smiled.

"Good, we'll cover a little higher up so you faggots can play with yourseleves. Alright, get back in the fucking truck, we're moving out!" Stone shouted to his own guys.

Stone's guys then started back into the truck as Stone turned and looked back at the driver.

"Take care now," Stone said sarcastically as he waved, then turned and walked back to his truck, "...fuckers."

The moment Stone got into his truck, he slammed the door and then floored it, causing the tires to screech as they drove off. The loudness of the truck caused Tommy and Jasmin to flinch as it raced past them. As soon as Stone's truck sounded like it was far enough away, Ray then aimed his gun at the men with the ski masks.

"Okay. Bob you take the driver; Steve and I will get the rest, understood?" Ray asked over the radio.

With Stone's truck now turning down another street and the engine of the other truck off, it was very quiet as the men in the ski mask stood very still, slowly looking around.

Suddenly it all seemed very quiet; the wind seemed to instantly die down and nothing but silence lifted up into the dark and smoky sky. And in that moment Jasmin and even Tommy thought they were out of the woods...and that's when curiosity got the better of Jasmin and he slowly lifted up his head.

"Is the coast clear?" Jasmin asked.

Tommy then lifted his head up, not seeing the men in masks at first.

"Yeah, I think the truck is gone," Tommy said as he whipped his head all around.

Tommy whipping his head got Ray and Steve's attention as they saw him moving in the car, and that meant that if they saw Tommy, so did the guys holding machine guns right in front of him.

And sure enough they did. The driver of the truck instantly snapped his neck into place as he saw Tommy's movement from the corner of his eye.

"Uh oh," Bob said as he looked through his scope.

Tommy turned his head and looked out the back window of the car, only to see nothing. But once he saw that view, he took a deep sigh of relief as he put his hand over his heart.

"We're good, Jas," Tommy said as he then lifted his hands and started to wipe his eyes.

Jasmin shook his head and then picked up the clear rubber object that had been touching his nose ever since he landed in the car. He looked at it, then lifted up to his face and smelt the brownish tip of the object...and he realized that it smelt shitty.

"Hey Tommy?" Jasmin asked.

"What?" Tommy asked as he finished up wiping his eyes.

"What's this?" Jasmin asked as he lifted up the object.

Tommy took his fingers out of his eyes and focused on the object that Jasmin had held less then an inch away from his face...then his eyes widened when he realized what it was.

"JAS! That's a used condom!" Tommy shouted at the top of his lungs and then quickly knocked it out of Jasmin's hand.

Tommy gagged as he watched the condom fly out of Jasmin's hand and hit the driver's window. The noise of the condom hitting the window caught Tommy's attention, causing him to look through the window, only to see the men with ski masks aiming their machine guns at him.

"Oh, shit," Tommy said just before Jasmin suddenly vomited.

The men all aimed at Tommy and got ready to pull the trigger, smiles on each one of their faces, when suddenly several quick flashes came out of the darkness from both sides of the car. Tommy ducked and dropped back down onto the messy floor of the car, landing in the puddle of orange vomit.

As Tommy landed in puke, the men outside suddenly dropped to ground dead, blood flowing from the bullet holes in the head of each masked man.

"Good bye," Bob said as smoke wafted from the end of his sniper barrel.

As the last man dropped to the ground, a bullet lodged in his skull, Ray lowered his gun and then wiped his forehead.

"Alright, Tommy, Jas get the hell out of the car," Ray said as he stood up and walked over.

Tommy flung open the door behind the driver seat with his foot, took his head out of the car and vomited the moment his head was out of the car. As soon as Steve and Ray saw the vomit splatter all over the floor, they both stopped walking toward the car, but they were already too close and quickly began smelling the horrific smell.

"Oh, Jesus," Steve said as he turned away.

Ray quickly turned to Bob as he saw Bob running over.

"Stay right there, Bob." Ray said as he lifted his hand.

"Why, what's going...holy shit what's the fucking smell?" Bob suddenly asked the moment he got a whiff of the foul order.

Tommy then lifted up his head and looked at Ray.

"Uh, Jas found a used condom in the car and decided the throw it in my face!" Tommy shouted as he slowly began to stand up. "Then he fucking puked all inside the car."

Jasmin then opened the door behind the passenger seat and slowly exited the car. "I didn't know what it was!" Jasmin said in explaination.

Tommy then looked at Jasmin.

"Jas, how the fuck could you not know what a condom is?" Tommy shouted.

Bob then turned to Tommy.

"Hey come on Tommy, don't make the man out to be an idiot," Bob began.

"Thanks, Bob," Jasmin said.

"He's foreign! Of course he doesn't know what a condom is," Bob finished.

Steve and Tommy chuckled.

"Like I said: thanks Bob," Jasmin said again.

Ray then cleared his throat and got everyone's attention.

"So now that we have that out of our system, why don't we get the hell out of here before more men arrive?" Ray asked.

Tommy wiped off the chunks that were remaining on his lip and then looked at Ray.

"Should we move the bodies off the road?" Tommy asked.

Ray shook his head.

"No, the apartment building should be right down the street. So let's make sure we're in and out."

Tommy reached back into the smelly car and picked up his shotgun, which thankfully was clear of any type of vomit. Once he grabbed it he quickly looked back up at Ray.

"Alright, let's go," Ray said as he pointed to the direction of the apartment.

They turned and began to head in the direction that Ray had pointed.

"Torque?" Ray asked over his radio.

"Yeah?" Torque responded in very heavy static.

"One truck is down. Now we're approaching the apartment complex. ETA is two minutes," Ray said.

"Copy, we just arrived," Torque said.

"You at the back?" Ray asked.

"We are."

"Okay, we'll be right there."

"Copy that. We'll be waiting for you. Keep your head down, Christ only knows what else is out here."

"Hopefully we don't have to find out," Ray quickly said back even though he didn't believe a single word.

Chapter 16: Strength In Numbers

Even though it only took Ray and the rest of the team about three minutes to reach Torque and the others, it seemed to be a much longer wait, to Torque at least. During the whole wait, Torque feared that instead of Ray or Steve emerging from the shadows, it would be another one of those damn trucks. So Torque was more then relieved when Ray, Steve, Bob, Tommy and Jasmin emerged from the shadows behind them.

"Hey, what kept you?" Torque asked as Ray and everyone approached them behind the tall building.

"Jas had to get some things out of his system," Tommy quickly said as he wiped the last of the vomit off his back.

"What?" Torque asked in confusion.

"Ran into a few of those trucks," Ray said.

"You sneak past them?" Torque asked.

"Snuck past one. Had to deal with the other," Steve answered.

"And there's more of them out there, so let's get in and out," Ray said.

Torque nodded in agreement.

"What floor was the apartment on again?" Tim asked.

"Third floor, number 307," Bob said.

Ray then cocked his gun before he turned and looked at everyone.

"Alright, safeties off and stay close," Ray ordered.

As the guys nodded and then took the safeties off their guns, Ray reached for the rusted door of the back entrance of the apartment building, only to find that it was locked. Ray quickly looked up and around to make sure he couldn't see anyone else around, and then lifted up his machine gun and double tapped his trigger, causing two bullets to jet out of the barrel of his gun and hit the knob of the door. The first shot made a loud ping noise, while the second shot was able to blow out the lock in the knob. As soon as the shell of the second shot landed on the ground, Ray pulled open the door and then rushed in, followed by the rest of the guys.

The long hall was dark and quiet. As the guys started piling in, Ray could see that the hall would turn completely dark the moment the rusted door closed behind the last person in. And sure enough as soon as Jasmin stepped in, the door shut behind him, leaving them all in pure darkness.

"Wow, it's really dark in here," Jasmin said.

"Nothing gets past you, Jas," Bob said.

"Anybody got a light?" Scotty asked.

"I got a lighter," Bob said as he dug into his pocket and started to pull out the yellow lighter.

"No, I meant a flashlight," Scotty said, correcting himself.

"I left mine back at the shop, didn't think I would need it," Tommy confessed.

"Me too," Jasmin said.

Suddenly just as Jasmin and Tommy dug into their pockets to make sure they didn't have anything, a flashlight beam emerged from the darkness and rushed up onto the ceiling...it was Ray. Then another flashlight beam emerged just off of Ray's left side.

"Thought I might need this," Steve said as he shined the flashlight on his face.

Then one last beam rose out of the darkness just behind Tim. The light startled Tim for a brief moment, causing him to jump, but then he realized it was Torque who had just turned on the light.

"Oh, Jesus," Tim said as he patted his chest.

"Didn't scare you, did I?" Torque asked.

Tim cleared his throat, clearly embarrassed.

"Um...no, not at all."

"Glad to see some of us came prepared," Steve said.

Torque smiled as he pointed the flashlight beam onto the cracked ceiling.

"Staircase should be at the end of this hall," Ray said as he shined his flashlight down the quiet and almost spooky white hallway.

Steve handed his flashlight to Bob, and Ray then turned forward, keeping his eyes focused on what was lit up in his flashlight beam.

The long hall, that at one point must've been a beautiful part of the once beautiful building, was now covered with chipped dirty white paint, holes in the walls. Probably from the tenants Ray thought. Large, what looked like water stains, covered the red carpet; clearly the good days for the apartment building were a thing of the past. And the smell in the air gave the place that extra feeling of old.

"Smells like sewage," Bob said as he shined the light on a huge hole in the wall on his right side.

"Smells like me mum's house," Steve confessed as he walked right behind Ray.

"Smells a lot better then Tommy does...what the hell is all over your back man?" Torque asked as he shined the flashlight on Tommy's back and was clearly able to see a large orangish spot on his back.

Tommy rolled his eyes. "Don't ask."

As the guys continued making their way down the rest of the hall, Jasmin couldn't help but think about how the hallway reminded him of something out of a horror movie.

"Little scary in here, huh?" Jasmin asked.

Steve rolled his eyes.

"Oh please, Jas. This is nothing compared to Chernobyl. You don't know the definition of scary shit until you walk through that place at night," Steve said.

Ray was going to agree with that when he turned the corner and saw a large black door with a glass window in the middle. The heavy looking door looked very unwelcoming as Ray walked up to it and began shinning his beam into the window. The window looked like it was covered with at least five different layers of dust; it hadn't been cleaned in years. Ray had to rub a clean spot on the window with the palm of his hand and then shine the light into the window in order to realize it was the door they were looking for, the staircase door.

"Guys, this is it," Ray said as he held open the door for Steve and then shined his light all the way up the long spiral staircase.

"Holy shit, that's a long ways up," Steve whispered to Ray.

"You can say that again. Bob, Torque, shut your lights off before you start up the stairs alright?" Ray said to them.

"Think anybody is here?" Bob asked.

"Let's hope not but if there is, the last thing we need is for them to see our flashlight beams lighting up the joint." Ray shut off his beam of light, leaving the guys in darkness again.

Once all the guys made it through the door, Torque then carefully closed the door to avoid a loud bang.

"It's gonna be hard to make it up those stairs with no light, Ray," Steve said as he looked up the staircase.

Ray knew that, but he also knew that if anyone was guarding that third floor, they could easily see flashlight beams heading up toward them. That's when Ray decided to take out his cell phone and turn on the screen. Once he did that he shined the screen onto Steve's face and then smiled.

"Knew there was a reason why you're the boss," Steve said to Ray, before turning and looking at the guys. "Turn your cell phone screens on and stay close guys."

"Cell phone screen?" Tommy asked as he pulled out his.

"Why a cell phone screen?" Tim asked.

"Because when you see a flashlight beam, you automatically know what it is, there's no denying that. A cell phone screen is a little harder to see," Ray explained.

"Done this before?" Scotty asked as he took out his phone.

Ray looked at Steve for a moment and then they shrugged their shoulders together.

"Once or twice...now stay sharp and watch your step. God only knows what's up here," Ray said.

The guys took out their pgones then aimed the screens down to their feet and began walking over to the staircase. Once Ray reached the long black first step, he shined his screen down and then started up, followed by Steve, who was literally one step behind him.

As Ray began to climb, he did his best to try and remain quiet, but it was a much more difficult task than he thought it would be. Each step he went up seemed to make a loud squeak, each louder then the previous one. He tried stepping up on them slower but it didn't seem to help at all. He thought about maybe trying to skip a step each time but with his bad knee and the poor lighting from his cell phone screen, it was a chance that wasn't worth the risk.

It seemed like a lifetime but once Ray got to another black door with a window in the middle of it, he slowly lifted his cell phone screen and was able to light up the large '1' that was plastered on the window of the door. But just as he made his way past the door, out of the darkness came a loud bang that made each and everyone of them jump out of there skins.

"Hold," Ray hissed as he shut his screen off just as the rest of the guys did the same thing.

The bang echoed throughout the stairwell, almost sounding like the noise was rising as it slowly started to drift away and up to the higher levels of the building...and then they were suddenly surrounded by pure silence...and darkness.

Ray couldn't see shit, but he attempted to at least try and look around to see if he was able to notice anything that could've made that loud bang. Steve very slowly started to creep over to Ray in the darkness and stopped literally a couple inches away from him.

"Hell was that?" Steve whispered as he also looked around but kept very calm.

"Not sure. Couldn't tell if it came from inside or out..." Ray softly said.

"I couldn't either."

The guys kept very still in the stairwell for a few moments, waiting to see if the noise was going to happen again, but it never did. After a decent amount of time passed, Ray knew he was gonna have to decide what he was gonna do next. While he didn't really want to move until he heard the noise again, he knew just waiting there was doing nothing more then wasting time, and they were already on a short enough time frame as it was.

"Let's move," Ray whispered to the guys as he turned on his screen.

The guys then turned there screens back on and then continued to follow up the stairs as Ray led the way but at a slower speed this time around.

"What floor is it again?" Jasmin softly whispered to Tommy.

"Three," Tommy whispered back.

Jasmin then exhaled.

"Oh thank God. I don't think I could make it if it was any higher," Jasmin said.

"Lazy bastard," Tommy whispered as he shook his head.

"I'm not lazy...I just get tired," Jasmin tried to explain.

"Gee I wonder why," Tommy sarcastically said as they walked past the door to the second floor.

While Ray led the pack up the stairs, it was Tim and Torque who were at the end of the line. With Tim lighting up the way with his cell phone, Torque decided it was best if he just shut his off; he didn't really need it anyway, Tim's screen was bright enough.

"Ever been on something like this before?" Tim whispered to Torque.

Torque shook his head.

"Yeah. Not with these guys, but yeah...what about you?" Torque softly asked back.

"A couple times...Roader normally doesn't take jobs that require a lot of sneaking around, but once in a while he does," Tim explained.

Torque nodded as he looked up toward Ray and saw him almost limping up the stairs each time he stepped up with his right knee. Clearly Ray must've been in pain but even though he was limping, he still kept going on steadily. It was a sight that gave Torque nothing but respect for Ray; it was clear nothing was going to get in his way.

But there was no denying it, Ray was in serious pain as he approached the third floor. The darkness was able to hide the sweat and the bright red color that was blotched all over his face, which was good—kept him from worrying about the others seeing him. Ray just wanted to rest even though he couldn't.

The arthritis in his knee had gotten a lot worse since the last time he had it checked out by a doctor. Even then, the doctors told him that it would only get worse with time if he didn't do something to fix it, but Ray didn't want to get it fixed. Not because he was worried that the surgery would make him unable to walk, or because it was too much money...it was because in Ray's mind if he had decided to accept the surgery, then it would be like Ray accepting the fact that he was getting old...and Ray had too much pride to ever say that to himself. His body might be pushing up into the sixties, but inside Ray was still just a kid. And nothing was going to take that away from him.

II

It took biting down on his lip to make it up the last step but once he did, Ray lifted up his machine gun and then reached for the large black door with the number three painted on the glass. Once he grabbed the old brass doorknob, Ray then looked at Steve. Steve was locked and loaded, ready to go. Ray could see that in his eyes. It made him feel good as he began to slowly pull open the door.

The door made a loud and rather horrific screech, ending the silence that had surrounded the guys all the way up. Ray tried to pull it a little slower, but that didn't help either; the screech only seemed to grow deeper. But as soon as the door was open enough, Steve took hold of the door and Ray went marching into the hallway as he quickly turned his flashlight back on. Then once he was through, Steve went, followed by the rest of the guys.

The hallway wasn't much of an improvement over the one on the first floor. In fact, it was even worse. This hallway not only had a horrible smell that was a cross between bad body order and shit, but also had large rats running all around as Ray shined his light down on the long red carpeted hall.

"Come on," Ray ordered as he took the first step down the hall.

Bob turned on his light and then followed behind Ray and Steve, while Jasmin looked around and covered his nose.

"Oh, it smells like shit up here," Jasmin whispered to Tommy.

"Smells better then the fucking orange vomit that's all over me," Tommy said as he looked Jas and then softly elbowed Jasmin's large belly.

"Not by much," Torque said as he closed the large black door all the way and then began to follow everyone down the hall.

The smell was starting to get to everyone by the time they were about halfway down the hall, even Ray was having a tough time dealing with it, but he just tried to keep focus on the door numbers as he jogged down the hall.

"303...304...305..." Steve softly said, reading out the golden numbers that were on the black doors of the apartments.

Ray was starting to get a rush as Steve said the numbers out loud. He knew the apartment was literally just before him and his mind was shooting all over the place. He first started to wonder what was just behind that black door. He started to tremble when he thought of the idea that Emily was in there, and he grew with rage when he began to think that Dutra could be inside...

Suddenly Ray put his left hand in the air, stopping everyone from Steve to Torque dead in their tracks...and they held there position as each one of them lifted up there weapons, ready to fire the very second anything so much as twitched.

The light from Ray's flashlight lit up the poorly painted door as well as illuminated the gold '307' that was going vertical up the side of the door.

Ray kept his eyes on the door, not even taking a moment to blink. Bob quietly yet quickly walked over to the left side of the door while Steve covered the right side, both aiming their guns at the bottom of the door. Bob gave the nod, then Steve gave the nod, symbolizing it was time to move in.

As Bob and Steve covered the sides, the rest of the guys all took aim at the door as Ray slowly began to lower his hand and then firmly grasped hold of his assault rifle. Ray took one more look at Steve, who nodded one more time...and then with all his might and anger Ray smashed in the door with his foot, instantly snapping the old door right off its hinges.

The door dropped to the ground with a loud crash as Ray quickly jetted into the apartment building. Bob and Steve quickly followed right behind him. Then the rest of the team rushed in.

The guys swept through the apartment from room to room. They noticed immediately that the apartment didn't look like it was being lived in: no furniture, no kitchen table, nothing.

Steve searched what appeared to be the bedroom but besides a broken queen sized bed and a small nightstand, the room was empty; the bed didn't even have sheets or blankets.

Tommy and Jasmin searched through the kitchen. Tommy quickly discovered that the kitchen cabinets were empty as he quickly opened all the doors to them; breaking one off it's hinge. Jasmin opened the refrigerator which clearly was older them he was, judging by the awful condition it was in. When he opened it, not only did he find out it was empty but he also found out that it wasn't even running.

Torque searched the bathroom, which was about the size of a bathroom on an airplane and turned up with nothing; the shower didn't even have a curtain attached to it. Not to mention that the toilet didn't have any water In It either.

While the rest of the guys kept searching, Ray made his way to what appeared to be a living room, only no such living seemed to be taking place. There was no couch, no coffee table, lamp or T.V. The only thing the room offered was a white carpet that was covered with brown, gross looking stains and a large window looking out toward the front of the street. But there was one thing in that small little room that instantly caught Ray's attention as he lowered his gun.

Directly in the middle of the room was what appeared to be an off white colored rotary phone resting peacefully on a small but rundown looking night stand which was chained in place and had one very small drawer right on the top. Ray kept his eyes on the phone, thinking that he hadn't seen one of those types of phones for years, but remembered them well. Once he quickly finished his trip down memory lane, he then started to question why the phone would be in the middle of the room...

"Ray..." Steve said.

Ray didn't hear Steve at first; for some odd reason, Ray couldn't get his eyes off the damn telephone.

"Ray!" Steve said again in a much louder voice.

The second time Ray heard Steve, raising his head to meet Steve's eyes.

"Find anything?" Ray quickly asked.

"Nothing," Steve responded as the rest of the guys walked in.

"Bathroom is clear," Torque said.

"Nothing in the kitchen," Tommy said as he and Jasmin walked over to Ray.

"Nothing in the hallway," Bob said.

"And nothing in the bedroom," Steve added.

Ray wiped his forehead and took a deep breath.

"Place is empty," Scotty said as he stood behind Tommy.

"No food, no pictures, no nothing. Don't think anybody lives here," Tim added.

Ray took in the news, rubbing his mouth with his right hand before turning to the window.

"Something feels off here," Torque said.

"What the fuck," Ray softly said to himself.

Bob looked at Steve and met his eyes just before lifting up his eyebrows. Ray cleared his throat and then looked out the window only to see mostly darkness, although he was able to make out the shapes of the buildings. He kept his eyes on the buildings as Steve walked over to him.

"Alright Ray, we gotta move out," Steve said as he patted Ray on the arm.

"No!" Ray said as he pushed Steve's hand off of him and turned to the guys. "No! There has to be some fucking reason why he would choose this spot! There has to be!"

"There's not, Ray." Bob said.

Ray looked at Bob with a pissed off looking face and then looked back down and began shaking his head in frustration. Steve then patted him on the arm again.

"There's gotta be a reason," Ray said in a lower voice.

Steve exhaled as he looked at Ray.

"Ray, I think he's just fucking with you...look around...there's nothing here..." Steve said in a soft, almost comforting voice.

Ray took yet another look around as the words sunk into him. It was in that moment when he knew that Steve must've been right. It was true; there was literally nothing there. They all thought at first that the apartment was going to be either a hideout for Dutra or even a base he was using but it was clear that nothing was there; it was like a bad prank.

Steve kept his eyes on Ray as he wiped his forehead and then looked back up at the guys, who were all waiting to hear what his next idea was going to be. Ray cleared his throat and then looked down, almost in shame.

"Alright you guys...let's head out," Ray said.

Torque shook his head and then turned toward the door and headed out...followed by everyone else. Ray watched the guys slowly head toward the exit, almost like he was frozen in place. It took Steve softly patting him on the stomach to get him back into it.

"Come on Ray," Steve said.

"Yeah," Ray said as he started for the door.

"Don't worry, we'll get back to the helicopter and try to get a hold of Roader. Hopefully he's got something," Steve said to try and raise Ray's spirit.

Ray was getting ready to tell Steve to shut the fuck up when he was interrupted by the old telephone, ringing with that extremely loud, ear numbing ring.

Everyone stopped dead in their tracks as fear shot through every single person in that room. And just when the fear started to go away, the phone rang again, sending yet another bolt down everyone's spine as they all turned around and looked at the old phone, their hearts pounding away with almost horror.

Ray looked back at the old phone, the small red light on the front lit up and everything. As it rang for the third time, the ring seemed to echo through not only the apartment, but also the entire floor. Once the third ring ended, Ray began to walk back toward the phone...and after looking back up at all the guys, who were frozen with fear, he picked up the phone and then lifted it to his ear.

Static filled his left ear as he waited to see who it was, almost hoping that it was either Roader or Sullivan, even though he pretty much knew there was no way that was possible. No, Ray knew exactly who was on the line; he knew the moment the phone rang. That's not what filled him with fear; it was knowing now what Dutra was now truly capable of doing that haunted him.

"Now, I warned you what would happen if you tried coming after me, didn't I?" Dutra said in a low frequency.

The anger built up in Ray, picking up where it left off the last time he was on the other end of the line with Dutra. Only a lot had changed since then.

"I fucking told you I would fuck and gut your daughter like a piece of fish if you kept after me! Did you think I was fucking lying to you? What you don't think I'll go that far?" Dutra asked as he shouted into the phone.

"No, I don't," Ray quickly said back.

"What?" Dutra asked to make sure he heard Ray correctly.

"No, I don't think you will go that far! You don't have the fucking balls," Ray firmly said.

"I don't have the balls? Have you looked around Ray? Take a look outside! Take a good fucking look outside!" Dutra shouted back.

Ray couldn't help but slowly turn his eyes back over to the large window in front of him.

"You see it? Do you see what I've done? What I've done to America, the strongest country in the world?" Dutra asked.

"A bomb and a couple of bullets can't bring down an entire country," Ray answered back.

"Well, if three men could prevent all out war for decades, anything's possible, isn't it?" Dutra asked as he turned and looked down to Emily, on the ground with her hands tied up, bruises all over her face.

Ray then stopped moving, stopped breathing, stopped thinking as what Dutra said processed in his mind and then exposed the fear that Ray always had about past sins returning for answers.

"Did you really think I didn't know what I was getting myself into? You really think I was just some stupid fuck who picked a fight with the wrong group of assholes? Well let me tell you this Ray: I've known you and Steve were two of the 'Dogs' for a while now. Just like I've known it was you who ambushed me in Bosnia," Dutra said as sinisterly as he possibly could.

Ray slowly turned to Steve, who could clearly see the look of fear trapped in his eyes.

"And now that I have your attention, I know what's coming next...and all I can say is I hope you're ready. Now with that said I'll ask you again: Did you think I was lying to you when I said if you didn't stay away, I would cut your daughter into pieces?" Dutra asked once again.

And for the first time in his life...Ray didn't have an answer. His mind was completely blank, and nothing seemed to be popping into his head. Dutra had come prepared this time round. But in the middle of the silence, as Ray waited to come up with a response, he heard a nose that once again sent a shock of fear down his spine. On the other end of the line, Ray heard a gun cock.

"No!" Ray quickly shouted, being the only thing that he could think of.

Dutra then turned and looked down at Emily as a tear began to run from her swollen eye and down her cheek.

"Ray. You are not going to believe...the shit...I intend to do to her. It's just a damn shame you won't be alive to see it," Dutra said.

"What makes you think I wont be?" Ray asked, almost mockingly.

"Well, twenty of my men are surrounding the apartment building as we speak..." Dutra began.

"Twenty? That's it? I've killed twenty men on my own before Dutra," Ray shot back.

Dutra shook his head and then shrugged his shoulders.

"That's nice, but my men are only there to make sure that the bomb in the drawer under the phone you're currently holding goes off," Dutra finished.

Once the words whipped the little smirk right off of Ray's face, he looked down and then open the drawer a crack, only to see the drawer was wired with plastic explosives and a red timer was counting down from twenty seconds right in the front.

"I'd be carefully opening that drawer though, any major movment will cause it to explode before the timer hits zero...and if my calculations are correct, that should be in sixteen seconds...right?" Dutra asked as he smiled.

Ray quickly turned to Steve as the timer hit sixteen seconds and then kept falling. Steve leaned in and then saw the bomb.

"Oh, shit," Steve said as his eyes widened.

Dutra smiled and he looked down at Emily.

"Goodbye Ray...rest in pieces," Dutra said as he chuckled and then hung up.

Ray dropped the phone and then turned to the guys. The guys looked at him and then when the timer on the explosives started to beep they all quickly looked down and saw the bomb.

"What the fuck is that?" Tommy quickly asked.

"Looks like C-4," Jasmin answered.

"What!" Scotty shouted.

Ray started to look around and the guys began to panic. Steve then looked down at the timer.

"Ten seconds,." Steve said in a calm voice.

"Great!" Tommy shouted.

"Everybody out! NOW!" Ray shouted.

Tim, Scotty, Bob and the other four guys of Roader's team quickly headed out to the apartment as fast as they could.

As the guys raced out of the apartment, Ray quickly lifted up his machine gun and fired multiple shots into the large window of the living room, causing the glass to shatter and then drop down onto the dark street.

Once Torque saw Ray shoot out the window, he turned and headed back for the bedroom, which also had a rather large window. He quickly caught up to Jasmin and Tommy who were just getting ready to turn for the apartment door, when Torque suddenly body slammed Jasmin, which caused Jasmin to bang into Tommy, pushing Tommy into the direction of the bedroom. Suddenly Torque lifted up his machine gun and fired several shots into the window before Tommy reached it.

"Torque, what the fuck are you..."

But before Tommy could finish his sentence, he reached the window and Torque pushed them and himself out, sending each of them into a sudden free fall.

"Oh, shit!" Tommy shouted on the way down.

And just as the timer got close to the end, Steve and Ray did the same thing, leaping out into the dark street, hoping they were about to land on something relatively soft. And not even before they were halfway down, the timer hit zero.

III

Instantly, a large yellow and deep orange fireball shot out of the windows of the entire top of the apartment complex, sending out a deafening roar into the night sky and echoed for what sounded like miles.

Bob, Tim, Scotty and the others made it out of the apartment and all made it to the end of the hall, avoiding any type of impact from the blast. Torque, Tommy and Jasmin were able to land in a large dumpster, which broke their fall. But the only thing Steve and Ray could land on was the ground...and that's exactly what they landed on.

The two of them both grunted hard and lost every bit of air in there bodies as they landed on there backs, looking up at the large, bright fireball. Not even half a second after they landed onto the ground, they felt a rush of extremely hot air come down and meet them on the ground, causing both of them to lift up their hands and cover their faces from the rush of heat.

Torque, Jasmin, and Tommy stayed very still in the dumpster, despite the fact that Torque was literally on top of Jasmin and Tommy. Normally Tommy freaked out when people would invade his space in such a way but in the moment, he let it slide. He was just happy (and actually surprised) that he was still alive. But he was getting really tired of falling out of buildings.

Once the great ball of fire lifted higher into the air, it suddenly was consumed by the dark night sky and thick black smoke. The apartment, along with the top floor of the building, however, was completely engulfed with flames, generating an eerie shade of soft orange light down upon Ray, Steve and the rest of the street.

It took a moment (or two) for Ray to get the breath back in his system to even attempt to roll over. He didn't get far on the first try, but on his second try he was at least able to roll onto his side and look at Steve.

"Steve...you alright?" Ray asked as he slowly began to move.

Steve was in a little bit of better shape then Ray so he was able to at least lean up before answering Ray.

"Fine," Steve said as he wiped some of the dust off his arms.

Ray then coughed, clearing his throat, and then slowly lifted his hand up to his ear.

"Is...is everybody alright? Bob? Tommy...Torque?" Ray asked over the radio.

While Ray waited for a response, he lifted himself up and then looked up at the burning building with Steve.

"Wasn't excepting that," Steve said as he slowly turned and looked at Ray.

Ray nodded as he felt something, almost like water, trickling down the right side of his forehead.

"You're head's bleeding," Steve said as he pointed.

Before Ray had the chance to react, the radio in his ear suddenly filled up with static.

"Ray," Bob said.

"Bob? You alright?" Ray quickly asked.

"Yeah, I'm fine. I got Tim, Scotty and the rest of Roader's team with me." Bob said.

"Where are you?" Ray asked.

"Still inside the building. Made it to the stairwell before the bomb blew. You outside?" Bob asked.

Ray then softly placed his hand over the large bloody cut he had on his forehead.

"Yeah. I'm with Steve," Ray said.

"Is Tommy and Jas with you?" Bob asked.

Ray and Steve then turned to one another.

"No. They're not with you?" Ray asked in a panic.

"No," Bob said.

Steve shook his head and then stood up.

"Alright, make your way down to us. Come meet us in the front of the building," Ray ordered.

"Copy that," Bob said.

As soon as Bob got the orders from Ray, he got right on them.

"Okay guys, we're moving out. Same way we came in," Bob said to the guys in the dark stairwell.

"Everyone made it out?" Tim asked.

"Ray and Steve did. Haven't heard about the others," Bob said.

"Think the others guys did?" Scotty asked.

Bob shrugged his shoulders.

"Let's just get downstairs," Bob ordered.

"Yes, sir," Scotty said.

Ray groaned as Steve helped him up.

"Cut looks deep," Steve said.

"It's fine," Ray quickly said as he looked around.

"So...now what?" Steve asked.

At that point Ray simply had no idea. He honestly wasn't sure of where to go next. To him it felt like any type of a lead or clue as to where the fuck Dutra was burnt up in that apartment. He felt like he was right back at square one, like he's been in a hole ever since this whole situation started and every time he tries to jump up and reach the top, he loses his grip and falls back down to the bottom. But Ray quickly sprinted into action when he heard a loud bang come from down the alley that was on the right side of him.

Ray and Steve quickly turned their bodies and pointed their machine guns into the position of the loud crash. Ray's heart began to pound as his knee began to throb, he could tell that his knee was on it's last stand, but made the effort to completely ignore it long enough to slowly creep up to the alley with Steve and then suddenly jump into the alley just in time to scare the shit out of Torque, Tommy and Jasmin.

"Oh, shit!" Tommy shouted.

As soon as Ray knew who it was, he and Steve quickly lowered their guns.

"Jesus Christ, I nearly shot you," Steve exhaled.

"You guys alright?" Ray asked.

Torque looked at Tommy and Jasmin.

"Yeah, I think we're good," Torque said.

"Speak for yourself. You're not the one who had Jas land face down on your crotch," Tommy said.

"Not a fun time for either of us, Tommy," Jasmin said as he cracked his neck.

Torque then looked up at the fire that continued to burn the apartment.

"Bob alright?" Torque asked.

Ray nodded.

"Yeah, he's on his way down with the rest of the guys," Ray said.

Before Ray had the chance to say anything else, Bob's voice suddenly filled his eardrum.

"Ray," Bob firmly said over the radio.

"Yeah?"

"We got company," Bob began, as he looked out one of the small windows in the staircase and saw multiple truck lights heading in their direction. "I'm counting at least a dozen trucks heading our way."

"Oh, shit," Ray said, instantly remembering about the trucks that were roaming around.

"What?" Torque asked.

"We got company coming," Ray said just before a bright beam from one of the trucks lit up the far end of the alley.

"Oh this can't be good," Jasmin said as the lights started to get brighter.

"Everyone get to cover now!" Ray shouted.

The guys took no time at all to do what Ray said, they all ran out of the alley and split up in every direction.

"Bob," Ray said into the radio.

"Go ahead, Ray." Bob quickly said.

"You still in the building?" Ray asked.

"Yeah."

"Good, stay there. Make your way to a window and cover us in case this gets ugly," Ray ordered.

"Copy that," Bob said before he stopped going down the stairs, causing Tim, Scotty and the rest to stop also.

"Bob, what's wrong?" Tim asked.

"New plan...you guys follow me," Bob said and started back up the staircase.

"We're going back up?" Scotty asked.

"Just trust me kid," Bob said as he ran back up the stairs.

Scotty looked at Tim to see what his reaction was, only to see Tim shrug his shoulders.

"Come on, hurry!" Bob shouted from the top of the staircase.

IV

As Bob raced to get into a good sniping position, Ray and Steve quickly ran over to the opposite side of the street and took cover behind a black car as Torque took cover behind a cement set of stairs that led up to the apartment building next to the one that had just blown up.

After their issue from earlier, both Tommy and Jasmin decided it was best if they stayed out of a car this time and figured it would be best to stay rather close to Steve and Ray. When they saw Steve and Ray take cover behind the black Ford model car, they did the same thing.

Ray kept his head low but his eyes up as the lights in the alley grew brighter and brighter with each passing moment. He felt like they were in a good spot, they would be able to take the guys in the truck out easily the moment they stepped out. But Ray was so focused on the lights in the alley, he didn't even notice the ones coming down the street...but Torque did.

"Ray, we got more trucks coming down the street, heading right toward us," Torque said over his radio.

"Shit, stay down everyone," Ray ordered over the radio.

The truck that was heading right towards them also clearly had the high beams on, which lit up the street like it was the middle of the afternoon. Torque knew that if he stayed in the same position he was in, the truck lights would light him up like a Christmas tree, so at the last moment he dropped to his stomach and rolled behind two trashcans that were just off to the side of him.

The truck in the alley had finally emerged into Ray's view and it stopped right at the end of the alley as the truck Torque was hiding from also was slowing down. Ray then turned and looked at Tommy, Jasmin and Steve.

"Safeties off," Ray whispered.

The guys nodded and then did as Ray asked but while Jasmin was taking his off, he noticed another light coming up the street from behind them.

"Uh oh, Ray?" Jasmin asked into his radio even though he was right behind Ray.

"What?" Ray asked.

"Another vehicle coming from behind us."

"Oh, shit. Bob?" Ray whispered into his radio.

"Yeah?" Bob asked.

"Steve, Tommy, Jas and myself have taken cover behind a black Ford in the front of the building. You in position?" Ray quickly asked.

"Just about," Bob said, running down the second floor hallway that led to the front of the building.

"Shit," Ray said as he ducked.

Once the driver of the third truck got close enough to the building, the truck stopped and then the engine shut off. They heard the truck doors open, not just the one behind them, but from the one in the alley as well as the other that had driven past Torque.

Bob finally made it to a window in the hallway that was looking down upon the front of the building and he was able to see with his own eyes the men getting out of the trucks. Tim, Scotty and the rest of the guys then caught up to Bob, only to stop right behind him and see the sight for themselves.

"Oh shit," Tim said as he looked at the trucks that were surrounding the building.

"Uh...Bob?" Scotty asked as he walked over to another window that was on the edge of the left wall.

"What?" Bob asked without taking his eyes off of the trucks.

"We got another problem," Scotty said.

Bob turned and looked at Scotty.

"What?" Bob hissed, but the he looked past Scotty and saw for himself.

More trucks were coming down the street, and fast.

"Damn it. Ray?" Bob asked.

"Tell me you're in position," Ray whispered.

"Yeah. But we got another problem. I'm counting seven trucks heading your way from the North...maybe more."

The very second Bob's words sunk in, Ray felt that shiver of fear run down his spine like he had before, only this time it was stronger.

"What are we gonna do Bob? We're completely outnumbered," Scotty said.

Bob thought about it for a moment as the trucks approached. There was no denying that they were outnumbered, they were outnumbered just by the amount of guys that came out the first three trucks. Bob knew their was no chance now to deal with this quietly like Ray was hoping. The best thing, the only thing he could do now was attempt to give Ray and the guys enough of a window so they could move.

"Scotty, head down to the end of the hallway and stay at that window. Tim, take the rest and cover the windows in the rest of the hall. I'll stay at this window and deal with these trucks. You guys just focus on protecting the guys behind that black Ford car when I give the order alright?" Bob asked.

The guys nodded their heads.

"Get into position," Bob quickly said.

Scotty, Tim and the others ran down the hall and covered the windows throughout the hallway as Bob walked over to the window and carefully put down his sniper rifle on the ledge.

"Okay Ray. I'm right above you...I'm counting twelve guys that have gotten out so far and the other trucks are pulling up now," Bob said as he closed his eye and looked through his scope.

Bob kept his sights pointed at the trucks that were now stopping. And once they stopped, more men started to get out. Each one had the same thing on, black ski masks in black clothing, holding black assault rifles. But it was Stone that got out of the driver seat in the first truck that Bob quickly locked onto.

"Ray, it's that loudmouth from before," Bob said over the radio.

Ray very slowly looked up and then saw it was Stone, that same guy they had banged into before they took out the other truck. As Stone exited the truck, he took out a cell phone from his jacket pocket and lifted it into his ear.

"Yeah?" Stone asked.

"Search around the apartment building. Search every alley, every car parked on that street, every possible goddamn place that someone could hide! I want you to make sure that there's no possible way anyone survived that explosion. Do you understand?" Dutra asked firmly into Stone's ear.

"I know how to do my fucking job. Don't forget who called who. Now what do you want us to do once we finish searching the street?" Stone asked.

Dutra paused briefly for a moment.

"Do what you normally do...." Dutra ordered.

Stone smiled. "With pleasure," he said before hanging up.

As Stone put the phone back into his jacket pocket, Bob kept the cross hairs of his scope directly on the back of Stone's head.

"Alright, listen up!" Stone shouted to the all the men. "Vacca wants us to clear this whole area before we take off! Clear it, then burn it to the fucking ground! Every single goddamn building! Make sure they're dead! You hear? You hear that out there, you bastards? You're gonna die! You're gonna fucking die!" Stone shouted into the night as his long black hair fluttered in the gentle wind.

"Great," Steve whispered to himself.

"Ray?" Torque asked for the radio. "How we gonna do this?"

Ray thought hard.

"Bob, how many can you see?" Ray asked.

"At least twenty," Bob responded.

"You think you'll be able to cover us?" Ray asked.

Bob didn't respond right away, he wanted to be sure before he answered. Bob had been a sniper every since he was a late teenager, there was probably no one better than him. He could fire the gun like nobody's business. If anyone could get Ray and the rest of the guys out of the situation alive it was Bob. But there were also close to thirty guys down there...all with automatic weapons and itchy trigger fingers.

"Bob?" Ray asked again as Stone looked up at the burning building.

Bob then lowered his head almost in disapointment.

"It'll be cutting it close Ray. I can't guarantee it. I'm sorry Ray," Bob said.

From Ray to Jasmin, Bob's apology echoed into every eardrum over the radio as the men surrounding the trucks began to walk over to Stone, making the gap between each other smaller and smaller.

"Ray," Torque said over the radio as he aimed his gun from the ground at the group.

Steve slowly took his eyes off of Stone and the rest of the men and then focused them onto Ray's back, imagining not only the thoughts racing through his head, but also the type of look he had on his face. Ray was scared shitless, maybe even more then he ever was in Vietnam, but he still kept calm. But to Steve he looked like he needed some type of reassurance, so that's exactly what Steve did. He softly placed his hand on Ray's shoulder.

"Ready when you're ready, Ray," Steve softly said.

Ray nodded his head softly and then exhaled deeply and then lifted his gun up into a firing position when suddenly a strange noise came out of his radio in his ear. The noise was worse then nails on a chalk board, causing everyone to groan and grab their ears.

"Bob, was that you?" Ray asked.

Bob didn't answer.

"Bob...Bob?" Ray asked again almost in a panic.

He feared that the radios had gone out and all lines of communication between him and Bob were now gone, which made his heart pound away into his skull when suddenly everyone, from Ray right down the line to Tommy heard a voice that sent butterflies up into their stomachs.

"Ray...are you there?" The voice asked.

Ray knew right away who the voice belonged to, God knows he's heard it enough times but in that moment, being outnumbered by that many, it took a second to convince himself that Roader's voice was real.

"Roader?" Ray quickly asked.

"Looks like you could use a little help, my friend," Roader said with a soft chuckle.

Ray quickly turned and looked at Steve who was also just as confused as him.

"Yeah. Wait, where the hell are you?" Ray asked.

"Right above you," Roader said.

Ray, Steve, Tommy and Jasmin all looked up to figure out what the hell Roader was talking about. Ray didn't see anything at first, in fact none of them did, all they saw was the fire in the apartment burning and the yellowish tint it was projecting onto the building next to it. But finally, when Ray's eyes made it to the top of a nearby building, they quickly focused and found Roader, who was on the roof, aiming an assault rifle down at the group of men.

"Good to see you Roader," Ray said with a smile.

"Welcome to the party," Steve shot back.

"Thanks guys...good to see you too. That's quite a shit show you have down there."

"Nothing gets past you, Paul," Ray said.

Tim then looked down and saw Stone and his men slowly starting to break apart from each other.

"Guys, it looks like they're beginning to split up," Tim said over the radio.

"Kid's right Ray. You want to take them out, you'd better do it now. Will be damn near impossible once they start scattering everywhere," Roader said.

"Well in case you didn't notice Roader, we're still beyond outnumbered," Bob said as he continued to look through his scope.

"Don't worry...I made a few stops along the way," Roader said.

"What are you talking about Paul?" Ray asked into the radio.

He was expecting to hear Roader's voice, but the voice he got was probably the last voice he ever would've thought he was going to hear.

"How ya doing, pal?" Joey suddenly asked over the radio.

Ray quickly got confused. "Joey?" He asked before looking up at Roader again.

Ray locked his eyes on Roader who was still locked and loaded with his sights aimed down at the group of guys, when suddenly his eyes shifted and he saw Joey emerge from Roader's right side. But it wasn't just Joey who emerged...it was also Sullivan and what appeared to be about a dozen American military soldiers too. And the view brought a huge smile Ray's face.

Both Joey and Sullivan lifted up assault rifles and aimed them down at the men standing near the truck and the soldiers followed suit. When Steve saw the sight, he couldn't help but pat Ray on the back.

"Bad ass," Jasmin whispered as he leaned close to Tommy.

"Guess this means the gang's all here," Steve said as he lifted up his gun.

"You can say that again," Tommy said.

From the roof Joey and Sullivan both began to move their weapons and than aim at two separate targets.

"Ready when you are Ray," Sullivan said.

Ray then turned and looked at Steve. Steve nodded.

"Let's do this," Steve said.

Ray smiled and then turned back and looked up at the apartment building.

"You ready, Bob?" Ray asked.

"Yep," Bob quickly said.

Ray nodded and then took one last deep breath.

"Alright...light it up!" Ray shouted at the top of his lungs.

Instantly Roader, Joey, Sullivan and Bob fired simultaneously, clearly aiming at well thoughtout targets. Sullivan and Joey both fired at two separate trucks right near the gas tank, causing both truck to suddenly burst into flames and lift up into the air, while Roader got a headshot off of the closest guy to Ray.

Bob fired his shot at Stone but Bob wasn't expecting Stone to turn his head when he heard Ray's yell, causing Bob's shot to blow a large chunk of Stone's cheek off instead of blowing a hole directly through his head. Blood squirted out of Stone as the chunk of cheek flew up into the night sky before he dropped to his knees and Bob fired another shot into his back.

As the two trucks lifted up into the air and blew up, the blasts instantly caught those who were close to the trucks on fire, their horrific screams lifted up into the night air while their flesh began to seer.

Then Ray, Steve, Tommy and Jasmin stood up and began to fire into the rest of Stone's men. As Ray shot two guys in the chest, Steve fired three shots into the guys by the truck in the alley. Two of his shots hit the windshield of the truck but his last one was able to hit the kneecap of the driver of the truck.

Jasmin began firing at the truck that was behind him, only to have bullets sprayed back at him. As Jasmin ducked for cover, Tommy quickly stood up and blasted one shot from his shotgun, blowing off the arm of the guy who fired at Jasmin.

Up in the apartment building Bob kept firing off rounds that were hitting a different target each time. Tim, Scotty and the rest of Roader's guys also started firing down upon Dutra's men, killing many that had emerged from the same truck that Stone came out of.

With hundreds of bullet shells falling down on him from Roader and the rest of the guys on the roof, Torque stood up and started aiming at the rest of Dutra's men, firing single shots out of his assault rifle, killing three men in a row with chest shots.

Joey aimed down his sights and fired, blowing up another truck as Sullivan and the military soldiers sprayed bullets all around. Sullivan kept firing until his clip ran out, then he reloaded it and suddenly ducked when some of Dutra's men from below started firing up at the roof, killing one of the soldiers and causing his body to fall lifelessly off the roof. Joey then put a bullet into the head of the guy who killed the soldier.

As blood flowed out of his face and back, Stone began shaking and attempting to try and move away from the gunfire. He very slowly lifted his right hand and put it over where his cheek use to be, attempting to stop the bleeding, but once he felt the loose skin dangling off his face, he knew there wasn't a chance for him to stop it just from applying pressure. And just as he began crawling away, the vehicle next to him suddenly blew up thanks to a well aimed shot by Ray.

Once the area around the black Ford was clear, Ray, Steve, Tommy and Jasmin broke from cover and quickly ran over to the trucks, firing their weapons all around. Jasmin fired three shots, killing the last two guys who were in the alley as Tommy took aim at a guy trying to run away and fired, blowing a huge hole through his back. And Ray got the last kill, firing his entire clip into the driver of the last truck as the man attempted to get back into the truck. And once Ray's gun was empty, the street quickly got silent again.

Steve, Tommy and Jasmin looked all round to make sure they didn't miss anyone (or anything). Ray reloaded his gun as he walked over to the last truck and looked inside only to see that it was empty.

"Clear," Steve said.

"Clear up here," Bob said.

"Same with us," Roader said.

Ray then lowered his weapon and placed his hand on his ear.

"Bob, head on down," Ray said.

"Copy," Bob said and lifted up his sniper rifle. "Alright let's head down, kids."

Ray wiped the sweat from his forehead and then looked up at the roof only to see Roader looking down at him.

"Thanks," Ray said into his radio as he looked up at Roader.

"Anytime, pal. Now come meet us by the fire escape," Roader said, looking down at Ray with a smile.

V

As Bob and the rest of the gang made their way out of the burning apartment building, Ray, Steve, Torque, Tommy and Jasmin quickly ran down the right side alley of the building that Roader, Sullivan and Joey were on top of. As the guys approached the fire escape, they saw Roader step off first, followed quickly by Joey and then Sullivan. Once Ray was within arm's reach, he patted Roader on the back.

"Looks like you owe me now," Roader said.

"We'll talk about that later," Ray said as he patted Roader on the shoulder.

Ray looked at Joey with a serious face. Joey also kept a serious face as he waited to see how Ray was going to act. But the tension quickly broke when Ray suddenly smiled and went in for a hug. Joey also quickly smiled and gave Ray a quick hug.

"Good to see you, Joey," Ray confessed.

"Didn't think I was going to leave you hanging, did you?" Joey asked.

Then Ray looked at Sullivan. Sullivan forced a smile at Ray and then lowered his head. Ray did the same and then extended his right hand. When Ray's hand made it into Sullivan's eyesight, he quickly looked up with a surprised look on his face. Then he shook Ray's hand.

As Ray shook Sullivan's hand, they all began to hear a noise, a very loud noise that sounded like it was coming from the sky. Ray looked up first, followed soon after by the rest of his guys, even Bob who was halfway down the alley. Suddenly from out of the night sky a large, military style helicopter raced past the alley, followed by another one before the two helicopters began circling around above them.

"Don't worry...they're with us," Roader said to Ray.

"Thought you guys were following a lead in D.C." Ray said to the guys.

"It was a dead end," Joey quickly shouted as the helicopters began to slowly to descend onto the street behind them.

"Come on, this way!" Roader shouted to everyone as he began to turn and head for the helicopters.

"Soldiers were a nice touch of class," Steve said to Joey as he started walking toward the helicopter.

"You liked that, huh?" Joey asked with a smile.

As the guys began to walk toward the helicopter, Sullivan walked to Ray.

"I had one of my guys run a wider search on Jonathon Street while we were in D.C. Turns out Street uses an alias by the name of Bill Couture, and once we searched that name another address came up," Sullivan shouted.

Ray stopped from walking towards the helicopter and then turned to Sullivan.

"What's the address?" Ray asked.

"48 West 54th street ...here in New York...satellite pictures show it's a fifty floor skyscrpper at the far end of the city...the only part of the city that wasn't heavily impacted by the explosion. Blue prints say a large penthouse is up on the thirty-third floor," Sullivan explained.

Ray took it all in as he looked back at the helicopters. Then he quickly locked back onto Sullivan's eyes.

"Emily's there," Ray said.

"Yeah, probably. Along with Dutra's entire army, but yeah," Sullivan said.

"I'm going," Ray firmly stated.

Sullivan shook his head up and down.

"I had a feeling you might say that," Sullivan began just before dozens of military convoys and undercover police cruisers pulled onto the street. "So I figured we might need a little bit of back up..."

Ray quickly took his eyes off the convoys and cruisers and looked back at Sullivan.

"We?" Ray asked.

"You've always said you were waiting for the day I do something more then just sit behind a desk. Looks like today is your lucky day pal," Sullivan said.

Ray smiled as his eyes almost began to fill with tears. Sullivan returned the smile and then patted Ray on the arm.

"Now let's go bring Emily home," Sullivan ordered.

Ray wiped his eyes and then the two men quickly hustled to the helicopters. As they approached, Ray saw two black SUV's pull up in front of the helicopters with red and blue lights flashing away on them before he watched Joey open the pilot door to one of the helicopters and jump in. Ray then walked toward that helicopter.

"My guys get into this SUV," Roader shouted over the roar of the helicopter as he jumped up into the helicopter Joey was piloting.

Ray then turned and saw his guys; all his men standing by the helicopter, waiting for orders. Ray pointed to the empty SUV.

"You guys get into the other SUV. Jas, you drive. I'll give you the address once we're up in the air." Ray said.

"You got it boss," Jasmin said.

"Alright, let's move," Ray ordered as he clapped his hands.

Jasmin quickly ran to the driver side door as Tommy headed for the passenger door. Torque and Bob then took the backseat. Ray watched them all get inside and for the first time since this all started with Dutra, Ray felt like their was now a solid chance to not only save Emily but also put Dutra in a grave once and for all. Ray lost his thought suddenly when he felt a tap on his shoulder. He turned and saw it was Steve.

"You heading up with Paul and Joey?" Steve asked.

"Yeah. You going with Bob and them?" Ray asked.

Steve chuckled under his breath.

"Figured I'd stick with you. Haven't left your side before, no sense in doing it now," Steve said.

Ray smiled and then nodded at the helicopter.

"Come on, let's get this asshole," Ray said.

"Yes, sir," Steve said as they began walking toward the helicopter.

"How many times do I have to tell you to stop calling me sir?" Ray asked.

"It's better then old man, right?" Steve quickly asked.

"Yeah, but not by much."

Once Ray and Steve reached the helicopter, Roader and Sullivan extended their hands out and helped the two of them up. Ray smiled at Roader and then looked down at the mounted M134D-H aiming out of the entrance of the helicopter and Sullivan looked at the M134D-H on the opposite entrance.

"Everybody ready?" Joey asked from the cockpit.

"Move us out, Joey." Sullivan ordered.

Joey nodded and then began to lift the chopper off the ground. Sullivan loaded up the large mounted machine gun and cleared his throat while Ray lifted his hand to his radio.

"Jas, the address is 48 West 54th Street," Ray said.

"Copy that, we're on our way," Jasmin said back as Tommy punched the address into the GPS in the SUV.

"Drive safe," Ray added.

"You too...well you know what I mean..."

"Yeah...I know what you mean Jas."

As Joey lifted the helicopter into the dark night sky, Ray took one last look down as the two SUV's started to move. Once they turned into nothing more than small spots in his eyesight, Ray lifted his eyes up to the view of the dark and gloomy New York.

It gave him chills knowing that somewhere among all the skyscrapers Dutra lay patiently waiting. But Ray didn't focus on the chills for very long. Instead he was able to focus on the fact that he wasn't going to stop until Dutra was dead. It was all going to end right then and there...and as Joey flew the helicopter deeper and deeper into the city, Ray not only accepted that, but he promised himself that if he ended up dying he wouldn't be dying alone; Dutra would be going with him.

Chapter 17: War

The night air was quiet. The wind had died down across the city. Power flickered in the buildings just outside of the blast area. Apart from the sound of fires burning, the city was blanketed in silence, a shocking contrast to the once crowded but now abandon streets.

The city had truly turned black. It was a horrific, apocalyptic moment for not only the city, but for the entire nation. A nation that would look a lot different the moment cell phones and internet connections were back up and running and the word got out of what had happened.

New York had lost its voice, but up high in his office, Dutra relished the silence that he had brought down upon the city. Meanwhile Vincent and a small army of men, locked and loaded with machine guns, surrounded the entrance of the tall skyscraper.

The street was also barricaded with trucks and SUVs, and since the skyscraper was the last building on a dead end street, all the vehicles in Dutra's grasp were able to block the entrance very effectively. With the street blocked and the dozens and dozens of men not only outside but inside as well, Dutra felt confident that nothing was going to get through, at least in one piece.

As Street opened the door to Dutra's office, Emily trembled in fear on the floor. Her right eye had completely closed up from the swelling, making it look like she had just gotten out of a boxing match.

Street closed the door and then looked at Dutra, noticing that for probably the first time, Dutra was very quiet. He wasn't looking around, moving or even looking like he was breathing...he was just there.

"Sir...still no word back from Stone," Street said.

Dutra then looked up, Street's words pulling him out of the state of mind he was in, but once again didn't answer right away.

"...Sir?" Street softly asked.

Dutra then exhaled before he chuckled under his breath.

"That motherfucker."

Then Dutra turned and looked down at Emily, on the floor with her hands tied behind her back, bleeding from several cuts on her face.

"Well...looks like he just killed his own fucking kid," Dutra said to Street. He said it loud enough for Emily to hear it, but she was in so much pain from the beating, the words didn't even register in her mind. At that point, probably for the first time in her young life, the only thing she wanted was to see her father. She was still confused with everything going on, not really knowing why the hell this was happening to her, but deep inside she had this feeling in her gut that if anyone could help her, it was Ray.

Dutra turned back to the window and pulled out his cell phone. He looked down at his men on the street as he waited for Vincent to answer.

Down below Vincent kept his eyes on the street, ready to stop anything that pulled onto the empty road. Then his cell phone began to vibrate in his pocket. Vincent reached into his pocket and then took out his phone.

"Hello?"

"Lock and load...now," Dutra ordered.

"Yes sir."

Dutra then hung up as Vincent turned to the small army behind him.

"Lock and load!" Vincent shouted into the night air.

Suddenly the quietness of the street was broken by the noise coming from all of Dutra's men loading their guns and cocking them. Vincent was doing the same, putting his cell phone away and then cocking his large assault rifle, when he suddenly heard a noise coming down the street.

Vincent looked up and saw what appeared to be a dark colored SUV pulling onto the street with the high beams on. It began heading in Vincent's direction, not fast but not slow either.

"Heads up!" Vincent shouted into the night sky.

All the men suddenly locked onto the SUV and put their fingers on the triggers of their assault rifles. Vincent aimed directly at the driver's side of the windshield and softly exhaled. He then fired one shot at the windshield, and the moment the loud shot rang into the air, all the men behind him did the same.

Bullets began hitting the front of the SUV, taking out both headlights as Vincent kept shooting into the windshield. He fired until his clip ran dry. He quickly reloaded and then fired one last shot into the windshield as one of the guys behind him shot out the passenger tire.

As the passenger tire blew out, the SUV began losing control, swerving across the street before it suddenly turned left and violently smashed into a street lamp, the lamp sparking as it met the SUV. And when it stopped dead in its tracks, Dutra's men stopped firing, bringing silence back to the street.

Vincent slowly stood up, still aiming at the SUV. A few of the men behind him walked up to Vincent and stood at his side, each also aiming at the SUV, just waiting for someone to step out.

Smoke began to lift out of the hood of the vehicle but their still was no movement. Suddenly a loud screeching noise came from the direction of the crash, but it wasn't the SUV. It was the street lamp. It's bottom had snapped, causing the entire lamp to come crashing down, hitting the street with a loud boom before the top half began sparking behind the SUV.

With all the bullets fired into it, it's hard to imagine that anyone in the

SUV could still be alive...but Vincent wasn't taking any chances. Dutra had taught him many things over the years, and eliminating the chance of a target being alive was the very first thing.

Vincent then took aim at the SUV again, but he aim at the windshield this time, or anywhere near the front of the vehicle. He took aim at the back right, around where the gas tank was. And with a smile on his face, he fired one shot.

Suddenly the SUV blew into flames, sending a large fireball and a mass of thick black smoke up into the air. Vincent lowered his weapon and looked at the guys next to him.

"That's how we finish the job boys!" Vincent shouted.

The fireball could be seen thirty floors up. Dutra smiled the moment he saw the explosion. He almost felt proud in that moment, happy that his men moved so quickly...almost like soldiers, which is what he's always wanted. He then turned and looked back down at Emily, smiling as she trembled in fear.

"Looks like daddy won't be saving you after all buttercup," Dutra said with a smile as he looked down at her legs.

Dutra examined Emily's body before turning back and looking out the window, taking a deep breath of air as he smiled and looked out across the city. In the distance he could see a glow of fire from where the Manhattan Bridge proudly stood. It was the moment Dutra had been waiting for and he enjoyed it; it seemed to him that nothing was in his way.

Suddenly, as Dutra was looking out the window, a huge explosion came from the tall building across the street, sending a huge ball of fire up into the air as the top half of the building blew up, causing Dutra to duck from the window as large pieces of debris came raining down.

The noise of the explosion rocked the street. Vincent looked up and saw the top half of the building beginning to fall toward the street. Some of Dutra's men covered their ears, due to the loud noise generated from the explosion.

"Everybody move!" Vincent ordered.

All but one of Dutra's men were able to get out of the way before the top of the building crashed down onto the street, sending a cloud of smoke into the air and instantly crushed the guy who didn't move in time.

Vincent looked at the debris, but his attention was quickly directed into another direction when he heard a loud humming noise come from up in the dark sky.

The noise got louder and louder as Vincent searched the night sky to figure out what it was. At first he couldn't see anything, partly due to the fact that he was still in a haze from seeing the explosion from the building. He kept his eyes on the sky as the noise grew louder and clear. Suddenly just as his eyes adjusted to the darkness in the sky, a large helicopter appeared overhead, causing all of Dutra's men to look up.

II

From the helicopter Ray, Steve, and Roader looked down, locating Dutra's large force of men standing in front of the tall skyscraper. Then they all took aim at the targets.

Ray began firing the mounted gun down upon the men as Steve and Roader fired their machine guns. The noise from the gun Ray was firing was nothing short of deafening, but that didn't stop him from raining down bullets.

Steve was able to hit two guys in the chest, Roader got three in the stomach and neck but it was Ray's bullets that were hitting everything around the street, blowing holes into Dutra's men as they attempted to get to cover.

Joey kept the helicopter steady for as long as he could before he turned the helicopter and began to fly right above the group. As he turned the helicopter Sullivan cocked the mounted gun on his side of the helicopter and then also began firing down, blowing up cars and hitting the guys who were near the entrance of Dutra's skyscraper.

Vincent hastily got under cover, ducking behind one of the cars barricading the street as the chopper flew above him. As soon as the helicopter passed him he, along with the men next to him, quickly lifted up their weapons and began firing up at the helicopter.

Dutra stood up from the floor in time to see the helicopter fly right past his window, groaning with anger as Ray and Sullivan continued to fire down upon the street and into Dutra's men. As Ray's helicopter flew past his window, Dutra looked up, only to see another helicopter flying in.

He knew the helicopters were going to be a problem, he honestly wasn't expecting a helicopter (let alone two) so he knew he was going have to act fast if he was going to keep the street locked down.

Dutra quickly turned to his desk and opened the top drawer, removing a 9-millimeter handgun. He then quickly inserted a clip into it and turned to the balcony door at the far end of his office.

Vincent and the rest of his guys continued to fire up at the helicopter. Joey began turning the helicopter away as bullets ricocheted off metal. He turned the helicopter toward the group of men on Ray's side. Ray took the opportunity and started firing back down at the street.

"Get to cover! Hurry up!" Vincent shouted.

As Ray fired, Steve quickly reloaded. As he put the clip in his gun, he looked up and saw the other helicopter approaching and firing down on Dutra's men.

"Joey, move us out of the way so the other chopper can make a pass!" Steve shouted.

"Alright, hold on!" Joey shouted.

Joey moved out of the firing zone. Then the other helicopter made its pass, the pilot holding down the machine gun button and spraying bullets all around.

Vincent kept still as the helicopter flew past, killing one of the guys on the opposite side of the car he was behind. Like Dutra, Vincent also knew that they weren't going to last if the helicopters kept coming in like they were. But even though it was a long shot, once the chopper passed, he stood up and began to fire up at it.

The helicopter finished its pass with a boom, blowing up another car and killing five or so people from the explosion. Then the helicopter began to lift up and the pilot smiled knowing he had taking out a good amount of targets.

The chopper lifted up higher and higher until it was near the top of the skyscraper. Once he was high enough he turned his head and saw Joey's helicopter making its way back.

"Ready for you," the pilot said as he turned the helicopter back to the direction of the building.

The pilot looked down at the smoke coming from the street and smiled, not even noticing Dutra standing on the balcony aiming up his gun. The pilot leveled off the helicopter and kept it still. Then he slowly turned his head and looked down and saw Dutra aiming.

"Oh shit!" The pilot said, and began to turn the helicopter.

But it was too late, Dutra was already locked on and then fired one shot from his handgun, the bullet easily breaking through the windshield of the helicopter and hitting the pilot directly in the forehead. As the pilot dropped his head, his hand on the throttle pushed down and began to descend, and fast. Joey was the first to notice as he circled back to the building.

"Oh, shit," Joey said.

Ray then stood up, groaning from the pain in his knee and leaned over to Joey.

"What?" Ray asked before he looked up and saw for himself.

Joey stopped the helicopter as the other made one last turn and then began to nosedive right toward a building about a hundred yards away from where the SUV had crashed earlier.

When it hit the building, the helicopter disappeared in a ball of fire. Roader, Steve, and Sullivan turned and looked in the direction of the blast and saw the large flames soar into the night sky.

As the helicopter exploded, massive chunks of the building it crashed into blew out onto the street, causing Vincent and the guys near him to duck for cover as little pieces began landing all around them.

"The hell was that?" Roader shouted.

Ray quickly turned.

"The other chopper," Ray answered.

"The hell took it down?" Steve asked.

Ray and Joey were looking around to try and find what took the helicopter down when suddenly a bullet shot through the windshield, missing Joey by inches.

"Oh, shit," Joey said as he ducked.

Ray also ducked and grabbed a hold of Joey's seat as Joey lifted the nose of the helicopter up just before more bullets started hitting them.

"Hold on!" Ray shouted to everyone on board.

On the balcony, Dutra continued to fire at the chopper until his gun ran dry of bullets.

"Shit," Dutra said as he ejected the empty clip and took out another one.

Joey heard that the bullets had stopped and quickly lowered the nose back down to its normal elevation. Ray took the chance to take a glance out the windshield.

"Right there on the ledge!" Ray shouted. "Quick Joey, get us closer!"

As Joey began to fly the helicopter toward the balcony, Ray went back to the machine gun.

"Steve! Paul! Get on this side!" Ray shouted.

Steve and Roader turned and then quickly got onto Ray's right side. Steve reloaded his gun as Roader looked toward the building.

"Alright, here we go!" Joey shouted and began turning the helicopter.

Dutra snapped another clip into his gun as the helicopter turned. Once it was in, Dutra then began to shoot, firing at an alarming rate of speed and aiming for the propellers of the chopper. But once the chopper turned all the way, he noticed Ray, Roader and Steve aiming at him with their machine guns.

Suddenly Ray began firing, followed by Steve and then Roader. Dutra ducked behind the stone wall at the edge of the balcony as bullets began spraying all around him, destroying the chairs and glass windows on the balcony.

When Ray saw Dutra duck behind the wall, he pointed the M134D-H at the wall and began firing with all his might, shouting into the loud noise of the gunfire while Steve and Roader also kept firing.

Dutra kept his head down and reloaded his gun. Meanwhile, back down on the street, Vincent quickly got out of cover and then looked up after hearing the guns being fired from the helicopter. He quickly lifted up his gun and began firing, and the rest of the men on the street also began firing up at the helicopter.

Ray kept firing at the wall where Dutra was hiding until the mounted gun ran out of bullets, instantly stopping the noise form the gun dead in its tracks. Ray then quickly looked at the gun, almost surprised that the gun was out of bullets already even though he probably should've known he was low.

"Shit," Ray said before taking his hands off the machine gun and looking around.

Suddenly a bullet shot the assault rifle right out of Roader's hand, dropping out of the helicopter.

"Damn it!" Roader said as bullets from everyone down on the street started to hit the chopper.

Dutra heard that the gun had stopped and quickly stood up and began firing at the helicopter, shooting out the windshield.

"Oh shit...Ray! We gotta move! We're taking too much heat!" Joey shouted.

Steve pointed his gun down and began firing down at the street.

"Joe's right, Ray!" Steve shouted as bullets hit the bottom of the helicopter.

As the bullets hit all over the helicopter, Vincent and the guys next to him kept firing up into the sky.

"Come on! Shoot that fucking chopper down!" Vincent shouted.

More and more on the street joined in until everyone on the street was firing up at the chopper.

"Ray! We gotta move!" Roader shouted as bullets bounced in and out of the helicopter cabin.

Vincent took aim at the propeller of the helicopter, aimed very carefully and got ready to pull the trigger when suddenly a bullet blew right through the head of the man standing next to him. Blood splattered all over Vincent's left arm.

Confused, he then turned to the man on his right, only to see him get shot right in the throat. Vincent spun around and saw two SUVs racing down the street.

"Oh shit," Vincent whispered.

III

Standing up through the sunroof was Torque with his machine gun as Bob held his gun out of the window, each firing into the group. As soon as

Vincent saw them, he ducked out of the line of fire.

"How close should I get?" Jasmin asked.

"Close as you can!" Bob said as he reloaded his gun.

Torque also reloaded his gun and then started firing again as the military convoys—and what was left of the New York City police department—followed right behind, flying past the building that was hit the by helicopter.

Vincent started firing at the SUV, bullets quickly cracking across the windshield. Tommy ducked as Jasmin swerved out of the line of fire. Bob also brought his gun back in as the bullets began hitting the SUV.

"Little closer Jas," Bob said, looking up and seeing they were rapidly approaching the blockade of car.

Another bullet hit the windshield, but that didn't stop Jasmin from getting closer. Torque came in from the sunroof and quickly reloaded as he sat down and exhaled. Bob looked at him.

"Fun, right?" Bob asked.

Torque looked at Bob.

"Okay guys, this is it!" Jasmin shouted before pushing his foot as hard as he could onto the gas petal.

The SUV roared with power and quickly accelerated. Jasmin aimed head on for the car Vincent was hiding behind.

The moment he crashed into it, the car was pushed out of the way and off to the side, leaving a large enough gap in the blockade for two cars to fit in. The driver's side of the car was all smashed in, but the SUV, minus a few dents and broken headlight, was fine.

Just as he cleared the blockade and began taking gunfire, Jasmin then suddenly turned the steering wheel all the way to the left, causing the SUV to begin spinning. It spun around two times and then finally stopped about ten feet away from some of Dutra's men with the passenger side of the SUV in their direction. Before the men had even the slightest chance to react, Tommy flung open the passenger door and fired his shotgun, blowing a bloody hole through one of the men. Torque and Bob then quickly opened the back door and also began firing.

Jasmin put the car in park and then shut it off before getting out and grabbing a hold of his assault rifle. He turned and saw the other SUV pull up right next to him. As Tim, Scotty and the rest of Roader's men came out, they all began firing their guns at Dutra's men. Jasmin couldn't help but smile.

"Bad ass," Jasmin said to himself before he lifted his gun up and began firing.

Ray smiled as he looked down and saw the guys joining the firefight, and not a moment to soon as far as he was concerned. In fact, he kinda wished they had shown up a little earlier.

"Looks like the guys made it!" Steve said as he continued firing down at the street, shooting two men in the chest.

Ray then looked back toward the balcony, only to see Dutra quickly standing up and running back into his office. Ray then turned to Joey.

"Joey! Take us down!" Ray shouted.

"You got it Ray," Joey said.

Ray turned and looked at Steve, Roader and Sullivan as Joey began turning the helicopter.

"What are you thinking, Ray?" Roader asked.

"We're gonna head in from the main entrance," Ray said.

"Why not have Joey drop us off on the roof?" Sullivan asked.

"Because more then likely the entire building is crawling with his goons. If we chase him down, we're gonna run into resistance and that's gonna slow us down," Steve said.

"But if we come in from the bottom and work our way up, there's no place for him to go," Ray said.

"He could always jump," Sullivan said.

"Let's fucking hope so," Steve said.

"Alright boys, we're coming in," Joey shouted to them as he began to lower the helicopter.

Ray then turned to Sullivan.

"How many rounds do you have left in the mini?" Ray asked.

"Hundred...give or take," Sullivan said.

Ray nodded.

"That should give us a small window," Ray said.

"Small? Fucking narrow is more like it," Steve said.

"And I need a weapon," Roader said looking at Ray.

Ray turned to Joey.

"Joe?"

"What?" Joey quickly asked.

"You got a sidearm?" Ray asked.

Joey reached over to the holster on the right side of his hip and pulled out his nine millimeter and handed it to Ray, who then handed it to Roader.

"Kinda hoping for something bigger," Roader said as he cocked it.

"That's what she said!" Joey shouted to him.

Roader chuckled.

"Okay here we go!" Ray shouted as bullets began hitting the helicopter.

Steve quickly reloaded his assault rifle as Ray then took his off his back and then cocked it.

"Just like old times huh?" Roader asked Ray as they watched the ground get closer and closer.

"Something like that," Ray smiled.

"Exactly like that!" Steve shouted.

Just before the helicopter officially touched down, Ray took one last look at Roader and Steve. He didn't say anything, there wasn't any time, but everything inside of him hoped that the two of them knew how much they meant to him. And with a smile, the three Dogs of War turned and watched the helicopter reach the ground.

"Sullivan, go!" Ray shouted.

Sullivan then cocked the mounted gun and began firing into the street, bullets slicing through bodies and blowing limbs off, creating a deafening sound throughout the entire street. As Sullivan fired, Joey took out his spare sidearm pistol and also began firing onto the street, effectively giving Ray, Roader and Steve enough time to exit out of the helicopter.

Roader quickly ran toward a red truck for cover, firing Joey's handgun until he reached the truck. Suddenly as he got to the front, one of Dutra's guys emerged and took aim at Roader. But Roader was able to get out of the line of sight, pushing the end of the gun away from him before taking hold of the man, head butting him and then smashing the man's head hard onto the truck. As the man dropped to the ground, Roader quickly threw Joey's piece of shit handgun onto the ground and picked up the man's SIG 556 PSD.

"This'll work," Roader said as he lifted it up and began firing.

Ray ran as fast as he could over to Torque, who was shooting behind a black Dodge truck. Once Torque ran out of bullets, he ducked for cover as Ray ran to him and also took cover.

Sullivan kept firing the mini, shooting everyone and pretty much everything in its path. The noise from the gun and explosions distracted him so much, he didn't even realize he was just about out of ammo...until the firing suddenly stopped. He then looked down at the gun.

"Oh, shit," Sullivan whispered.

Silence filled the street as the echoes of the last rounds Sullivan fired trailed off into the distance and disappeared beyond the surrounding buildings.

"RETURN FIRE!" Vincent suddenly shouted into the night sky.

The silence was murdered as Vincent and the rest of the men taking orders from Dutra began to return fire, shooting multiple police offers that had pulled up right along side Jasmin's SUV.

"Goddamn it!" Sullivan said as he ducked his head and exited the helicopter. "Joey, get back up in the air! Can't afford to lose you too!" Sullivan ordered.

Joey nodded and began to lift the helicopter off the ground as Sullivan quickly went for cover behind a white Oldsmobile Intrigue with Steve.

"Come on, get your head down Sullivan!" Steve shouted, grabbing Sullivan's hand and pulling him behind the Oldsmobile.

Bullets were wreaking havoc upon the SUVs the guys had pulled up in, destroying everything, from all the windows to the tires. But much of the gunfire was focused on the police cars and military convoys, many bullets taking down the remaining officers as they tried to get to cover.

"Jesus Christ!" Torque said as the back window of the Dodge truck he was behind got shot out, causing glass to fall all over him.

Bullets sprayed onto the helicopter as Joey did his best to lift it back up into the sky as fast as he could. Once he got it up, he let out a big sigh of relief before looking back down at the street.

"Joey!" Ray yelled over the radio as bullets hit all around.

"Yeah?"

"You got any rockets left?" Ray quickly asked.

Joey smiled.

"Way ahead of you..."

Joey turned the helicopter so it was facing toward the street in a slightly slanted position. Not as many bullets were reaching the helicopter as before but Joey still ducked each time he heard one bounce off the chopper. He put his right hand on a lever with a red button directly on the top, smiling as he looked down.

"Ka boom," Joey said under his breath before pushing down the red button. A large rocket came shooting out, blasting its way back down to earth, taking aim at one of the last remaining vehicles in the blockade that wasn't on fire before hitting it.

The rocket hit the engine of the American made truck, exploding on contact, causing the truck to lift up off the ground and flip onto its side. Joey was too far away to be able to actually see, but he was positive anyone near the truck had been eliminated.

The rocket provided a brief break in the shooting, Vincent and many others ducking as the large explosion lit up the street. And that quick moment was all Ray and the others needed, all taking the chance, standing back up and firing back at Vincent in the others, hitting many.

"Move up!" Ray shouted as he and Torque shot two of Dutra's men on the opposite side of the truck they were crouching behind.

Steve, Sullivan, Scotty and Tim, along with Ray and Torque, quickly moved, covering one another as they made their way closer to the entrance of the skyscraper. Bob however stayed back just in front of the blockade of police cars and providing sniper fire for the guys as they moved up, successfully getting a headshot on a guy who was just a few feet away from Ray.

"Thanks, Bob," Ray said into his radio as he saw the entire top of the man's head blow off.

"Yeah, Steve on your left..." Bob barked.

Steve spun left and saw one of Dutra's men appear right next to him. Steve quickly elbowed the man in the privates before quickly pulling out his side arm and firing three rounds into his chest.

"Impressive, old man," Bob said, chuckling, before blasting another sniper round into the neck of another poor bastard.

"I'm moving up, cover me," Ray quickly said to Torque before stepping out from cover and firing at Vincent.

Torque also quickly stood up and not only returned fire, but also followed Ray as Ray got down on his knee behind a large SUV. Just as the two of them reached the SUV though, they instantly started to take heavy fire from Vincent.

The gunshots instantly grabbed Steve and Sullivan's attention. They both quickly started to fire at Vincent from where they were. Sullivan wasn't able to see Vincent from his position but he tried to fire where he thought the shots were coming from.

IV

From up on his high balcony Dutra starred down at the war zone. From that great height, everyone looked like small shadows, but he could tell that his men were losing ground...and quickly. He paused, questioning if he thought his men had the chance to take back control of the street, but when he saw the large group of soldiers and police officers advancing to Ray's position, he knew in that moment that he was losing the fight. With anger and a touch of fear nested in his mind, Dutra quickly ran to the glass door and headed back in his office.

"Lock down the building," he ordered Street, who was sitting behind Dutra's desk.

"Yes, sir," Street replied before turning to his laptop and quickly getting into the security system for the entire building.

Dutra watched impatiently as gunshots echoed from outside.

"Hurry!" Dutra ordered.

"Almost there," Street said, typing as fast as he could.

Another explosion down on the street brought Dutra back to the window. He looked down, only to see another ball of fire fly up from the street and into the sky.

"Street!" Dutra shouted.

"Got it!" Street said as he typed in the final code to initiate the lockdown.

Suddenly alarms quickly blared throughout the entire building as red lights began flashing, casting an eerie red glow over the entire building.

The loud alarm caught Ray's attention as he fired a shot into a man's chest. He turned and looked at the entrance, which was only about forty feet away. Then he saw the red lights beginning to flash inside.

"The hell's going on?" Torque asked Ray.

Ray shook his head.

"No idea...Sullivan?" Ray asked into his radio as Torque stood up and began firing.

"Yeah?" Sullivan asked as he reloaded.

"What's up with the alarms inside the building?" Ray asked.

Not sure what Ray was talking about, Sullivan glanced up and then saw the flashing lights and could even hear echoes of the alarm going off just inside.

"Oh shit..." Sullivan said to himself, before putting his hand up to the radio in his ear. "Looks like the building is going into primary lockdown."

"In English, Sullivan. What does that mean?" Ray asked.

"That means that if you don't get inside before the gates close, the building will be sealed from the inside. Once it's sealed there's no way to get in, which pretty much means we're fucked Ray!" Sullivan shouted into the radio.

"Shit." Ray looked back up at the entrance and saw that only about half a dozen people were in front of it.

As Bob got another headshot, Ray quickly reloaded his gun and then placed his hand back up to his ear.

"Roader, Steve, Sullivan...I need you guys to cover me while I make a run for the door. Bob any help from you would great too.," Ray said.

"Copy, that Ray," Bob said as he reloaded the sniper rifle.

Just as Ray was getting ready to make a run for it, Torque quickly grabbed his arm, causing Ray to turn and look at him.

"What are you doing?" Torque asked.

"If that door seals up before I get in, we'll never be able to get inside," Ray said, impatiently.

"Ray, even if you make it in, there's probably dozens of his men inside."

Ray shook his head.

"I'll cross that bridge when I get to it." He turned and looked back at the entrance.

"I'm coming with you then," Torque suddenly said.

"No, stay here," Ray shot back.

"No you're gonna need help in there...face it Ray, you can't do this on your own," Torque said.

Ray exhaled and then looked up at him.

"Keep up then."

"Yes, sir."

Ray then looked at Sullivan who was directly across from him.

"Okay, you guys ready?" Ray asked.

"Ready," Sullivan said.

"Bob, you ready?" Ray asked.

"Locked and loaded," Bob answered.

"Alright...one...two...three!"

On three, everyone from Ray and Torque, Sullivan and Steve to Tommy, Jasmin, Tim and Scotty stood up from cover and began firing back as Ray and Torque hightailed it to the main doors just as the gates began coming down.

Bob fired one shot, hitting one of Dutra's men in the neck as Torque fired, killing two more.

While Ray and Torque made their way to the door, Vincent saw his men standing by the doorway getting shot and falling to the ground. As he watched the men drop to the ground, bleeding from their chests, heads, and necks, he also saw the gate coming down.

"Fuck," Vincent whispered to himself, and he broke from cover and began running to the entrance himself.

Ray and Torque fired until their clips were dry. Steve also kept firing, but quickly stopped when he saw Ray and Torque run out of bullets at the same time. They were taking fire, the bullets missing them by only inches as they reloaded.

Steve knew that he had to do something, or else Ray and Torque wouldn't make it much further. Even though he was also getting shot at, he knew he had to risk it, just like he knew Ray would risk it if the situation were reversed. Steve quickly fired back at the street, stood up and then ran toward Ray and Torque.

"Steve? Steve!" Sullivan shouted, trying to find out what he was doing.

Sullivan kept his eye on Steve until he realized he was going toward Ray and Torque.

"Goddamn it," Sullivan said before turning to Roader. "Ray's in trouble, cover me."

Roader nodded.

"Right behind you."

Sullivan stood up and began firing at one of multiple gunmen shooting at Ray and Torque. He shot one of them in the chest as Roader shot another gunmen in the stomach three times.

Ray and Torque were reloaded. Torque turned and fired, and with the help of Steve, Sullivan, and he was able to succeed.

Back on the SUV, standing out of the sunroof, Bob also did his best to keep the shooters at bay, killing anyone his sights came upon, but their were still a lot more than he could handle all by himself.

As Vincent quickly ran to the front entrance the gates were about halfway down. He turned and saw Torque and Ray running towards him. Without hesitating, Vincent lifted his machine gun up and was able to fire two shots before he ran out of bullets; he didn't have any more clips. He threw the gun out of his hands and then reached behind his back and took out a black handgun.

Ray and Torque had both stopped running, quickly firing back at the street, giving Steve, Sullivan and Roader the chance to catch up. But it also gave Vincent the chance to make sure the first shot counted. Vincent took aim at Ray's chest and began to squeeze the trigger.

Just then Ray ran out of bullets in his clip. He turned and saw Vincent aiming at him. He knew that there was really no way out of this one; nothing was around to even duck behind. His heart pounded as he looked into Vincent's murderous eyes.

Vincent's gun flashed, but the moment Ray saw it, he suddenly felt someone forcefully push him out of the way and onto the ground. Ray quickly turned as he fell, only the bullet Vincent fired didn't hit him...it hit Sullivan on the left side of the stomach.

"Sullivan!" Ray shouted as he saw the bullet enter.

In the crosshairs of his gun, Bob saw Sullivan drop to his knees from the shot. He turned the weapon to the staircase and saw Vincent getting ready to fire another shot. Quickly, without aiming for a mortal wound, Bob fired one shot, hitting the black handgun in Vincent's hand, sending it skittering away.

Shocked, Vincent quickly looked in the direction of the shot. He saw Bob, who was now really aiming for a kill shot. Vincent rushed for the door. As he opened the door, Bob fired one more shot, but hit the edge of the door as Vincent ran inside.

"Shit," Bob said.

Sullivan dropped onto his stomach as Ray stood up and rushed toward him. Sullivan looked down at his stomach as blood began to run onto the street, creating a pool. Ray grabbed Sullivan's arm.

"No, I'm okay! I'm okay! Get your ass inside! Go! Now!" Sullivan shouted up.

Ray took his eyes off of Sullivan and looked back at the door, seeing that the gate was now more then halfway down. He then quickly glanced back at Sullivan.

"Ray, go!" Sullivan said.

Ray turned and ran as fast as he could toward the door, followed by Steve, Torque and Roader while Sullivan began to breath heavily and put his hand over the gunshot wound.

As he was running, Ray took aim at the glass door and fired multiple shots into the glass, causing it to break and fall out of the door and crash on the ground, leaving a large opening in the door where the glass was. But Ray could clearly see that the opening in the door was getting smaller and smaller.

Despite the aching pain shooting out from his knee, Ray knew he had to get into the building, he *had* to. He could tell just by the amount of pain he was feeling that his knee was on its last leg, but he wasn't worried about that. The only thing he was worried about was getting to Emily...and killing Dutra.

Ray swallowed hard and prepared for the pain he was about to feel, closing his eyes as he reached the door. And the moment he reached the door, he dived directly through the opening of the door, landing right on his knee.

Pain shot up his leg, causing him to grasp his leg as he groaned and breathed heavily. He looked up and saw Steve heading right toward him. Ray rolled out of the way as Steve dove though the door opening. Roader also quickly ducked and barley fit through the small opening between the floor and gate.

Torque knew he wasn't going to be able to dive or duck in the same way as Ray, Steve and Roader, the opening was now to small for either one. As a bullet from outside missed his head by only inches, Torque instantly dropped down onto his stomach and began crawling in.

Torque's body was only about half way in when Roader looked and saw that Torque was about to be in trouble if he didn't move faster. Torque kept crawling but the gate just seemed to be moving faster. Torque looked up at the gate and realized it was literally only millimeters away from touching his body.

"Shit," He said.

Suddenly both Roader and Steve grabbed a hold of his hands and pulled him in as the gate closed.

"Cutting it a little close, my friend," Roader said.

Torque shook his head.

"Yeah, maybe too close..."

Steve smiled as he turned to Ray, who was almost in tears from the pain shooting out through his knee.

"Shit, Ray? You alright?" Steve asked as he walked over to Ray and knelt down.

Redness and sweat was plastered all over Ray as he kept his hand on his kneecap, breathing heavily and trying to remain calm.

"Yeah...I'm...fine. Just give me a second," Ray panted.

Steve shook his head and then looked at Roader, who was looking all around at the large lobby. Roader had just stepped forward when about a dozen men, all dressed in black and holding assault rifles, suddenly emerged from the far end of the lobby and began shooting. Roader, Steve ,and Torque quickly dropped to the floor as bullets began shooting all around.

Ray glanced up and made sure he was out of the line of fire before looking back at the entrance, which was now sealed. It was difficult to see through the gates but Ray's eyes we're able to finally find and then lock on Sullivan, who was still in the same position that Ray had left him in.

"Tommy! Jas! Sullivan's down by the main entrance! Can you get to him?" Ray asked over the radio as Torque began to return fire at Dutra's men at the far end of the lobby.

"Won't be easy!" Tommy shouted back.

"Well ,try damn it! Bob?" Ray asked.

"Yeah?"

"Keep Tommy and Jas covered," Ray ordered.

"Copy."

V

High up in his office, Dutra looked down at the street, disgusted by how quickly his men were losing ground. Dutra knew he had enough men to deal with Ray and his team but he hadn't been expecting more company, let alone two helicopters and damn near half of the U.S. military.

For the first time in his life, Dutra felt trapped. Some twisted knot in his gut was telling him that this was going to be a close call for him. Besides Bosnia, Dutra had been in quiet a few close calls, but something about this felt different to him. But the feeling didn't make Dutra nervous or even scared for that matter. In fact, it had quite the opposite effect. It really pissed him off and it only got worse when Street came running into the office.

"Sir!" Street said.

Dutra turned his head to the left, barley, but just enough so Street could see he had his attention.

"Sir...they're inside," Street confessed.

Dutra closed his eyes for a moment, trying not to completely lose all control, but not even he could contain it all.

"Show me," he growled.

Street walked over to Dutra's desk and opened his laptop, tapping the screen to wake it up. Once the screen lit up, Street quickly swiped away some of the apps he had open and then pulled up the security screens and tapped the one for the camera in the lobby.

As soon as it pulled up, Dutra leaned into the screen and watched as Ray quickly came out of cover and fired his machine gun, killing three men instantly. Dutra then leaned in closer until the screen was literally right in his face. He then watched as Ray looked up at the camera, then took aim at the camera and fired one shot, instantly turning the laptop screen black.

Dutra softly gasped as the screen went black. But instead of suddenly moving, he stayed in his position and looked at himself in the reflection on the black screen. Dutra then saw his face slowly change from calm to an unimaginable evil face filled with hate and anger. The sight sent a trickle of fear down Street's already sweaty spine.

Dutra slowly leaned back up and then suddenly looked down, realizing that the time had indeed come to set the final piece of his plan into motion. The thought brought joy into the madman's mind as he slowly took out his handgun...aimed for Emily...and then pulled the trigger.

"I warned him."

Chapter 18: Up And Down

Bob covered Tommy and Jas as they made their way closer to Sullivan's position. Tim and Scotty moved up from the far left side of the street, using the billowing smoke from the destroyed vehicles as cover.

"Two at one' clock," Tim quickly said and turned, taking aim.

"One, two...three!" Scotty counted before both fired at the same time, instantly killing the two men.

"Alright, go!" Tim shouted to Scotty.

Scotty lowered his machine gun and began moving down the street as Tim followed right behind him. For a brief moment they were in the clear as they made their way further on down the street, no bullets were being fired at them at all. It seemed a little strange but they didn't have the time to question it.

Up in the sky, Joey was circling around, doing his best to keep an eye on the guys on the street, but as more and more military soldiers began pushing closer and closer to the entrance of the building, it was getting complicated to figure out who was whom. Finally, it got to the point where Joey knew he couldn't really do anything without endangering the lives of pretty much anyone. The feeling left Joey feeling useless and he looked down at the war zone.

"Bob, you there?" Joey asked over the radio.

"Yeah what's up Joe?"

"It's getting difficult to see who's who down there. I don't think I can make another run, not without knowing where everyone is," Joey confessed.

Bob lifted his eye from his scope as dozens of soldiers ran past the SUV he was in and took cover behind the first set of cars from the blockade.

"I hear ya, Joe," Bob said.

"I'm gonna try circling around the other way, see if that'll get me in a better position," Joey said.

"Alright," Bob said as he put his eye back in his scope and fired one shot, hitting a man that was right near Jasmin.

"Holy shit! Thanks Bob," Jasmin said after blood landed on him.

"Yeah, careful you two, there's a guy heading to the opposite side of the car you're near and I don't have a shot," Bob said over the radio.

Jasmin got ready to stand up and fire, when Tommy quickly grabbed his arm.

"I'll deal with him," Tommy said.

"Okay," Jasmin said.

Tommy smiled at Jasmin quickly before dropping onto his stomach and crawling under the car.

"Tommy...what are you doing? Tommy?"

Confused as to what Tommy's plan was, Jasmin quickly lifted himself up and fired down the street, his bullets hitting many of the burning cars.

"Good job, Jas...I don't think you hit a single person," Bob said over the radio.

"Shut up Bob!" Jasmin said as he shook his head and then looked down only to see Tommy was out of his sight.

Underneath the car, Tommy crawled over to the passenger side, where he could see a pair of legs standing right in front of the passenger side door. Tommy made he sure stayed quiet, trying not to get caught as he slowly reached the opposite end of the car.

The man standing by the car then began firing his gun, causing empty shell cases to fall onto the ground, hitting Tommy's face and the tip of his shot gun as he carefully stuck his head out and then began to pull his gun out. Once he had just enough room to move his shotgun, he aimed it up at the man and cocked it. Curious from the sound, the man glanced down, only to realize he was looking straight into the barrel of a shotgun. Tommy smiled.

"Heads up."

The man swallowed hard, knowing what was about to happen and before he could do anything, Tommy proudly fired the shotgun, blowing off the man's face and a large part of his head.

Jasmin jumped from fright at the roar of the shotgun as Bob watched the large chuck of flesh and brain fly up into the air.

"Ouch," Bob said as he chuckled.

As the lifeless body dropped onto the ground, Tommy then pulled himself out from under the car, wiped the blood and chunks of flesh off himself before quickly standing back up and looking toward the direction of Sullivan.

In severe pain and discomfort, Sullivan slowly made his way over to an upside down car, leaving a trail of blood as he crawled on the street. With each movement, Sullivan could feel more and more pressure near the bullet hole, almost making it feel like half of his body was useless but he knew he had to at least get to a safer area.

"Bob, I got Sullivan!" Tommy yelled into the radio as he ran over to him.

Sullivan groaned as he stopped and then dropped onto his stomach.

"Sullivan!" Tommy shouted as he reached Sullivan and knelt down next to him. "You alright?"

"Fine, just get me out of here," Sullivan said before he began coughing.

Tommy nodded as he quickly looked up and noticed Jasmin a couple yards away.

"Jas!" Tommy shouted.

Jasmin quickly turned to where he heard Tommy's voice and then began to approach when he saw Tommy wave his hand in the air.

"Holy shit, that's a lot of blood." Jasmin said without thinking.

"Should see it from down here..." Sullivan said as he slowly rolled over onto his back.

"We gotta get him out of here...now...can you carry him?" Tommy asked Jasmin.

"Yeah, I think I can."

"Good, Sullivan...you think you can walk?" Tommy asked.

"I'll try...no promises," he said through the pain.

"Okay...Bob?" Tommy asked over the radio.

"You got Sullivan?" Bob asked.

"Yeah...think you can cover us?" Tommy asked.

"Alright...from here looks like you guys have a ten second window. Make it count," Bob said.

Jasmin lowered his gun and then took a hold of Sullivan's hand as he lifted his arm up.

"This might hurt," Jasmin confessed to Sullivan.

"Always does."

Jasmin nodded and then carefully but forcefully pulled Sullivan up. Pain shot through Sullivan's entire body as Jasmin lifted him up, Sullivan shouting from how intense the pressure was. But to both Jasmin and Sullivan's surprise, it only took one try to get Sullivan back on his feet. And once he was, Jasmin wrapped Sullivan's arm around his neck and then began to slowly move toward Bob while Tommy kept his eyes focused on the street, providing cover as Jasmin and Sullivan moved as quickly as they could.

II

Meanwhile, Ray, Torque, Steve and Roader made it down to the far end of the lobby and reached the elevators. While Torque pressed the button for the elevator, a door right next to it quickly opened and a man dressed up in a tie and holding a large machine gun emerged from the doorway. Before he could do anything, Roader lifted up his gun and fired, not just a couple times either, Roader fired almost half a clip into the man's chest and stomach. Finally, after the twelfth or thirteenth bullet, the man dropped to the floor in a puddle of his own blood.

"Think he's dead, Paul," Steve said.

Roader released the clip from his gun and loaded in another.

"Better safe then sorry," Roader said.

Steve smiled and shook his head at Roader while sweat dripped from Ray's face; it was obvious that he was in some serious pain.

"Hey...you alright?" Torque asked, softly patting Ray on the shoulder.

But before Ray answered, the elevator chimed, signifying that it had reached the lobby. Instantly Roader and Steve lifted their guns at the closed door, ready to take out anyone or anything that was unlucky enough to be on that particular elevator.

The doors opened, revealing an empty, all metal interior with a small light overhead and two speakers on each side, softly playing music. Roader and Steve lowered their guns and then looked at Ray. Ray looked up at them before turning and looking back at Torque.

Ray made the first move, stepping into the elevator and looking up and down, checking to make sure it wasn't a trap. He nodded at the guys and they stepped in. Steve went in first, standing behind Ray while Torque and Roader stepped in and stood on either side of Ray. Roader then looked down at the buttons on the right side of the elevator doors.

"Which floor?" Roader asked.

"Thirty-three," Ray said before cocking his handgun and then putting it back into the holster on his hip.

Roader pressed the button labeled '33.' As soon as he did, the light illuminated in gold and then the doors to the elevator closed, leaving the four of them alone with their thoughts...and classical music.

While Steve looked up at the LED display, counting up the floors, Roader wiped the sweat off his forehead and took a deep breath. Torque locked his eyes on Ray, who he could tell was in a little bit of rough shape.

Just by the way Ray was standing, favoring his right leg, it was obvious that Ray was in dire strain. Everyone in the elevator knew that (two out of three kept warning him to get the damn thing fixed while he still could) but it really wasn't the time to be bringing it up.

"Check your weapons," Ray said as he cocked the machine gun in his hand.

Roader double-checked his while Steve and Torque both took the old clips out of their guns and loaded a full new one in.

"Anything on Sullivan?" Roader asked.

Ray lifted his hand to the radio in his ear but all he could hear was static.

"Just getting static...metal from the elevator must be interfering with the reception," Ray said.

Torque took his eyes off of Roader and looked at Ray one more time before lifting his eyes up to the display, seeing it change from '10' to '12'...'13'.

"Seems like it moves faster when you don't want it to," Torque said.

Steve smiled and shook his head in agreement.

"Older you get the faster it goes...wait till you hit our age kid," Roader said.

"Yeah, you wake up one day and it's your twenty-first birthday, go to sleep, wake up the next day and suddenly you're looking at fifty," Steve added.

Ray then turned to Torque.

"Enjoy it while you can, Johnny."

Torque looked down at Ray and gave him a quick smile, showing that he would take Ray's words to heart. He then looked back up at the screen as elevator hit '25'.

"Alright boys...time to kill this son of a bitch," Ray said as he lifted up his gun and got ready for when the elevator doors opened.

"Been looking forward to this moment all day," Roader said as he also lifted up his gun, drawing down on the sights as the elevator began to slow down.

Steve and Torque also aimed and got ready for what would be behind those doors. Torque was kinda hopeful, thinking that maybe most of Dutra's men had been taken out on the street. Ray, Steve, and Roader however felt a little differently, having another idea as to what would appear when those elevator doors opened. And once the elevator came to a complete stop, the screen near the top of the doors flashed '33' and the doors quickly opened.

The moment the doors opened, bullets began spraying into the elevator, forcing the guys to take cover just off to the sides of the doors. The bullets shot all around, bouncing off the metal frame of the elevator as Steve and Torque covered their heads, hoping that luck was still on their side.

Most times they would wait for a break in the gunfire before they would return it, but each one of them knew they had no time to wait, the bullets bouncing in and out of the elevator were too dangerous to just stand and wait, they were just gonna have to risk it.

Ray took the first risk, quickly coming out of cover and firing back, hitting two of Dutra's security guards on the left hand side of the hallway. As soon as he saw them drop to the ground, Ray kept moving out of the elevator and headed for cover on the right hand side of the hall. As he moved to the spot, Roader also emerged and returned fire, doing his best to draw fire off of Ray.

As soon as Ray got to his position, he began to fire, giving Steve and Torque the opportunity to get out of the elevator. Steve and Torque stayed together, firing at as many people as they could while Roader quickly made his way in front of Ray, taking cover behind a metal trash barrel.

But as soon as Roader got to the barrel, he quickly began to take fire from a shotgun. The shotgun blast was powerful, blowing a large chuck off the top of the barrel and missing Roader by inches. Roader quickly fired back but after four shots, his clip ran out.

Roader dropped the machine gun after realizing he was completely out before Ray quickly stood up and returned fire at the guard with the shotgun, shooting out the large window that was just right next to him.

"Go!" Ray shouted.

Both Ray and Roader broke cover and ran straight into the direction of the gunfire as Steve and Torque covered them. More security guards entered the hallway. With Roader in front of Ray, Ray couldn't really clear a path up ahead for Roader, but Ray took aim at the guards just heading into the hall, shooting three out of five.

As Ray covered him from behind, Roader quickly ran right toward the guard holding the shotgun, driving headfirst right into the guard's chest. The guard fell back to the wall from the force of the push. Then quickly Roader grabbed the guard's arm as he raised the shotgun up and twisted it, snapping the bone and yanking the gun right out of his hand.

The guard instantly screamed bloody murder as blood began pouring out of the large opening in his arm. Roader cocked and then aimed the gun at the guard's stomach before pulling the trigger. Flesh, skin, organs and blood soared out of the guard's body and right out the window that Ray had shot out...just before the man took a few steps backwards and then fell out of the window himself.

"Bye," Roader sarcastically said as he cocked the shotgun.

Ray finished up about the same time as Roader, shooting the last guard directly in the forehead, blowing off the entire back piece of the guard's skull. Once the guard's lifeless body hit the white floor, Ray, Roader, Steve and Torque were suddenly surrounded in silence.

Ray took the opportunity to quickly reload his assault rifle while Roader, Steve and Torque walked toward Ray. As Ray loaded the clip into his gun, he looked down at his hip and realized it was the last clip he had.

"That it?" Torque asked as both he and Steve slowly walked up to Ray.

"Can't be," Ray answered back, not taking a chance on letting his guard down.

"How much further down?" Steve asked.

"Should be right around the corner." Roader said, pointing down the long hall.

"Keep it tight," Ray said, taking the first step down the hall.

The guys carefully but steadily headed down the hall, checking the corners of the hall and carefully keeping an eye on every doorway they passed as the power began to flicker overhead. The speed they were going was a little too fast, a speed they would never go in any other situation...but this wasn't just another situation.

Suddenly a noise from the end of the hall grabbed everyone's attention. Roader and Steve quickly turned their guns to the end of the hall as Torque quickly lifted up his gun and locked his eyes in the sights. As they reached the end of the hall, Ray did the same thing.

When they got to the end of the hall, Ray heard what might have been whispers, and then he heard footsteps. In that moment, Ray knew he was going to make a move...and fast. With a deep breath, Ray quickly entered the hall.

Time seemed to stand still in that brief moment. What should've been a second or two felt like an hour. In that brief moment, there was no sound, there was no noise...there was just a deafening silence as Ray's eyes slowly locked on to Dutra's.

Even though Dutra had traces of doubt inside of him, it was impossible to see it in his face, a menacing smirk growing out of his goatee while his dark brown eyes latched onto Ray.

The look on Dutra's face sent both chills and anger shooting through Ray's body. He kept his eyes on Dutra, overlooking the fact that Street and four other security guards dressed in body armor and holding assault rifles surrounded Dutra. Ray could clearly tell Dutra was heading to what appeared to be a staircase that went up, most likely to the roof...and Ray knew what that meant.

Suddenly the moment was over as fast as it began. Dutra ended the silence by taking aim at Ray with a black handgun and getting off one shot before Ray even knew what hit him, not to mention before the guys were able to return fire. Ray broke eye contact as the bullet grazed his face, slicing a large cut across his left cheek.

The bullet was a wake up call to Ray and not a moment too soon. Just as Dutra was getting ready to fire again, Ray quickly lifted up his machine gun and began firing, hitting two of the guards in front of Dutra as he turned and ran to the staircase.

As soon as Dutra made it through the doorway, Street quickly followed behind him as Ray and the rest of the guys fired at the guards with everything they had. Ray fired the last of the rounds in his gun as Torque aimed for a headshot and then took it.

Street got into the doorway, turned back to the door and closed it as fast as he could, turning just in time to see the last of the remaining guards get hit with bullets. Once the last guard was down, the bullets then began hitting the door as Street was closing it. But just before he closed it all the way, Dutra took one last aim down the hall while Ray did the same thing. The two of them quickly locked onto one another and then both fired, just as Street finished closing the door.

Ray's shot was close but too wide, missing Dutra by inches, bouncing off the outside of the doorframe. Ray knew just by the sound that he missed. As he dropped his now empty machine gun to the floor a gasp from one of the guys caught his attention.

"Steve?" Torque asked as he lowered his gun.

Suddenly Steve dropped to his knees, groaning in pain as Ray and Roader turned to him, only to see a bullet hole directly in the center of his chest.

"Steve?" Roader asked, moving quickly to Steve.

Steve let go of his gun, letting it slide out of his hands before he reached up to his chest.

"Motherfucker," Steve groaned as his face began to turn red.

Ray dropped down onto his good knee and then reached for Steve's hands, trying to move them so he could see how bad the wound was.

"You alright?" Ray asked even though he knew the answer already just by looking at the wound.

"Yeah...I'm fine," Steve slowly said as he lifted up all the layers of clothing to reveal a bulletproof vest. "...Never leave home without it."

Roader nodded at Steve and then turned back down the hall, looking at the door that Dutra had escaped through. He knew it would be a long shot that the door would be unlocked but he went for it anyway, hoping Dutra was becoming careless in his desperation.

Roader went for the door, walking down the rest of the hall as Ray helped Steve back up to his feet. Steve cleared his throat and then wiped the sweat off the top of his forehead before looking back up at Ray.

"Had me nervous for a second," Ray said.

"Had myself nervous for a second," Steve confessed, chuckling as he bent down and picked his machine gun back up.

Ray then pulled out his sidearm, a black nine-millimeter pistol. Torque looked down at it before lifting the strap of his machine gun over his head and handing it toward Ray.

"Here," Torque said.

Ray waved his hand.

"Naw its okay, this'll be fine," Ray said.

"You sure?"

"Yeah. Besides, you're gonna need that."

Roader kept walking down the hall, aiming his shotgun from down at the guards to the door, keeping an eye out for anything. He was pretty confident that Dutra was long gone, close to roof by now, but what he wasn't so sure of was the guards lying on the floor. He carefully watched as he kept walking toward them.

But his attention was quickly taken off of the guards when he looked through a passing doorway to make sure nobody was in there. The last thing he was expecting was to see her in a pool of blood in the middle of the floor. Emily appeared to have a bullet wound in her lower stomach. The sight not only took Roader by complete surprise, but also got him thinking about another woman he found in a pool of blood many decades ago. It was a sight he could never get use to...no matter how many times he's seen it.

"...R...Ray!" Roader shouted, clearing his throat.

Ray took his eyes off of Steve and then lifted his head up to Roader, only to see a stunned look on Roader's face, almost like he was shot. In fact, Ray even looked down to make sure he hadn't been. By the look on Roader's face, Ray knew it couldn't be anything good.

Roader broke eye contact, looking back at Emily as Ray rushed down the hall toward him, he couldn't bear to look Ray in the eye for this, and he knew it was going to get rough. Roader exhaled, pulling his eyes down as he tilted his head down as Ray ran up to him.

"What is it...?" Ray quickly asked before he turned and looked inside Dutra's office and saw the sight for himself. "Oh Jesus, Emily!"

Ray rushed into the office, dropping to his knees as he reached his daughter. Torque stood with Roader as Steve walked toward the door Dutra had escaped through.

"Emily?" Ray asked, carefully moving her right arm off her bullet wound so he could see it himself.

The wound (not to mention the puddle of blood she was in) didn't look good. Ray could tell right away that she was going to need immediate help...if she was still alive.

Tears began filling up Ray's war-scarred eyes as he looked down at his daughter. Even with blood all around her, Ray couldn't help but think that she looked so much like her mother, the sight destroying what was left inside of Ray's heart and spirit.

"Come on, M." Ray pleaded as he began to put pressure on the wound.

The sight broke Torque's heart as he stood there helplessly, hoping, praying that she would be okay. Even though he had only met her one time...in that moment...to Torque...it felt like he had cared about her for a lifetime.

Torque began to look around the office, breaking away from Roader and walking all around, searching for anything. Torque couldn't just stand and watch anymore, he had done enough of that over in Iraq.

Roader walked over to Ray, slowly kneeling down next to Emily as Ray lifted one hand up from her bullet wound and then put it on her neck, checking, hoping for a pulse.

"She's alive," Roader said as he watched Emily take a very weak breath.

"Barely, we got to get her out of here!" Ray said.

Roader took his eyes off of Emily and then looked at Ray before Steve quickly entered the office.

"The door is reinforced steel. No way in hell can we get through that," Steve quickly said before looking down and seeing Emily. "...Oh Jesus, Ray."

"Steve, help us get her up," Ray said as he stood back up and then took hold of Emily's feet.

Torque made his way over to Dutra's desk, looking for that one thing that just seemed to be out of place. Torque was having a hard time putting his finger on it, but he could tell something just wasn't adding up right.

Torque then moved his eyes down the right hand side of the desk, quickly noticing the top drawer was slightly open, not enough to see what was actually in the drawer but just enough to grab his attention. Torque swallowed hard before taking his hand off his machine gun and reaching for the drawer.

He honestly didn't think about what could possibly be in the drawer as he began opening it, he almost opened it out of curiosity and habit. Torque had seen a lot over in Iraq, everything from schools full of dead children to suicide bombers, so it took a lot to surprise Torque...but when he opened the drawer...he was surprised. It took a moment to click in Torque's mind before he realized what exactly he was looking at. But once he did, his heart quickly began thumping away in his chest.

Inside the drawer was a brick of C-4 explosive, with a timer wrapped in black electrical tape counting down from twenty seconds. The numbers were bright and clear as day, lighting up the drawer a haunting red as is it hit fifteen seconds.

"Bomb!" Torque quickly shouted, lifting his head up towards Ray.

"Shit, come on! Everyone out!" Ray shouted as he, Steve and Roader carried Emily quickly toward the door.

Torque closed the drawer just as the timer his ten seconds, jumped over the desk and ran out of the office as fast as he could.

"Hurry Torque!" Ray shouted back into the office.

Torque pushed himself as hard as he could and was able to get out of the office and catch up to Ray and the guys just in time.

The timer struck zero and the desk completely exploded, blowing up not only everything inside the office, but also blowing the door frame of the office clean off the wall, sending chucks of dry wall and sheetrock in Ray's direction. The blast was so powerful, it also blew right through the office window and a large part of the surrounding wall.

A ball of fire escaped through the window and walls of the office, and was released up into the nighttime sky, quickly grabbing everyone's attention down on the street. For the briefest second all the firing stopped as each person watched the fire lift up into the air. The fireball grabbed Joey's attention too as he finished circling the building.

As the building rocked from the explosion, Dutra and Street stopped running up the stairs, aimed their guns and looked down toward the door they had escaped through, checking to make sure no one was following them.

"Think it worked?" Street asked.

"Let's get to the roof...come on!" Dutra ordered. He lowered his gun and continued up the stairs.

Street took one last look at the door before quickly following in Dutra's fast footsteps, rushing up the stairs as fast as they could to the roof.

III

Ray wiped the dirt and ash off of Emily's face as fire entered the hall from Dutra's office. The others struggled to their feet.

"Holy shit," Torque said.

Roader looked at Torque and then bent down to pick up his shotgun, while Steve wiped the sweat from his forehead and then looked down at Ray.

"We gotta get her help!" Ray shouted.

"Ray, what about Dutra?" Steve asked.

"Fuck him, she's gonna die if I don't get her out of here," Ray said.

Roader turned to Ray and walked toward him.

"Steve's right...we have to get Dutra," Roader firmly said.

"My daughter's life comes before that asshole!" Ray said, pushing Roader as Roader stepped closer.

"Ray, Ray! Think about it!" Roader began as Torque heard a noise coming from the office. "If we let Dutra escape, we'll never have another chance at getting him...think about it!"

Even though nothing could get Emily off his mind, Ray, knew Roader was right. Letting Dutra go at this point would be a complete waste. Everyone in that hallway knew it.

"What am I supposed to do, just leave her here?" Ray asked.

Roader looked down at Emily, clearly seeing that even though he was right about Dutra, Ray was also right about Emily: she needed help...and soon.

"I'll bring her down," Roader said.

Roader met Ray's eyes and then quickly turned and looked down the hall at Torque, who was standing in front of Dutra's burning office.

"Torque and I will take her," Roader said as he looked back at Ray.

Ray briefly looked down at Emily as she inhaled a very weak breath. Then he shook his head.

"No...I can't leave her," Ray said as he kept his eyes locked on her.

A large crash from inside Dutra's office grabbed Roader and Steve's attention, causing them to break off of Ray and look toward the office as Torque watched a bright light appear through the large hole in the outer wall.

"Ray...I've never let you down before...and I'm not planning on doing it now. We may not be as close as we once were, I know that's probably my fault, but despite that...you know that you can trust me with your daughter...just like I know you'd do the same it this was my son," Roader said. "Only you can stop Dutra."

Torque entered Dutra's office as fire began burning up the wall. The heat from the fire made it feel like a sauna in the burning office, but that still didn't stop Torque from walking over to the hole in the wall, trying to figure out what the light was.

Torque kept looking through the hole as long as he could until so much smoke was rising out of it that he could no longer see. He quickly raced across the office floor, jumping from the piles of fire in his way until he reached the balcony door. He rushed out onto the balcony and lifted his hand above his eyes, trying to shield his eyes from the light.

As the light got brighter and brighter he started to hear the spinning of a propeller. Suddenly the light lowered just enough for him to get a glimpse and see who, or what it was.

"Joe," Torque whispered.

From up high in the sky, Joey shined the large light onto Torque and saw him standing out on the balcony before Torque began waving his hands in the air.

"Torque?" Joey asked over the radio.

"Joe! Ray needs your help, anyway you can land down here?" Torque asked.

Joey looked down at the balcony, trying to figure out if the helicopter would make it.

"Not sure the balcony is big enough, but I'll try," Joey said.

"Alright, I'll grab Ray." Torque turned and rushed back inside.

In the hall, Ray took a step closer to Roader.

"Keep her safe for me Paul," Ray said.

Roader nodded.

"You have my word."

Ray nodded and then pulled out his handgun just before Torque ran into the hall.

"Ray!" Torque shouted. "Joey's on the balcony...there's still a chance to get to the roof."

Roader turned toward Ray and Steve.

"You guys go. Torque, I'm gonna need your help bringing her down," Roader said.

Ray tore his eyes away from Emily, but quickly stopped when he heard Roader.

"Ray," Roader said.

Ray turned and looked at Roader.

"Kill the bastard once for me, will ya?" Roader asked.

Ray nodded before turning to Torque who was shaking his head as he tried to catch his breath. He looked at Torque and waited for Torque to look at him.

"Take care of my daughter for me John," Ray said.

The words both satisfied and haunted Torque. He was grateful to hear that Ray trusted him with something so important to him, but it also frightened him because it almost sounded like a goodbye.

Before Torque could question the meaning of the words, Ray took his hand off of Torque's shoulder and then both Ray and Steve rushed toward Dutra's office.

"Alright, think you can carry her on your own?" Roader asked.

Torque then turned to Roader and looked down at Emily.

"Uh...yeah."

"Okay, if you carry her, I'll cover you, just stay behind me the whole time alright?" Roader asked.

Torque nodded his head.

"Okay...let's get her up."

As Roader and Torque carefully lifted Emily up off the floor, Ray and Steve rushed through the fire and smoke that was consuming the office and opened the door to the balcony where they saw Joey touch down in front of them.

The wind from the blades blew the smoke all around as Ray and Steve rushed towards the helicopter. Joey looked around to make sure nothing was too close to the propellers. Ray was the first into the helicopter, jumping just to the right of the empty mini gun quickly followed by Steve.

The jump wasn't the greatest feeling on Ray's knee but so much adrenaline was rushing through him, he honestly didn't even feel it. Ray turned and looked at Joey.

"Joey! Get us to the roof!" Ray shouted over the roar of the helicopter.

Joey nodded.

"Going up!" Joey shouted, quickly pulling the helicopter up off the balcony and up towards the top of the skyscraper.

Ray kept his eyes locked onto the balcony as it got smaller and smaller with each passing second. Ray was so focused on the balcony; he didn't even see Steve walk right up to him. It took Steve tapping him on the shoulder to get Ray's attention.

Ray looked at his shoulder and then looked up to see Steve standing over him. As Ray made eye contact, Steve put out his arm and held out his assault rifle. Ray looked down at it and then slowly took it from Steve's hand.

Ray examined the rifle as he took it in his hands, hoping it would be the gun that ended Dutra's life. Ray clicked the switch on the left side of the gun and changed it from rapid fire to burst before looking up at the tall skyscraper. His heart began to beat hard in his chest when he saw they were about ten or twelve floors away from the roof. It was clear that they were at the final stretch...and whatever ending that lay ahead for each of them was on the horizon.

Ray took a deep breath and cocked the assault rifle as the helicopter approached the top of the building.

Chapter 19: Endgame

Back down on the street Bob and the rest of the guys were making progress, but the last of Dutra's men refused to give up without a fight, taking aim at anything that moved.

The soldiers Sullivan had brought only suffered a few casualties but the same couldn't be said for the police officers that also came to the fight. Between the wounded and the dead, not many were left standing. Ray and Roader's guys were trained for intense combat to the fullest, and the soldiers were also used to gunfire, but the same could not be said for the officers of the New York Police Department. Sure many of them had been shot at before, but nothing compared to what was happening on the street just in front of Dutra's skyscraper.

"They just fucking keep coming, man!" Jasmin said to Tommy, who was right beside him, shooting another one directly in the forehead.

"Part of the fun, Jas!" Tommy said, before firing his shotgun at one of Dutra's men, blowing his right arm clean off. "How's Sullivan?"

"Bleeding pretty good...doesn't look good," Jasmin said after firing another shot.

Tommy nodded and then began to quickly reload his shotgun as Jasmin stood up and fired down into the street, shooting two in the stomach and one in the neck before bullets began hitting the opposite side of the car.

"Almost out of ammo," Jasmin said as he took the clip out of his machine gun and reload a full one.

"Yeah so am I...could be fucked, Jas!" Tommy said in a funny, sarcastic tone before lifting his hand to his ear. "Bob?"

"Yeah?"

"Jas and I are low on ammo...there any way you can cover us so we can find some?" Tommy asked.

"Where are you?"

"Down by the green Mazda 3 directly in the middle of the street."

Bob aimed down in his sights and began looking for the green Mazda. Smoke was still coming from a lot of the cars that had been blown up, thick smoke too, and it made it difficult for Bob to see in certain areas. Bob was also several hundred yards away from them.

"Directly in the middle?" Bob asked over the radio.

"Directly in the middle. You do know what a Mazda looks like right?" Tommy asked.

"Yes I know what a Mazda looks like, smart ass! I just can barely see from all the smoke," Bob said.

Tommy rolled his eyes as Jasmin stood up and fired a few more shots before quickly dropping back down.

"Tommy...eleven shots left," Jasmin said, looking straight into Tommy's eyes.

"Bob?" Tommy quickly asked again.

"I'm trying! Any way you can fire a shot?" Bob asked as he looked around.

Just as Bob asked Tommy that question, a man in a black ski mask jumped out right next to Tommy. Once the man saw Tommy, he began turning and aiming his weapon, but Tommy was faster, aiming his gun up at the man's head and pulling the shotgun trigger, blowing the man's head clean off and up into the air.

Bob heard the blast and turned his gun just enough to see the head of the man fly up into the air and land a few yards away from where the shot came from. He aimed his gun in the direction the head had popped up from.

"Alright I found you," Bob said.

Tommy looked at his now empty shotgun and then through it onto the ground before reaching over and picked up the machine gun of the man whose head he just blew off. He then began to dig in the man's pockets to try and find any more ammo, but came up empty.

"Jas?" Tommy asked.

Jasmin fired another shot and then looked at Tommy.

"What?"

"How many rounds you got left?"

"Five."

Tommy took out the clip of the machine gun and then looked to see how many bullets were left, only to see the clip was actually empty.

"Of course," Tommy said as he threw the gun across the street.

Jasmin then fired the last of his rounds, quickly dropping back down the moment he realized he was out. Once he got down to his knees he turned and looked at Tommy.

"I'm out."

"Like I said Jas...we could be fucked," Tommy said before taking his eyes away from Jasmin and looking directly ahead in the direction of Bob. Jasmin did the same thing, both guys thinking it was pretty much over for them when suddenly two machine guns dropped in front of them from out of nowhere.

"Sounds like you boys need some help," Tim said over the radio.

Tommy and Jasmin leaped up and grabbed the machine guns. When they stood up they saw Tim and Scotty a few feet in front of them firing down the street.

"Well that worked out nicely," Jasmin said before running around the car and catching up to Tim and Scotty.

Tommy then lifted his hand and put it back on his ear.

"Bob, we're set," Tommy said.

"Copy that, I'm gonna move up from the right. I'll let you know when I'm in position," Bob said.

"Alright, were gonna keep heading down the street with Roader's guys."

"Copy," Bob said before lifting up his sniper rifle and lowering himself down from the sunroof and into the car.

Tommy joined Jasmin, Tim and Scotty. As Tim fired on the left, Scotty fired from the right while Jasmin fired from the middle. Tommy looked behind and saw the soldiers catching up. He knew they weren't going to have any issues from behind, so he quickly stood right next to Jasmin and began firing with him.

"Five bucks says I get more kills," Jasmin shouted to Tommy over the gunfire.

"Let's live a little Jas...make it ten," Tommy said as he smiled.

Jasmin chuckled, shaking his head as he turned back around before the four of them fired their weapons in all directions.

II

Back inside the skyscraper Roader and Torque remained quiet as they rode the elevator down. Roader kept his eyes locked on the screen showing what floor they were passing while Torque kept his eyes locked on Emily as she kept still in his arms. Torque kept his eyes on her chest, hoping and praying that it would keep moving up and down as he tried to keep his sadness at bay.

"Come on come on. Move faster damn it," Roader muttered to himself. Roader kept his eyes on the screen as the elevator went past floor five. He then quickly looked down at the buttons just under the screen and pushed the number '2' button, causing the button to illuminate up in white.

"Why'd you press the second floor?" Torque asked.

"First floor will be crawling with security guards most likely. Would be like walking into a trap," Roader said.

Torque shook his head.

"You think the second floor will be better?"

As the elevator reached the second floor, it slowly came to a dead stop and surrounded Torque and Roader with silence, until suddenly bullets began hitting the elevator door on the opposite side, causing Torque to jump as he held onto Emily.

"Probably not," Roader answered before he cocked his shotgun. "When the door opens, keep low and stay right behind me, understand?"

Torque nodded, swallowing hard and holding onto Emily tighter as more bullets hit the opposite side of the door.

"Alright, let's go!" Roader shouted.

The door opened, revealing dozens of Dutra's security guard all scattered around the large open area of the floor. From behind large beams to behind the long reception area, Dutra's men were nested in well, locked and loaded as Roader emerged from the elevator.

Roader quickly lifted up his shotgun and fired once, hitting a part of the reception area. Then he fired two more times down the hall. The shots were misses but they were enough to provide a moment for both Roader and Torque to jet across to the other side of the floor, taking cover behind another set of desks near the balcony that overlooked the main lobby on the first floor.

As soon as they got behind the desk, Torque dropped to his knees and carefully put down Emily as they began to take fire once again. Roader covered his head as the bullets hit the top of the desk, causing a large potted planet to break and send soil all over him. Roader shook the soil out of his hair and then stood up and fired once, hitting the man that shot the plant in the stomach. Roader tried to get another shot off but the gunfire was just too much.

"Shit," Roader said as he ducked down and cocked the shotgun. He looked over towards Torque who was just finishing up putting Emily down. "Torque! Gonna need you."

Torque nodded his head and then picked up his machine gun. Roader looked at him and then nodded.

"Okay...now!" Roader said.

Instantly the two men stood up and began to return fire at Dutra's men, Roader hitting two while Torque got headshots off on four. Roader cocked and fired the shotgun as fast as he could, blowing through much of his ammo as he started to notice the guards slowly trying to retreat. Once he was sure they were far enough away, Roader then stepped out of cover behind the desk and then began walking towards them.

"Roader!" Torque shouted as he watched him following the guards.

"Stay with her until the coast is clear!" Roader shouted back.

Torque exhaled and then quickly ran back to Emily, not even seeing the elevator door, next to the one they came out of, opening.

"Oh shit...Emily...?" Torque softly asked as he carefully brushed the hair off of her face.

Even with blood and bruises all over her face, Torque tried to smile and remember the girl she was back in the bar. It was tough to do but Torque did his best to not focus on the negative of the situation, he kept trying to be positive, telling himself that everything would be fine.

But that train of thought quickly came to an abrupt halt. Just as Torque stood up, Vincent suddenly body slammed him, violently pushing him away from Emily and sending him straight to the edge of the balcony. Torque was so caught off guard, he didn't even have time to process what was going on, let alone react to what was happening. All he could do was tag alone for the ride. And as they picked up speed, Torque's lower back hit the edge of the balcony, sending pain down the lower half of his body before Vincent quickly lifted his left fist and punched Torque across the face.

Torque dropped to the floor as blood began to leak out of his nose. Vincent's punch had taken out much of Torque's energy as he rolled onto his painful back before wiping the blood that was running down into his mouth. He looked up at Vincent, hoping Vincent would see the anger building up in his eyes, but Vincent wasn't focused on him; he was focused on Emily, smiling as he looked down at her.

"Well, well...isn't this one hell of a coincidence..." Vincent said as he reached into his jacket, pulled out a black handgun and then cocked it. "But don't worry, I'll finish it this time."

Torque moved his eyes off of Vincent and onto the gun as he aimed it at Emily. Judging by the height of Vincent's arm, Torque could tell that Vincent was most likely aiming for her chest. He knew that if he didn't act fast, he was going to lose her. Before Vincent was able to take the shot, Torque lifted up his leg and kicked Vincent on the back side of his knee, bringing Vincent' body weight and aim down to the ground.

As soon as Vincent hit the ground, Torque grabbed him, trying to get the gun out of his hand. Vincent tried to push Torque off but Torque's grip got firmer as he pulled away.

Torque fought to get hold of the gun. He could see that it was still pointed in the direction of Emily. He knew he had to get the gun at least pointed away from her, but he knew if he took his hands off of the gun Vincent would get the shot he wanted...and Torque wasn't going to let that happen.

Torque turned his head and butted Vincent in the side of the face, taking Vincent completely off guard. He lost his grip and the gun flew out of his hands and across the room. Torque looked up and saw the gun land about ten or twelve feet away and thought he might be able to get it. But before he could act, Vincent turned and punched Torque in the face as hard as he could.

The force of the punch sent Torque spinning to the ground, landing on his stomach. Vincent stood up, looking down at Torque with a sadistic smile (a smile he no doubt learned from Dutra).

The punch left a large red mark and cut across the right side of Torque's face. He groaned, trying to quickly get back to his feet. It took some serious effort on his part but Torque was able to find the right amount of willpower to help him not only get to his feet but also get ready to face off with Vincent.

"Let's see what you got punk," Vincent said with a smile.

And with all his might, Torque lifted up his fists and lunged at Vincent. Torque was fast...but Vincent was faster, quickly blocking Torque's punch with his left arm, taking Torque off guard and giving Vincent the advantage.

Vincent swung his right fist, hitting Torque directly in the face. The force of Vincent's punch caused Torque to groan and fall back. Before Torque even had the chance to do anything, Vincent swung with his left hand, hitting Torque in the face again.

Blood splattered out of Torque's mouth as Vincent's fist met his cheek. The punch pushed him back even further than the first punch. So did the third and fourth punch. As blood began to run from his nose and lip, Torque knew if he didn't do something, the next punch would do him in; he had to fight back.

Torque lifted his head up only to see Vincent bringing his right arm back down and aim for his face...but when Vincent's hand was close enough, Torque suddenly grabbed it and quickly pulled Vincent's arm down and then elbowed Vincent directly in the face.

Caught off guard and surprised, Vincent groaned as Torque lowered his elbow. Torque then quickly lifted up his left fist and sent it soaring up into the air, smashing into Vincent's jaw.

Vincent's head bobbed up as his lip spurted blood. He looked back down at Torque and then punched him in the face again, spinning Torque around from the force. Vincent smiled as he lifted up his leg and kicked Torque in the stomach.

Torque painfully groaned, dropping down onto one knee, trying to catch his breath. Blood began dripped onto the floor as Torque lowered his head down and coughed from the pain coming from his stomach.

Vincent smiled as he walked over, standing over Torque like Torque was his trophy. Vincent looked over at Emily.

"Think I'm gonna fuck her before I kill her. But don't worry...I let you watch," Vincent said, and he started to laugh.

The words shot through Torque like a hit of drugs, instantly shattering what very little patience he had left inside and giving his adrenaline the little boost it desperately needed.

Torque stayed kneeling down, waiting, as Vincent lifted up his fist and then brought it swinging back down at Torque's face. Just when Vincent's hand was close enough, Torque suddenly blocked the punch and quickly lifted himself and his right fist up and punched Vincent in the stomach.

The breath in Vincent's lungs shot out of his body the moment the punch impacted...and he didn't even have time to try and catch it. As soon as Torque finished that punch, he quickly took another shot, hitting Vincent in the face...then another...and then another. With each punch Vincent was stumbling further and further back; the fifth punch causing him to bang up against the balcony.

Blood began dripping out of Vincent's mouth. He managed to block Torque's left hand, forcing Torque to punch him with his right fist as fast as he could while Vincent held onto his left hand.

With each punch blood came faster out of Vincent's nose, cheek, mouth and lip. He began to feel weaker with each hit. And just as Vincent looked up, Torque's fist came racing down and smashed him directly in the face, shattering his nose.

Vincent let out a horrific cry as the pain shot through him. Then with one last effort, Torque quickly made eye contact with Vincent before his left hand plowed right into Vincent's jaw, not only knocking him out but also sending his entire body over the balcony. With a loud crash Vincent landed on the first floor, his upper back landing on the edge of the lobby desk, snapping his spinal cord in half.

Torque groaned in pain as he wiped the blood from his face and then walked over to the edge of the balcony, looking down.

"Fuck that, you piece of shit," Torque said, and turned back toward Emily.

Down the hall, Roader fired his shotgun twice into a guard's chest before realizing the rest of the way was clear. With the long hall quiet, Roader looked around to make sure he hadn't missed anyone. Once he was sure that they were alone he quickly turned and ran back to Torque and Emily.

Roader's loud footsteps coming down the hall spooked Torque, thinking that it was a guard coming down. He quickly turned, grabbed Vincent's gun and aimed up, as the footsteps got closer. But right when Roader emerged the hall, Torque lowered the gun.

"Hall is clear, we should move now," Roader quickly said.

Torque nodded his head in agreement as he stood up, revealing his beat up face.

"Shit what happened to you?" Roader asked.

"Got into a little fight."

"How's the other guy?"

"Dead."

Roader shook his head then looked back down the hall, double-checking that no one was coming as Torque bent down and slowly picked up Emily.

"You good?" Roader asked.

"Yeah, I'll be fine."

Roader gave a quick smile, turned and then started down the hall with Torque right behind him. As they walked, Torque looked around at all the bodies that were on the floor, there was probably at least twenty, all scattered throughout the hall, and none of them were in one piece; many had holes in their chests or parts of their head blown off.

"Jesus Christ Roader, a little trigger happy?" Torque asked as they got to the end of the hall.

"Shotgun works pretty good," Roader said as they got to a staircase. "Alright this should bring us down to the lobby. Stay right behind me. God only knows what's down there."

Once Roader gave Torque the order, the two men started down the staircase to the main lobby of the building. Neither said anything to each other, but both men were happy to know they were about to reach the lobby. Torque however was also worried about Emily, because he could tell just by holding her that her breathing was getting slower and slower.

III

Roader and Torque made their way down the staircase but Dutra was going in a different direction, rushing up the last steps to the top floor. He and Street stopped when they reached a gray metal door that led onto the roof of the building. Street quickly looked down, checking to make sure no one was following.

Dutra looked at the numbers pad directly above the doorknob and typed in the passcode for the door. As soon as he put in the four-digit number code, the small light right above the keypad went from red to green. He passed through the door and Street followed. As soon as Street walked out onto the roof of the building Dutra quickly closed the door and began to look around.

Steam was rising out of several of the heating vents, the large fans screeching loudly as they spun around at great speed. But besides the multiple fans inside the vents, it was pretty much quiet...no helicopter around like Dutra thought there would be. Street also looked around, trying to figure out why no chopper was up their waiting for them.

"Where the hell is the helicopter?" Street asked.

But before he could get an answer, a bullet suddenly shot into his forehead, killing him instantly, spraying blood all over Dutra. As Street dropped to the ground, Dutra took cover behind a three-foot high cement wall that was surrounding a large generator.

The moment Dutra bent down he began taking fire himself from Ray, as Joey kept the helicopter level. Ray fired again with the machine gun, a burst of bullets hitting all around Dutra as he kept his finger on the trigger.

Dutra ducked his head down even further as bullets bounced all around, lowering his eyes and looking down at Street who was now in a large pool of thick red blood with chucks all over his face. For a brief moment Dutra actually felt sorrow for Street. Dutra still didn't give a shit that he was dead, but even he couldn't deny that after working with someone for so many years, it was hard to think they wouldn't be around anymore. And for Dutra that was his moment.

But that all changed when Dutra lifted his eyes up slowly and saw the machine gun Street had been carrying just off to his side. Dutra quickly went for it but stopped when Ray began firing directly where he was, proving that if he went for the gun, he would be shot. Dutra had to wait until Ray needed to reload. And to Dutra's surprise that moment came sooner than he thought it would.

"Shit," Ray said as he pulled the trigger and realized he was out. "Steve, another clip."

Steve quickly pulled a clip out of the holster he had attached to his hip and handed it to Ray.

"Last one Ray," Steve warned.

"Great, keep it steady Joe!" Ray shouted.

Dutra looked up when he realized he wasn't taking any gunfire and saw Ray in the process of loading the new clip into his machine gun. Dutra knew that would be the only chance he was going to get to grab Street's gun...and he took it.

Dutra suddenly emerged, lifting up his black handgun and returning fire at the helicopter, shooting as many shots as he could with his right hand while his left reached for Street's gun. Even for not aiming, Dutra's shots were too close for comfort, hitting all around Ray before shooting out the glass in the door that led into the pilot seat just as Dutra picked up the machine gun.

"Jesus Christ!" Joey said as glass shattered all over him.

"You hit?" Steve shouted, looking up at Joey.

"Not yet. Come on, Ray!" Joey shouted.

Ray then jammed the clip into the gun and quickly took aim only to see Dutra already aiming. Dutra fired one shot up at the helicopter, the bullet quickly clipping the side of Ray's gun, creating a large, bright and very hot spark. And the moment it sparked, Ray quickly dropped the gun.

"Fuck," Ray shouted as he and Joey watched it fall out of the helicopter and race down to the street.

As soon as Dutra saw Ray's machine gun hit the ground, he quickly took aim at the helicopter and began firing.

"Get down!" Steve said as he pulled Ray down.

The bullets shot all around the helicopter as Steve and Ray covered their heads. Bullets also began to hit all around the pilot seat, making Joey flinch as he attempted to not get shot. But Joey knew that since Ray lost his gun he was going to have to do something...and ducking down wasn't an option. He wasn't quite sure what he could do; he'd used up all the bullets in his machine gun going back and forth down on the street. As another bullet missed him by an inch or two, Joey quickly locked eyes onto the little red button just above the machine gun trigger. Since he hadn't been able to use them down on the street, Joey completely forgot that he had missiles left. He then looked up and smiled before he started turning the helicopter toward Dutra.

"Hold on!" Joey said as he suddenly spun the helicopter around.

"Joey! What are you doing?" Ray shouted.

"Killing this motherfucker!" Joey firmly said.

When the helicopter started turning toward him, Dutra stopped firing as he looked up and then made eye contact with Joey.

"Joey?" Ray asked, straightening up.

Joey then put his hand on the red button and suddenly grew a huge smile on his face.

"Adios, Mother Vacca!" Joey said to himself just as Ray looked in the pilot seat and saw Joey's finger on the red button.

"Joey, no! No!" Ray shouted trying to warn Joey.

But it was too late. Joey had taken aim...and so had Dutra.

"Oh, shit," Steve said as he kept his eyes on Dutra.

Joey pushed the red button down, causing a large rocket to come shooting out of the bottom of the chopper, aimed directly at Dutra. Joey was positive that the rocket would head right in the direction of Dutra, and it did...Joey just never thought that Dutra would actually *want* that to happen.

A fraction of a second after the rocket shot out of the helicopter, Dutra fired one carefully aimed bullet, not at the helicopter but at the rocket. The bullet shot through the night air and quickly met the rocket, hitting it directly in the center of the tip, causing it to blow up instantly.

Fire engulfed the air as the force of the explosion reached the helicopter and pushed it back and off to the side. Ray, Steve and Joey held on tight as the chopper began spinning around in circles before the smaller propeller on the back of the chopper hit part of the building, snapping it clean off. Suddenly warning sirens filled the inside of the chopper as Dutra lowered his weapon, smiling as he watched the helicopter spinning around.

"Shit I can't control this thing, guys!" Joey shouted, trying to level out the helicopter.

Ray looked down and saw that even though they were spinning all around, the top of the skyscraper was still right below them.

"Joe, what's the plan?" Steve asked.

"I'm gonna try and get you as close to the roof as I can!" Joey said as he began descending despite still violently spinning in circles.

Dutra watched as the chopper spun all around with that awful grin of sin plastered across his face. Even he could hear the warning sirens from where he was standing. He had no intention of shooting; he just wanted to watch it all play out.

He took his eyes of the helicopter to reload his weapon, as Joey descended down toward the roof. The top propeller spun directly into a large vent that was standing out. A horrific screech sound, almost like nails on a chalkboard, rushed out into the air as the blade hit the vent, sparks spraying all around. The noise quickly grabbed Dutra's attention and he lifted up his head, only to see a small piece of the propeller flying directly at him. It snapped his machine gun in half, the force of the blade knocking him to the ground.

"Okay guys, this is it! Go!" Joey shouted at Steve and Ray.

They quickly got to the edge of the helicopter and then jumped down as Joey unbuckled himself from the pilot seat, opening the door and jumping out himself as the helicopter began to fill up with thick, black smoke.

Steve saw the roof coming and tried to brace himself but before he could get into a good position he hit, slamming down onto his back while Ray landed on his stomach and hit his knee on the ground. And Joey was the last one, landing on his side before the helicopter landed right next to him and suddenly exploded as it made contact with the roof.

Instantly, a huge fireball lifted up into the sky, shooting smoke and ash up into the night air. The roar from the explosion grabbed everyone's attention. From Tommy and Jasmin, to Torque and Roader who were just exiting the building. They all looked up and saw the light from the blast.

"Holy shit," Tim said as he and Scotty looked up at the large blast.

"Oh man..." Jasmin said as he sighed.

Tommy nodded his head.

"...Yeah..."

None of the guys actually said it, but they all were thinking the same thing: if anyone was on board that helicopter, there was no possible way they could've survived. Everyone down on that street had thought about the fact that the explosion they just witnessed might've killed Dutra, but it might've killed anyone else up there too...

Chapter 20: Dutra

Smoke enveloped the roof of the tall skyscraper, as what was left of the helicopter continued to burn. The smoke sat heavy and thick as silence filled the cool night air.

Down on the rooftop Ray kept still for a moment before he lifted his head up and looked around, only to see nothing but smoke surrounding him. He wiped the ash and pieces of sheetrock from his face and then began trying to slowly move. But he quickly stopped when an extreme amount of pain suddenly took over his body.

Ray's knee was gone; the level of pain he was in trying to move only confirmed that. It was now nothing but bone rubbing up on bone and it hurt like hell. Still, he tried to slowly rise. As he did, he began looking around, hoping to see Steve or Joey but both were nowhere to be found. It was just him and his bum knee.

Ray's knee slowed him down considerably, after what felt like ten minutes, Ray had only made it to a push up position, trying to keep any type of weight off his knee, which made it difficult for him to get to his feet.

Suddenly, Dutra appeared from the smoke, kicking his right leg into Ray's stomach as hard as he could, sending Ray right back down onto his back. Ray groaned in pain but quickly began to get up, despite his knee, but Dutra once again kicked him in the stomach, sending Ray right back down.

Enraged from the blows he was taking, Ray began to get up much faster this time, but it wasn't enough. Dutra kicked him again only this time in the chest, sending Ray back to the ground and causing him to hit his knee violently on the ground. He groaned again in pain as he grabbed his knee without thinking, trying to hold it until the pain went away.

Dutra looked down at Ray's knee and then smiled, knowing he had found a weakness. He could tell just by the expression of Ray's face that it was a sore spot on him. Dutra lifted up his right foot and sent it stomping down, directly onto Ray's bad knee.

Ray let out a horrific scream as the pain shot through his entire body. He screamed even more loudly when Dutra began twisting his foot on the knee. Ray tried to get Dutra's foot off but the pain just took the energy and breath out of him.

Dutra took his foot off of Ray's knee, lifting it high for another strike, but before he was able to bring it down Steve rushed out of the smoke and body slammed Dutra. Caught completely off guard, Dutra soared into the side of a large AC unit.

Dutra hit with a loud bang just before Steve slammed into him with all his might. Steve lifted up his arm and then violently pushed it into Dutra's throat, pushing down as hard as he could, chocking him with all his might.

Dutra began jerking all around, trying to get out of Steve's firm grip, but he was having a very hard time moving due to Steve's body pressed up against him and the AC unit. Dutra could feel his face was starting to turn red and purple. He knew he had to find a way out of Steve's grip if he was going to fight back. He looked down at the ground and saw a way to get out.

As Steve pushed on Dutra's throat even harder, Dutra suddenly lifted up his right foot and stepped on Steve's foot as hard as he could. Steve quickly groaned in pain, loosening up his grip by mistake as the pain shot up through his foot. Dutra quickly pulled Steve's arm down and swung his left fist into Steve's face.

The force of the punch caused Steve to fall back a few steps, and Dutra quickly stepped forward and then punched Steve in the stomach with his right fist before bringing up his left fist and punching Steve in the face again.

The forth punch knocked Steve into another large AC unit, his back smashing into it as blood began to run down from his lip. The force of the hit was painful but Steve was still able to block the fifth punch Dutra quickly sent in his direction, grabbing Dutra's right hand and stopping the punch in midair. But as soon as Steve stopped one fist, Dutra hit with the other.

Steve attempted to keep up and managed to block a few more brutal punches, but all in all he was nowhere near fast enough to keep up with Dutra, the best he could do was stay on his feet for as long as possible.

And Steve was able to do so until Dutra landed an uppercut as hard as he could to Steve's jaw. The force and the surprise of the punch were devastating, dropping Steve to the ground, where he began coughing blood from his mouth.

Dutra quickly looked down at Steve, smiling at the fact that he was able to take Steve, one of the dogs, down so quickly. It was obvious that Steve was gonna need a moment or two before he was able to get back to his feet, but Dutra had no intention of giving Steve those brief moments.

But just as Dutra was getting ready to act on that murderous urge, Ray suddenly body slammed him away from Steve, sparing Steve a stomp on the face from Dutra's steel toe boot and giving him the chance to get back on his feet.

The force of Ray's hit pushed Dutra all the way to the edge of the building, crashing into the five-foot-high brick ledge that surrounded the roofline. Dutra groaned as he hit the wall, and tried to stand all the way back up. But before he even had the chance, Ray suddenly slammed into him again, pushing Dutra right back onto the brick wall with full force. Pain from the hit shot all through Dutra's body as Ray's body weight continued to crush him.

Ray pushed into Dutra as hard as he possibly could. As Dutra tried to break free, Ray pushed onto Dutra's body harder, trying to stop him from getting out of the position. Dutra then moved his hands and began trying to get a punch to Ray's face. The two punches Dutra threw were misses, but only just. Judging by the force Dutra was giving out, Ray knew it was only a matter of time before Dutra got a hit in, so Ray very quickly took his elbow out of Dutra's stomach and then took hold of Dutra's neck and began to squeeze with all his might.

The pressure from Ray's large hands caused Dutra's face to turn red again as Ray's grip tightened like a python. Panicking, Dutra again tried to swing at Ray, throwing up another three punches but all missing. And the more punches Dutra threw up at Ray, the more Ray began to squeeze. Frantically, Dutra lifted up his right boot and sent it soaring down onto Ray's bad knee.

Ray let out another horrific cry, breaking his grip to grab at his knee. As soon as Dutra was free from Ray's grip, he quickly turned and grabbed Ray by the shoulders, latching onto him and jerking down as he lifted up his right leg, kneeing Ray in the face before slamming him into the brick ledge.

Dutra then began to unload onto Ray, punching him everywhere from his face to his stomach. Ray tried to grab Dutra's arm just before he could make the other punch, but Dutra head butted Ray, knocking his head back.

Ray dropped his grip on Dutra's shoulder as his head bounced and pain shot into his nose. Dutra swung his right arm all the way back and then pulled it forward, hitting Ray on the left side of his face. The moment the punch hit him, Ray fell right to the ground, landing on his back.

Dutra leaned down to Ray but from behind Steve quickly Dutra's left arm and then whipped his right arm around Dutra's neck, squeezing while Ray tried to stand back up.

Steve kept pulling tighter, but just like last time he could feel Dutra's strength slowly starting to empower him again. Steve had Dutra in a good position but it wasn't going to last, Dutra was already starting to break free.

"Ray!" Steve shouted, groaning as he held Dutra.

Ray stood up on his bad knee only get a sudden rush of pain, causing him to stop.

"...R-Ray!" Steve said again.

Though it killed him to, Ray stood up as fast as he could, turned and looked at Dutra and Steve.

"Do it Ray...now!" Steve said struggling.

The anger in Ray once again built up as he moved his eyes down to Dutra. He limped to them and began unloading his anger— punch after punch into Dutra's gut as hard as he possibly could. Ray was nowhere near as fast as Dutra but his hits were hard and powerful.

Dutra groaned as another punch hit his lower stomach. Between Steve's chokehold and Ray's punches, Dutra was losing his strength...and fast. He kept trying to jerk his way out of Steve's grip but Ray's punches stopped him dead in his tracks.

Suddenly Ray quickly took aim and threw a hard punch right into Dutra's face. Dutra groaned as the punch made his head jerk to the left. Ray then sent another heavy punch right into the other side of his face.

Dutra could tell even though Ray was in pain from his knee, he wasn't going to stop punching. He could see the fury in Ray's eyes, but Ray wasn't the only one who could get angry...and with each passing punch Dutra started developing his own rage. And just as Ray was getting ready to make another hit, Dutra attacked.

Ray pulled back his arm, getting ready to punch Dutra in the face again but before he could, Dutra suddenly lifted up his right leg and kicked Ray right in the testicles before thrusting his head back and head-butting Steve in the face.

Ray groaned as he fell back, holding his privates as the pain kicked in. The pain was so bad, Ray almost lost his footing and fell to the ground but he was able to stay on his feet and deal with the pain.

Dutra's head-butt hit Steve right in the nose, taking Steve by complete surprise, making him take his arm off of Dutra's neck.

Dutra turned and punched Steve in the face, his fist smashing the left side of Steve's face before he punched Steve again...and again...and again. Dutra made one last fist with his right hand and then swung it down as fast and as hard as he could, hitting Steve in his left eye, the punch spinning Steve around before he tripped over his own feet and fell, smashing his head into a large metal pipe, knocking him out instantly.

Dutra cracked his neck as he looked down at Steve, watching to make sure he wasn't going to get back up. And he wasn't, he was knocked out for sure. The pool of blood beginning to form around his head made Dutra think he was dead, which was fine by him.

A groan from behind made Dutra turn back to Ray, who was still trying to recover from the blow to his crotch. However, Dutra's attention was taken off from Ray when a loud noise began to roar across the roof.

The ten large AC units that were side but side began to start up, the fans inside creating a loud roar almost like a jet engine was passing by. Dutra walked over to them as a clever idea began to sink into his mind.

As he was walking to the AC units his left foot banged into something. Dutra looked down and saw it was a metal pipe about a foot and a half long. The pipe was snapped at the end; most likely it had broken off when the debris from the helicopter was flying all around.

He reached down and picked up the pipe, examining it as held it firmly in his left hand. He smiled when he saw how sharp the pipe was from where it had broken off. Dutra lowered the pipe and then walked over to the AC units.

Dutra threw the pipe onto the top of the first AC unit and then lifted himself up onto the top. He had a little bit of trouble lifting himself up, mostly due to the height of the unit but once he was on top he then bent down and picked the pipe back up.

The pain in Ray's balls was finally subsiding. He was at least able to stand back up all the way. He then looked up and saw Dutra walking on the AC units. He didn't want to, but he knew he was going to have to get up there himself if he was going to face Dutra.

He began to walk toward the unit, limping from his shit knee. But his knee was the last thing on his mind. Ray knew just as much as Dutra did that this was it. This was the end of the line for one of them.

Ray quickly looked down at Steve as he walked past him. He wanted to bend down to make sure he was all right, but he knew his knee just wouldn't let him. All he could do was hope Steve would be okay...but with all the blood, it didn't look good; Ray had a bad feeling in his gut.

Ray finally got to the AC unit, which was just above his stomach. It wasn't going to be easy for him to get up, but he knew he had to. He lifted up his right leg and bum knee and then rested it on top of the unit, grabbed the top with both hands and then pulled himself up, groaning as he did. And even despite his leg and his age, Ray was able to get himself up and didn't even hurt his knee.

He then stood up as fast as he could, trying to make it seem like nothing was hurting him, even though pretty much everything inside was aching. Once he finally stood up he then turned and looked toward Dutra. His heart began to beat fast from what he saw Dutra doing.

Dutra was walking down all of the AC units, kicking off the black vents that covered the large fans, exposing them as they spun at what looked like a hundred miles per hour. He kicked off another and another before he reached the last one and kicked off the vent as hard as he could. He then turned around, smiling as he made eye contact with Ray.

Ray swallowed hard, and then began to walk toward Dutra. Dutra doing the same thing. He didn't look it, due to the smile on his face, but inside even Dutra was a little nervous.

II

The two met in the middle, maintaining eye contact with each other the whole time. Ray sighed and then made a fist as he kept his arms at his side. Dutra looked down and saw Ray's fist. He then lifted up the pipe and looked at it, Ray seeing the sharp tip for the first time. But suddenly to Ray's surprise, Dutra dropped the pipe to his feet and then looked back up at Ray.

"It'll be more satisfying to kill you with my bare hands," Dutra said over the roar of the fans.

Ray kept eye contact with Dutra as he slowly lifted up his fist. Dutra followed suit as he also kept eye contact with Ray. Ray then began to step closer to Dutra, keeping his guard up. Ray took one step closer, which brought Dutra into his range of punching. But Dutra suddenly took the first shot; punching Ray once in the face with his lightning right hand.

The punch took Ray by surprise and he shook his head, trying to shake off the pain. He quickly put his fists back up but Dutra struck once again, hitting Ray in the face again. The hit again took Ray by surprise and with the punch being stronger then the first, it almost knocked him down.

Dutra saw that Ray was in a bit of a daze from the punch and took the opportunity to finish the job. He quickly rushed up to Ray and then punched him in the gut twice before punching Ray in the face. Dutra then swung with his left hand but Ray blocked it. Ray kept his grip on Dutra's hand until Dutra suddenly kicked the side of his leg, knocking Ray down.

Blood started to drip in Ray's left eye from a large cut above his eyebrow. Between his shit leg, his age, and everything else in between Ray was starting to doubt he could take Dutra on.

Ray slowly made it back up to his knees as Dutra wiped the sweat from his forehead and then looked back down at Ray. His sinister smile grew back on his face as he watched Ray struggle to get to his knees.

"What's the matter old man? Christ, your daughter put up more of a fight," Dutra chuckled.

Ray looked up and made eye contact with Dutra. The look in Ray's eyes took Dutra by surprise...but not as much as when Ray, despite the pain from his knee, quickly stood up and then charged at him.

With a loud war roar Ray swung as hard as he could with his right hand. Dutra quickly lifted up his right arm and blocked the punch before bringing his elbow down and hitting Ray in the face. He then quickly hit Ray in the face with his other elbow.

Ray lowered his head and then body slammed into Dutra's chest, knocking both of them down. Dutra let out a soft groan as his back hit the top of the AC unit before Ray landed on top of him. Dutra let out a deep groan when Ray landed on him.

Ray was able to quickly get himself up to his knees and sent his right fist down, hitting Dutra in the face. Then he sent his left one, which hit Dutra on the other side of his face. Ray began to swing down his right fist again but Dutra blocked it, but once he did Ray quickly used his left fist and smashed Dutra's face again.

Blood began to run down the left side of Dutra's lip as he kept hold of Ray's fist, trying to somehow get him off his stomach. Ray brought down his left fist again but to his surprise, Dutra quickly grabbed his fist before it hit.

Ray began to push his hands closer to Dutra as Dutra tried to push them back. Ray's face quickly began to turn red as he pushed down, trying to overpower Dutra's strength. Dutra was also having a difficult time trying to keep Ray's hands from hitting him. It was clear that Ray was going to win the struggle.

Ray pushed his hands closer and closer to Dutra's face, thinking he was stronger than him, but when his hands were a few inches away, Dutra suddenly pulled Ray's left hand to the left, let go of it and then sent his right hand into Ray's face, knocking Ray back and off of Dutra's stomach.

Ray fell down, his head leaning over one of the spinning fans inside the AC unit. Dutra then began to stand up as Ray rolled over on his back and also began to stand back up. When Dutra got to his feet, he quickly wiped the blood off of his face and then spit the rest out that was in his mouth.

Even though the punch was a good one, Ray was able to get to his feet rather quickly too, before he turned and looked at Dutra who was standing only three feet away from him. Ray wiped the blood off of the large cut on his forehead...and then charged.

He swung at Dutra's face but Dutra blocked it. Ray lifted up his left fist and punched Dutra's stomach. He then used the same hand again to punch Dutra in the face as hard as he possibly could.

Surprised and pissed off by the punch, Dutra quickly hit back, hitting the right side of Ray's face. Ray's head and body quickly jerked to the right, but Ray used his left hand to backhand Dutra in the face.

Dutra then swung, hitting Ray in the stomach.

Ray then punched Dutra in the face.

Dutra smashed Ray in the stomach and face.

Ray elbowed Dutra in the face.

Dutra kicked Ray in the stomach.

Ray punched Dutra in the lower gut before standing back up.

Dutra grabbed Ray's hand before another punch hit his face and then head butted him.

It went on and on.

III

Dutra's face was a mess, from his bloody lip and nose to a cut on his right cheek. It was clear that Dutra had taking a beating. But his face was a far cry from what Ray's face looked like at that point.

The cut on Ray's forehead was bleeding heavily, his right eye was beginning to turn black and blue, his lip was getting swollen and most of all, his knee was beyond fucked; it was a miracle he was still standing.

Ray sent another punch into Dutra's stomach before trying to get another punch in, but Dutra was able to block it, bring it down and then pull up his left hand and smash Ray right in the jaw.

The punch to the jaw was it for Ray, he had nothing left...and it was obvious not only to Dutra but also to Ray; even he knew he was in trouble.

Ray spun around and then fell, landing on the pipe Dutra had dropped, groaning as his body hit the pipe. He then began to cough, trying to catch his breath. Blood began to drip down from his face and onto the AC unit.

Dutra smiled as he walked over to Ray, looking down at him with disgust. Even though Dutra was pretty black and blue himself, he felt like he had won not just the fight with Ray but the one down on the street. He couldn't have been any prouder of himself.

"Not bad for an old fuck...but not good enough," Dutra said as he walked over to Ray.

Ray coughed again, still trying to catch his breath. He began to move his hands very slowly onto the pipe as Dutra approached.

"Dogs of War, huh? Judging by your face must not have been a very big dog," Dutra said as he laughed.

Ray shook his head, trying to shake the blood off of his face as he grabbed hold of the pipe with both hands.

"You took everything from me back in Bosnia, now I'm gonna do the same fucking thing to you...looks like we found out which side God chose to be on after all," Dutra said as he reached Ray and stood over him.

Dutra slowly lost his smile and made a fist with his right hand while Ray took a deep breath. Dutra bent down and then swung his fist down...but Ray suddenly turned over, lifted up the pipe and smashed it into Dutra's hand, instantly stopping the punch from reaching him.

Dutra briefly shouted in pain and fell back, giving Ray enough room to leap up. Dutra grabbed his hand, trying to stop the pain, and didn't even see Ray lift the pipe and swing again, hitting Dutra in the stomach. Dutra groaned, much deeper this time, clearly in pain.

Ray swung again, hitting Dutra in the shoulder before lifting it back up and hitting Dutra in the face, the sharp tip of the pipe made large slices across Dutra's face as it hit him. Blood shot out of Dutra's face as Dutra shouted. Ray then hit the other side of his face with the tip of the pipe, which also created large bloody slices.

Ray lifted up the pipe one more time and then swung it down as hard as he could and smashed it right into the right side of Dutra's head. Dutra spun around and then fell down, landing on his stomach with his head dangling above the spinning fan of one of the AC units.

Ray dropped the pipe as he breathed heavily. He kept his eyes on Dutra to make sure he wasn't going to get back up, and clearly he wasn't. Ray did however notice Dutra jerking around, trying to lift up his head. The first thing Ray learned in this business is to never leave any loose strings...and always make sure the target you go after is dead...and Dutra was still jerking around.

Ray walked over to Dutra, thinking about everything from the death of Kevin to the fact his daughter may not make it. Once he got to Dutra, he bent down on his bad knee and grabbed Dutra by the neck. He lifted up Dutra's head and then quickly pushed it down into the spinning fan.

Blood instantly splattered everywhere as Dutra's body began to violently jerk. Ray kept his eyes on Dutra's head as it quickly started to get sliced off. The propellers of the fan turned a bright red as skin and hunks of flesh flew out. Once the blades of the fan reached Dutra's brain, Ray pulled Dutra's face up and looked at what was left of it.

The entire top left half of his head was gone, with some of the right side also gone; his left eyeball dangling down to his nose. Ray then looked into Dutra's right eye and saw it was staring right at him. Then it blinked.

"Rest in pieces...motherfucker," Ray firmly said before violently throwing Dutra back down.

IV

With a soft groan, Ray slowly stood up and closed his eyes, taking a well-deserved moment to process everything. His face was bloody and bruised, his leg was shit and he had a massive headache but looking down at Dutra's lifeless body was well worth the pain he was in. It was in that moment Ray finally told himself it was over.

"Ray!" a voice shouted out through the smoke.

The smoke from the helicopter was only getting thicker and making it harder to see, but when Ray looked around he saw Joey emerge from the smoke, his face all cut and covered in soot from the helicopter exploding.

"Joey?" Ray asked.

Joey limped over to the AC units and then pulled himself up onto it. Ray smiled as he looked Joey over, making sure he wasn't fatally injured anywhere. His smile got bigger when he realized that besides a few cuts and burns, he would be fine.

"Jesus, what happened to you?" Joey asked, looking at Ray's bloody face.

"You should see the other guy," Ray said.

Joey looked down at Dutra and saw what was left of his head.

"Oh, shit...someone's having a bad day," Joey said as he looked back up at Ray.

"Glad you're alright Joe," Ray said.

Joey smiled and then patted Ray on the back and then began looking all around.

"Where's Steve?" Joey asked.

"Oh shit!" Ray said before turning and heading over to the end of the AC units. "Steve!"

Ray quickly got to the end and carefully jumped down and turned...only to see Steve starting to slowly get up. Ray let out a huge sigh of relief, happy to see Steve was still in one piece, unlike Dutra.

"Steve," Ray said.

Steve looked up.

"Ray," Steve said as he began to slowly stand up.

Joey jumped down from the AC unit and then helped Ray pulled Steve up to his feet.

"Oh...boy do I feel like hell," Steve groaned as he wiped blood off of his forehead.

"You look like it too," Joey said.

Steve turned and looked at Joey.

"You don't look much better yourself kid," Steve said just before coughing.

Ray wiped some of the debris out of Steve's hair and then put his hand back on Steve's shoulder.

"You alright, Steve?" Ray asked.

Steve cleared his throat.

"Yeah, I'll be fine, just have a massive headache," Steve said before looking all around. "Where's Dutra?"

Ray smiled as he looked in the direction of Dutra's body.

"Well...he's got a bit of a headache himself," Ray said.

Steve looked at Ray and saw Ray looking behind, so Steve turned and also looked, his eyes meeting the faceless body right away.

"Oh damn...he's gonna need a shit ton of Ibuprofen to shake that off," Steve said as he chuckled.

Joey and Ray also began to chuckle as Steve looked down at Ray's leg. "How's your knee?"

"Gone," Ray said, and then laughed some more.

Steve chuckled and then looked around before taking in a deep breath of air. And then the three of them stop talking, taking a moment to gather all their emotions as they looked around the top of the roof. They then all looked out toward the city. Smoke was still rising up into the night sky, but the once clouded over sky was now giving way to the stars. In that moment all three of them took a moment to send up a prayer.

"Everything will change after tonight...wont it?" Joey asked.

Ray nodded his head.

"Yeah...lots of changes on the horizon," Steve said as he shook his head.

Ray then took his eyes off of the view and looked back down at Steve and Joey.

"So...how about we get out of this hellhole?" Ray said as he and Joey began helping Steve walk.

"Thought you'd never ask," Joey said.

Ray smiled and then the three of them began to head toward the door to the staircase, each of them happy to be walking out.

Chapter 21: Partially Reunited

And finally, after everything...the war was over. And just like every other war, the end was far from pretty. Bodies were scattered all around, cars were burning and questions were still in the air about who survived...and who didn't.

Bob stood up after firing the last shot of the battle. He heard a loud noise from behind and quickly turned his head. His eyes took a moment to adjust and when they did, they saw dozens and dozens of ambulances, fire trucks, and military convoys driving up to the scene.

The noise from all the sirens engulfed the street, grabbing Jasmin and Tommy's attention as they stood up. Jasmin wiped dirt off of his shoulder as Tommy lowered his shotgun to the ground and smiled.

"Look who decided to show up," Tommy said.

Jasmin also smiled as he watched the approaching emergency vehicles.

"Better late than never," Jasmin said.

Tommy chuckled and then patted Jasmin on the shoulder.

"Looks like we made it through this one Jas," Tommy said, before he turned and walked toward Bob.

Before Jasmin followed Tommy, he took one last look behind him, taking in all the destruction, amazed that they actually survived this time. Jasmin had been through a number of fights with Ray but this one easily topped the list. It took a while for Jasmin to actually realize he had lived through it all.

The ambulances pulled up to the entrance of the skyscraper. The lights from the sirens reflected of the windows of the building like diamonds. And as soon as the first ambulance pulled up, Torque and Roader quickly ran to it. Roader yanked open the back doors of the ambulance and Torque quickly climbed in and put Emily down on the stretcher.

"What do we got?" Asked the paramedic.

"Gunshot to the lower abdomen...she's lost a lot of blood," Torque confessed as he looked down at Emily.

"Alright..." The paramedic said just before he lifted up her shirt and examined the bullet hole.

"...How's she gonna be?" Torque asked, almost frantic.

The paramedic shook his head and then looked up.

"Not sure. Gonna have to get her over to the hospital," he confessed.

Torque shook his head and then looked back down at Roader.

"Should we wait for Ray?" Torque asked.

Roader sighed.

"Don't think we can. She needs to go now. Ray will understand that," Roader said as he turned and looked toward the entrance of the building.

"You go with her, Torque."

Torque turned and looked back at Roader.

"What?"

Roader step closer.

"Ray wouldn't want her to be by herself...and since he trusted you to get her out, I don't think he would have a problem with you going with her."

Torque nodded and then looked back at Emily.

"Alright..."

Roader nodded his head and then began to close the doors to the ambulance.

"Hey Roader?" Torque asked.

Roader looked up.

"Yeah?"

Torque smiled with gratitude.

"Thank you."

Roader nodded and then closed the ambulance doors. Torque turned and grabbed onto Emily's left hand as the paramedic put an oxygen mask over her face. Torque wiped a few tears out of his eyes while he looked at her, praying that they weren't too late to save her.

Roader watched as the ambulance pulled away and headed down the street; hoping for the same thing Torque was hoping.

"Roader!" Tim suddenly shouted.

Roader turned and looked as both Tim and Scotty walked over to him, each covered with dust and sweat.

"You guys alright?" Roader asked as he quickly hugged both of them.

"Yeah...we're alright," Scotty said, shrugging his shoulders.

Roader shook his head and then looked down the street, amazed at all the destruction that was surrounding them.

"Pretty big mess...anyone else on our team left?" Roader asked as he took his eyes off the destruction and then looked back up at them.

Scotty lowered his head, almost in shame while Tim cleared his throat and made eye contact with Roader.

"Afraid it's just us, boss," Tim confessed.

The news was tough to hear, but with what was just before him, he wasn't surprised by the news.

"Well...at least you guys made it," Roader said after exhaling deeply. "What about Ray's team?"

Tim lifted his head back up and nodded his head to the left. Roader turned and when he saw the view he shook his head and smiled.

"I'll be damned," Roader said as the smile grew bigger on his face.

Out of the thick smoke came Bob, Jasmin and Tommy. Each one of them—with the exceptions of a few cuts and bruises—were unharmed. Roader found it to be a welcoming sight to see after hearing about his own team. And his smile only grew larger as they walked over.

"You guys okay?" Roader asked.

Tommy and Jasmin nodded.

"Yeah, we're fine...good to see you two made it," Bob said to Tim and Scotty.

Tim nodded. "Yeah...you too."

"You get to Emily?" Tommy asked.

"Yeah, Torque and I brought her down. The ambulance just left with them in it." Tommy and Bob shook their heads.

"What about Ray...and...Steve?" Jasmin asked.

Roader slowly turned his eyes and looked into Jasmin's.

"They followed Dutra up to the roof while Torque and I brought Emily down," Roader said.

Jasmin shook his head and then looked down as Bob lifted his head up to the top of the skyscraper, only to see smoke and fire rising from it. The sight put chills in Bob's gut as he began losing hope that they were still alive.

Roader noticed that everyone from Bob and Tommy to Tim and Scotty had the exact same look plastered on their dirty, sweaty faces. It was a hopeless look; you could tell that their spirits were crushed.

"Hey," Roader said, quickly getting everyone's attention. "Stay positive. You know how strong, how stubborn both of them are."

Tommy and Bob briefly smiled as Roader attempted to comfort them. Even though it was a failed attempt, everyone thought it was nice of Roader to at least try. Roader was getting ready to add onto what he said but his attention quickly shifted to a soldier walking up to him.

"Excuse me...sorry but can anyone here tell me where I can find Caption Roader?" He asked.

"You're looking at him...and you are?" Roader said.

"Sergeant Hanson, 101st Airborne. The President sent us down figuring you might need a little more help," Hanson said.

Roader looked at the guys quickly before looking back at Hanson.

"Situation is under control down here, but the building isn't secure yet," Roader said.

Hanson shook his head as the rest of the 101st Airborne Division walked over to them.

"Okay, my men and I will take care of that," Hanson said.

Roader nodded. "Thank you Sergeant."

"Sir?"

Roader stopped and turned back to Hanson.

"Yeah?"

"There any of your guys left in the building?"

The question took the breath out of Roader while Tommy and Jasmin held their heads down, Jasmin fending off tears. Bob also was having difficulty keeping his emotions at bay as he looked up at Roader. Roader cleared his throat and looked up at Hanson.

"...Uh...I'm..."

Just as Roader was getting ready to answer Hanson, Tim suddenly interrupted him.

"Look!" Tim shouted as he pointed.

The guys—Roader, Bob, Jasmin, Scotty and Tommy—quickly turned around and then looked to where Tim was pointing. Roader then shook his head in disbelief as he focused on the sight.

Stepping out of the main doors to the building, bruised, bloody and black and blue were Joey, Steve and Ray. Tommy and Jasmin were the first to smile. Bob also had a bit of a smirk on his face and for the first time in a very long time...Bob actually wasn't trying to hide his emotions.

Tim and Scotty weren't smiling though, they were stunned. Both could only imagine how rough it was up in the building; the street was bad enough. As they watched Ray, Joey and Steve walk over they immediately had a new respect for the men before them. It was clear they were truly the Dogs of War everyone talked about.

"Guess now we know who the Dogs of War really are..." Scotty said as he leaned into Tim.

Tim nodded in agreement. "Yeah...I think we do."

Roader's smile grew as the guys walked right up to him and looked at him. Roader looked at Joey, then to Steve...and finally looked into Ray's tired, bloodshot eyes.

"Welcome down, Ray," Roader said, echoing the very same thing he said to a much younger Ray in Vietnam at the bottom of Hamburger Hill.

Ray exhaled deeply.

"Good to be down," Ray said with a straight face.

Roader nodded, smiling that Ray also remembered what he had said back in Vietnam, and then extended his hand for Ray to shake. Ray lowered his eyes and looked down at Roader's hand. But instead of firmly shaking it like they've done for decades, Ray lifted up his hands, stepped toward Roader and then gave him a hug. Roader returned the gesture with honor.

As a few more ambulances pulled up, Ray and Roader let each other go and Ray looked back at Steve, patted him on the shoulder and then looked up at Bob, Tommy and Jasmin.

"Tommy...Bob...Jas..." Ray said to each of them.

"Good to see you Ray," Tommy said.

"You too..." Ray said as an ambulance pulled up next to them. "You guys get checked out alright?"

"You sure you're alright?" Jasmin asked.

"I'll be fine. Just wanna make sure you guys are too," Ray said.

Bob nodded his head and then the three of them turned and walked toward the ambulance. Roader looked at Tim and Scotty.

"You guys get checked out, too," Roader said.

"Yes, sir," Tim said before turning and walking over to Bob and the other guys as Tommy stepped up into the ambulance.

Roader then turned and looked at Ray as another ambulance pulled up next to them. Ray looked at the ambulance and then quickly turned and looked at Steve.

"Okay, I don't care what you say, you're getting your head checked out," Ray said.

Steve looked at him and rolled his eyes.

"It was a slight fall," Steve said.

"Bullshit, I heard it, and I was twenty feet away from you."

Joey nodded in agreement.

"He's right. Besides you can't afford to have any more brain damage," Joey said with a smile.

"You know what Joey? I kinda liked having you passed out somewhere. It was definitely a nice change of pace," Steve retorted as he stepped toward the ambulance.

As Steve took the first step up the stairs, he began to lose his balance, but before he lost it all the way, Joey grabbed him and helped him up.

"You're welcome," Joey sarcastically said as he walked Steve over to the ambulance.

"Yeah, just don't get any ideas, pal. I don't have anything against your kind, but don't be rubbing up against me," Steve said.

"Hate to break it to you Steve, but I'm not interested in dating someone that's my grandfather's age." Joey began to laugh, and so did Steve, shaking his head as they made it to the ambulance.

Ray kept his eyes on them until Steve made it on the ambulance. As he lowered them he met Roader's eyes, which were also bloodshot.

"You sure you're alright?" Roader asked.

"Fine, what about Emily?" Ray said.

"We got her out safe, got her into an ambulance and they already took her to the hospital," Roader said.

"Torque made sure nothing happened to her?" Ray asked.

Roader shook his head.

"Ray, Torque not only made sure of that, he probably saved her life a dozen times as we came down. I'll tell you the kid may be a kid, but he's a damn good one. Don't think I would've been able to get us down if it was just Emily and I," Roader confessed.

Ray shook his head and then looked around.

"I gotta get to the hospital, make sure she's alright," Ray said, looking around for a vehicle.

Roader turned.

"Hold on...stay here and I'll grab us a car," Roader said before quickly running off into the crowd of military soldiers and firefighters.

Ray stayed in his spot and cleared his throat as he impatiently waited for Roader to return. What was only ten seconds left like twenty years to Ray in that moment, all he could think about was getting to Emily and making sure she was alive. Ray kept telling himself to remain calm, but his mind was going a hundred miles per hour.

After a few more seconds of waiting for Roader, Ray then walked down from the stairs impatiently. He exhaled, trying to remain calm and then lowered his head down.

He noticed blood on the ground. Not just a little bit of blood either, but a whole trail of it. Ray looked around, checking to see if it was coming from anyone behind him. As he looked back down, his eyes followed the trail of blood and to Ray's surprise, it went into an alley just before the skyscraper.

Curious, Ray began following the bloody trail down the alley. Ray kept walking down the dark alley, even after realizing he had a fucked knee and no type of weapon whatsoever. He turned around, quickly thinking he should at least grab a handgun, but he decided against it when he saw just how far he was in. He turned back and kept following the blood.

As he got closer, legs began to appear from behind the trash barrels and bags just under the light. Ray slowly reached to his side, only to once again remember that he didn't have a weapon. He quickly looked back and carefully took steps toward the barrels, clenching his fists as he moved closer. As he got closer, he began to see more and more blood collecting around the person.

Ray stepped closer and carefully focused on the person's chest and saw that is was moving in and out heavily. Ray took one last step and then quickly turned and looked down at the person. He unclenched his fist.

"...Oh, Sullivan..."

From the ground Sullivan slowly lifted his head up and looked at Ray. But before he could say anything he suddenly began coughing, blood coming up with each hack and running out of his lips as he breathed heavily.

Ray's knee was gone; literally nothing but bone rubbing up on bone, but that didn't stop him from kneeling down at Sullivan's feet. He lowered his eyes down and saw the bullet hole in Sullivan's stomach; blood flowing out like a river. He then looked back up at Sullivan's face.

"You...look like shit Ray," Sullivan said with a very slight smile.

Ray shook his head as he kept his eyes on Sullivan.

"Kinda feel like it, too."

Sullivan chuckled.

"Well...make sure...Joey...gives you guys some time off."

"Why have Joey do it when you can do it?" Ray said as he turned and looked down the ally, only to see no one was there.

Sullivan cleared his throat.

"Ray...I'm not gonna..."

"Yes you are Sully! Yes, you are!" Ray said before he turned and looked at the end of the ally. "Help! Down here! Help!!"

"Ray? Ray...Ray!" Sullivan said as loud as he could.

Ray turned and looked back at Sullivan, clearly worried...and scared for him as his eyes met Sullivan's.

"...Don't," Sullivan softly said.

"What do you mean don't? Sullivan you got to get to the hospital," Ray said.

"...It's not worth it..."

Ray lifted his eyes up from Sullivan's stomach and then looked into Sullivan's eyes.

"What are you saying?" Ray asked.

Sullivan cleared his throat softly as his breathing began to slowly down.

"I'm saying let me go, bud."

"But we can get you to a hospital," Ray began in a softer voice.

"It's too late for that Ray ...I can see it in your eyes...just like you can see it in mine."

Ray's eyes began to water up as he looked away from Sullivan to wipe them.

"What can I do?" Ray asked helplessly.

"Forgive me." Sullivan said as he lowered his head down.

"For what?"

"For everything...this...whole...situation is my fault," Sullivan said as he looked down at the blood coming out of the bullet wound.

"Sully none of this was your fault. Hey...you hear me? You're not to blame for anything that's happened."

Tears began to run down Sullivan's face as Ray leaned in closer.

"My son...Garrett...you'll watch over him...keep him safe?" Sullivan asked as he began crying.

Ray nodded with a smile as tears began to drip from his eyes.

"Tell him...I loved him...and that I'll always be with him," Sullivan said.

Ray nodded softly.

"You have my word, Sully. I promise he'll know the kind of hero his father was..." Ray said, as he kept his eyes locked into Sullivan's.

Sullivan briefly smiled as he thought about Garrett growing up and learning about him. It was something that Sullivan always wanted to do himself but in that moment he was more than satisfied with having Ray take over that dream.

Ray then broke eye contact with Sullivan, leaned in and hugged him. Sullivan very slowly lifted up his left arm and put it around Ray as the two closed their eyes and held one another. Tears fell from each other's eyes as they said their silent goodbyes together. And very slowly...Sullivan's breathing stopped...as Ray's breathing picked up, sobbing into Sullivan's shoulder as he felt the life leave his body.

II

While Emily was rushed into surgery, Torque was left waiting in the waiting room, which to his surprise wasn't busy at all. He paced back and forth waiting to for a doctor to come out of the doublewide doors. For the first time in his life, Torque was scared, not just for Emily but also for Ray. He knew it was going to be a rough night for each of them.

Torque walked over to the end of the waiting room and looked out of the large windows that over looked the city. The darkness from the night hid the destruction well, even the smoke off in the distance was tough to see. Torque moved his eyes all around and then stopped when he found Dutra's skyscraper, smoke and fire lifting into the air from the roof.

He began to wonder about Ray, which took his mind off of Emily for a brief moment. He thought about the explosion he saw when he and Roader were walking out of the skyscraper. He wasn't up there but he was pretty sure Ray was. Along with Steve and Joey.

With no clock around, Torque wasn't sure how long he had been there. When he looked up, though, he could see the sky getting brighter off in the distance. He began to worry even more, trying to figure out if being in surgery that long was a good thing or a bad thing.

He turned his head when he heard a noise coming from down the hall. Clearly someone was running but Torque wasn't sure if it was just a person or someone being rushed into surgery. He turned his head and then looked toward the window, losing interest as he focused on the horizon that was a beautiful blue. He didn't even see Ray and Roader rush in.

"Torque," Ray said.

Torque turned his head, saw Ray, and quickly stood up.

"Ray!" Torque said with a bit of a smile.

Ray limped over and gave Torque a hug. Torque returned it, patting Ray on the back as they hugged.

"How is she?" Ray asked almost in shame.

Torque exhaled deeply.

"Haven't heard anything yet. She's still in surgery."

"You alright?"

"Yeah..."

"Did you get him?"

Ray turned and met Torque's eyes. Ray didn't answer, he just kept his eyes on Torque but in that moment Torque knew what that look meant. He remained calm but inside a part of him was jumping for joy while the other part wished he could've been there to help.

Torque was getting ready to speak when the double doors opened. Ray and Torque quickly looked and saw a doctor in blue scrubs walk out and look at them as she took off her blue cap from her head.

"Are you here with Emily Gagnon?" Dr. Henderson asked.

"Yes," Ray said, "...How is...um...how is my daughter?"

Dr. Henderson looked into Ray's bloodshot eyes.

"She'll be fine," Dr. Henderson said.

Both Ray and Torque took a deep breath of relief as the words sank in, while from off to the side Roader smiled.

"She lost a lot of blood. But thankfully the bullet didn't hit any major organs...she's very lucky," Dr. Henderson continued.

Ray smiled as tears began to fill up in his eyes, happy that she would be okay. Torque, also filled with excitement, patted Ray on the shoulders. Ray lifted up his head and wiped his eyes before he looked back at Dr. Henderson.

"Thank you," Ray said with a smile.

Dr. Henderson nodded.

"Would you like to see her?"

Ray nodded.

"Yes...very much."

Dr. Henderson smiled as Ray and Torque looked at each other and smiled.

"Thank you Torque," Ray said as he patted Torque on the arm.

"Anytime Ray...now go see your daughter."

Ray then quickly hugged Torque again before following Dr. Henderson through the double doors. Torque watched him as he walked away, excited to see Ray so happy, and knowing he was a part of that only made the moment that much better. Torque smiled and then sat back down.

Roader leaned up from the wall and walked over to Torque and then took a seat right next to him before patted Torque on the left leg. Torque then turned and looked at Roader.

"He won't forget this," Roader softly said.

Torque nodded before breaking eye contact and looking out the window and seeing the beautiful sunrise that was taking shape on the far horizon.

"Guess this means it's over," Torque said.

Roader shook his head.

"For today at least."

III

As Dr. Henderson led Ray down the hall his heart began to beat faster with each step forward. No words could express how thankful Ray was for Emily being alive, but now he had no choice; he was going to have to explain everything to Emily. He knew it was going to be a lot to take in, he knew that back when she was in grade school. The only thing that had changed since then was that there was just more to explain.

"She'll be pretty groggy when you go in, so just expect that," Dr. Henderson explained.

"That's fine...as long as I can talk to her," Ray said with a bit of a chuckle under his breath.

"Well, hopefully you don't talk to her about anything to important...there's a good chance she may not even remember if she keeps going in and out," Dr. Henderson said.

Ray nodded and then looked around as they both walked deeper into the hall as doctors rushed all around.

"Yeah..."

"You should probably get looked at yourself," Dr. Henderson suggested.

"I'll deal with that later," Ray said.

Dr. Henderson nodded and then turned to a doorway on the left side of the hall.

"Right in here," she said.

Ray smiled.

"Thank you."

Dr. Henderson shook her head and then walked away to her next patient. Ray very slowly peaked his head in the doorway only to see Emily lying on her back on a bed in the middle of the room. Ray smiled for a brief moment, happy to see her alive. At first he thought she was sleeping because she stayed so still.

Ray kept his eyes on her as he rehearsed his attempt to explain everything. He'd always wanted to, but he was never sure if he could get the words out for it all to make sense.

But as he kept looking at her, his smile began to fade. He tried his best to keep it, but the thought about Emily getting hurt because of him wiped that smile away, just like it had ever since he found out Dutra had her.

Thinking about Dutra being dead brought some type of closure into his heart for a moment, but it didn't last long. Ray had always been honest with everyone, including himself, and he knew the truth about the situation he was in: Dutra may be dead today but someone else will most likely take his spot tomorrow. It's a never-ending job...and a never-ending risk.

Ray didn't want to admit it but he had to: Dutra had won. His face may have been shredded off like a piece of cheese in a cheese grater, but he still won the game; Ray couldn't deny that. Dutra being dead didn't change the fact that Ray's and everyone else's name was now out in the public for all to know...and that alone would be a serious issue for the team in the future.

Ray knew he needed to make a choice. It would be a choice that would affect how he lived the rest of his life. He gave it serious thought as he kept his eyes on Emily, trying to figure out what was the best thing to do. He thought about that fact that he was retiring and would be able to finally stay with her and spend time with her, which was what he always planned on doing when he got out...but he also had to take the hack—and everything that it could bring—into account. And in that moment, he made the choice to stop running from her. The threat was serious, but Ray knew if he walked away from her again, he would never live it down. He took a deep breath and walked into the room.

As he approached he noticed her eyes were closed, so he tried to keep quiet. When he got to the side of the bed he stood over her as tears filled up his eyes; the sight of her all beat up and hurt broke Ray's heart. Ray wiped the tears from his eyes and then very carefully lowered his right hand and softly touched her face, causing Emily to groan and then slowly open her eyes.

Emily's eyesight was a little blurry but she was able to turn her head and see Ray smiling down at her.

"...D...Dad...?" Emily asked in a very tired voice.

"Yeah baby...it's me."

"What...what happened?"

Ray exhaled.

"Emily...it's a long story...but the short version is that...I'm not a body shop manager. Never have been. Truth is...I work for the government. Remember when you were little and before bed you always asked your mother and I to close your bedroom window because you were afraid that a bad man would come in, and your mother would tell you that no one would because the soldiers known as the Dogs would stop anyone from coming in?" Ray asked.

Emily didn't say anything, but she did remember and kept her eyes on Ray as he lowered his head, almost in shame.

"I was one of them...I was one of the Dogs. It wasn't because I was cheating, or because I was a horrible husband...I just wasn't around because I was off trying to make the world a better place for my family...just never thought I would lose them along the way." Ray wiped a tear from his face and cleared his throat. "And so now you know...now you know why..."

Ray lowered his head even more, doing everything to avoid making eye contact with his daughter. He tried to hold back tears but he was unsuccessful, several of them landed on the floor next to his boots.

"Dad..." Emily said in a very soft voice.

Ray quickly wiped his eyes and then looked up at her.

"Why didn't you tell me?"

Ray exhaled.

"Because your Mother asked me not to...she was afraid that if you knew, you would become a target."

Emily began to get teary eyed as she looked back at all the years that had past and how she had thought that when her father wasn't around he was either off gambling or having an affair.

"I'm sorry for not being there for all these years...but I just wanted to keep you safe as best as I could. I don't expect you to understand...but at least now after all these years you now know the truth."

More tears began to flow from Emily as Ray turned and looked towards the door. There was so much that Emily wanted to say in that moment, but she didn't know where to start. She could tell Ray had more to say, but couldn't bring himself to admit anymore for one day.

As Ray kept his eyes on the door, Emily slowly lifted up her left hand and placed it down onto Ray's dirt-covered hand. When he felt the touch, Ray turned and looked back down at her, almost confused. But before he said anything, he looked into her eyes and she smiled.

The smile took Ray by surprise. It not only lit up the room but also brought a bit of light into the darkness that surrounded Ray's heart. And with tears in his eyes, Ray gently took hold of Emily's hand and smiled back as they both spent those few minutes in silence, enjoying the fact that, for the first time, it felt like they were father and daughter.

*   *   *

IV

After close to twenty minutes with her, Ray walked down the hall and back towards the waiting room, wiping tears from his eyes and smiling. As he walked out of the double doors and into the waiting room, Torque looked up and quickly stood when he saw Ray come out. Ray limped over to him, clearing his throat as he approached.

"Hey," Torque said.

"Hey...where's Roader?" Ray asked.

"He took off...got a call saying his son woke up."

Ray shook his head.

"Good."

"Yeah...so how'd it go?" Torque asked.

Ray exhaled.

"Uh...think it went alright...a lot to take in, you know?"

Torque shook his head.

"Yeah..."

Ray briefly lifted his head up and looked out the window at the beautiful sunrise.

"Well, least now she knows," Ray explained.

Torque patted Ray on the arm.

"Hard parts over then..."

"Maybe...still have to figure out how to deal with the fact that our names are out there now," Ray said.

"We'll deal with it when the time comes. Maybe when Dutra got our names, he only used them for himself..."

"He didn't take yours."

"What?" Torque asked.

"When he hacked into the F.B.I. server, he got our names but your name wasn't in that file. Sullivan didn't get a chance to put it in because I never processed the paperwork...so no one knows about you," Ray said.

Torque shook his head and then looked back down.

"Guess it's kind of a good thing you didn't like me at first," Torque said, chuckling.

Ray smiled as he looked back at the double doors.

"Hope I'm not too late to be there for her," Ray said as he exhaled.

Torque shook his head and then looked back up at Ray.

"She needs her father Ray—every kid does, no matter what age."

Ray shook his head and then swallowed.

"Hope you're right, Torque..."

Ray patted him on the shoulder and then walked away. Torque kept his eyes on him as he walked away, hopeful that maybe this was Ray's chance to finally be happy.

Ray fought to hold back tears again, but he somehow found the willpower to keep his eyes dry as he headed into an elevator, pressed the first floor button and waited until the metal doors closed in front. Torque turned and walked toward through the double doors and started to head down to Emily's room.

V

The E.R., located on the first floor, was filling up fast. Everyone from victims of the bomb to officers and military soldiers injured at the shooting were down there. Towards the back end of the large room was Tommy and Jasmin, who were both getting checked out.

"Ow!" Jasmin said as the doctor touched a deep cut on the side of his head.

"Come on Jas, don't be a baby," Tommy said as a doctor stitched up a cut over his eyebrow.

"Shut up Tommy!" Jasmin said.

"You shut up, Jas," Tommy quickly shot back.

"How about both of you shut up?" Steve asked from the gurney next to both of them.

They both quickly stopped talking and took their eyes off of each other; Steve smiled once he saw them do that.

"Wow, you really got a good size mark on the back of your head," the young doctor said. "What happened?"

Steve shrugged his shoulders.

"I was saving the world and the bad guy got one good hit in," Steve said.

The young doctor chuckled.

"Oh yeah?" The doctor asked.

Steve turned and looked up at him.

"Oh yeah," he said before he turned and saw Ray walk into the E.R. "Am I all set?"

"Yeah, just take it easy alright...no saving the world for a few days."

Steve turned and looked at the doctor as he stood up from the gurney.

"Kid, if I stopped for a few days, there wouldn't be a world left to save," Steve shot back before turning and walking toward Ray.

As Steve walked over, he could clearly tell Ray was in pain from his knee, just by the way he was limping. It was a hard sight to see, but now wasn't the time to start bitching that Ray should get it fixed.

"Everyone good?" Ray asked as Steve walked up to him.

"Yeah, everyone is good. Bob's fine, Tommy needed a few stitches, Torque must be fine I'm assuming, and Jasmin is being a baby."

"Am not...Ow!" Jasmin shouted as a young female doctor inserted a needle into his left arm to take out some blood.

Steve chuckled.

"How about you?" Ray asked Steve.

"Never better."

"What about your head?"

"Just a slight tap, nothing major...what about you?" Steve asked.

"Going to get checked out now. Think it's time to get this old knee looked at," Ray confessed.

Steve lifted up his eyebrow, surprised that Ray actually admitted it.

"Oh...alright then...good. How's Emily?" Steve asked.

"I think she's gonna be fine."

Steve smiled.

"Good...good," Steve said as he turned and looked back at the guys.

As Tommy and Bob laughed with Jasmin, both Ray and Steve smiled just watching them. The both of them had worked with a lot of people, but they each agreed that the guys with them in that moment were the best they'd ever had.

"You're gonna miss them," Steve began.

Ray turned and looked at him.

"What makes you think that?" Ray asked.

"Because I would," Steve answered.

Ray shook his head.

"You're not going to miss guns, the long trips away from home, or being shot at...but you will miss moments like this," Steve said.

Ray looked back at the guys. He didn't say anything but he knew Steve was right. Ray would miss those moments. He'd never thought about it until then, but it was those kind of moments that had kept him in the business for so long, and it was those kind of moments like that made it easier to deal with the fact that his family was always put second.

Steve then turned and patted Ray on the back as Ray kept still, watching the guys make fun of one another. Then they both saw Tim and Scotty walk up to the guys and stand next to them.

"Might have found a few more guys," Steve said, pointing at the two of them.

"Good luck explaining that to Roader," Ray said before he groaned in pain from his knee.

Steve looked down and then put his arm on Ray's back.

"Alright, come on...time to get that knee looked at," Steve said.

Ray looked up at him.

"Yeah...maybe it is," Ray said.

Steve smiled and then helped Ray over to the nurse's station as Ray took one last look at the guys, smiling at them as he slowly walked away.

Chapter 22: Maybe

A lot had been done in six months in New York. Much of the debris had been picked up, the Manhattan Bridge was already in the process of being rebuilt and the lies of what really happened seemed to be sticking. Many people, including Steve, Joey and Roader, weren't sure if people would believe a gas explosion could do that, nor did they think people would believe that the Manhattan Bridge fell due to rust and corrosion...but they did.

It seemed everyone believed the other stories as well. Everything from saying a gas explosion also happened in Boston, a lone gunman shot up the JKF airport because he was mad about the seat he had on a flight, to a Secret Service agent accidentally firing a rocket into the White House. It was one lie right after the other but it kept the country from panicking and that was fine by everyone in Washington.

All the news stations were told the same thing; at least that's what it sounded like when Ray was watching it in the hospital after his knee replacement. Ray didn't agree with the choice to hide everything, but he could see where everyone in Washington was coming from. But instead of dwelling on it, he did his best to just focus on resting up so he could leave the hospital and it paid off for him; he was walking just a few days after the surgery.

To Ray's surprise, his recovery was short. The only thing that he was still having some trouble with was long periods of running, but since he was retiring, he figured he wouldn't need to be running anymore. And that was fine with him; running always tired him out fast anyway.

Now that his retirement was official, there was a part of Ray that was excited, a part that kept bringing a smile to his face as he drove to the body shop. He hadn't really been in contact with anyone over the six months, aside from Steve and Emily popping in every now and then. But other than them, Ray hadn't seen anyone else since. Even though he would've liked to have seen everyone, he knew that they were just giving him space so he could rest up.

As he got off the exit for the body shop, he reached down and touched his knee and was yet again amazed that there was no pain at all. He wished he would've listened to everyone and had it done earlier...of course he would never admit it to anyone, not even Steve.

The view of the shop up the street made Ray start wondering if he should've waited and returned when all the guys were there, so he could officially say goodbye to each of them. He would've like too, but in his opinion if he said goodbye to them it would've felt like he was ending the friendships they had and he didn't want that; adjusting to retirement was going to be hard enough.

Like always, Ray pulled up to the body shop and parked in the same old spot that he always did and opened the door to his truck. He stepped out and looked up at the sun as it approached the evening horizon. He then lowered his head and looked around, trying to take as much in as he could before he made his way to the side door.

With a loud grunt, Ray opened the door all the way and then stepped inside. The place was pretty bright for the time of day, sunlight filtered through the skylights and the windows in his office. He looked all around before he made his way across the shop and over to his office. The conversations, the laughs, the jokes, the heartaches and the pain all playing through his mind as he made his way across.

Even though his mind was roaming all around, he was still able to keep his emotions in check...until he stepped into his office. His eyes began to tear up as he walked in and looked around. Those walls held a lot of memories, just like the shop did, only the memories in the office were much deeper than anything the wall of the shop had.

But instead of reliving the past completely, Ray decided to cut it short and just get what he went in for: the photo of his desk of Emily when she was a baby, and his wristwatch in the top drawer of the desk.

He went for the picture first, picking it up as he walked over to his desk. He lifted it up and then began to smile. The photo was over forty years old, but even forty years later it still brought a smile to his face. He was so focused on the picture; he didn't even hear Joey walk in. Joey carefully knocked on the door frame, causing Ray to look up and turn.

"Oh...hey Joe," Ray said as he lowered the picture.

Joey smiled.

"Hi ya doin?" Joey asked.

Ray shrugged his shoulders.

"Alright...you?" Ray asked as he walked over to the front side of the desk and opened the drawer. "Sorry, just came for something."

"No problem and I'm good...you know, staying busy," Joey answered.

Ray grabbed his wristwatch from the drawer and then closed it as he looked up at Joey.

"Good," Ray said with a smile.

"Yeah...uh...they...promoted me to Sullivan's position," Joey said.

Ray nodded his head.

"Yeah, Steve mentioned that last time he came to visit me. Congratulations."

"Thank you...yeah uh...it's gonna be difficult...pretty big shoes to fill," Joey confessed.

"Well, if anyone can do it, it's you Joe. I think Sullivan would be pleased to know that it was you who took over his position," Ray said as he smiled.

"Thanks, Ray," Joey said before changing the subject. "So...how you feeling about retirement? Nervous?"

Ray shrugged his shoulders.

"Naw. Not as bad as I thought it was going to be...think I'm actually getting used to the idea."

"Good, glad to hear. Any big plans?"

"Gonna head on up to New Hampshire and see Sullivan's kid. Broken a lot of promises in my life but this is one I plan on keeping. After that...just live in peace, or attempt to anyway," Ray said correcting himself.

Joey shook his head as he looked around the office.

"Yeah, I hear ya..." Joey said.

Ray looked down at the wristwatch.

"What made you come down here?" Ray asked.

Joey looked back at him.

"Was hoping I would bang into you," Joey confessed.

"Okay, any special reason?" Ray asked.

"Just wanted to double check and make sure you haven't changed your mind about your replacement. It's a big job to step into and I don't want the guys—and by guys I mean Steve—getting all pissed off about it."

Ray cleared his throat as he smiled.

"I know the guys will be fine with it and as for Steve...I don't think you have to worry about him."

Joey lifted his eyebrow.

"What makes you say that?"

"Steve also chose him; in fact, Steve insisted that I choose him," Ray said.

"Really?"

Ray chuckled.

"Yeah, hard to believe but yeah, he did. And he thinks he'll be a damn good leader too."

Joey smiled.

"What about you...? "

Ray looked up at Joey.

"Yeah, I think he will be too," Ray said before he looked down at the photo of Emily.

Joey smiled as he looked at Ray admiring the photo of his daughter.

"How is she?" Joey asked.

Ray looked up and saw Joey pointing at the picture.

"Oh...uh...she's alright. Still a bit shaken up after everything I guess," Ray said.

Joey looked down at the aged photo.

"Yeah...I bet. It's...a lot to take in all at once. To us it's just another day at the office, but to everyone else...it's...well, intense to say the least."

Ray nodded.

"Yeah...but she's getting better. Think I've seen her every day this week; going to see her now as a matter of fact. Might actually have a chance to fix everything I broke throughout the years...maybe."

Joey smiled.

"Good, I'm glad to hear that."

Ray nodded as he took one last look around the office. Memories from all the conversations, midnight chats and bonds he experienced in that office played through his mind. As he looked around, Joey shook his head and then looked down.

"So...guess this is it," Joey said.

Ray looked at Joey.

"Guess it is...feels a little weird...kinda starting to think I'm going to miss it all," Ray confessed.

Joey smiled.

"I think we might miss you too, but it's time for your next adventure...only this time I think you can manage this one on your own for once."

Ray chuckled as he stepped closer to Joey.

"Yeah, and I know you and the guys will be fine without me. I have no doubt about that," Ray said with a smile.

Joey nodded as Ray patted him on the shoulder and then began to walk away while Joey looked down for a moment before he turned back to Ray who was just about out of the office.

"Ray?" Joey asked.

Ray stopped and turned back to him.

"Yeah?"

Joey briefly smiled.

"Thank you."

"For what?"

"Saving the world every day. I know you said you did it for your daughter...but her life isn't the only one on the list of people you've saved. My name's on that list too," Joey said.

Ray then walked back over to him.

"Thank *you*...for everything Joe."

"Anytime Ray," he said as he smiled.

Ray smiled as he lifted up his right hand so Joey could shake it. Joey looked at it and then firmly shook it.

"Well...I better get going...don't want to be late for dinner with Emily and Torque," Ray softly said.

"Yeah I probably should get going too," Joey said.

Ray walked towards the door as Joey followed. When they got to the door and stepped out into the shop, Ray turned and looked at Joey as they headed for the exit.

"Take care of yourself, Joe."

"You too Ray. Make sure to keep in touch."

Ray smiled.

"Maybe..."

As Joey walked next to him, he began to think about everything that Ray went through in the time that they've known one another, and it was clear that not only had the man prevented countless wars, but he had also saved the lives of hundreds of thousands...maybe even millions. It was in that moment that Joey wished the side of history that would never be written would one day be told...because like he said to Ray...he would be on damn near every page.

When they got to the door, Joey pushed it open and walked out. Ray also stepped out, but stopped for a moment and then looked back into the shop one more time. The thoughts made him smile as he remembered all the laughs he and the guys shared together.

Ray shook his head, still confident that retiring was the right decision. A part of him was still a bit sour to the idea but he knew it wasn't truly goodbye, he promised himself he would stay in touch, not only with Joey but the guys too. And with that promise, he took hold of the door handle and then pulled the door closed, sealing another chapter in his life and moving him on towards another more promising one.

September 2nd 2014-May 29th 2015

Afterword

Over the past few years, I've written a lot of things, some good, some not so good but I have to say *The Dogs of War* was by far the most fun I've ever had writing. Everything from the story to the dozens of characters; it was just pure entertainment for me and kept my mind more than occupied throughout the eight months writing it.

To be honest, *Dogs* started off by accident. I was in the middle of typing a story about my drug and alcohol abuse and halfway through I had to stop. At that point it had been close to four years, but it was still too soon to relive it. I decided to place that idea on the back burner and start something else, so I opened a new document and just started typing. I typed so much, by the end of the day the first chapter was done...and that's how it all started.

I didn't have a big plan and layout for the book like some authors do (I personally don't believe in doing that because I feel like it limits your imagination if you stick to the same thing. You gotta give yourself room to roam and see where your mind takes you, not plan it out exactly and execute it). I can honestly say I winged every part of the book; with the exception of the fight between Dutra and Ray (course at the time I didn't know it would be them). Some days it was scary to not really have an idea of what was coming next and others days were flawless.

After the second or third chapter, I knew I was going to need to write the names down of all the characters; otherwise I was going to forget who was who. But I didn't want to just have made up names because then I felt like I couldn't relate to them...so I decided to use people I knew in real life. As it turned out most of them were the former guys from a produce department I use to work in. Some find it hard to believe but its true: Joey was my manager, Steve was my supervisor, Bob was the assistant manager, Tommy and Jasmin were both part timers and Kevin worked nights (the only characters I had to make up was Dutra, Roader and Sullivan).

When I decided to use all of them as my inspiration I knew it was going to work out. The dialogue between the guys (especially Tommy and Jasmin) had pieces of things we actually said to one another in real life. It was funny then and it was funny as I typed it; it was like I could hear them saying all this to one another all over again. That's why I loved writing the dialogue more then I loved writing the action scenes (because to be honest the action parts were draining to type).

The inspiration, background (and name) for Ray came from my grandfather. Like Ray in the book, my grandfather is also a decorated

Vietnam Vet who survived the bloodiest battle in the war (he also is in need of a knee replacement himself). He has always been a hero to me, so this seemed like the perfect way to say thank you to him for all the years of watching over me.

Probably one of the more difficult things about writing *Dogs* was trying to make sure that each character received their 'fifteen minutes of fame' so to speak. Some characters were obviously guaranteed that (Ray, Steve, Dutra) but I didn't want to overlook any of the others; I wanted to make sure every character was covered so none would feel like a cardboard cutout. But since there was like fifteen of them, it got a little tricky to do at times.

I knew that the book would be called an action/thriller book but I didn't want it to be an all-out action book; I wanted real character development, real emotions and real situations that would test all of these characters. So personally, I look at the book as more of a drama then a full on action book.

When I wrote the book, I have to admit I was in a dark place. Suicide was on my mind every day. I guess life was just not working out like I wanted it to. There were a couple of scary nights during the writing of this but the thing that stopped me from doing something stupid was writing this book. I felt because it was so exciting and fun, it would be a waste to kill myself and leave it unfinished...and that's what kept me going. So I think that's why I'll always look back at it with fond memories.

I think my own thoughts of suicide are the reason why the book ends the way it does. I always told myself I would never leave a suicide note, because to me, leaving a note is a way to get attention and I didn't want that. I knew by not leaving one, however, it meant I would be leaving a lot of questions for people in my life, and living with unanswered questions is not something anybody should have to live with, so that's why I wrote the ending I did. It was like my goodbye was imbedded within the characters' goodbyes...and to me that's what makes the ending that much more meaningful.

But of course that all changed when I started talking to my good friend Chris. His friendship was that kickstart I needed to get my mind out of the gutter and see just what exactly was in front of me (it's hard to see what you're missing when you spend your whole life wishing you were dead). As we really got to know one another, I started to question if I should change the tone of the ending (even began to) but the attempt to change it just didn't feel right. It felt forced and out of place, so in the end I chose to stick with the original ending; which looking back I think is a good thing because it reminds me of where I was then and it reminds me of where Chris has led me to now. And I can't think of anyone else who has been able to do that for me in the way he has, which is why I had to include him in the dedication.

So as I close this and move on with my writing, I know for an absolute fact that I will always look back and embrace the moments, the feelings and ideas I had when I wrote *Dogs*. I never would've thought that a quick one-page idea would become my first novel...but life works in mysterious ways...so I've been told.

-Matty

www.ingramcontent.com/pod-product-compliance
Lightning Source LLC
Chambersburg PA
CBHW030919050726
47498CB00003BA/814